The Grimoire's Heir

The Grimoire's Heir

Craig Walston

Gearbox Inn Books

Contents

First Printing, 2024

Dedication

For my wife Rachel, who first inspired me to write this story while stargazing.

Prologue:

Desperation clawed at Octavian as he searched the night sky. His eyes darted from his pocket watch to the dimly lit street. All around, snowflakes landed and instantly melted. Beads of sweat dripped off his chin and soaked onto his dampening collar. His crisp shirt was buttoned up tight and tied with a lace cravat. Such an outfit had cost him several months' income, an investment he had hoped would pay off. He felt ridiculous in it, but it's what his buyers expected. Unfortunately, it would surely be worthless by the end of the night at the rate he had been perspiring. He paced back and forth as if he were a fresh recruit about to be sent into battle.

*I have staked everything on tonight going well. The cost for the Wardens alone sent me into the red, and if the Embers get wind of this....*He shuddered at the thought, *all of this work undone by an idiot thief who I hoped could be trusted with a simple job...well...*he confessed to himself, *I guess it wasn't simple.* His thoughts were interrupted by a young attendant tapping him on the shoulder.

"Master Octavian? Your guests are growing restless."

Octavian spun around to face the boy, who now shrank seeing Octavian's face, knowing he had made a mistake.

"Ah! And you think that you are the one to keep me on schedule?" He demanded, "Well far be it from me to keep you and my guests waiting."

The boy's eyes went wide, he was far too surprised to say anything in his defense. Octavian knew it wasn't his fault, he had likely been told to go find him, really he was just following directions. But Octavian felt like being cruel, it usually helped him to relax. Tonight though he couldn't afford it for more reasons than one. He composed himself, straightening his jacket and took a deep breath, "My apologies, Mister...?"

"Gregory, sir."

"Yes, thank you Gregory." Octavian shifted his demeanor, "I am quite aware of the time and the guests. I acknowledge your desire to be of assistance, but I do not require it from you or any of your kind. Now go and make sure everyone's drinks are filled."

The boy rushed off, glad to be out of Octavian's presence.

Octavian decided to give up on the belated thief and get the evening started without him.

Entering the room, he plastered on a face of confidence and enthusiasm with great effort. He was further emboldened by the sight of the crowd, which was larger than he expected. The main room was warm from the torches despite it being a cool fall night. Octavian kept it well-lit but was selective in how much light made it outside. It had to look lavish, so as to not offend his deep- pocketed clientele, but could not attract unwanted attention. He stationed his own guards, dressed as the poor, outside with strict instructions to rough up anyone foolish enough to ask questions. Attendants rushed back and forth with well-paid-for smiles on their faces carrying various cakes and wine. Every one of them avoided his gaze and they were wise to do so.

The former library was a perfect place for this kind of affair. Shelves long since emptied and taken away, now it only housed vagrants. Once they were swept away, he could transform it into something grand...at least for a night...then they would come crawling back after his business was finished. It wasn't a perfect job but he was serving enough alcohol to make everyone miss the more incriminating details. Being far too preoccupied with what was going to be auctioned to notice or care, his clients filed in. They knew this gathering was illegal, but when you wish to buy unnatural items of antiquity, you have to make small concessions; like spending your evening in a cleaned up homeless shelter.

Octavian took a moment to congratulate himself as his lips formed the beginning of a smile. He already felt better, deciding to move on from his last few minutes of worry and focus on what was going well. This night, barring a few hitches, was going to make him a lot of clips. Maybe enough to buy his way back into polite society. He even secured a low-level Warden to ease any lingering doubts that he had taken care of everything.

The Warden stood silently against a far wall watching the evening transpire. Periodically guests would come by and thank him for his presence and tell him how nice it was that this affair was so legitimate. He politely shook hands and patted shoulders making everyone feel more comfortable. The Warden wore a suit that vaguely resembled old military garb from a forgotten time, but with far less pageantry; simple gray trousers with well-polished buttons and a solid gray button-down dress-shirt. He had a black belt that caught the light and there was a small insignia of the city on his shoulder. The uniform stuck out in the room like a flower in a garden that was never given color.

Octavian approached the official and tried to project confidence, "Well, Warden Richmond? Didn't I promise you this evening would be a boon for the city?"

The Warden looked carefully at Octavian and extended his hand in greeting, "You cannot possibly deliver what you promised. Which is why I am so interested in this event." Octavian shook his hand as the Warden chuckled, "Your thief will not show...he is most likely ash by the hands of the Embers as we speak." The Warden's words pierced Octavian like an arrow and he yanked his hand back. "Now that is just...they can't and they wouldn't...who do they think...there are laws..." He sputtered. Again, Octavian took two slow, deep breaths, and looked back at the Warden. "He will be here, he is not ash, and you will have earned your bribe".

"My administration fee," Warden Richmond corrected.

It was all the same to Octavian.

——————————————————————————————————-

A bell chimed through the Library and conversations hushed as the attendees took their seats. Octavian walked briskly over to the main stage and greeted the room with a feigned smile. A thin podium awaited him. As he took his place behind it, he spoke in an even and measured tone. "Welcome one and all to our fifth auction of rare artifacts and relics acquired by Aquina's Venture Firm in collaboration with Horace inventions." He paused for applause but was greeted with none. Clearing his throat and went on, "What you will see here tonight, if wielded properly, can bring you more glory and fortune than the richest and most famous in all of Magnadun! Ever since we remade contact with our neighbors we have had all manner of curiosities come to our attention."

He motioned forward at the dramatically covered items up for auction in front of the crowd. "We will now begin the listings, once all the items have been presented, we will start the bidding round. As exciting as our items are, please hold all bids till the appropriate time. Now let's begin with our first listing! Tonight, bear witness to a lithe dagger that when unsheathed illuminates a room!"

An attendant brought it forward in a wooden box lined with black velvet. The knife had a silver blade with an ivory handle, two small gold rivets secured the tang. Octavian took the box and held it at an angle for all to see. The attendant removed the sheath and light emitted from the blade. It was hard to tell if it was just catching reflections or truly generating light. Octavian covered his eyes dramatically as though it was too much. He paused for reaction. A few raised eyebrows, but none showed the astonishment he had hoped for.

These people are getting harder to impress, he thought.

He swiftly moved along to the next item, "A fine cedar box that can store twice what it appears... handy for hiding keepsakes from nosey relatives." He added the last part hoping to spice up his merchandise. Admittedly, a box that was larger than it looked was not the most exciting, even if it could be useful. It garnered less reactions than the knife.

Switching to a deeper tone for effect, he continued, "From the far north we have an ancient mace made thousands of years ago. Time hasn't touched it and it is believed that the wielder also will not age while holding it." Sometimes a complete fabrication was necessary. Lies like this worked well because he told the truth more than not. Besides, this one would take years to prove wrong. The crowd muttered in approval.

He went on, "A statue that is so well carved it will be the centerpiece in any foyer." He made a show of whispering, " And as your guests admire it, the statue will also calm their nerves and make them feel at home, excellent for potential business partners." This caused a stir in the audience, some were aghast, others were audibly impressed. "And trust me the statue isn't at work right now," he laughed with a large smile and the audience did as well, although theirs was more nervous than his.

"And finally, a genuine teleportation cloak from Valdannon. The wearer can transport themselves short distances with only a puff of smoke to indicate it has been used. The intricacies will be lost on the common observer but its deep violet base color hides an intricate weaving the match of which I have never seen. It radiates Magnincy and is likely one of a kind." There were considerable limitations to the abilities of this cloak but none he needed to disclose until someone purchased it. Even now the crowd rumbled and gasped in approval at the implications of what it could be used for.

Octavian was about to continue when a boy caught his attention with a raised hand just off stage.

Octavian paused and turned to the crowd, "My apologies ladies and gentlemen. As you can see, we have a great many things in store for tonight and because of their unique nature, I am needed to oversee them. Please pardon me and welcome my assistant to finish the listing." He motioned for the boy to come up on stage and take over. The boy's eyes went wide with fear. Clearly, he was not the right substitute, but Octavian did not have anyone better at the moment. His regular staff that worked his legitimate business had no idea he ran an underground black market. So, he had to hire less-than-qualified men.

Octavian rushed off stage and went directly into the back. He saw a small crowd speaking in hushed tones. A panicked voice arose from the center of the huddle that had no intention of being polite or subdued. The thief had arrived, his face ashen gray, and he was talking wildly to whoever would listen. Octavian marched directly to him pushing the crowd aside and grabbed him by the shoulders. The thief was still looking around wildly and babbling, Octavian drew back a hand and slapped him across the face. Speaking to him through gritted teeth he said, "We will speak of your tardiness later, did you get the item?"

The thief wouldn't look Octavian in the face and fell silent. His hands moved into his bag and pulled out a lantern made of black metal with a withered white candle in the middle. Octavian looked at the lantern then back at the man. His eyes narrowed and his lips pursed. He spared a brief second to look back and forth from the crowd to his attendants and said quietly, "Back to your stations." The men quickly dispersed leaving the thief and the auctioneer alone.

"What is this supposed to be?" He hissed.

"A lantern, sir. I know the instructions were to steal a book from their libraries but..." He trailed off getting lost in thought.

"But, what!?" Octavian demanded.

"Well, I got into the college just like I promised I could...but," he began to trail off again. This time, instead of shouting, Octavian just squeezed the man's shoulders digging his fingers into him.

"Ahh! Sorry, sorry, the building didn't make sense! Doors that I had used just moments before were gone the next second. Shadows didn't work right and voices filled my head! It was making me crazy just to be in there. The map was useless. I grabbed this lantern and finally found a window to jump out of. Nearly broke my leg when I landed." He rubbed his leg as he said it. "I know I didn't get what you asked, but I believe the lantern is something special. It seems to not need to be replaced with new wax! Probably enchanted or something like that."

Octavian was seething, "The candle...doesn't burn wax...that is what you brought instead of what I asked?" The thief, knowing how badly he had failed, gave a weak nod as he looked into his captor's eyes for mercy. Octavian released him and began to take deep breaths; slow and measured, desperately keeping panic from taking over. *This is worse than I had anticipated. My reputation will take a serious hit when I can't deliver as much as I advertised. That terrible little Warden will mock me for this... he may even try to fine me despite the handsome bribe I already paid.* His breathing became labored and just as he was about to pass out the torches all around the room dimmed in unison. The thief's voice squeaked out, "Oh, also, I may have been followed..."

———————————————————————————————————-

Ember of the Arcane Flame and Chief Researcher of the Lost and Forgotten, Bartelby Maddox, had heard enough. Rising to interrupt this gathering of fools and their patrons, he leaned over and whispered a final instruction to his apprentice. She leapt from her seat and ran from the room. It would have made a scene had the crowd not already been stirring from the sudden drop in illumination. Maddox loved doing that. It was so simple and always unnerved people. It helped in what came next.

Maddox stood up and shot his hands straight out and back with practiced speed. Suddenly, the boy who was speaking horribly on stage was spared any more embarrassment as he began to gasp. His eyes went wild with alarm, but the Ember's attention had already turned away. He was scanning the room, searching for someone.

Maddox's voice boomed out with great authority, "Would the proprietor of this little gathering please come forward?" His words crackled through the air, even with all the commotion they cut through the din. "Come out now, Octavian, I have wasted half my night on this already." From behind a curtain, a man wreathed in sweat stepped out breathing strangely. Not even a small measure of his confidence was left.

As the nervous host inched forward, Maddox continued, "And everyone else in the back, all of your attendants, boot polishers, booze pourers, and the guards outside. Everyone. Come in here now!" The Ember's fingers taped together like a spider climbing a web. His robes hid most of his body except his hands and face. He liked it that way. It fit people's expectations of what an Ember should look like and it usually made them speak to him with respect. However, tonight was not about that. Tonight, was about finding a thief.

The room filled hastily and when the last man entered Maddox addressed the crowd. "A thief broke into the College of the Arcane Flame this evening. That alone is an egregious crime, but he stole something of great value. I am interested in finding out how this was done. This is not the kind of research I prefer and therefore, I wish to be done here expeditiously, as I am sure, you all do as well. This need not take any more time than it has already." He looked at the auctioneer, who was clearly about to faint from hyperventilation, "Octavian, go get Sigmund from the back. He is trying to open a door, but he will find that task impossible." As the nervous proprietor scrambled away, a middle-aged merchant with graying hair and a shocking amount of gold adornments stood up and stammered, "You...Embers walk around and pretend like you are the ones in charge! You don't have any real power. Just tricks that scare children and the superstitious."

Maddox did not look at him. If it had not been so quiet, one would have assumed he had not heard the man speak at all. But that was impossible. Maddox waved dismissively in his direction and stated icily "The nescient may not speak now..." The merchant began to gasp as the substitute auctioneer had moments earlier who was now passed out after he clattered off the podium.

Just then Octavian returned dragging along a diminutive man who looked absolutely sick. The smell hit Maddox first. Then it became obvious by his lite green complexion and the residue on his shirt that this man had vacated the contents of his stomach. Strange that such a talented thief would also be such a coward. Typically, those two things do not go together. Maddox smiled warmly at Sigmund the thief and commanded, "Give me what you stole." While he spoke, Maddox held out his spindly fingers in an open grasp. Sigmund gave the lantern to him and looked down at the ground. Maddox looked at the lantern with a flat stare and returned his attention to the thief. "Do not play games with me boy, give me the book now or you will know great torment." His words left no room for doubt. Sigmund looked back and forth and suddenly stammered, "But that was all that I took!"

The torches exploded into hues of various colors, engulfing the room in a roar.

"Lie to me again and this whole room burns with everyone in it!"

Panic crashed into the room like waves onto rocks.

People climbed over each other, clawing wildly trying to find an exit. Soon they realized there was no escape, so they turned on their host. "Just give it to him!" "Can't you see he will kill us all!" The wealthy stammered with torn cuffs and smeared makeup. The merchant who had spoken up was clawing at his own throat while only weak gasps escaped. Fear had replaced pride and their words were soaked with it.

"How dare you threaten our lives!"

"What gives you the right?"

"You aren't half of what you claim to be!"

"Just charlatans who prey on the ignorant."

"The merchants and the entrepreneurs run this city!"

"This was a legitimate auction, the presence of your warden proves it!"

"You let us out of here right now!"

Maddox shot his hands forward again, seizing something the others couldn't see.

Contempt filled his eyes and he whispered "Nescience." to himself. When his hands opened the crowd collectively gasped. Squeaks of shock and bewilderment moved like a wave through them as they struggled to breath. .

The thief wiped tears from his eyes, and pleaded "Honestly, all I took was the lantern!"

Maddox's face turned grim. He loathed when it came to this. Octavian broke his composure as well and began to shake Sigmund yelling, "Just tell him and end this madness!"

A revelation crossed Maddox's features. He lowered his head and resigned himself.

"He can't," Maddox stated in realization. "He's not the thief, just a clever diversion."

A sickening silence permeated the room as most of the guests flailed on the floor.

Maddox shook in uncontrolled fury. A long line of wardens filed into the library. Without turning to them, Maddox issued an order. "Take them to the tower, they will be made to serve the sacred flame!"

At that command the crowd collectively breathed again after having it be stolen from them. The room's torches snuffed out and the once grand library dropped into total darkness.

1

Old and Young

Huxley settled in for a tedious lecture.

"You really are a fool, you know that?..." Ember Palithur said while stroking his chin, he continued, "oh and also an embarrassment. To both me and yourself...probably all of Mayburn now that I think about it. Not to mention your ridiculous family. Perhaps it has escaped your friends' attention, they seem incapable of noticing."

"Umm sir?"

Palithur's weary back hunched deeper, said "Again with these futile attempts ..." he lost his thought as a new one occurred "Wait you're nearly twenty-one now, hardly a boy, although you still act like one." Then he returned to his first thought, "You'll just embarrass yourself again and me by extension."

"I...I think that-" Huxley began.

"No!" He interrupted, spittle bursting out of his aged lips. "I think. I think so well and so clearly that I have unraveled the cosmos. I have grasped the fires of knowledge." Huxley wondered if he ever noticed he did that when he got angry.

"You serve me," he spat and a few frothy drops landed on Huxley "just like all of Mayburn. You serve so that I don't have to waste my time doing whatever it is that you are doing. The only clever thing you've ever done is finding this...loophole..." The last word was spoken with deep contempt.

Huxley cursed to himself. He knew Palithur was in a more sour mood than normal. But today was the deadline to apply for entrance. It really was a clever loophole he had found. Every resident can take the entrance examination while in their final years of city-mandated education, but after eighteen you need special permission or extenuating circumstances. Working for the office of an Ember was one of them, even if you were nothing more than a glorified maid. Under the law, he was technically an Ember's attendant which allowed him to take the exam until twenty-five. Seven failures in a row to reach even the minimum requirements had not slowed him down, although his resolve weakened. Huxley knew one thing for certain. Ever since he was a boy, he believed the only way to get his questions answered was to become an Ember. That was the only way for anyone to be truly educated so far from Danador. Mayburn was at the end of a far line of important cities, born to a family that cared for education but only enough to get by. He was lacking any real means to advance his life in any meaningful way. His friends knew this, his family knew this, and most importantly, he did. It didn't seem so bad when he was young but now life was forcing him down roads he didn't want and so he fought it with whatever means he had.

Right now, that was with loopholes. No matter how much it made his superiors irate, Huxley was determined to persevere. Most others would likely have given up after so many failures. Huxley was different...or maybe he was just as much a fool as the Ember described...either way he was going to take the test again. He had figured out that he could excel in general knowledge and spend the majority of his time there, leaving the more specialized sciences for whatever time he had left. This way, if he could clear the lowest requirements, he could maybe move a city closer to Danador. Even as a child, he never allowed himself to dream of entering the College of the Arcane Flame. That was nearly exclusively filled with Ember's children, high-ranking wardens, and exceptionally gifted students, all of which he wasn't. But if you did well enough you could be deemed worthy to serve in higher capacities. Like what he was doing now with Mayburn's Grand Protector and Savior of Civilization, Ember Palithur.

Palithur, at the moment, was giving Huxley the deepest and most meaningful glare of contempt and annoyance that he had ever seen. Palithur had only sent one student to the College to train. That student's name was Onders. A year older than Huxley, he had barely known her before she tested well enough to train. Palithur talked about his "Star Pupil" often and how he had identified the shine of her brilliance early on. She was only a girl when she left. It had been well over ten years now, but if you talk to Palithur, it was as though she had just left. Her departure left a vacancy of brilliance, a hopeless void, an emptiness that was only exacerbated by Huxley's attempts to prove to be up to Onder's level.

"Yes sir, but since I am allowed to, I would like to try again," Huxley stood firm.

Ember Palithur huffed in frustration that Huxley knew the legalities. He had stubbornly kept applying knowing that rule existed. In all of his time studying how to get in, he had never heard of anyone actually achieving it so late in life. Perhaps it was there just to appease the poor into thinking they had some chance. Huxley held his resolve regarding his request and insisted he be tested. The old Ember may be a bit slow and even teetering on madness, but he was always excellent at paperwork. He would make sure Huxley's name was on the next exam if Huxley pushed him hard enough.

The two squared off, each disliking the other's stubbornness, neither willing to relent. But then Ember Palithur swayed and lost his balance. Huxley forgot his defiance and grabbed his hand helping him into his seat. He scooted up to his desk and began scribbling notes. There would be no more words from him today. The Ember wasn't a kind man or overly pleasant, but he had at one point genuinely saved the town from destruction. Huxley and Mayburn owed him a lot. That was part of why he served in this role despite the abuse. He respected the older man's position greatly. Some days Palithur got emotional and would be prone to outbursts. It was always then that he shut down and mutter to himself for the remainder of the day.

That was why it surprised him when he stopped writing, looked up at Huxley and said, "You'd better get to your training. Leave this to me."

Palithur's normal flat-lined lips curved into a faint smile. Huxley had nearly forgotten that it was training day. The only other thing Huxley was worse at than academics was militia training. The Ember enjoyed hearing how badly Huxley was doing and made sure to include it in the list of things Huxley can't do well. He was tragically right. Huxley turned away and headed for the training grounds, his muscles began to ache just thinking about it.

———-

In a jumble of arms and limbs, Huxley splashed into the mud. He considered not getting back up as he lay sprawled out on his back. His cheek and shoulder throbbed with pain. A few good-natured laughs from his friends penetrated the mud caked in his ears. Laying there for much longer would be grounds for mockery, so Huxley summoned his strength and stood up. He was greeted by a barrel-chested man with an out-stretched hand. Captain Pilch's forced smile stretched his thin mustache to the edges of his jowls.

"Ooo, that was a solid strike Huxley my boy! Keep your guard up. Plant your feet. Move with the flow of combat."

"Wait, how can I plant my feet and flow at the same time?" Huxley balked.

The Captain thought for a second while rubbing his ample chin and replied, "Hmm, well that's what training is for, to answer questions like those. Okay, one more time."

His eyes scanned the squad. "Huxley and...Bennett!"

A determined boy with black hair cropped short stepped out of the crowd. Bennet stood straight and rolled his shoulders back, he was nearly a head taller than Huxley. His friends cheered, "Get him, Benny!" The rest of the boys cringed. It was no secret that Bennett was the best fighter in their class, probably in all of Mayburn. He was strong and fast, but he was not cruel. Huxley knew he would stop the attack when the spar was won, unlike others who wailed on him when he went down. Hefting his shield high to cover his throbbing shoulder, he raised his practice sword in a defensive stance.

The exchange ended fast.

Bennett swung high knowing Huxley would take a step backward to avoid it. Bennett stepped forward rapidly covering the ground and used his right leg to sweep Huxley's feet out from under him. Bennett leaned into the move, shoving Huxley with his shield which knocked him to the ground. It was a solid strategy that Huxley respected in theory. In practice, it left him with more bruises.

He splashed into the mud again. On his way down he thought he caught a glimpse of sympathy from Bennett. That's what every great warrior wanted right? To be pitied. The boys cheered Bennett's inevitable victory while a few helped Huxley back up.

Captain Pilch yelled to the boys, "Alright, that's enough for today. Clean up and head home. Good work, we will be ready if any wild brutes attempt to breach our walls!"

Huxley wasted no time hustling to the armory, racked his gear, and began taking off his cuirass. As he lifted it over his chest the shoulders caught his ears. They pinched them upwards and then his shoulders began to burn. It was almost worth the pain of wearing it to experience the relief of having it off. He had been so excited to get the armor a few months ago. Huxley thought about the first time he walked out of his room with it on. He looked at himself in the mirror and saw a fierce warrior. It was a good look for him. Unfortunately, it all ended when he saw everyone else. Their armor did not move back and forth like his did. Theirs fit securely. His was tightened to the last notch and he still had wiggle room. Huxley had always been small, not sickly or scrawny, just not as big as everyone else. His ears were the exception and had always outpaced his contemporaries. He grew his hair long to try and cover them. His mom called it sandy colored. He had never really seen a beach but he liked sandy more than dirty blonde which is what most people called it. The current fashion didn't include long hair on boys, but the shoulder length did wonders for covering up his ears. The tradeoff was he was sometimes mistaken for a girl. An additional tradeoff was, his hair now felt like it housed ten pounds of mud. Washing it all out would take forever.

He looked at himself in the mirror, had he got bulkier? He flexed his arm stealthily so no one else would see him checking. He shook his head...no, but maybe soon.

It seemed like guys his size had left for university or found a way to get out of mandatory militia duty, probably accompanied by a generous donation from their parents. The thought of it was enough to ruin his night. The other boys chatted with vigor about the upcoming evening's events. They finally had a night off and they wanted to relax, as though anyone could truly relax knowing what was waiting just beyond the city gates. Scouts estimated an army of over two thousand warriors at least. They showed up out of the Fecundity over a month ago. One day all was well, the next, Mayburn was under siege. There were no demands for surrender, no communication at all really. Everyone feared the worst. That made days "off" hard to come by. All young men of age had been called into militia service. It was usually just light training with the occasional patrol. Mayburn was located at the end of an immensely long line stretching out from Danador. The town was so far away they rarely got proper military protection so it fell to the citizens to do most of the heavy lifting, even if they weren't particularly suited for it. This was different though. No amount of training could stop the size and scale of what waited outside the city walls. They would need Embers' support. Their job was to hold the gates until such reinforcement arrived.

The constant pressure made those in the militia uneasy. They needed to blow off steam. Most of his friends did that with late nights and ill-gained drinks from their parents' cabinets. Huxley preferred quiet and when he could get it, time at the library. The contrast was stark and his friends took every opportunity to goad him about it. Huxley couldn't help it. He was naturally inquisitive. His mind never seemed at rest. He burned with a desire to know.

As they made plans for the evening Jonah, a longtime friend, quieted everyone and said, "So Huxley...are you excited to see the librarian tonight? I hear she got even older since the last time you saw her. She is positively ancient now. I can see why you would want to hang out with her instead of us. It's the only girl you can get to spend time with you!" Jonah laughed and his hair swished back and forth. He laughed often. When Huxley grew tired of his jokes he would just watch his hair swish. Jonah liked to be the center of attention in a way that was usually harmless, but if no one was responding to his joke, he would get meaner to illicit reactions. That wasn't Huxley's judgment, even Jonah recognized on occasion that he did that. Despite this, he was an easy to like person. With a near constant smile and boundless enthusiasm, he could make a boring training session entertaining. He was smiling so often his face looked strange when it wasn't. He was even the perfect middle ground of Huxley and Bennett. If Huxley was on the scrawny side and Bennett was...well not. Then Jonah landed in the middle.

Even if they were teasing him, they were right. He was going to the library because today the library got a new shipment of books from the train. Its arrival was greatly anticipated as everyone expected platoons of soldiers or Embers to come pouring out to protect them but instead, all they would get is books. He was probably the only citizen of Mayburn happy about that. He had already torn through all the books he was interested in and felt like a buzzard picking at the bones of whatever was left. Not anymore. Tonight the library was supposed to receive old editions from the College. They would, of course, have been read so many times that it wasn't new or valuable information to anyone in Danador. But to a few in Mayburn, it was pure gold. To top it all off, his parent's shop was closed so he did not have to come help clean up and close for the night. Tonight, he would have four uninterrupted hours of reading. Huxley forgot about his aching body for a moment as he became lost in thought. Suddenly, a shoulder slammed into him jarring him back to reality. It was Captain Pilch. He clapped a large arm around Huxley making him almost disappear in his armpit. The hug brought a smell with it that was stronger than he was. Pilch was a kind man, but he was also a focused man. That focus rarely centered on good hygiene.

Pilch's first words to Huxley were muffled as he squirmed free of his inner arm.

"It's really an honor to train your group and see everyone come together as one! It's enough to make an old soldier like myself get teary-eyed. So how about it lad? Are you enjoying your time here?"

Huxley paused a second to collect himself and murmured "Umm, yeah, I guess, although I feel pulverized daily."

Instantly, the arm returned, this time thumping him on the back with a hand that felt like a sack of sausages. The slap was accompanied by a thunderous laugh, Pich's cheeks undulated with mirth. Talking to the Captain was like tangling with an enthusiastic, joyful elephant.

His laugh trailed off and the Captain added, "Hey! You can be honest with me! I know this place wasn't your first choice, or heck even your second, third or fourth. But you are really coming along. A natural soldier!"

Huxley stared. "You can't be serious?" Huxley searched for signs that the Captain was goading him now too.

"Oh, but I am! The other boys are strong and brave and can follow orders to the letter."

Huxley's face fell and Pilch tried to recover with: "But you can be that way too! Just keep at it and don't give up. You were an absolute wreck when you started, but today you hit a milestone!"

"What milestone was that, Sir?" Huxley wanted to know.

"You got knocked down only half as much as you did when you first started. That might not sound like the praise you want, but progress is progress, right?"

"Yeah. I guess so."

Captain Pilch began to come in for another hug. Huxley saw it coming this time and leaped back stating, "Well thank you so much for the encouragement and leadership sir, but I have to be running!"

Huxley turned and swiftly exited. He heard the Captain yell after him, "Of course! But don't forget about the benediction!"

Of course, he forgot about that. It was a recently tacked-on practice that every official in the town just started taking part in. It was harmless enough, but it felt strange to Huxley. Religion and prayer had only been practiced by travelers who visited the town. They would hand out some pamphlets, but would lose interest when everyone would return them or simply not make eye contact. Religion did not seem to have a place in small towns like his. The ancient people that had once been here appeared to have a complex religion, but it was gone along with them. Maybe there were still religious people in the woods. Here it just felt like trying to teach kids not to squirm in their seats. It is just not going to happen. His people asked too many questions that focused on the factual and religion only offered the opposite.

Huxley walked back to the central sparring yard and saw his class forming ranks in front of the looming and ever-present Ember statue, Ember Mayburn Palithur of the Arcane Flame. The statue was a smaller one that stood in the city square. He had memorized Palithur's face as a child. Every official building or state-controlled property wasn't without either a statue or picture of his face. His stoney demeanor always stared forward resolutely. His one hand held an open book and the other pointed forward. It was meant to inspire and remind everyone just who gave them this city. Somedays Huxley looked at it with contempt but most days with awe and respect. Ember Palithur may be a shadow of who he once was but Mayburn, the town, and his namesake was safe because of him. And for that, he deserved a few statues in Huxley's opinion.

He hustled to find his place so as to not be the last one. Then Pilch stood up front under the statue's shadow. They all raised their hands mimicking Mayburn's stance and slowly lowered them while stating, "Through knowledge and will he keeps madness at bay, his mind is our savior and our protector. Sundered lands be made whole again, MAY IT BE RECLAIMED!" The last part had to be yelled at the top of your lungs to emphasize the commitment. Huxley had thought benedictions would be more somber. This felt like a mantra for the mayor or some other bureaucrat. At least it was short.

2

Mail and Fools

With the bruises he endured, Huxley should have just wanted to crawl into bed. Instead, he discovered a new reserve of energy. He hurried down the road that would take him to the library. Most days he would walk home with his friends. They took longer than he did taking off gear, usually wrapped up in discussion and not worrying about the time. But he was too excited to wait today. He would most assuredly get ridiculed for it. No one else really shared his love of books. He tried at first to get everyone interested. He would work his favorite stories into conversation, finding even the loosest connection to something he was reading. Huxley felt it was clever in the moment, but was typically answered with laughter at his attempts. After quite a few tries, he gave up. In the capital city of Danador information had been monetized so greatly that it changed the interest of literature and science. Rare books were worth their weight or more in clips. But the ones Mayburn received could not even be called uncommon. And so there wasn't much interest. It was all for the best really. His status allowed him to stay late and even granted him access to books unavailable to the general population. Not that he could make sense of them, they were so advanced reading, they only confused him further. But the rest of the library was his. It felt like his own private study.

Huxley never felt more alive than when he absorbed himself in a book.

His life was nothing terrible to complain about, but that was just the problem. Nothing ever happened in Mayburn. Current events notwithstanding, it was a boring life, barely passable. He finished primary school and began work as his father's assistant cobbler. It was decent work, but at twenty years old, his mind grew restless with the atmosphere. He did not have access to many books growing up. Books were rare for most people and the ones they had were usually a recipe book or instructional manuals. They had one book in their house that was of great interest to him as a kid. A relative of his, some years ago diagrammed strange creatures that he had encountered in the Fecundity. It was fascinating to Huxley, but his mother locked the book away from him after he added a few doodles and notes of his own. It was an improvement in his mind. But now he understood why doodling in books was frowned upon.

Huxley followed the path which took him over the top of the hill that overlooked a large portion of the town. He paused to check one last time that his parent's shop was closed. Even though he confirmed it with his mother this morning, he would feel bad if they decided to open anyway and he was not there to help. He squinted in the sunlight and saw that the lamps were out and the door was closed. That was good enough for him. He looked over the town and breathed in deeply and sighed. Smoke from the campfires from beyond the wall were rising now. It would have been a welcome change of scenery if not for the threat they posed. He looked away to try to stay untroubled. Mayburn stretched out before him. Rolling hills and houses surrounded a small and cozy downtown, with a large trainyard off in the west. It was a simple town and everyone had a place, but Huxley was still looking for his.

The library could have been easily missed by most travelers. It was a small building that was off the main road. Sun-bleached and flaked, the sign that tried to draw attention to it had seen better days. There were much larger and newer signs near it that commanded more attention. But to Huxley, it stood out like a beacon. It was one of the few signs that once had color. Brown wood with green lettering. It had become chipped and faded, but to him, it was beautiful.

Huxley had felt robbed in a way. Other towns had thousands of books that he could have spent his whole childhood reading. He could have made so much more of himself, perhaps a government official or even a scholar. He had been amazed when he found out it was someone's job just to study one subject and learn all they could about it. He would often lose himself in the thoughts of what could have been. Education was a double-edged sword. The more he learned, the more he realized how little he knew. Nothing had been more painful than realizing an opportunity had been lost. Whenever he thought about it, his mood soured so he tried to forget. What good would it do now anyway? He was glad that he got the opportunity to read whenever he could.

As he pushed open the wooden door a tiny bell rang softly and the familiar smell of books filled his nostrils. There was more commotion today because the library received several crates of books. He walked in, hung his bag on a hook, and began to look around for the librarian. She was a sweet lady who seemed to be the only person who shared his interest in reading. Agnes was undersized with salt and pepper hair and a kind smile. She had the remains of a once freckled face. Spending so much time indoors had made those freckles fade, but a keen eye could spot them. Her dresses were a confused fashion that mimicked her. She always wore long-sleeved garments with high necklines, and with colorful patches. She often wore scarves and mismatched jewelry that was quite playful and sometimes silly. She simultaneously dressed well and like a person that was splashed with paint by accident, it fit her personality. The rules of her library were strict and unbreakable, but she had a habit of breaking her own rules and periodically demanding attention so that she could read aloud a new favorite poem she found.

She was not in the main gallery, but Huxley hoped to find her unloading books in the back. His heart raced with anticipation. Huxley found the well-worn leather chair that he frequented and got comfortable. He had already read through most of the adventure novels and practical skills books. He could work more on chemistry and the physical sciences, but he yearned for something different. His thoughts were disturbed by a shout that sounded more like a scream. The noise cut through the silence of the library. Huxley hastened towards the back room, his senses alert. He peeked around the corner.

"Hello? Is anyone hurt?"

No response. He decided to investigate. He made his way past some old bookcases and found the librarian, Agnes, collecting a pile of books off the ground. She appeared unhurt, but disheveled and frustrated.

"Huxley!" She yelled at him, almost sounding like an accusation.

"Yes?" He replied.

"Very sorry for the ruckus. I'm trying to pack things up and I'm not quite as strong as I used to be." She stooped down to pick up some more books.

"Pack things up? For what?" Huxley asked.

"Huxley, don't tell me you've forgotten already?" She looked at him unamused.

He thought for a second and it all snapped back. "The kinship revival festival!" He said while breathing in.

Agnes continued stacking books.

"Yes, of course. We discussed it two weeks ago. You said you would help me. I've already picked out the perfect spot for our 'mini library.'"

Of course, Huxley remembered now. Guilt stabbed him for forgetting, but moved on to the disappointment of realizing tonight would not be the quiet evening of study he had hoped for.

"Of course, I remembered Agnes. I must have just gotten my head hit too hard today in training."

"Oh, yes? Are you still going to that awful place? It would make sense that the one other person around here who appreciates books would go out and get his head caved in by some brute who can't even read."

Agnes had always been outspoken in her disdain of the militia.

"It's not that bad Agnes. It's good exercise."

"Well, it's no matter, you're here now. Would you help me with this next case?"

Huxley felt his evening drifting away. This realization hit hard. Harder than practice. He pushed down his disappointment in hopes of it not showing and said, "Of course Agnes."

He certainly did not want to help, but she had been so sweet to him, how could he really leave her here to work alone while he studied? Besides, his help might endear him enough to her to let him take home a few of the research books she almost never let out of the building. Their work took an hour or so. It went a little faster than expected and Huxley felt a well of hope spring up. Maybe he would get at least a few minutes of reading. Those thoughts were dashed when Agnes told him that she wanted to close early in order to get a jump on the next day. She all but pushed him out the front door while he made attempts to stay late. Agnes' tone was not one that would be bartered with. She had a plan and intended to keep it. Huxley gave up and the door shut in his face. He breathed a sigh and turned around to walk home disappointed. Agnes surprised him when she burst back out the door and called after him.

"Oh Huxley, I forgot to give you your package!" Huxley blinked in surprise. She shoved it into his hands and said "Feels like a book!" Before he could respond, Agnes had scurried back inside and locked the door. Huxley stood there surprised, clutching what felt like a book wrapped in brown paper and tied with twine.

His imagination consumed him for the whole walk home. It had to be a mistake or maybe his friends playing a trick on him ... or maybe someone really did send him something. Maybe Agnes was so impressed with his scholarly pursuits that she wrote a letter to the nearest University vouching for his intelligence and drive and they wanted to extend an invitation! That last thought was certainly a daydream. No one from any learned place even knew his name.

––

After rushing home, Huxley finally arrived at his street. The houses were humble and old, which was true of most of the town. New buildings were expensive and required skilled teams and architects. Such skilled craftsmen stayed away from towns like his. Instead, the people here favored simple buildings that were blocky and would not require much upkeep. Knowledge was usually reserved for the wealthy or powerful and Mayburn had little of both. Most residents lived in the older buildings that were here before the Embers took the land back from nature. Just rip out the vines and sweep out the dirt and you have a home.

His house looked the same as the rest, except for a tell-tale pile of shoes out front. His family's storefront wasn't far but when your shoes are broken the walk would be terrible. So they accepted shoes that were dropped off at all hours and returned in the same way. "Make it easier for them to give you money." Huxley's father always said. He was right, it had certainly made a steady income but it also meant a pile of shoes near their doorstep...always.

He opened the door and the aroma of dinner hit him. It was tangy and sweet smelling, which was most welcome. His mother had been hard at work. On days when the store closed early, his mother enjoyed experimenting with new recipes. His stomach grumbled at him for ignoring it for so long. Ordinarily, he would try to sneak up to his room for some peace and quiet and come down later, but not tonight. His parents were not big supporters of him being so busy, but he was too hungry to bother hiding or avoiding them. He walked right into the kitchen and greeted his parents. Hugging his mom, he snuck a look at what was cooking. It was a mixture of greens with roasted chicken and potatoes. After his day, it was the most welcome thing he could think of. His father asked him to set the table as was his customary job. He was already at work getting it done when his sister rushed into the room. Oakley was a wild auburn-haired twelve-year-old girl who loved to talk and loved to bother Huxley even more. She was almost always smiling even when upset. She was sweet most days, but Huxley had begun not paying as much attention to her as he once did and that brought the imp out of her. She routinely mocked his hair, his style, his ears, his lack of a girlfriend, and really anything that occurred to her. Huxley took it in stride, even gave sass back on occasion. Today was not a great day for it, but Oakley had not sensed that.

"Hey, Huxley! Where have you been? Mom and Dad think you're wasting your life, so do your friends, and so do I, actually. Is it true? Are you wasting your life? It sure seems like it. WAIT don't respond, answer this question. Were you at the library or were you with an actual girl?"

Huxley sighed deeply and said, "it's not--"

"Hah! I knew it. 'Ooo my name's Huxley and I prefer to read about other people's lives than living one of my own.'" Huxley just turned and left the room. He could hear her call from the dining room, "Aww come back. I didn't mean it!" But she did. He knew she did. The words did not hurt so much as he just did not have the energy to keep up with her. Best to leave it alone. Huxley's mom met him while she was carrying most of their dinner in a large pot and said, "Huxley get back in there and be nice to your sister! She misses you while you're away."

Huxley rounded on her and said, "Me be nice to her?" He emphasized hard to make his point. But his mother was gone before he could defend the matter further. His father was next. He was a tall man with hardly any hair left and a short well-kept beard that had been tailored to make a point at the end of his chin. He had small glasses that rested low on his nose, and he was almost always dressed in his work clothes. Shoemaking was more than his career. It was his passion, hobby, and interest. He was a loving father and husband, but his heart was in shoemaking. Huxley expected it was because he could understand it easily, unlike his family.

He looked at Huxley carefully and said, "Welcome home son, your mom is in a mood. Keep your head down." He gave Huxley a wink. As if to say "Just ride this night out." Huxley could not have agreed more. He just wanted to eat dinner and go up to his room.

He rejoined his family at the dinner table. Oakley chattered from the very beginning to her dad and he paid attention for the most part. In between mouthfuls, he would offer an "Oh my," and "That's so interesting." That was all Oakley needed to continue. Huxley was not paying much attention to Oakley, instead, his full attention was on the potatoes. They ate potatoes on most nights, but finding good herbs to season with was rare. This batch was seasoned in such a way that the smell alone made his mouth water. They only got new spices when a trader came through town and for a week or so they greatly looked forward to dinners. Huxley was reaching for a second helping when he caught his mom's eyes shooting glances his way. It was not uncommon, but the looks seemed intense, more than normal anyway. He thought he was just imagining things and continued to eat quickly and quietly. The meal continued and the food shrank while their bellies filled. The conversation lulled and a strange quiet descended on the room. The feeling was one that any son could recognize. His parents wanted to talk. Maybe they were moving, maybe mom was pregnant, maybe we were getting a new dog? Probably not. Dogs were forbidden in his household after the first attempt left many destroyed shoes. Huxley decided to test the waters, "So Mom, Dad, are you excited about the kinship revival festival coming up?" Festivals were always a good thing to talk about. It was good for business and it was a lot of fun. Who would not be excited? They both looked up from their meals and exchanged glances. "Yes, we are Hux, are you?"

"Well yeah, last year there were about fifty carts with different shows and shops. Remember the guy that could catch a knife that was thrown right at him?"

Oakley bellowed out, "Oh, my goodness, yes!"

His parents nodded along. That was a good sign.

"Or how about those animals that were so big they were busting out of the cages?" He added

His mother snorted, "Unseemly creatures of the wilds, those things were."

"Or the guy that could freeze water like snow and make it something that we could eat?" Huxley continued.

His mom smiled and said, "Oh yes, he also liked to charge enough to buy a new house."

"Well, it was a special machine that freezes ice Lamria." His dad said placatingly.

"Well, I have a special machine that melts ice, it's called a fire!" She snapped back.

This was not going as Huxley had hoped. His mom's good mood was slipping away. It always did when they talked about spending clips.

Huxley decided it was time to try to slip upstairs.

"Well, if everyone is finishing up, I'll start the dishes..." Nobody responded and right as Huxley began to move he saw the table bump and his dad wince. Great. This was all he needed today. Another talk with his parents about his potential path he was headed on in life.

Just relax, don't get mad. Just agree that I need to work harder.

His dad cleared his throat and began, "Umm just a second son, we wanted to talk to you."

"Yeah! Let's have a little chat." Oakley said with a big grin.

"No, not you Oaks, you go to bed."

"Ugh, fine. Night Hux! I hope you don't get kicked out." And with that, she darted off.

His mother scrutinized him. He knew she was mad or disappointed or something. He could endure it. Huxley sat down and prepared himself.

"Ok...what is it?" Huxley asked, tensing over what was to come.

"Where were you this afternoon Huxley?" His mother asked with a cold tone.

"This afternoon!? Right after practice I walked over to the store and checked again that we were closed. I even asked you this morning and you said that we were closing early."

His mother's voice remained the same. "That's not why I asked. I said, 'where were you this afternoon?'"

Huxley looked confused for a minute and said, "I went to training after work and then went by the shop to make sure everything was closed up, and then..." He realized now that they might not love that he was spending his free time at the library. "...I went to the library."

When he spoke it his mom and dad looked at each other confirming their suspicions.

"Son, your mother and I are concerned about how you spend your time. Training and then heading off to read, it's not good."

"What's wrong with the way I spend my time?" He could feel the anger growing inside him.

"Your mother and I are concerned that you don't have a good path set up for your future. We don't understand why you don't want to learn more about how to run the family business. If you are going to take over in a few years you need to know the accounting and the craft far better."

Those words surprised him. What had ever given his father the impression that he wanted to take over the family business?

"Dad...Mom...surely you know..." He searched for the right words.

He had lost his train of thought. What if he offends them? Was this the right time for this conversation? But he was too tired to be diplomatic. ".... you know I don't want to take over the business right?"

His father did not react, but his mother threw her hands up in the air and stood up pushing her seat back, nearly making it topple. Huxley heard a squeak from up the stairs. Oakley was listening. But that was the least of his concerns.

"Huxley. Hewlun. Durant. What do you mean by that? So, what then? You want to be a traveling salesman or a librarian or go run into the Wilds and join bandits!?" She practically screamed.

He held his hands up to calm her down and said. "Mom, no! I don't want any of those things. I don't know what I want. I just know I don't want to be a shoemaker."

"What options do you think you have? You never did well in school. You barely passed your final year, I hear that you are only an adequate militia man. Imagine that? You can't even excel at the job where someone tells you exactly what to do! So...I'm curious, what do you think you will be doing instead of taking over shoemaking in a few years. Something, by the way, that most of your friends will never get in their lifetime. Handed such a great opportunity only to be thrown away? Well, maybe we should just sell it now and move so that Huxley can be alone!" She seemed to be talking to herself at this point.

This was going worse than he imagined. What was getting her so upset? This was not new information to her. He had never hung around the shop more than he needed to. She was acting bizarre even for her.

His father spoke in a loud and clear voice. "Huxley, let's step outside. Lamria, clean up. I will talk to him." His mom began muttering, but mainly just reiterating what she just said as she left the room.

Huxley stepped outside and was met with the cold night air. It was so placid and still compared to the room he just left. His Dad followed behind him, clearly agitated.

Huxley took a seat in a rocking chair. His father sat in the one next to him. "Sorry about that."

"Where did that come from?" Huxley asked.

His father took a few seconds to think about it.

"Well Huxley, for the past few months your mother and I have been talking about your future. As she said, we had hoped that you would be the one to take over the shop. We have trained you enough and with a little more focus you could be as skilled as I am. Aren't you interested in that at all?"

Huxley knew that this conversation would happen one day. Not today, but one day. He knew he had to let his father down, but how to put it?

But his father continued. "My guess is that you aren't."

Maybe his father had been paying more attention than he thought.

"But if not this, then what? It's true, Captain Pilch tells us you are good at following orders and respect his position and others, but you aren't a stand-out soldier. You were never one for academics, you don't even like running around with your friends, although you do make friends so that's good but not...great you know?"

"Good but not great? Why is that bad?" Huxley asked.

"It's not exactly, I guess what I'm saying is, you've only ever been...passable."

Huxley did not know how to take that.

"Passable?"

"Yes, but don't take that the wrong way! I don't mean it as an insult. I mean it as a compliment."

"As a compliment?" Huxley asked indignantly.

"Yes, I mean, you have never been great at anything that you attempted, but you've been good enough to be passable. You never quite fail, which is something many people do." He added that last part hastily. "You seem to be at least good enough in most categories, which I think is kind of rare. I'm actually quite proud of you in that regard. But the problem is, as your father, I want more than that for you. If you go out on your own and try to be more than you are, you will experience failure for the first time. And let me tell you, *it hurts*. We are concerned about you spending time at the library because we know that you aren't a scholar and certainly not an Ember. I'm worried that you might be filling your head with grand notions of what is possible, when it isn't. When your mother and I started here in Mayburn it was our third try at a business. We had to work hard for many long hours and ate sparingly just to get ahead. And now that our business is well established and thriving we want it to continue to succeed." His face softened and he looked right into his son's eyes. "We think it is the best way for you to be happy and comfortable and able to raise a family of your own. Do you understand?" His father looked at him with kindness, but also concern.

Huxley responded with a quiet answer, "yes."

Huxley did not know how to feel. Only just passable? That was perhaps that harshest criticism he had ever received. People have said meaner to him, but this felt like it was a well-thought-over opinion, like it was the end result of a lifetime of measure. What hurt the worst was, deep down he knew it was true. It stung. To his surprise, his eyes began to mist up. He blinked to dissipate it and he looked straight up into the sky. The stars shone brightly. Were they shining brighter than normal? It was probably just his eyes filling up and catching the light. Mercifully, his father did not press for an answer. He put his hand on Huxley's shoulder.

They sat together for what was probably close to an hour. They talked a little bit about their day but it was mainly trying not to acknowledge what they just discussed. His father shifted in his seat, looked over at Huxley, and said, "I love you son, and I want the best for you, so does your mother. Let's talk more about it tomorrow." And he got up and left the porch leaving Huxley alone. Huxley had been thankful for him changing the location of this conversation. He had always found the stars relaxing. It helped to look up at the night sky and see that his problems were small compared to the vastness of the sky and the stars. As he gazed at the shimmering stars Huxley suddenly remembered the package waiting in his room.

Daring to hope for one thing besides potatoes to be good about his day, he hustled to his bedroom. Settled at his desk to inspect the package, he picked it up. The packaging crinkled in his hands and he looked it over. No label, just thick paper wrapped with twine. Was this definitely for him? He was too curious to wait. He undid the twine and the paper fell away revealing a book. Anges was right, but it was not like any book he had ever seen. It was brown leather bound and had two blackened well-worn thick leather buckles going around the sides and the spine, clasping over the front. The book was weathered and looked ancient. He checked the spine and saw some faded symbols that he could not decipher. A musty aroma met his nostrils. Huxley breathed it in as he prepared himself to look inside. He undid the buckles with care. He could not be sure how old the book was and he feared damaging it if opened too clumsily. He slowly lifted the cover, the book opened with a crackling of pages on the spine. A note was inscribed on the first page.

Upon my death or madness, deliver this grimoire to its heir.

"Oh no," Huxley said out loud. Every part of that sentence was unnerving. Death or madness? A grimoire? An heir? What even was a grimoire? Huxley thought he had read that word once before, but not recently. Huxley made a mental note to ask Agnes about the meaning and origins of the word later. *I can't be its heir.* He thought, *The only thing I'm heir to is a business that I don't want.* Should he read on? If this was not his property he probably should leave it alone. His desire to know more about this grimoire drove him to continue.

Well, it isn't a diary. He reasoned, *And reading it will probably help me figure out who's it is.*

He flipped the page and was astonished to realize the book was hand-written. He had never held a hand-written book before. They are incredibly rare, printing in mass production started about forty years ago, hand-written books became obsolete. Huxley had thought only the rich and powerful had access to what was left of the handwritten books for their collections.

It seemed the more he read the more questions he had. The Grimoire was incomprehensible. Huxley's frustrations swelled as his inability to make any sense of this madman's scribbles gave way to the haunting words from his parents. After a while, he could not ignore it anymore. His parents were right. He had gotten his hopes up when he discovered his love of books, but he was routinely baffled by their context. Some science books were impossible to follow from page one. Books of poetry were so colorful and packed full of imagery, he always got lost in their meaning. He was not a secret scholar or a great fighter. So, what was he? That question would not be answered tonight. It would have to wait until morning. Huxley put the grimoire in his bag, perhaps Agnes could give him some insights. He made his way upstairs and collapsed onto his bed. His eyelids grew overly heavy and he could not hold back sleep, nor did he want to. Perhaps tomorrow will be better. How could it be any worse?

3

Paper and Leather

The morning was as awkward as the night before, maybe worse. Everyone avoided each other and got ready in relative silence. Oakley was the exception, she was never silent. She asked about his training. She wanted to know the difference between a cutlass and a rapier. She wondered whether or not he would become part of the Mayburn Guard or maybe the elite scouts and attempt to tame the outlying wilderness area. He tried his best to satisfy her curiosity. He did not know the answer to most of her questions. That didn't seem to bother her, she might have just liked asking them. He was glad for the good company and tried to enjoy it. He guessed work would not be as pleasant.

The Durant's shoe store aptly named, "Durant's shoes," was full of shoes and no customers. Huxley's father never liked the idea of flashy over-thought names for stores. "Why shouldn't we be clear in our messaging? It's SHOES made by the DURANTS! Was his typical response when pushed for something more interesting. The majority of the business was done in the afternoons when most people were out of work. It was well organized in the front, with each shoe prominently displayed for inspection. Every day they were cleaned and the shop swept. Sunlight poured through the two front windows illuminating every last speck of dust. Durant's Shoes was not a large place, but it was certainly the cleanest thanks to his efforts. The back room was a different story. Huxley was used to the piles of shoes in various degrees of repair or creation. It didn't seem a mess at all. It was a well-organized workroom but the uninitiated would see it differently.

Located near the town square, it was actually a cozy place, dark wood floors with red display cases. A brightly lacquered desk to talk with customers and long benches that creaked every time someone sat on them. Like most of Mayburn when the town was reclaimed from the Fecundity's outgrowth it had likely been another place before. But when Huxley's dad bought it, all he could see was the showroom floor. He would go on and on about how important the location was, optimal for all routes of business and not too far from their house. It was nearly in central Mayburn, his father was right about traffic. It was surrounded by other businesses of course, and they weren't much bigger than theirs. In truth, it fit in just right. Durant's Shoes became a constant reminder of what Huxley was supposed to be.

The Wardens and some engineers had recently been outfitting all of downtown with gas pipes to allow constantly fed lanterns and not the oil pumped kind. His father still hadn't done it citing daylight as his preferred light source. He always resisted change, like it was a creeping rot that could only hurt and not help. Huxley could tell his mom liked the idea but rarely disagreed with his father when it came to the business.

Huxley's hours at the shop were uncomfortable. His family was not great at idle chat already, but they were even worse at dealing with arguments. This is probably the reason why normal conversations ended up building into explosive talks.

The minutes of the day ticked away, and when what felt like an eternity passed Huxley checked the time. It had only been an hour since he got started.

When Huxley had finally dusted the store twice and couldn't possibly think of something else to do, he gave more thought to the idea of taking over. The more time he spent thinking about it, the more he was sure he did not want to. It was a quiet life which was a good thing in a way. An occasional grumpy customer might complain about how tight his toes felt, but most days it was repetitive and reliable work. Huxley began to question himself. *Why don't I want this? I could work, then go to the library. I could have more free time than most people get and have a stable income. Certainly, this would be beneficial to finding a wife and raising a family. Doesn't everyone want this? What is holding me back? Why was the idea so...repulsive?*

Just before lunch, he realized he had to start waking his brain up. He had to be ready mentally for training. It was a three-hour block of his day where laziness in mind or body would not be tolerated. He viewed it as a test in endurance. If he could get through his time there he could get through anything. At two o'clock he began packing his things up. Just then, his mother approached after a whole day of silence.

She finally wanted to talk.

She walked right up to him, hugged him, and said, "Huxley, I'm sorry for last night. I just worry about you so much." She sniffed and began to cry.

"It's alright mom."

"No, it's not. I need to be more patient. You'll come around. I'm sure of it. You'll be ready when the time comes."

"What? When what time comes?" Huxley asked in confusion.

"Huxley. Your father told me that you came around last night and you indicated that you would likely be ready in a few months, a year at the most..." She trailed off while looking for his dad at his workbench. His chair was empty and was still swiveling. "Arthur Durant you coward!" She chased after him. Clearly, his dad told his own version of last night's talk and fled the scene when he needed to back it up. Huxley took the opportunity to do the same. He ran out the front door and made his escape.

––

Huxley's friends were waiting for him outside the gear room. Captain Pilch made them wait while the other squads racked their gear. Jonah, Bennett, and about twenty other guys were all milling around, joking and laughing. It seemed like this kind of thing came easily to them, perhaps they even looked forward to training. Huxley had been preparing mentally for the last three hours. His friends greeted him with hugs and punches, as was a tradition which he hated but accepted. It was a welcomed normalcy after last night.

After a few minutes, the boys started getting restless. Was the Captain late? No, he was never late. What time was it? Huxley glanced at the sun and did a trick to guess the time. If he raised his fist straight up in the air that should be noon, and if every fist stacked hand by hand to the sun counted as an hour he could make a rough guess.

While he was doing this, Jonah began to make fun of him, "Hey Huxley, did you read that in a book somewhere?" he said in a mocking tone.

"Actually, yes, Jonah." He answered.

Jonah looked side to side, "Well, I bet that makes you so..." Bennett punched him in the arm harder than normal, cutting off his speech.

"Shut up Jonah, I want to know what time it is too." Said Bennett.

Huxley did the measurement a few times. "It's close to three. Honestly, where is the Captain?"

Right as Huxley finished the question the doors swung open. Two high-ranking Wardens were talking with the Captain and speaking in hushed tones. He only noted their rank because truthfully, Huxley hadn't seen those except on paper. It chilled him. Wardens ran most parts of the government but in Mayburn the highest-ranked Warden wasn't even close to these guys.

"Very well, then. We will be ready." Pilch spoke in short certain sentences and he gave a well-practiced salute.

The two Wardens returned the salute while gazing out over the young soldiers. Then they swiftly walked away.

Captain Pilch thought to himself a second and then shouted out, "Sorry for the delay everyone. Go ahead and gear up, we're late!"

The group moved slowly when one voice called out, "Sir, is everything alright? Are we under attack?"

Huxley was glad someone asked. And the Captain responded, "Everything will be fine, but we need to talk. Get ready! I will see you in the main yard."

That answer was insufficient to say the least. The obvious answer was bad. Mayburn was a quiet place and relatively free from conflict, but skirmishes did happen on occasion. Periodically, beasts who'd grown mad from the Fecundity would make their way out of the forest. Huxley was certain he heard a shakiness in the Captain's voice that he had never heard before and that unnerved him. It had been years since an actual attack. Why would they call up trainees? The guard had been enough to stop bandits in the past. Surely, we aren't prepared. But in a crisis, no one is ever prepared. He'd given his oath that he would stand in battle, his hand shook, and he could barely hold his sword steady let alone swing it properly.

By the Arcane Flame, I hope it's not an attack.

Speculation ran wild in the few minutes away from the Captain. As they geared up the questions flew.

"Maybe it's hazing from the older soldiers to welcome us?"

"Maybe it's one of the ancient beasts from the eastern wilds!"

"Maybe your mom has run out of pastries and we have to subdue her. Obviously, the entire Guard can't stop her."

"Maybe that warlord I heard about is at our gates right now!"

It went on and on. How could they be so cavalier about this? Surely, Mayburn was ill-equipped to handle a real threat. It was the talk of young men, full of excitement, bravado, and naivety. They hastily made their way into the practice yard curious for information.

Captain Pilch was waiting for them. They fell into their training formations, eagerly awaiting news. Pilch's face betrayed nothing.

Just as they thought he would not wait any longer he yelled, "LAPS!"

The boys looked back and forth confused and slowly began jogging. Laps were the way they started every day. The excitement faded. Practice proceeded as normal though Pilch was quieter and more precise shedding most of his jovial demeanor. Something was definitely wrong. But, it looked like they would not get answers until it was absolutely necessary.

At the end of training, they all cleaned up, racked their gear, and met in the middle of the yard for their end-of-the-day prayer. Instead, Pilch held his hand up for silence. This was it.

"I'm sure you lads are worried. I can see it in your faces. You needn't be. A few scouts have reported movement in the east. Likely, they are packing up to move out." He paused to let the excited chattering stop. "Okay, calm down. Nevertheless, we need to be on alert. Ember Palithur has issued a standby alert to all militiamen, and that includes you all. I'm sure we won't need you, but, regardless, you should be ready. If he needs our support then we will give it. As an Ember of the Arcane Flame, he can handle a small group of unorganized wild men."

Another burst of chatter and Plich lost their attention.

"Ember Palithur might actually fight!"

"We might SEE Magnincy!"

Huxley couldn't contain himself. As much as he hated to see the town attacked, he wanted morbidly to see Palithur use Magnincy. He'd never actually seen it, he only read stories, tons and tons of stories. To actually witness all that vast knowledge put to use would be a wonderous thing.

The Captain wrestled control back and said in a too-loud voice. IF YOU HEAR THE BELLS RING..." His voice faded once theirs did. "Then show up here as soon as possible! That is all. I'll see you all tomorrow."

He turned to walk away when a boy said, "Sir, what about the prayer?"

"Hmm? Oh yes!" Pilch trotted back over.

He raised both hands and the boys followed as everyone repeated, "Through knowledge and will he keeps madness at bay, his mind is our savior and our protector. Sundered lands be made whole again, MAY IT BE RECLAIMED!"

There was less excitement and more worried discussion. The boy's curiosity was satisfied, but it was replaced with a dose of fear. Pilch was probably right. What would a real army want with them? They didn't even have riches to take. There were stories of wild men trying to attack cities instead of travelers. It was rare, but it happened. What if this was one of those times?

Huxley heard a loud crack as Bennet climbed onto a wooden box that he just slammed down. He stood up to his full height and commanded attention.

Bennett looked at the squad and said, "I know what you all are thinking. And to be honest, I'm worried too. But this is precisely what the last few months have been about. If we let fear shake us, then we are playing right into their hands. If we are to meet the enemy in combat we will do it as a unit and as brothers! I have seen this group turn into a real platoon of soldiers. No, we aren't the most experienced or skilled but we are strong, brave, and determined. Mayburn is our home and we won't let marauders come and take it! Who's with me?" He waited and got a smattering of cheers which swelled into the whole squad cheering. Even Huxley felt his fear shrink. They needed this moment. Bennett changed everyone's attitude and showed what a small amount of bravado could do. Huxley felt the camaraderie swell around him. Maybe they could handle anything the wilds could throw at them. The boys dispersed and Huxley went home, his spirits lifted.

———————————————————————————————————-

It was a Tuesday which meant Huxley would have some work to do in the shop before he could head to the library. But when he got there they were already locked up for the night. This was peculiar, but Huxley knew it was most likely due to the fight they were having earlier. One of the benefits of owning your own place is setting your own hours. Huxley was glad for the additional time to pour over the Grimoire. There were a few things in life that felt better than unexpected good news, like getting an extra hour of sleep or finding extra clips in your pocket. After the stress of work and training, he welcomed this chance. The library was bustling with activity, unlike yesterday. Agnes had been up all night, packing and getting ready. Stacks lay semi-organized and half-packed. Agnes was running all over, looking disheveled and tired.

"Hello." Said Huxley.

Agnes stopped suddenly and looked at him. "Oh, Huxley. Hello as well! Welcome to the chaos!" She laughed while gesturing around herself. "Please have a seat and enjoy a good read. We have the new editions available. Sorry about yesterday. I think I finally have a good system for packing."

"I'm glad to hear it. So, you don't need help then?" He asked sheepishly.

"Oh no, I'm nearly finished. Thanks!" Agnes said.

Huxley did not hesitate, he went and sat in his favorite leather chair and pulled the mysterious tome from his bag. The grimoire had a weird sense about it. Almost like it wanted to be read. He did not know how to interpret that. It clearly could not want anything; it was just a book, but it just felt that way. Like it wanted to be understood by him. He unbuckled it and laid it across his lap.

Huxley hadn't read a book like this before. The Grimoire was a part journal, part encyclopedia, part science textbook and part naturalism collection with sketches of creatures observed. The biggest problem was that the subjects and thoughts were disconnected. He understood the words as written but when put together they made no sense. It really might have been written by a madman as the note implied, but it also stated that if he did go mad then the book should be given away. Perhaps, this was his descent into madness? If so, was this book useless? Huxley was determined to get something out of it. His confusion only grew. It was like an artifact from another time. There were schematics for machines that used sources of power he had never even heard of. He couldn't even pronounce the names of most of them. "E-lek-tric" he tried saying a few times. It was presented as a source of movement like steam. There were others but they were more advanced. He pulled out some paper and began taking notes. He wanted to see if he could connect the thoughts. There was a main text on every page. Those were in immaculate penmanship. Typically, it was accompanied by a loose sketch of the subject. Those were helpful but they were also imprecise. Some were musings of a theory and the others were mathematically sound schematics. There was a whole section on the Fecundity and the animals and flora found inside it. The animals had growth patterns that shaped them into horrible monsters over time. He understood this part best. Everyone had a horror story of something terrifying crawling out of the Wilds. It was deeply unnerving that the Grimoire supported their existence. If he truly encountered some of these creatures, he probably would not have time to sketch them out properly. There were objects detailed as well. One was a sword that seemed crystalline in property. Like it was carved instead of forged. It was interesting. Huxley wondered if that could really be done.

His notes continued for a few hours. The book was fascinating at first, but over time he grew frustrated. Why was he unable to make the connections? Did he just not have enough of an understanding? The more he read the more he became sure there was a common thread, but he could not see it. Most baffling were the pages that contained exact thoughts on science. There were pictures of fires and small notes that point to specific regions, as though an individual lick of flame could be studied. Others were directions of seeds and fruits. Some looked straight out of a history book from the old days. The last page was a complete enigma. Huxley had to reread it a few times. It had a symbol on it. The symbol was a tangled knot with a burning orb in the middle. This page repeated itself often and seemed agitated, yet reverent. Was it a religious symbol? Religion had been a part of the past but the more people learned in science the more it faded away. So why was the Grimoire, obviously a scientific book tied together with religion?

His frustration grew. It felt like he was a toddler grasping at understanding how to cook, it was just too far out of his understanding.. But worse than that, it confirmed to him that he was probably not the heir to this grimoire. He would need years of instruction before he could understand these concepts.

But every time his mind told him to find the true heir or maybe even just tell someone like Palithur, he stopped himself. As though a quiet whispering voice said "No." It even sounded real in some moments. Like it was next to him, a quiet voice urging him not to quit.

Whenever he heard the "No" in response to quitting it steeled his resolve to go on. He was hopelessly out of his depth but perhaps, with enough effort, he could figure it out. Like a puzzle, overwhelming at first, but once you connect enough pieces, it becomes easier. It had already shown him so much that was possible. The Grimoire made his imagination kindle in a way nothing had ever done before. He may not understand the minutiae of it, but he could certainly see that it contained wonders. In fact, it might contain the greatest secrets that Magnadun had to offer.

His understanding had not grown but his certainty did. Certainty, that there was no going back, and as this realization sank in, he became determined. *I am going to figure this out, every single word of it...somehow.* He settled on his new mission and buckled the book shut. He slid the grimoire into his pack and looked up. It was dark outside. He gulped realizing he had lost track of time.

He blinked. His eyes had grown so dry while reading the Grimoire. His focus and drive had made him forget to blink more often. He wanted to slip out of the library. He felt, for some reason, that the grimoire ought to be kept secret and he did not want Agnes to get nosey. Fortunately, Agnes was busy preparing for the festival. Seeing Agnes reminded him that he had hoped to ask her about the meaning of the word grimoire. He hesitated in a moment of indecision. He needed to keep the book a secret. She turned and noticed him, so Huxley took a chance and blurted out, "Hey Agnes, what's a grimoire?"

Oh, you fool.

She looked right back at him. She did not seem surprised by the question.

"A grimoire? Hmm a grimmmoooiirree". She sounded the word out emphasizing the middle. *Good job, Huxley. Maybe she will start yelling it to townsfolk next.*

"Oh. yes! I remember. A grimoire is a book of magic spells or incantations."

She said that as though she was reading it. It made sense. That seemed to fit the very personal nature of the book.

"Oh, alright thanks." He turned to leave, but of course, she followed up.

"Why? Is that what you got in the mail?" She asked coyly.

He decided to lie. "No, not at all. That package was just something for the store I forgot I ordered. I am here so much I put this address so that I got it delivered more directly." Not a bad lie either. That was pretty believable but if she scrutinized more, it might fall apart.

"That makes sense. It's a little disappointing though. It would have been interesting to read a grimoire, but I doubt they actually exist." She turned back to her work

Huxley smiled to himself, pleased with his answer but the temptation to ask another was too strong. "Why do you doubt they exist?" He asked.

"Oh" She laughed and said "Only Embers have Grimoires, and they don't send them in the mail. They keep them in the Tower of the Arcane Flame. I've never even heard of one outside the tower."

Huxley thanked her with a nervous nod, and rushed out of the library, not caring how strange or obvious he looked. He gripped his newly gifted Grimoire knowing for certain now that he wasn't the recipient. In it were all manner of concepts he did not understand because it was intended for an Ember! That confirmed it wasn't for him but he was not ready to give it up yet. He would learn every secret it carried first.

———————————————————————————————————-

That night Huxley's mind tormented him. Had he just lucked upon a treasure trove of knowledge? If he sold the Grimoire, he couldn't count the amount of clips it might fetch.

Huxley's heart sank as he considered that it might be a cleverly drawn children's book. Afterall, people had done that before. Forgeries and fakes were a huge business in Danador and the inner cities. They were skillfully made to fool someone long enough to trick them out of clips. But it was awfully detailed for a forgery. He wasn't sure it was genuine but if it wasn't, he was holding a well-crafted fake.

Huxley plopped down on his bed, grabbed the Grimoire, opened the buckles again and looked at the note.

"Upon my death or madness, deliver this grimoire to its heir."

He read it to himself a few times. His face scrunched up reading it over and over. If he died it would make sense to leave it to someone. But if he went mad, who would trust his words? Who would really follow the will of a madman? And how would they determine his heir? Huxley thought this was too difficult to answer without more information. So he turned his attention to the book.

He studied late into the night and made pages of notes. He felt like his mind had been switched on for the first time like something deep within him had been sleeping and was now finally awake. His progress was like crawling up a mountain. He knew progress was happening but was unable to tell how much. The strangest part was no matter how difficult he found the subject matter, it only emboldened him to try harder. In the past such a difficult chore would have defeated him. Studying the Grimoire didn't have that effect, the opposite in fact.

It was well past midnight when he finally grew too frustrated to keep going. Once sleep started to set in, the more he read, the more confused he got. Huxley glanced at the first page before closing up the book. At the top was an entry. The title there read: "Eyes that see what others cannot". Another portion read, "the veil must be witnessed, and expulsion of intended recipients." Huxley considered a veil as a thin piece of fabric people wore to cover their head or face, so perhaps he needed to wear a veil while reading these pages? Like a cypher? He imagined himself wearing a veil and reading the grimoire and laughed at himself. I will put that in the "maybe" category. He looked again at the "expulsion of intended recipients" section. What could that mean? The rest of the text was mired in ambiguity. He could read all of the words individually, but together they made nonsense. Then his understanding shifted and his heart sank.

What if this was a joke? What if the grimoire didn't contain secrets of the arcane but was rather a wedding etiquette guide?

Eyes that see? Veil? Expulsion? It was the management of a wedding and when to bring out the bride and when to move the guests, just written in poetic language.

Huxley swore.

Jonah probably did this!

They would think it was so hilarious that Huxley got a fake book full of mysterious things meant to torment him. And if he asked them about it, they would pretend like they knew nothing and try to convince him that he found something special. If he had not been so angry he might have agreed that it was funny. He slammed the grimoire closed and did not bother to buckle it. Huxley lay in bed, mood ruined and feeling foolish.

He was too angry with himself to go to sleep now. Huxley climbed out of bed and walked over to his window. It overlooked his front yard and had access to the front veranda. Outside the stars were in full regalia accompanied by a crescent moon. He opened the window and the cool night air drifted in. Oddly enough, he felt compelled to climb out. Huxley, by nature, was not a huge risk taker, but with how good the air felt and how appealing the night sky looked, he decided to climb out onto the veranda.

The roof sagged up and down but held his weight. Huxley laid down and breathed deep. What a couple of days it had been! He'd been beaten up, robbed of reading, yelled at, scared to the core, and pranked. And there was no end to the cycle in sight. He needed a vacation, or maybe just a day without anything going wrong.

He rubbed his eyes and really drank in the starlight. They reminded him of a few books he had read. There were endless theories about what they were. One was that they were great warriors or knights of the past looking down on us. Another was that it was part of a large network of celestial bodies. One crazy one was the boats of souls lost in the sea in the afterlife. His personal favorite was that it was the lights of eternity itself and the black sky was a huge blanket that covered it up. The lights poking through were small holes in the fabric so we could catch glimpses of the light. He imagined deities in eternity walking around and blocking out the holes periodically to make them twinkle. It was the silliest, but also the most comforting. Someone was watching. Someone was looking out for him. It made his problems seem miniscule. He thought he saw a brief wrinkle in the sky, like a ripple in a pond. When he looked again, he realized it was his eyes fading out from sheer exhaustion.

Huxley could not be sure when he fell asleep but it wasn't the sun that woke him up. Bells were clanging all over town. Mayburn was under attack.

4

Wood and Flame

"Reaching for what could be while accepting what is, leads one to burn bright but remain the same which is no bad thing."- **Page 1 Excerpt from the Grimoire**

The clanging bells ripped Huxley from his sleep. His training kicked in and he leaped to his feet, almost losing his balance on the veranda. His body was stiff from sleeping on such an unusual surface and his clothes were soaked in dew. He couldn't believe how well-rested he felt despite it all. He climbed into his room, threw on his trousers, and put on a long white linen shirt. Huxley heard shouts coming down the hall telling him what he already knew. He beheld the grimoire still lying on the ground. Was it beckoning to him? He sensed a pull from somewhere deep inside him to take it. He shook his head, clearing the thought away. What good would a book do? Huxley slid the grimoire under his bed. Joke or no, he did not want anyone to know about it yet. He dashed from his room while throwing his long hair back in an unkempt ponytail. His parents tried talking to him on the way out the front door but he was too fo-cused and worried to hear them. His mother seized him and hugged him tightly which he did not have time to return. It wasn't out of anger, but a nagging thought began to gain ground. What if the walls were being breached right now and his squad needed him?

"Sorry, mom I HAVE to go!" Huxley yelled.

He tore himself away and raced out the front door. He could faintly hear his mother weep behind him as he sprinted toward the unknown. He would be sure to apologize later, but he had to focus now. Huxley ran faster than he thought he could. It looked like all of those laps and weight training had begun to pay off. His stamina *was* improving. It was the comparison to others that made him think less of himself. He was glad for all those long hot suffering days in the heat now. He would likely need every ounce of strength before the day was out.

A trumpet blew through the streets and shook the trees hard enough that snowflakes fell off the branches. Huxley covered his ears and stopped in his tracks. He had never heard anything that loud before. It was from the enemy outside the gates. When he collected himself another horn blew from off in the distance. It vibrated his stomach and shook the air around him.

He heard screams nearby and people hurried to get to safety. The sound caused chaos everywhere. He felt the ground shake underneath him and Huxley feared that the enemy had already broken into Mayburn. That thought evaporated as a large group of Mayburn soldiers on horseback came thundering past. A mixture of pride and fear rushed through him. They had the symbol of the Warden's office on them. Likely they were personal guards or some elite officers. Huxley followed the horses and arrived at the training yard in a few minutes. Captain Pilch was busy with other squads, barking orders and sending them off.

The horn sounded again. This time it was a little less unsettling, but it did cause commotion in the ranks. He did not know what to do with himself, without his gear on he felt naked. Still, he managed to stand at attention awaiting orders. The rest of the squad fell in following his example. A younger boy rushed over with a cart full of practice armor and training weapons and set it down.

"Equipment for Squad D, delivered!" He said it aloud, but not to anyone in particular. The boys looked around for instruction only to find

Pilch gone. A few of the boys moved to pick up their used leather armor, and spears when Bennett's voice rang out.

"Okay men, just like we trained for. The Captain is obviously busy! GEAR UP!" The squad was eager for leadership and accepted Bennett's direction without hesitation.

Moments passed as they instinctually did what they had trained for. Getting dressed for battle was surreal. Huxley never really thought it would happen but here he stood.

Suddenly, they spotted an officer approaching their squad. His armor was unlike anything Huxley had seen before. It had metal plates that were attached with large leather straps and a helm with only a narrow slit to see out from. His shoulder pads bore the symbol of Danador! Resembling a knight from an old storybook, his armor gleamed in the sunlight. Clinking with each step, he stopped at the front of their formation. He must be an agent sent from The College of the Arcane Flame. Perhaps even a member of the Vanguard of Danador, whose warriors had protected the city since its founding! He had strange-looking weapons, or perhaps tools, hanging from his belt. Long metal tubes with grips and a mechanism for use. It wasn't a crossbow. And it certainly wasn't a cannon unless it was made in miniature. No matter who he was, this man seemed unafraid of the teeming masses threatening to break through the walls. The officer lifted his faceplate showing a wide thin mustache and a sweating jowled face. It was Captain Pilch. Only he had no trace of his jovial self, the Captain had shed his kind demeanor entirely. He towered over the fledgling group of soldiers. Huxley wondered if his armor forced him to stand so erect or if his posture was naturally that way. No trace of fear or trepidation invaded his face. This man wasn't just a soldier, he was a warrior.

He looked them over, stone-faced and self-assured and when he was satisfied, he addressed them.

"Men, we are indeed under attack." His tone was matter-of-fact. "Our scouts say a large army hailing from beyond the Fecundity, likely from Dathu, is amassing at the south pass."

A few gasps escaped the brave faces.

"Follow my instructions without hesitation to survive. This is our duty and our sworn privilege, likely they won't make it past our crossbows but we have to be ready. To the walls!"

He took out his strange weapons and dashed away obviously expecting us to follow. The squad scrambled after him in a flurry. They ran in semi-formation to the south wall. Huxley was uncomfortable with how close his family's house was to the South Pass. After a short but tense jog they arrived at the final hill before their destination. There are three main entrances into Mayburn. The main one being the eastern entrance. It was well-guarded and fortified. It could be held with twenty well-trained men. The northern entrance had river access. If attacked in earnest it could be made a viable entrance but the water helped to serve as a natural barrier. That left the South Pass. The South Pass was only defended by a small wagon gate. Despite being double thick, this gate stood between them and the Wilds. Any army attacking this gate would be bottlenecked coming in. It was used by farmers and small traders who didn't need to bring in large wagons. The field outside the wall was grass and a few shrubs with about a hundred yards to the tree line. This meant that the crossbows would have ample targets and the invaders had nowhere to hide. He took a measure of happiness from this. His job would probably be keeping the crossbowmen stocked with bolts and providing water.

His squad followed the wall and climbed the hill. They got to the top and looked down and their hearts plummeted.

"Where is it?" Someone asked.

"It's gone," Jonah stated coldly.

The gate that had stood for decades was splintered on the ground engulfed in flames. Huxley could see it plainly in front of him, yet couldn't bring himself to believe it. Fear and panic surged through the group like a burst dam. Where the wall had stood was a huge pile of broken logs and fires that billowed black smoke. Blood spatter from under the ruined gates, where the guards had stood. The city walls weren't just breached, they were gone.

Seizing the situation a commanding voice stirred them back to lucidity.

It was Pilch. "Madness and damnation! Men, quit pissing yourselves and form up!"

Suddenly, the wall next to them exploded inward.

Huxley was flung into the air as wood and flames surrounded him. He was thrown against a nearby building and felt something in his body crack against it. Huxley nearly lost consciousness, his vision faded, and only his racing heart managed to keep him lucid. He tried to shake it off. Training took over and he struggled to his feet. Smoke clouded his vision. His ears rang with a high-pitched whine. He saw his friends littered around him like discarded sacks. A few began to stir and pick themselves back up, some screamed in anguish as they assessed their injuries. Others were unscathed, just shaken. His whole squad had just been taken out by an explosion. Who had weapons that could do something like that?

Huxley winced as he stood up straight. There was pain in his ribs. It might have been a scratch or cut. He felt down with his right arm searching for the wound and froze. A piece of the wall was lodged in between his ribs. It flew right inside the lace of his chest and back armor. Huxley felt himself going woozy at the sight of it. If not for the shock and pain he might have passed out. Fingers shaking, he reached down and grabbed it.

His body registered a wound so sharp it pierced his mind and all other thoughts retreated.

In a panic, his fingers gripped the piece of wood and yanked at it. Pain curled through his chest. Huxley lost his grip on it and angrily tried again. This time he got a good grip and pulled it out. White light flashed and his eyes watered as blood spurted out. Luckily, the wound wasn't deep. It didn't get directly between his ribs. It just got caught on one.

Huxley cast around for his weapon when he heard heavy, determined footfalls approach. It must be Pilch, come to retrieve them. He looked up into the smoky haze and saw not his Captain, but a monster. The creature loomed over Huxley, breathing in snorts and gazing down at him. Huxley blinked hard as hot breath streamed into his face. He saw it wasn't a monster of the wilds, it was a man that just looked more creature than man. He seemed so large that if Huxley hadn't been sure he was in shock, he would have said he was ten feet tall. His tangled mess of hair concealed a pair of eyes that hunted back and forth, bloodshot and full of rage. An enormous two-sided ax hung over his naked shoulder, the rest of his body could barely be considered clothed. A string of sewn-together furs covered segments here and there. All of his exposed skin was horrifically scarred. His gnarled body looked to have healed from countless injuries, some so devastating it was a wonder he had survived. The man-creature towered over Huxley and stopped in front of him. Soaked in blood and sweat, the creature dripped both on Huxley, hungrily as though sizing him up. He inhaled one gigantic sniff and shoved Huxley. Another shot of pain surged through Huxley's ribs as he slammed to the ground.

Was this one of the soldiers that were attacking us? What could we hope to do against giants?

Huxley watched the man-creature move from one member of his squad to the next, looked them up and down, and tossed them aside. Most were barely getting to their feet, except one. One stood definitely facing him.

It was Bennett.

Bennett stood stone-faced and resolute. Obviously injured, like the rest, though he didn't show it. Bennett hefted his spear, pointed it at the creature, and charged. Stumbling at first he soon picked up speed. Gripping his spear, he surged forward. Bennet was what Huxley could only hope to be.

Hope swelled within Huxley. The man-creature took no notice of Bennett as he advanced. The spear was only inches away when Bennett's target lunged sideways, dodging it. He knocked the spear away with his free hand and snatched Bennett's neck, lifting him off the ground. Bennett gasped as his spear clattered to the ground. He produced a hidden blade from under his greaves and drove it into the man-creatures shoulder. The man-creatures lips peeled back, baring its teeth through its thick beard. His fingers tightened around Bennet's throat. Huxley heard a popping sound. Bringing Bennett's face close he said in a gravelly voice, "Is this all that tall walls and comfy buildings have produced? You're just a pup...where are your fighting men?"

A crackle tore through the air and a puff of blood shot out the back of the man-creature. He immediately dropped Bennett, flipped the ax round in his hands, and threw it in the direction of the attack. The reaction was so violent and sudden, Huxley barely could follow. He didn't even see the ax in the air, only where it landed.

It had crunched into Pilch's chest, caving in his armor. The Captain's small metal-tubed weapon was smoking. Huxley still wasn't sure what the weapon was but it hadn't worked. The man-creature howled in rage. Huxley saw the rest of the warriors from Dathu climb through the newly blasted hole in the wall. Despair claimed Huxley's heart. How could there be so many of them? One was bad enough. The others didn't seem quite as big as the first, but they did appear just as vicious. They wore furs, feathers, and bones. all arranged differently. No one looked the same. Some wore masks made of animal bones over their faces, others had given themselves war paint in bizarre patterns. None spoke, they just watched, perhaps waiting for instruction.

The man-creature inspected the small hole in his chest made by Pilch. Upon looking closer at it, the creature smiled then reached up and pulled Bennett's blade out of his shoulder with a chuckle. He straightened himself and said to the others, "What are you waiting for?! There are no Embers here. No fighting men. I alone could defeat them. This was a waste." The man-creature turned to leave but suddenly stopped by Bennett's ragged voice. He croaked out "You'll be hunted down for what you have done here! The militia of Mayburn will rally and defeat you!"

He had propped himself up on his discarded spear, a massive handprint around his neck where the man-creature had grabbed him.

The invaders turned their attention to Bennet with their leader turning last. His face was unreadable. Huxley choked out of fear for Bennett.

"You have no warriors, just soft men protected by books. Where are your Embers? He wasn't one of them was he?" the man-creature growled, gesturing to Captain Pilch's body.

Bennett tried to respond but his throat had been badly damaged making it difficult. He could only issue a few mumbles before the man-creature reached down and lifted him up again. Face now murderous, He raised Bennett to eye level. The man-creature leveled his ax's central point to Bennett's neck and said "Victory has killed you today. The Embers claim to be your protectors but they cower in their city instead." Its eyes measured Bennett again and reported, "As one of the bravest here, we will give you the dignity of her talons." The man-creature motioned for one of his own to join him. Another warrior dressed similarly to himself stepped forward. This one was clothed in feathers with an owl-shaped helmet. His beard, tied into three long braids hung well past his chest. He hefted a clean trident that bore similar beaded braids at the handle. "She does not find truth and strength in the slaughter of the weak," he argued back.

The bloodlust abated and the leader drew himself up to his full height, bringing Bennett with him. Bennett's legs now hung two feet from the ground, which he used to deliver a few kicks to his assailant. They were ignored. Bennett struggled but managed a few choice words, "Then your religion is as feeble as you are Grubmush." The ax raised and Bennett stared violently back. The weapon stopped at its peak when a weak and frightened voice interrupted. It was a voice that Huxley was surprised to hear ... His own.

"Stop! Just go...please. You're right, we are too weak to fight you." Huxley said feebly.

The man-creatures glanced at the ruined guard who dared address them and roared in laughter, except the one who had protested a moment ago.

Huxley felt stupid, was that really the best he had? It was a plea that wouldn't have worked on schoolyard bullies.

Huxley had to do something, He couldn't watch silently as Bennett was murdered. Mind racing, he was seized by two man-creatures for his outburst. One savagely threw him to his feet and yanked his hands behind his back. Then the other stepped forward and slammed his fist into his stomach. Huxley's abdomen convulsed and his wounded ribs screamed. His vision darkened and they threw him face-first onto the ground. The laughing continued. He felt his thoughts reaching desperately for something that would help him, and came up empty. His skills were no match. He couldn't believe just minutes ago he'd remarked about his own strength as though it meant anything against this enemy. His friends were scattered and Ember Palithur had abandoned them.

Hope faded.

Huxley felt his breath heavy in his chest. Through great effort, he pushed himself onto his back. The night sky greeted him. Smoke clouded his vision thanks to the fires burning around him. Light caught the smoke and made it look like it was dancing. Huxley felt his mind washing away. Right at the precipice between consciousness and the abyss, Huxley realized he could see the stars in the sky with the clarity of book illustrations. It washed into view, not just pinpricks of light but truly millions of stars in a vast array of the cosmos.

This was it.

He was dying.

His mind began to swim between lucidity and focus not knowing which was which. Then one of the stars shone brighter than the others. Distinguishing itself, it floated towards Huxley, vacating the cosmos and soaring down to him. Huxley watched its journey as it approached. The closer it flew, the more Huxley became sure it was something else. It looked like a star, but it didn't behave like one. It seemed to have a mind of its own. Always floating towards him but also weaving around as though it were restless. The glowing white orb hovered right over him and paused. Its surface was smooth like a river stone but its skin was moving in ripples. It hung right outside of his reach.

I'm dying, he thought, and now I'm hallucinating.

The orb beckoned to him, as though it was there just for him.

He reached upward.

It danced just beyond the reach of his fingertips, zipping back and forth. Huxley felt a stab of pain from his injuries and in frustration snapped his hands forward in a grasp. He felt his fingers curl around the star suddenly. He expected it didn't want to be caught and held it tightly, but the orb stopped as soon as he tightened his grip. In fact, it settled suddenly and waited in his hand. He felt a sense of connection with it like it was a part of him; not just a part even but an extension of him. It was what he could be and what he was at the same time. He knew at that moment what he was supposed to do with it.

Huxley forced himself to stand. His legs almost gave out, but with a sudden sense of purpose and motivation, he willed himself forward. The warriors had amassed around their leader. Instead of trying for an intimidating threat he simply spat some blood from his mouth and yelled at his attackers.

Only a few glanced toward him, but most took no notice.

Huxley hurled the orb at them.

It burned bright white as it arced over his fallen friends, illuminating them as it passed by. It cleared the first two invaders and landed right into the middle of the horde. A cacophony of sounds broke the silence. Dozens of blinding white spikes erupted from the orb skewering all of them. The man-creature who led the invasion caught the centrality of its spikes. He was torn to pieces instantly. The one with the trident was impaled through his stomach making his body drop limp.

After it completed its job, the orb dissolved into nothingness. Gone as quickly as it came, taking many lives with it. Half of the warriors nearby fell dead while the rest retreated with fresh wounds from spikes that impaled them. Huxley was as shocked as they were. His hands began to shake and he turned his palms upward, studying his hands and searching for answers. Seeing men fall dead by his hand overwhelmed his mind. He stumbled backward. The Grimoire ran through his head, its pages flapping furiously until they landed on the last page bearing that strange symbol. The symbol drew something from him that caused his mind to stagger like his body had, it was too much. Huxley fell onto the burning battlefield.

5

Trees and Gears

Elatress reached out and drew her cloak tight as a chilly autumn breeze rustled the leaves on the trees around her. In the dwindling half-light, her silhouette stuck to the deepening shadows of faded stalks of hickory and oak to conceal her presence. She had walked over two miles since stepping off the train. She could still hear the steam shuddering and the occasional whistle over the wind, but only faintly now. She needed to choose her hiding spot with care. She was plenty familiar with untamed places and nature, it had been her home for years but she had to hunt differently out here.

Nature was strange in the Wilds. It behaved in ways that nature shouldn't. A timely breakdown in the engine guaranteed her at least an hour. The engines were loud and powerful, but just like loud and powerful people, they required a lot of maintenance. Abernathy could fix just about anything but given this rare opportunity to explore the heart of the Wilds, Abernathy would probably afford Elatress as much time as possible.

Abernathy knew of her desire to hunt. He had tried distracting her as best he could, always helping her to make friends and be sociable. The only people Elatress wanted to be friends with were other hunters. She'd also make an exception for skilled warriors or maybe an Ember. But she felt she already had a friend and didn't really require more. She was certain Arktos felt the same. They were both natural-born hunters.

That's why when Abernathy and Elatress heard the engine sputtering, they raced to the window to see what opportunities were nearby. That's when they spotted the chancey tree. A chancey tree would have a wide variety of one-of-a-kind plants surrounding it. Abernathy had hastily scrawled down a list of items to forage. It seemed to her that he was already plotting to slow down the repairs of the train because the list he gave her was too long for just a simple repair. She rammed the list into her sack and took off. A chance-driven tree was a valuable find. Abernathy had given up arguing with her that trees had proper names, and that a tree doesn't take chances. But she always recognized chance takers and some trees just were. That's how you knew it had valuables. Elatress darted off into the Wilds headed straight towards it but got sidetracked when she got a whiff of something that she just couldn't ignore. Abernathy's list would have to wait. Right now, she smelled rabbits.

She sniffed viciously, filling her lungs. Her eyes scanned back and forth. She retreated deeper into the low foliage of a willow tree. Elatress shivered, she wasn't really dressed for cold. Her cloak covered her, stretching down to her ankles and preserving her body heat. She declined shoes for this trip. She could feel her surroundings far better without them. Her trousers and shirt were nearly the same color and had been stitched so many times, they were barely holding together. In stark contrast, her fine leather rucksack was well-oiled and the straps and buckles were all in place. It was far larger than what most ladies her size would ever carry, but she needed to carry more than most. At her side hung twin hatchets attached to her belt with leather loops.

While waiting out her prey she dug her toes into the dirt. She could feel the beginnings of mushrooms sprouting in the soil. She was curious how many there were just under the surface. She wiggled her toes deeper into the dirt to try and see. A small bug, probably a beetle, scurried over her left foot in a dash. She didn't dare look down for fear of missing her prey. They would come out any second now. The rabbit's scent was almost overwhelming. Then she saw it, two unmistakable ears sticking straight up, alert, listening for danger. Thoughts of the mushrooms ceased and her whole body tensed. She would have preferred something bigger to hunt, but this would do.

The whole family of rabbits had woken up for the evening. She felt victorious, in Autumn rabbits are hard to track. You have to rely on your nose. If only it had been snowing, then the tracks were unmistakable. The breeze picked up again. This time she let her cloak catch it. She wanted to be totally sure which way the wind was blowing. It would be an awful shame to let them get away because of an errant gust. More rabbits hopped out of the burrow. Elatress almost jumped with excitement.

"Two, three, four...maybe up to seven" she counted.

You could kill at least half. The mad voice told her. *Maybe wound some of the children and it will draw out the parents. I wonder if they scream like gophers do.*

"Damn," she said in a flash of irritation.

She hadn't meant to speak. Luckily the rabbits hadn't heard. She had hoped for more time than this. Once her inner voice started talking to her, it would take a lot of focus to suppress it.

No, she said in her mind, *I only need one...maybe the adolescent there.*

He's a runt, he'll be picked clean in minutes. Light a fire and smoke all of them out.

Hah! She thought as a smile formed. *That would work actually.*

Yes! Now, where can you get tinder? Surely there is a good amount around here somewhere. Kill two and smoke out the rest. Grab your hatchets and kill those two right there. You can throw that distance in less than a second. Throw them, THROW THEM NOW!

Elatress smiled at the thought and reached for her hatchets. When she touched the cold steel her mind sharpened and she violently shook away the thoughts. The larger, and likely male, rabbit paused and looked her way.

She froze.

Everyone has instincts, an internal drive that guides actions, but not a voice that actually speaks back. It began about two years ago. At first, she embraced it, believing it made her special, which was unfortunately true.

She had become a more masterful hunter with its guidance. It was only recently that she and Abernathy figured out what it really was. She would need to silence it before she could deal with the rabbits. It would sleep for long periods but once it woke up, it only got louder. And if it gets too loud, it would start messing with her emotions and disrupt her focus. When hunting rabbits, you never want to take your eyes off them. Their ability to hide was nearly as good as their hearing. The best method was snares, not hatchets, but you take opportunities as you find them. And her "opportunities" were beginning to sense her presence. Their little noses sniffed the air around them in rapid and constant motions. Hunger would keep them from retreating for now, but a rabbit's awareness of danger always won out against its hunger.

She collected herself. Remember what Abernathy taught you. Elatress spoke to her voice. *No, I only need one. People like me and other nice girls only need to kill one animal at a time. It's savages and beasts that kill for sport. I am not a savage or a beast...I am a nice girl. I am pleasant at parties and social gatherings. I bathe indoors and wear clothes. I never fight unless threatened and even then, words are important and I should use...* She paused to remember the ending. *...th-them often to be understood. When I do kill it, I will cook it like a lady. I won't listen to or note its screams. I am doing this for survival only and not because it's in my territory. It is not important to store up fat for the winter, nor will my enemies be frightened by my many carcasses. Now silence.*

She held her breath a moment and listened. The voice only gave a low growl back at her.

Good enough for now, I suppose.

Elatress gripped her hatchets tightly, feeling the nervous sweat push in between the handle and her palms. The smooth metal and well-sanded handles felt good as she deftly unhooked the matching hatchets from their loops. She worked under her cloak to mask her movements. The male rabbit that had sensed something earlier had returned to searching for food. His body seemed more rigid. She had better not miss.

YES! And kill the rest of them when they are vulnerable and frightened. Use your hands and hatchets to dig down after them and pull all of them out! Do it! ATTACK! The voice came roaring back into her mind, nearly taking control.

"No, I only need one. I wish it was something bigger, but people like me and other nice girls only need to kill one animal at a time. It's savages and beasts that kill for sport. I am not a savage or a beast...I am a nice girl. I am pleasant at parties and social gatherings. I bathe indoors, and wear clothes."

Her mental exercise was interrupted by a bone-crunching chomp in front of her.

The family of rabbits, terrified, ran into their home, now fatherless, as a prodigiously sized grizzly bear, blood covering its mouth and paws, loudly gulped down the last of its newly killed rabbit dinner. It looked carefree while licking its lips and turned its gaze in the direction of Elatress.

Elatress tensed. Her hands tightened on her hatchets and she rose out of her place of concealment. The bear studied her, recognition and something else flooded its eyes and strangely human-esque expression.

The two hunters held each other's attention for a moment longer until Elatress exploded.

"Arktos!" Elatress screamed.

Arktos immediately turned tail and fled.

———————————————————————————————————————-

Abernathy watched Elatress sprint into the forest with Arktos scampering behind. Before he closed the door, he leaned to the side of the train car, about six cars up a group of workers were shouting at each other. He could hear the engine laboring to boil. It reminded him of someone about to sneeze, all wind up and no payoff.

"Of course." He spoke into the night air.

No one was around to listen, but he said it anyway. He moved back inside and slid the door closed. Abernathy's car was filled with cargo and luggage of all varieties. Whenever the train shook, he always braced for a cave-in. It rarely occurred, but one had only to experience it once to not wish for it again. Most of the windows were blocked off from sunlight by the cargo. Four precious windows remained unperturbed through which he could take in the sights. He was guaranteed space for himself and three guests on every train. Usually, it was just him and Elatress with Arktos in the caboose, which allowed him to stretch his leg out. At first, he had been insulted by the arrangement. What was so bad about him that he had to be stowed in the back like a suitcase? He realized in no time that it was the best possible place. Plenty of room to work on side projects as he rode. There was a serviceable workbench with tools enough for express work and if he needed sleep it was relatively quiet. Not to mention, there were fewer rich folk for him to be forced to mingle with. Abernathy was unused to wealth and how it changed people. It never sat right with him how once someone gained a bit of financial independence, it changed how they viewed their fellow man. Readjusting himself in his seat, he reclined back and reached down to find his pipe and tobacco. Perhaps he could get a few puffs in before he was disturbed.

It would take a few minutes for them to finish arguing and decide that they should just go ask him what to do. He would have to solve this problem for them, which would give Elatress a much longer time to get his list of ingredients. Traveling in the Wilds was troublesome on the best days and downright dangerous on most. They may have secured this track line for now, but keeping it secured was a titanic effort. At first, Danador employed military soldiers to beat back the growth and maintain safe travels. That lasted less than six months. Maulings, poison, and outright exhaustion tore through the ranks until none would take on the task no matter the pay. It wasn't until they realized that by keeping the train going with only short stops for maintenance, they could keep the lines open. With just one train on the tracks, there was no risk of collision. The only nagging issue was what to do when Abernathy wasn't around. The train ran great on any given day, due in no small part to his hard work and insight into engines. But that was the problem, he had fixed it so well that only he could seem to grasp its more delicate systems. Perhaps the Embers or a well-educated Warden might be up to the task, but this kind of work was beneath their station. Better to make a foreigner like him do the dirty work. He huffed at the thought of it and began to tinker on a little toy.

Abernathy did, in fact, get a few good puffs into his pipe before a young man covered in soot, grease, and sweat opened his door. Concern peeked around the corner of his eyes, but he did well to keep it at bay. A frightened engineer would panic the passengers. A few others followed him, it seemed he drew the short straw and had to be the one to speak with Abernathy. They were good boys, hard-working, driven, and inquisitive, all the makings of good engineers. Abernathy even thought they would design fine engines on their own someday. It is a shame it would take so long. For some reason, mechanical engineering was not taught in Danador. For that matter not much was taught, the Embers kept all the knowledge to themselves. They only seemed to let discoveries out if it profited them directly. It made their society lopsided in technology. Some things were quite advanced like the railways and architecture, but some were woefully behind like chemistry, biology, and engineering. He figured they put too high a priority on Magnacy in their schooling. It was all about the volume of knowledge and not practicality. This was the result of such oversights. A few stand-out geniuses and a lot of people without a foundation in a society struggling to stay moving.

"Uh, excuse us Grand Craftsman and Lord Engineer of the Sacred Railways, Savior of the Crag villages of Valdannon, we need your help."

Abernathy leaned forward so his mustache would cover his grin. That title was utter rubbish. They had looked at him with such awe when he got involved with their locomotive restoration. Abernathy became annoyed at their ignorance, so he had to do something to make fun moments for himself. It brought some relief from all the frustrating parts. They had to call him that as part of the arrangement.

He stifled his laughter and put on a serious tone that would fit a Grand Craftsman and Lord Engineer...whatever that would be.

"Yes, son, how can I help? What have you all done to my engine?"

"We followed your instructions to the letter sir, it's just, well, the boiler...it's not...boiling. He looked away in shame, partly because of how silly his statement was.

Abernathy didn't take the opportunity for ridicule and rubbed his chin feigning to be in deep thought.

"Mmmm, not boiling you say? Well, that is a problem...by the sounds of it I would guess the crown sheet, or maybe the ashpan hopper." Abernathy thought out loud.

"Apologies sir, but no. We are sure it isn't one of those."

Abernathy dropped his hands from his beard. "You are quite sure of this?"

"Uhh, as sure as I can be without climbing into the engine itself, Sir."

Abernathy sighed and made a face that he hoped looked confused. "What do you mean you haven't climbed in yet? That's the first step to being a great engineer son! You can't be afraid to get dirty." He barely held back a laugh.

The boy just stared at him trying to process what had been said. A moment passed as he searched for an answer. The boy yelped in pain as he was slapped on the back of the head. Behind him another young engineer said, "He's messing with you, the Grand Craftsman and Lord Engineer is known to joke with new trainees. That would kill us instantly."

"Shut up! I knew that! I just didn't follow the Grand Craftsman and Lord Engineer's joke..." he said, rubbing the back of his head.

Abernathy looked over the boy's shoulder and yelled, "Hey, who's that? Ronald? You spoiled my game!"

"Apologies Grand Craft-"

"Enough! Just Abernathy for now." He waved his hand at them dismissively.

"Yes, sir, uh, Abernathy. We have tried those things. We believe it is beyond our skill and training." Ronald stated.

"Oh well, why didn't you say so? Let me see the problem." Abernathy leaped to his feet and grabbed his toolbox.

Elatress rushed forward, "MY RABBIT! You hulking, smelly, fat, lazy, jowly, drooling, lay-about thief!"

Arktos gave a low growl and averted his eyes.

"You were hungry?! You ate two hours ago in the train car. I fed you a whole haunch of beef!"

The grizzly groaned, this time while looking at his stomach.

"Your stupid chow tank is always empty. When we get back to the

Gearbox you are going on a diet. Turkey only, or maybe only the mutton that doesn't get eaten."

Arktos blinked.

"I'm serious! Look how big you are, you block out most of the light of the moon."

Arktos lowered his head and sniffed, his breath rustled the leaves underneath him.

Elatress folded her arms and stood straight.

Arktos remained in his downtrodden stance when Elatress realized maybe she'd hurt his feelings. But she was incensed, how could he not even split that rabbit with her? Now she had to run two miles back on an empty stomach, accompanied by a bear with hurt feelings.

"Okay...only half serious." She relented.

That was enough for Arktos. He looked up and began to plod over to her his warm breath producing plumes of moisture that reminded Elatress of the train.

"Easy, don't knock me over." And she opened her arms for a hug.

His snout moved right under her outstretched arms and his head and neck wrapped around her torso. At his touch, she felt the voice go silent again. Not like before when it was quieted, but truly silent. Thank goodness for that, she thought as she returned the nuzzle. Being embraced by a bear was by far the best thing anyone could experience. His damp and warm fur enveloped you. Arktos radiated heat like a furnace no matter the temperature outside. The low rhythmic breathing of his chest could make anyone fall asleep while standing. Keeping a bear has a great many challenges, not the least of which is when they are hungry, they interpret all food as theirs. The greatest challenge was loving him so much, but not letting him be with you all the time. People were always so uncomfortable with bears. Some bears are vicious and bloodthirsty. Not Arktos though, she'd barely ever seen him more than annoyed. People should be afraid of people. There are hundreds of varieties, and rarely is the variety pleasant. They lie, betray, steal, murder, and tell you to wear shoes. How could they be so happy with tons of people walking around a city, but freak out whenever a bear came trotting through? At least with a hungry bear you know what he's thinking. With people, you can never tell.

Elatress aptly located the items on Abernathy's list and hiked back to the train with Arktos following in the moonlight. The Wilds are a dangerous place, even more dangerous than cities. But they had lived out here for a while and nothing ever happened that they couldn't handle. Her pace slowed as they grew closer to the train, hoping for a few more minutes away from the screeching sounds and revolting smells. She had been so elated to have an unplanned run and hunt through the forest. That elation seemed like a distant memory now.

Arktos was a bear of the Wilds and he was very much a product of it. She wasn't sure how old he was, where he was born, or even if he had a family. He never told her about any of that, so she assumed it didn't matter. Seems like if he did have a family, it would have come up in conversation, or at least grunted about. Elatress was positive he was a grizzly most days and so was he. But on occasion he would be a different bear, always the same on the inside but not outside. During the winters his fur would turn white like the snow, and brown again for the summer. He didn't hibernate. She was pretty sure most bears did, but not Arktos. He even got cut wide open once on his shoulder. Elatress sewed him up and spent the whole night worried about him. In the morning, his wound had healed into barely more than a scratch. How was that even possible? Once he even turned black and white overnight. That was a strange day. When he slept, sometimes he would wake up different; bigger, smaller, fatter, stronger. Even in the Wilds, bears didn't do that. A grizzly was a grizzly, but Arktos was just Arktos. It's probably why he didn't have a family...until now. He didn't match most understandings of bears, and she didn't match most understandings of people. It's probably why they got along so well. They understand one another, and really, that is all Elatress needed in a companion. Elatress hadn't felt understood most of her life. It was like people heard her, but through a wall, all muffled. Yelling didn't help, it just caused more confusion. But walking in the Wilds with Arktos...she was understood here. Here, no one told her to be someone else. She doubted Arktos' opinion of her would ever change no matter her circumstances. She felt the same way about him.

Elatress and Arktos emerged from the tree line, and both had to shield their eyes from the light of the train. The train may have been loud and stinky and full of people, but it was always a sight to see. Something man-made existing in the Wilds, seemed impossible even as she stood looking at it. The Wilds definitely didn't want it here. She doubted the train was too keen either. She looked towards the caboose and nodded her head toward it. With a huff, Arktos ambled forward. He had to ride in the back, which was a special allowance since Abernathy was the on-call Engineer. He had written in the agreement: "Passage for myself, Elatress, and the bear." They would never let Arktos ride in the passenger cars, so he had a little area in the caboose. It was an arrangement no one loved, but everyone accepted. He plodded towards his entrance, and they parted ways. Abernathy stood at the opening behind one of the cars waiting.

"You've got blood on your cloak." He said flatly.

"Oh, yeah, it's a rabbit's," she responded.

"You okay?" He asked.

She rolled her eyes and said, "Of course...rabbits aren't vicious."

"No...are you okay?" He said with a knowing look. "No episodes?"

"None worth mentioning." She replied as she lifted herself onto the train car.

Abernathy had reached his hand out to help her up, but she didn't notice.

"None worth mentioning, huh? Well, let's mention it more in the car."

"What about you?" She glanced over her shoulder. "You are covered in grease and soot. What did they do to our train?"

"Actually, it wasn't that bad," he said with a shrug, "the boys did good work. Some are even handsome, you know." He winked at her. She stalked into the train car pretending to not have heard that last part.

He slid the door closed and the engineer cried, "All aboard! Estimated arrival in two hours!"

The engine filled its lungs with steam and breathed to life. The train lurched forward leaving the Wilds and chugged towards Mayburn."

6

∽

Stars and Oceans

"Lateral undulation is produced via waves of horizontal bending propagated along the body from head to tail." **-Page 419 Excerpt from the Grimoire**

Huxley sat by the side of the ocean, the water gently lapped against his toes.

The battle felt like it was years ago. His wounds healed and the horrors he had seen were forgotten. His only concern now was how to prolong his time enjoying the ocean. Perhaps he could go for a swim, it was a lovely day for it. He stood up and stretched. He did not know how long he had been resting, but his legs felt stiff. Breathing in the salty sea air, he cocked his head, something was off, it didn't smell like the ocean was supposed to. He breathed in again slowly and then it clicked.

Beef broth veggie soup!

The sun melted away in front of him and the light plunged into darkness. The sky was illuminated with starlight now. The exact same starlight he had seen so recently. Or was it weeks ago? He looked at the night sky trying to understand, then his body screamed in pain.

Huxley shot awake with a scream blanketed in sweat-covered sheets.

His sudden movement undid some of his dressings on his arms and ribs. The pain surprised him. Fresh steaming soup sat at his bedside next to dozens of notes. His mother burst into the room.

"He's awake! Arthur, he's awake!" She yelled down the hallway.

Huxley's mother ran to his bedside, tears welling up in her eyes. She sat down and immediately looked him over.

"Don't move too much now, you're just beginning to heal."

Huxley didn't say anything; he was just happy to be alive. Wait, how could he be? Wasn't he just surrounded by enemies and then he...

"Mom, what about Dathu? Are they outside? Is Mayburn destroyed?" Huxley dreaded the answers, and he was having a hard time collecting his thoughts.

"Destroyed? Goodness no, no, no. They left some time ago. Yes, we are safe...and my boy is awake and well again." She spoke the last part seemingly to herself as though he wasn't there. His mother refocused and looked at Huxley. She slowly became overcome with emotion and kept touching his head and patting him while grasping his hand. She squeezed it so tight it began to hurt. Before he could protest, his father came stomping into the room.

"Huxley my boy! Up and 'attem I see! Course you are. No attack on Mayburn could stop my proud soldier!"

His dad declared to the room as though hundreds were gathered to hear it. He looked at him with a broad smile. It was the look of a father's pride in his son. It felt undeserved to Huxley, but it was so welcome after the last few days.

"So, how did it all go down? Did you run across the battlefield striking fear into the enemies' hearts and with a mighty roar pushing them back into the wilds?"

He mimicked the motions while relaying the events.

"Or maybe the line was breaking and at the right moment, my son, the hero of Mayburn, burst through with a spear leading a countercharge!"

His mother shot a withering look, the kind that left no room for interpretation, it was time to stop. He had seen that look often enough to know it.

Her face softened and she turned back to Huxley saying, "You don't need to tell us anything. Just focus on getting well again. In the meantime, I will get you some fresh soup, and maybe change your bandages."

Just then, a creak from the hallway gave away someone's presence. Oakley must be waiting impatiently outside, under orders from their parents to be silent.

His mother and father glanced towards the door and tensed up becoming obviously uncomfortable. His father cleared his throat and said, "Must you speak with him now? He just woke up."

A short bald man poked his head in eagerly. He surveyed Huxley and said, "Oh don't be worried at all. I just want to talk to him while he is fresh. My superiors are quite eager to hear about his adventure."

His smile and voice sounded kind, but the way he approached reminded Huxley of a snake that had just noticed a field mouse out of cover. In fact, he even moved like one, his feet flowed over the floor silently while his eyes remained fixed on him. Huxley shrunk as the man approached. He had the uniform of a Warden of the state. It was a well-pressed gray suit with black accents. It had polished buttons and a small badge on the shoulder with the crest of Danador. He carried a small bag overflowing with notes, ledgers, and every kind of stationary. Wardens of his rank were almost never involved in the workings of Mayburn, and if they were, it was usually limited to the tax offices. But he had seen the two other high-ranking ones earlier. Perhaps there was more happening than he realized.

The memories of the battle flooded back to him in droves. Word must have gotten out about the explosion he caused. Now he was going to have to answer for it. But how could he explain what he didn't even understand?

The faces of the men he killed clawed at his thoughts. He remembered them howling in pain and falling to their knees as life left their bodies. Huxley couldn't fathom it. He felt just as much of a monster as the attackers.

The Warden pulled up a chair and sat down right beside his mother.

"Again, it won't be but a moment or two. I just want to record his statements and thank him for his service to Mayburn, Danador, and Magnadun of course." His words sounded friendly, but his eyes revealed something else, a singular focus that unsettled Huxley.

Huxley's mother nodded and turned to leave. His father stopped and said, "Huxley are you okay with this? If not, we can probably reschedu-"

"Of course, we are fine! I'm so sorry to be a bother. Five minutes at most." The warden interrupted. Huxley looked at the Warden and then to his dad. He shrugged not knowing what to say.

"I will be right downstairs." His father said as he closed the door.

As it clicked shut, the Warden began scribbling in his notebook immediately. He had got set up in the blink of an eye with a pen and ink reservoir. He paused for a second or two and looked at Huxley and returned to his writing. His pen scratched at a furious rate. Was Huxley's appearance alone worthy of extensive notes? The Warden finished a sentence with a flourish, tapping his pen. He turned to Huxley.

"Hello Huxley, how are you feeling?" His serpentine eyes settled on the injured youth like his next meal.

"Umm, tired and hurt. I feel like I got hit by a train. Uh, how are you?" He felt silly asking, but he didn't know what to say.

"Fine." He retorted sharply. "Anything else? How did you hurt your ribs? Were you stabbed at any point? What did your captain tell you about the attackers before the battle? Please tell me everything to your best ability."

"The Captain!" Huxley yelped. "Is he ok?"

"Later...answer my questions please." His finger tapped on his notes.

Huxley had a hard time turning his thoughts away, but this Warden looked to be in no mood to be argued with. He took him through the details of what he could remember. The Warden was deeply interested in everything he had to say. Huxley knew he would ask soon about how he survived. Could he tell him the truth about what he did? This man did not seem interested in anything but facts. Perhaps it was best to stick with what he could explain for certain.

He recounted the story and all the while the Warden took notes, his pen a blur on the page. He was sure it must have been the same story as all of the other soldiers, save for him throwing a star.

He glossed over that part explaining, "When I was knocked down and fighting to stay conscious, I heard an explosion near the hole in the wall. I guess whatever they used to get through misfired and took a few of them out." Huxley didn't feel good lying to a Warden. If he was caught in the lie, he might be arrested or worse. But truly, no one could have known what he had done, Huxley didn't know himself. He'd only look like a madman.

As the story progressed, the Warden slowed his writing speed. His eyes lost sharpness and faded to disappointment.

Finally, the interview ended. The Warden packed up his accouterments with a well-practiced speed. He stood up and forced a courteous smile.

"Thank you for your time, Huxley. I must be off to see other soldiers like yourself. I thank you for your service to your country and its people. All of Danador is in your debt. Goodbye."

The Warden walked straight for the door and Huxley said goodbye.

He breathed out a sigh of relief and said, "I'm just glad that night is over."

The Warden halted.

He turned on his heel to face Huxley again.

"Oh, yes? That night is over?" Hunger returned to his questions; the disappointment vanished.

"Err yes...it was a terrible ordeal...I'm glad it's over." Before he could finish the Warden nearly ran back to his bedside. His entire demeanor changed. His smile broadened and showed teeth that probably remained entirely hidden on most days.

"Huxley, I am so sorry, I have acted rudely and was far too preoccupied with my workload. I didn't even introduce myself. I am Warden Ignatius Richmond of Danador's resource management offices." He said as he seized and shook Huxley's hand. The smile grew broader.

At first it weirded him out but after a minute Huxley felt different. This guy was just trying to help after a horrible situation. Was he kind of strange looking? Sure, but Huxley probably looked strange as well layered in bandages and covered in sweat.

"Huxley, may I ask you just one more question before I leave?" He insisted.

"Umm yes." Huxley felt curious himself. What had he said that would be worth this much attention?

Warden Richmond thought for a moment and said, "Do you know what time your battle took place?"

He thought for a minute, "Probably close to midnight."

"Are you sure? Why would you think that?"

"Well, the stars were out..."

Ignatius bounced a little in excitement. It was kind of cute. Like a student who just figured out a difficult answer on an exam.

"Yes, the stars were out..." Warden Ignatius trailed off then asked, "And in your sleep just now, did you see more stars or an ocean?"

Huxley was stunned. How could he know that he had that dream? He couldn't hide his surprise. Warden Richmond did another little bounce.

"Come now, answers please, stars or ocean?"

The answer was both. Huxley hesitated.

The Warden got overly excited not waiting for a response and said, "Huxley, are you aware that your battle took place around nine o'clock in the morning? Not close at all to your estimation. The fact that you saw the night sky at all is troubling. You may be a great danger to yourself and to others. Now tell me, in your dreams, did you see the night sky like you did in the battle or did you see the ocean?"

Sweat beaded up around his forehead. Fear and panic gripped him, but the Warden's glare demanded an answer. He wanted to be honest, but the warden just said he was a danger to everyone. Best not to mention more stars until he could figure out what happened.

"Ocean." He murmured after a moment.

"Are you sure? Nothing else. In your dream, you saw a large ocean. If yes, did you go swimming in it?

"No," he said quietly again.

The Warden stood upright like a human exclamation point. "I will return soon after you have recovered more. Think about what I said, and do not for any reason attempt to do whatever it was that you did again. I will help how I can. Until then, rest and try to relax."

"You want me to relax?" Huxley blurted.

"Yes, don't worry about your dream or my questions. I'm sure it was just a strange phenomenon that doesn't warrant further investigation. Or at least, that is what you should tell everyone. I will return soon to speak more."

Before Huxley could reply, Warden Richmond of Danador was gone. He could hear his footsteps walking with purpose down the stairs and out the front door. His parents' muffled voices rang out through the house in questioning tones. *Great. Now I have to explain another thing that I can't possibly explain.*

He would, however, take the Warden's advice. He would tell no one of his dreams or how he managed to throw an explosive star. He was thankful for the few days of bed rest. He felt like he could sleep for days and maybe in between he would have ample time to read the grimoire. Maybe it would have answers.

7

Bandages and Study

"Philosophy, Navigation, Natural Elements, Human Biology, Physics, Zoology. Broad subjects that require precise study. Master these and the erudite will be on his way towards ascension." - **Grimoire's table of contents**

Four long, slow weeks had passed since the battle. Huxley had not been able to leave his room except for the occasional attempt at stretching. The first week, he had received numerous visitors. Happily, a few of his squad survived including Bennett and Jonah. They were also laid up in bed. Oakley told him that Bennett tried returning to practice after only five days. Huxley wasn't surprised that he tried. Jonah was also injured but seemed fully recovered after only a week, although he insisted he needed more time to relax. Ember Palithur even visited. Huxley had hoped he would have been kinder, but the Ember had no sympathy to offer.

"Foolish...you know that right? I had everything under control." Palithur told Huxley a long story about how he was destroying the brunt of the forces attacking Mayburn. That the splintered group that got through was just going to be part of his mop up efforts. Every other account said he was nowhere to be seen, disappeared into his study the moment an alarm sounded. The old Ember continued his story and made

Huxley agree that he had saved the town from the foreign invaders and not the militia. When his story ended, he put a hand on Huxley's and said, "When will you be back in the office?"

"My mom says a few weeks."

Ember Palithur rubbed his chin and said "Well, a spot working for an Ember like myself is too important to leave unattended. You can reapply for your job when you recover."

"I'm fired?" Huxley gasped.

"No, you just can't do the job, so I'll find someone who can. You can reapply when you get better."

"That's fired!"

"Call it what you like. But I need my office working, always." The Ember added with no room for disagreement. Despite the finality, the Ember waited, eyebrows raised, as though expecting more. Huxley didn't know what he was waiting for. Palithur ran out of his already miniscule patience for him and spat, "You should probably ask if your foolish request to be tested again is still valid. To which the answer is yes. And I have heard the even more foolish rumor that you produced Magnincy."

How had he found out about that!

Palithur huffed and folded his arms. The old man reminded Huxley of an envious teenager. He crossed his arms and said, "Obviously you should disabuse them of that, you will only disappoint them as you have me for every day of your service."

Huxley looked like he was about to argue but Palithur cut him off, "Only a fool would think someone like you could wield it! Everyone was injured or dying right?"

Huxley shook his head.

Ember Palithur nodded in confirmation to himself "Hallucinations then, mad ravings of a terrified people. You are no Ember, Huxley, and you never will be. Anything they thought they may have seen was either a trick of the light or myself wielding the power of Magnadun."

This time, he didn't wait for more from Huxley. He got up and left with a speed that shouldn't have been possible for a man his age.

———————————————————————————

Life got back to normal for everyone in Mayburn; everyone except Huxley. He had a hard time keeping track of the days, they became so boring. Oakley would come in frequently and bother him. It was a perfect situation for her as he was a captive audience. He wouldn't admit it, but he began to enjoy it. It was a nice break from his study time. Before this, he had become convinced the Grimoire was a joke, but after what he experienced, he wasn't so sure anymore. It may have a wedding ceremony in it but it also had unfathomable insights into the workings of Magnadun.

Huxley had read through the entire grimoire at least ten times. Reading through it wasn't difficult at only three hundred pages. Understanding it was different. The language wasn't the problem. it seemed like the words didn't get along. As if the mind that thought up such sentences was teetering on the brink of insanity.

He created a primer to help him. When he felt like he followed a string of thoughts or ideas he wrote them down with their context. He then applied that context to other areas of the book. It was slow work. Fortunately, time was on his side. With each day spent in study, his understanding grew by inches. If he was the heir to this book then the bequeathed either had a high regard for his academic abilities, or it was meant for someone else. Working on something so puzzling was a welcomed distraction from remembering the screams of those who died in battle. Some days he convinced himself it was a dream just like the one he had that the Warden was so interested in. But mostly, he couldn't escape the truth. He was so sure that he had done it. He bore the scar and the memories as a testimony.

During week two, he was sure that what happened was connected with the Grimoire. It contained descriptions of stars and of bizarre abilities. None like what happened to him or at least not that he could understand. But it had to be connected. He was able to connect ideas and thoughts outside of each chapter. It was an amazingly good feeling to know he could crack the puzzle of this book with enough time.

During week three, he made the best progress on his primer. He tried making his own lunch, but his mother insisted that he be back in bed.

Week four was the real challenge. He reached a plateau in his studies. His primer was becoming cluttered. He began to think he had taken himself as far as he could without help from someone else. If only he could be holed up in the library. There he could maybe find some answers. The ability to wield Magnincy and the amount of secret knowledge you had were connected. He didn't know if it was that you just studied long enough, and they deemed you worthy to be taught the techniques. Or if you had to be given it through Magnincy itself, like a ritual or ceremony. All he knew for sure was that he had wielded something that greatly resembled Magnincy...and Palithur felt threatened by it.

———————————————————————————————————

On the twenty-ninth day of his recovery, a small rock tapped against his window bringing him out of his thoughts. Huxley looked around when another rock tapped. He pulled himself out of bed. His legs were stiff but strong enough for him to waddle over. He opened the window to see Bennett and Jonah standing in the darkness, their faces illuminated by his bedroom light.

"It's the savior of Mayburn himself! The great hero that held back Dathu!" Jonah cheered and faked a crowd's roar.

Huxley's heart leapt to see them. He had been told they survived and were doing well, but it was so good to be able to confirm it. It felt like it had been ages.

"What are you guys doing here?" he asked, trying to keep his voice low but failing in his excitement.

"Well, we just wanted to help you use your privy." Jonah said with what Huxley hoped was sarcasm.

Bennet punched his arm playfully and croaked, "The Kinship Revival Festival is tonight." His voice didn't sound the same. It was rougher. He sounded like he had been screaming all day. Bennett cleared his throat and looked away self-consciously.

"That's right! How could I have forgotten? Wait, wasn't it weeks ago?" Huxley asked.

Jonah rolled his eyes and said "Hux, are we going to talk all night through your window. The train will be stationed and will allow everyone to walk through it. We'll explain on the way. Just come downstairs and come have fun with us. You've earned it."

"Ok, I'll be right down." He turned to change when Jonah called back to him.

"Hey Hux!"

Huxley looked back at him.

"I heard you're an Ember now. Do a magic trick."

"I-wha? No, shut up, I'll be right down!"

Getting dressed was problematic. He hadn't worn real clothes in weeks and stumbled around as a result. The commotion hadn't gone unnoticed, and his mother appeared at his door.

"Going somewhere?" She said with a tone that Huxley knew wasn't actually a question but an accusation.

His excitement at the prospect of going somewhere overwhelmed his normal tact he adopted when dealing with his mother. He blurted out. "The Kinship revival festival is tonight!"

"... oh, yes?" she responded with a flat stare.

"It's tonight," he repeated.

"You aren't going anywhere. You're far too injured. And those monsters could be back anytime."

"Mom, I'm fine! Look." He lifted up his shirt. He was still bandaged but it only caused him pain when he twisted around. He tried to pretend the pain didn't exist, but his mother remained unconvinced.

"Not yet you aren't. Maybe next week we can go for a family walk." she said as though that would be enough.

Huxley's voice grew harder. "Mom, I will be fine. I'll be out with Bennett and Jonah." He motioned to the window. "They will make sure I'm taken care of." She walked directly to the window and leaned out of it.

"Go home the both of you! Leave my son alone. He won't be going anywhere tonight, and don't you dare try to get him to come out again until he is fully recovered!" She spoke through gritted teeth but still managed to yell.

Bennett immediately nodded apologetically and turned to leave but Jonah moaned a juvenile "awwww!"

His mother didn't react. She just watched them walk away.

Huxley grew angry and was getting ready to argue when his mom walked over to him and slapped his ribs. Pain shot like lightning through his side, and he nearly fell to the floor.

He gripped his bedpost for stability and his mother said coldly, "You will get back in bed until you are fully healed. After that, you are coming to work as your father's apprentice. No more fighting, no more late nights with friends, and no more libraries. It's time you accepted your place in this family. You nearly died out there and I won't lose my son to wild nights and stupid ideas. Now. In. Bed!"

Huxley stood there, mouth agape. He hadn't remembered the last time she had been this angry. Fearing she would slap his side again, he climbed into bed. She left the room as cold and rigid as her actions. His side throbbed.

Huxley knew he had to make the choice. If he stayed here and gave in that would set a precedent with him and his mother that he didn't like. He knew one thing for certain.

He did not want to be a cobbler.

He had experienced a new-found connection with his friends that he hadn't known before.

Perhaps being in battle is what bonded them together. He had read about that. And furthermore, why would she try to cut off his reading at the library? It seemed cruel and unnecessary.

"I'm going," he said quietly to himself. He needed to say it out loud. She was right, he was still healing. But right then, it didn't seem like such a big deal. What was wrong with a short break and seeing a spectacle? Surely surviving an attack from man-creatures had earned him a few indulgences. His mind was too excited with the possibilities of the evening. He got dressed as adroitly as he could, taking extra time with his shirt favoring his right side. As he laced his boots, another small rock hit the window. He raced over and saw Jonah standing there with a big grin on his face. Of course, he hadn't listened to her.

"Hux...come on!"

8

∽

Rivers and Drinks

"...taking the azimuth into account is of paramount import when navigating Magnadun from the cosmos." - **Page 47 Excerpt from the Grimoire**

Huxley climbed out his window onto the front veranda, careful to make as little noise as possible. He crept to the front and leapt the rest of the way. Not too crafty of an escape and it hurt when he landed but he didn't care. His mom would likely come check on him soon. He would deal with her later. He was too old to be this worried about his mom's opinion. Also he knew there was a mountain of disagreements forming between them, he might as well start with a bang.

Jonah ran up to him and hugged him earnestly. Joking aside, he did seem thrilled to see Huxley. He sported a cut above his eyes and some scabs on his arms but no worse than a night brawling with friends. He was lucky. His smile was still wide and his large brown eyes still eager for excitement. Huxley doubted Jonah would bring up the battle at all. They embraced for a moment and then Huxley noticed Bennett further down the street waiting. Perhaps he was afraid of being noticed by Mrs. Durant. Bennett stood tall and imperious as ever. His black short-cropped hair wasn't so short, he had let it grow longer. It was still far shorter than

Huxley's but it was a change for Bennett. Somehow, during recovery, he seemed to have gotten more muscular. *Of course, he did*, Huxley thought. He approached and shook Huxley's hand while placing his other hand on Huxley's shoulder.

"I'm glad you are well Huxley," he said in a gravelly voice.

"Well enough I guess, but what about you?"

Bennett smiled and said in a voice that was more than hoarse. "Me? Nah, I'm fine, just some bumps and bruises." He labored to keep the shake out of it.

That was obviously untrue. Huxley saw what happened, but let it go. He didn't want to talk about injuries either. Huxley then leaned in and whispered, "But we should talk about what happened...soon." Bennett had likely been the only real witness. He knew he couldn't lie to him. Jonah chimed in. "Hey guys, this is cute and everything, but I want to meet some women tonight, not hang out with two guys whispering on a dark street. Would that be okay? I mean, it's clear you have something going on here, but me personally, I'm not interested." Huxley and Bennett broke their handshake and started to walk towards town away from Jonah, who hustled to keep up. The three friends walked together toward a wounded city who truly had something to celebrate.

————————————————————————————————

The Kinship Revival Festival was in full swing by the time they arrived. It started first as a homecoming for the first explorers who made it back through the Wilds of the Fecundity. They'd come back with incredulous stories about people who looked like them but every thought and inclination were different. They called their country Valdannon. These people were terribly concerned with art. So much of their culture was rooted in art that it was practically their language. Danador had artists, but art was mainly for leisure, to rest your mind for things that were important like science. Valdannon's love for art was amusing but it revealed a far more worrying question. What had happened to Danador's sister nation, Disardia? It was supposed to be in the same location but it vanished a

generation ago, when the world shook and the Fecundity appeared. It took years to reorganize and mount an expedition through it. How did a whole nation just disappear overnight? It had somehow changed into Valdannon. Valdannon's people had the same issue as Danador. They claim there used to be an ocean near their town. No one could explain what had happened to it.

The term kinship wasn't quite true because everyone from Valdannon was not kin to Danador, in fact, no one could find a single relation. It was as though the world had shuffled itself overnight. Entire nations and oceans being shuffled is one thing. What was worse were the terrifying rumors of what lurked inside the Wilds. It was so upsetting that when the explorers returned with the friendly, albeit weird, people from Valdannon, Mayburn rejoiced. It was good to know that some of civilization survived and that it had not been all turned into the horrors of the Fecundity.

The festival was annual and always well attended. But this year was different. It was far bigger. It usually shut down a few streets and a good portion of the town showed up. For Mayburn, that was what qualified for spectacle. But now, with the knowledge of how close they had come to destruction...Huxley doubted anyone had stayed home. They were celebrating being alive as well as kinship. He could hear the celebrations a mile before he got there. The lights, laughter and roar of commotion greeted them long before the first vendors.

Huxley, Jonah, and Bennett looked at one another and smiled. Each of the young men had been away for months from each other. They all avoided the fact that they lost most of the squad. So many friends that they had trained, laughed and bled with were gone. Undone in moments. Huxley's thoughts lingered on what he experienced. His conscience was at odds with him enjoying himself. Maybe he should visit the families that lost sons instead.

He tried to dismiss it. After all, what would he say to them? *Sorry, your son died, and I didn't, but I hear this festival is great!* Huxley never handled delicate situations well. He imagined a grieving mother in front of him as he searched for thoughts that might help. Everything came up trite, or a cliché'.

The trio pushed through the masses in the streets somehow forgetting that just weeks ago they were on the brink of disaster. Most residents of Mayburn were probably far from the fighting and never really saw it, but the stories reached everyone by now. His side throbbed as if reminding him of what the town was forgetting.

What had been a chilly night was now warming up from the sheer amount of people in attendance. The air was thick and spirits were high. It was possible he had never been in a festival so big. It was like all of Mayburn was trying to fit in the town's cramped square. He tried pointing out how amazing this was when Huxley became acutely aware that he had separated from his group. Throngs of people moved about in every direction. Dozens of tents and attractions lined the streets. Some were serving up foods dripping with grease and butter. Others waved people in promising wares and to showcase wonders from the far reaches of Magnadun. Huxley had found himself drawn to such amusements as a kid. However, as he grew older and realized they were all fake, and he lost interest. Many people claimed to have left Danador and traveled far and wide, but most were just skilled charlatans. It was fun to look at their stuff anyway. The sheer imagination on display was good for a laugh. Huxley was looking for his friends when he noticed a booth that looked familiar. It distinguished itself from the rest, although not in the way it likely intended. A recently painted sign stood in front of it with colorful writing.

Mayburn Library!

...the most *valuable* treasures

Huxley smiled knowing there was only one other person who felt this way.

"Huxley Durant! You're up and about!" Agnes's voice yelled right into his ears, and she gave him a hug that rivaled Captain Pilch's.

His voice muffled; he returned her greeting. "Agnes! Your booth looks wonderful"

She was dressed in her normal attire. A once fine dress that had been sewn and repaired many times. On anyone else it might have looked strange but on Agnes, it seemed like she was born to wear it. A true representation of her personality.

"Oh, yes! My book emporium. It isn't quite as exciting as the others. But I've got a few people interested- HEY! Those are for show only!" She yelled at a group of kids flipping through the books and looking at them like they had just picked one up for the first time. Rolling their eyes, they put them back and left.

"Agnes, isn't that bad for business?" Huxley ventured.

"Business? Sweetie, that's not what libraries do. We provide the information so that others may broaden their horizons." He had heard her say that before, and he could tell she believed it.

"Of course," he said, starting to look around.

It was good to see Agnes, but he really did feel strange not knowing where Jonah and Bennett went off to. It seemed useless looking through the crowds. He reflexively took a step backward into the booth to try and see better. The crowd looked like a human river that he would have to ford through. Perhaps he could chat a minute after all...

Agnes seemed eager to talk, probably about the battle as it was the most noteworthy thing to happen to Mayburn in a decade.

"So, how is your mysterious book? Is it a romance? Or how about a swashbuckling pirate tale? Or a how-to book?" She said the last part with less energy than the first suggestions. Huxley shouldn't have been surprised. Why would Agnes care about anything else when there was a new book to discover? Then something dawned on him, and he asked,

"Agnes, did I even tell you it was a book? I seem to recall telling you it was just something that I ordered."

"Please, Huxley. You don't handle books every day without knowing what one feels like...especially after you have shaken the package as much as I did." Agnes admitted sheepishly.

"As a matter of fact, I did get a book and it has really helped to keep me occupied over the last few weeks. It's not a novel or a 'how-to' book either, it's more like a..." he was searching for the right word, but Jonah's voice interrupted him.

"Oh, by the Arcane Flame of pompous twits, he's over here! And of course, it's a library. Honestly, only you would go to the event of the year and decide to read a book." He burst into the booth walking right up to Huxley and stopped to look at Agnes.

"Oh, hey Ag...aggy...Agnatius? No, AGNES. That's it..hi, Agnes."

Jonah really was a talented guy, in one short outburst he managed to insult two people with unparalleled efficiency.

Huxley tried to save face and said "Jonah would you-"

"Yeah, hang on to that thought Huxley, listen." Jonah leaned in close to Huxley's face and said, "Ladies Hux." His expression was one of understanding, but Huxley just stared stupidly. "Ladies are here and want to meet you. Come on!" He grabbed Huxley's arm and pulled him after him. Jonah didn't contain much skill in the practical areas of life but his ability to find women at social functions and occupy their time was masterful. Huxley was dragged along. It wasn't that Huxley didn't appreciate it, he just always felt drowned out by Jonah. And every time the conversation went below the surface, he felt like he had nothing of interest to say which was a problem Jonah never struggled with. Huxley turned and glanced back at Agnes as he was pulled away and she gave a wave goodbye. With that, Huxley joined the river of people with Jonah as a guide.

—————————————————————————————-

The festival surged and Jonah, Huxley, and Bennett found themselves greeted warmly wherever they went. He had worried about being questioned about the battle but found most people shied away from direct questions. That came as a relief. It was strange, for the first time in his life he was recognized as somebody. He was a member of a respected group; the defenders of Mayburn. He started to think that maybe being in the militia wasn't all bad. The day in and day out of training was monotonous, but the gratitude he saw in people's eyes made him swell with pride. It was like a warm voice from within that let him know he had truly helped. It soothed his soul with a rightness he had been searching for. He didn't get that feeling working for his parents or from studying in the library. *I bet this is how the army of Danador felt when they and the Embers took back the land from the beasts of the Fecundity,* He mused.

The night stretched on and with each passing hour, Huxley grew more comfortable. Perhaps it was because he could trust Jonah to hold the conversation without his input. Maybe it was Bennett's aloof stoic presence that kept him grounded. Probably some of both. It was interesting how a couple of good friends by your side helped you to handle the hardships of the world, but even better friends could help you heal from those hardships.

———————————————————————————————————-

Huxley sat near the town square at a table waiting for Jonah and Bennett to get drinks. He let the noise and merriment of the night wash over him and even spared a minute to look up into the night sky. The stars shone brightly above. They were harder to see tonight because of the lights of the festival. Both torches and new gas lamps lined the streets which illuminated the air and muted the wonder of the stars. He looked up anyway. He thought it odd how they twinkled, were they truly shimmering or was it just a trick of the light? Some maintained their light while others flickered like a lamp low on oil. He noticed one that did more than shimmer, it appeared to move. He blinked a few times and watched closely. He was certain. It was moving. The star he had grabbed had reappeared.

The noise of the festival drowned out, and his whole body went rigid as it began to move in the sky. Not in the same way it had during the battle. That time it had flown almost directly to him. Now it danced back and forth beckoning to him. He dared not reach out, in terror of repeating previous events. It exuded a warmth that matched the emotional one he felt just a while ago. The feeling of rightness. Warmth grew to a pleasant burn and pages about star charts and navigation in the Grimoire flashed through his mind.

Suddenly, the star disappeared just as a huge mug slammed down in front of him spilling froth all over the table and himself. Jonah had arrived and was in mid conversation with a group of girls. Bennett trailed the group politely nodding with Jonah's flurry of words. He had somehow met up with a group of five girls who were absolutely enraptured with Jonah's bravado. "Ooo-ing" and "Ahh-ing" over everything that he said.

Jonah sat down slapping Huxley on the back.

"And this is the guy right here ladies! He is the hero of Mayburn. Took on a whole leg of the army himself. Incinerating all those in front of him like one of the Embers..." He turned to look at Huxley trailing off, realizing something was wrong. Both Huxley and Bennett stared daggers. Huxley faintly shook his head "no" hoping Jonah would figure it out. Jonah considered for a second and looked at the girls, "Ah, sorry everyone, I think my fellow heroes and I need a minute. Can we come find you all later?" He added with a wink.

The group begrudgingly left making arrangements to meet by the bar. When they parted ways Jonah, knowing he'd made a mistake somehow, turned to face the consequences.

"They just wanted to hang out with us. We're kind of heroes now and I want to capitalize on that. Everyone's going to want to see us and hear our stories! After all, we repelled Dathu single-handedly."

"Jonah, didn't you get knocked out after the first blast?" Bennett asked mockingly and then winced while rubbing his throat.

"Psh, yes...that was all part of my heroics. I absorbed the brunt of it to rescue my friends! See, it all makes sense. My soldier instincts kicked in and I leaped in front of the blast. At least, that's what I remember. Do you guys remember anything else? I've heard stories about you two. They said you guys led the counterattack, with my help, of course. But your names come up more often."

Jonah likely didn't remember anything except a moment before the explosion. Once Huxley thought about it, he barely remembered Jonah there at all. He really must have been knocked out cold in the beginning. It was probably for the best that he didn't have to experience what Huxley did, although it explained his eagerness to talk about it.

Bennett looked at Jonah and back at Huxley and said, "The battle was violent and frightening." He paused to swallow between sentences, it seemed a great labor to speak now. "We lost good friends that day."

He paused and took a sip from his glass. "We shouldn't use it to impress people or get what I'm assuming is free drinks."

He gestured at the mugs in front of them. "It was our duty and our honor to serve."

He winced between pauses and drank more. "Besides, we were no heroes. If Huxley hadn't acted, I would be dead right now, and so would you."

He coughed and drank again, after a moment he said, "So, if he doesn't want to talk about it we owe him that. We owe him way more than that actually."

Huxley was grateful for his candor but was concerned about him now. How badly was his throat injured? It may have been more than just bruised. Bennett was quiet normally, but he was always thoughtful and honest when he spoke. It was that trait Huxley found himself envying often. Huxley looked at Bennett and simply said, "Thank you."

Bennett nodded in return.

"Aw Huxley, I'm sorry," Jonah said. "I just got excited. Benny's right, I should calm down and just enjoy our time out. Getting knocked out and then being rescued isn't the best story, so I should probably cool it." Jonah turned thoughtful and said earnestly, "Is it true though Huxley...did you really save everyone? I'm surprised Palithur's been teaching you. You are kind of his apprentice, right?"

Huxley stiffened at the question.

"I fought just like everyone else." He said without conviction. "And no, I'm basically Palithur's maid. He hasn't taught me a thing, in fact, he-"

Bennett interrupted and said his voice barely more than a whisper now, "It doesn't matter, what matters is that we made it out. Right Huxley?"

"Uh, yeah I guess."

"So, you didn't wield Magnincy and destroy a hundred wild men?" Jonah blurted.

"A hundred? No! That's crazy." Huxley stammered, "...it was only ten or so."

"TEN? Wait, you actually DID do something? I thought it was just lies made up by others to sell a good story. You actually commanded Magnincy?!"

Bennett punched Jonah in the arm and pressed a finger against his lips. "Shhh! You Idiot!" Bennett reprimanded. "Huxley doesn't owe us an explanation."

There was no stopping Jonah's excitement, "Wait, Bennett saw it?" He asked while rubbing his shoulder. He turned intently to Huxley. "Ooo, does that mean that you can do it now? Do it! Something small so I can see it." He looked around and spotted a chair pulled out of place. "Like...make that chair catch on fire!"

"Start a fire in a packed festival." Huxley shook his head. 'It doesn't work that way."

"Well how *does* it work?" Jonah replied.

"It doesn't matter how it works, it's dangerous and should be left-" Bennett's voice cut out and he winced.

"Easy for you to say, you got to see it!" Jonah was wound-up now.

Huxley looked back and forth, said "Fine watch this!" He raised up his hands, placed a few fingers in an odd direction and started mumbling an incantation while pointing at Jonah. He made his eyes roll back and heard Jonah make a high-pitched squeal that reminded Huxley of a mouse getting caught in a trap. Jonah leapt backwards, knocking his chair down with a clatter. Huxley and Bennett burst into laughter. Bennett had tensed during the exchange, but relaxed once he realized Huxley's game. Jonah looked sheepish and bent to pick up his chair.

"Sorry Jonah, I just had to. You were being so stupid." Huxley said while wiping a tear from his eye.

"Well, excuse me for being excitable. Anyone would be, if they got a chance to see Magnincy." Jonah said.

Huxley composed himself and waited for the stares from nearby patrons to turn back to their own conversations. He took a long drink. It burned his throat. He tried his best to not let it show but couldn't help it. He could never handle alcoholic drinks. It seemed everyone else could drink it all down without so much as a twitch.

He put his mug down and said, "I don't know what happened. That is the truth. I have been trying to figure it out. I've never even seen Palithur wield Magnincy. He took the credit for what I did. I'm alone in this, and I feel like I have nothing to go on. I thought a book I got would help me but it only confused me more. Honestly you guys, I am more frightened about what happened than intrigued. I killed people, killers and murderers yes, but how fast I did it...it was easy, frighteningly easy. It shouldn't have been that easy. It's like one minute they were there picking us off one by one then...boom...dead. What if it happens again? What if I can't control it?" Huxley looked for an answer from his friends. Bennett rubbed his chin, he seemed troubled as well. Jonah even hesitated. But only for a moment.

"Well, I would say we should practice. If Palithur won't help you then hire a teacher. Surely someone knows about this."

"He's right." Bennett wheezed and motioned the two inward, so he only had to whisper. They obliged and shared a painful glance of pity. It obviously hurt him to speak but clearly decided it was necessary. "Yes, even Jonah can be right periodically. I saw what happened. At first, I thought I was delirious from the pain, but you did do something...unexplainable. Whatever it was that you did. It saved us. Dathu turned around immediately after it happened. There were cries of an Ember of Danador being here to defend the town. They probably thought we were all alone and relatively undefended. Which was true. But your attack convinced them otherwise." He took a long slow gulp of his drink. Paused to give himself a break, then fixed his eyes on Huxley and said, "You saved us...and you might have to do it again if they come back."

His words cut through the mood like raindrops during a picnic. Huxley didn't want to consider what Bennett was proposing. And for a moment, no one had anything to say. They finished their drinks trying to not make things awkward.

Jonah was the first to speak.

"Hey, Huxley?"

"Yes, Jonah?"

"What does your dad look like?"

Huxley found Jonah's eye line and followed it. His heart sank as he saw his father standing at the bar asking questions and scanning the crowd. Huxley ducked low.

"We have to get out of here." he whispered. The other two reflexively did the same.

"How much trouble are you going to get in, should we run?" Jonah asked.

"We should probably go fess up." Bennett offered.

"This time I'm going to side with Jonah, we should run," Huxley said while getting up from the table. He knew he was already found out, so he might as well enjoy the rest of the evening. "But where should we go?"

Bennett pulled them close and whispered. "I know where. It certainly won't be a place your dad will think to look. Come on!"

"Yeah, best not to leave it to Huxley, he would just go hide out with his books at the library." Jonah remarked.

He wasn't wrong. The idea had occurred to him.

"No, no libraries, no crowds. Follow me, I know just the place." Bennett said.

And the three friends disappeared into the festival.

9

Ɛ‹ა

Electricity and Makeup

The lights dimmed and a singular spotlight lit by a large gas lamp reflecting off of a shiny piece of rounded metal, illuminated the stage. A frayed red curtain with gold inlays was all that could be seen. It swooshed as feet hurried behind it setting the scene. The crowd murmured in anticipation. The train could be heard pulling into Mayburn, its echoing whistle and hiss of steam reverberating the rafters above their heads. Bennett's plan had been to mingle with one of the largest crowds in the festival. The over-the-top magic show was a signature event. It was standing room only so the boys found a spot in the back. Jonah passed the time chatting about what they might see.

"Three years ago, that guy came that would leap through a flaming ring, and then had his dog follow him. Now that was magic." Jonah said.

"How is jumping through a ring magic, even if a dog did it too?" Bennett wanted to know.

"Uhh...I said it was on fire! He didn't get burned at all or his dog! Dogs are covered in fur. He should have lit up like a bonfire, but no. Just a bit smokey. Now that guy was a performer." Jonah didn't try to hide the awe in his voice.

A stranger next to them overheard and said "hey, were you guys here last year? A real Magician came from Norun that had a coiled ring that could shoot lightning from it. The whole crowd screamed, about half fled. It would be amazing to see him again."

The boys continued to discuss possibilities, but Huxley wasn't paying much attention. He kept his eyes on the crowd. It would be hard for him to not feel like his father's eyes were narrowing in on him. He didn't know why he was so afraid. It's not like his father was a violent man. It was more frightening to think about what would happen at home. His mother would be so furious. Huxley had seen her in a bad mood often enough, but this was different. She was so cold, so controlling. She seemed like a different woman. No doubt, she sent his father. This was probably close to the last straw. Most boys moved out of their parent's home around his age. Militia men usually chose to live in the barracks or obtain affordable housing on the outskirts of town. Huxley didn't particularly love either of those plans, so he didn't want to move out quite yet. Although, after tonight, he might not have a choice. One phrase still lingered in his mind, *"...you've only ever been just passable."*

It more than stung him, it wounded far deeper than the attack had. If he was being honest, that was the real reason he was avoiding everyone.

His father meant it in a way that wasn't intended to hurt, he was too kind a man for that. It stung because there was truth to it. Huxley had never really excelled in much. It was hard for him seeing his friends find their niche and he ached inside when he thought about the future for himself. It was so uncertain. It almost felt like he was forced to put together a puzzle that didn't have a picture to follow. The worst part was that the puzzle was his life. Staying home and making shoes certainly wasn't right for him and joining the militia wouldn't work either. He had never actually been down the mines except for a school trip and even though the trip was framed to entice new recruits, it had the opposite effect on him. He was not a fan of being underground where the light dimmed as the rusty elevator slowly descended. No, the mines were certainly not for him. Anything else would be better. The problem was that he didn't think he was particularly good at anything else. His soul burned for something more, some height he couldn't see, some purpose that lay hidden from him, and until recently he didn't dare try and grasp what it was.

What was this push inside of him that told him to reach for something else. Something unseen. Like a weary traveler who knows his destination could be around the next corner. He couldn't give in now when there is likely something way better so close. He had to keep going.

There was so much to see and understand. How could a person ever be ok with fixing shoes every day? The idea bothered him because that was exactly where his life was headed. He could save up and buy a train ticket and leave Mayburn to find his place somewhere else but where would he go? It seemed any place he thought of had considerable bureaucracy and at best he could only go to work doing the same thing he would be doing here. In fact, up until four weeks ago, nothing remarkable ever happened in his life. The reality set in that perhaps the battle he fought would be the most exciting thing that ever happened to him. If he decided to make a career out of it he could bore recruits with stories of the one time the town was attacked and he defended it, just like Palithur. Huxley shuddered.

The seven piece band played a melody that was probably intended to be mysterious with long drawn-out moments making it seem like any minute something unexpected might happen. It did build a measure of anticipation. Instead of a leap though, a man casually walked out. He had crow's feet around his eyes and gray hair with wisps of black still holding on. The magician stared at the crowd; stone-faced. He had donned a costume that seemed a strange version of a formal suit that businessmen wore to fancy parties complete with a pocket watch and cummerbund. His suit jacket had two long tails that flapped behind him as he walked. His boots were polished and gave a distinctive thud-tap at each footfall. The man crossed to the exact middle of the stage, turned to the crowd and bowed low revealing a balding head who's scalp matched the deep ruby red color of his cheeks. He looked up and his smile seemed to belong to a far younger man. A sudden crack erupted from his hands and smoke shot into the air. The crowd gasped. The demonstration had silenced any remaining murmuring. When the smoke cleared the man was gone. As sudden as the last time a similar crack sounded at the back of the room and the man appeared amongst the crowd. The gas fueled spotlight spun to point directly at him, almost blowing out the flame in the process. He had appeared ten feet away from Huxley. The crowd cheered and he hurried his way back on stage. Rushing back, he announced, "Bear with me folks, that one required a lot of hustle." He nimbly hopped back up to the center stage again. He bowed lower this time. The crowd paused expecting something again when a large banner unfurled from above reading "The Magnificent Guliford!"

The crowd clapped again but this time with less enthusiasm. The man stood upright and said "Good evening Mayburn, and happy Kinship Revival Festival! I am Guliford, the magnificent, the well-traveled, the well-read, the patient, the mysterious, and the good tipper, although usually not all at once!" A few laughs emitted from the crowd, and he smiled. "It is true, I am well-traveled. I attend nearly every festival in Magnadun, even as far to the west as Sumine! Have any of you traveled further?"

Nobody made a sound. Huxley thought it impossible to have ever really traveled that far. Sumine? That place was on the other side of the world, and it was through miles of Fecundity. Almost as if perceiving his thoughts, The Amazing Guliford declared, "Doubt it if you dare, but do so at your peril. I am a man of many talents and abilities. Why, I have even trained with the Embers of the Arcane Flame in the college of Danador itself! But they declared me far too magical and wondrous to be trifled with. Your stalwart defender Palithur even acknowledged my strength just today!" Before the crowd could react to such an outrageous claim, the Magician threw his hands forward dramatically and made a huge show of wrestling something nonexistent from the air. He wrenched it back to his body, he pretended to be fighting an invisible creature. "I hold in my hands one of the rarest species from the Wilds that I have nearly tamed. The fire-breathing lizards of the crushing seaside depths! They have trained themselves to be invisible at all times while swimming through the water. They sneak up on their prey like a silent assassin. And just when the time is right…BOOM!" From the magician's hands erupted an inferno. Blazing so bright and loud that for an instant, Huxley thought the ludicrous story was true. The flame had only lasted for a moment. The crowd clapped with excitement and much to his chagrin, Huxley did too. Could he be the real deal? Was it possible that he really did study with the Embers? If so, perhaps he could help Huxley with some answers. Guliford went on with his act and began casually talking to the audience.

Just as Huxley started thinking about how to meet him afterwards, Jonah grabbed Huxley's hand, and threw it into the air declaring "This guy right here! He is the hero of Mayburn! He would make a great assistant!" Stunned, Huxley looked at Jonah who had a huge smile plastered on his face. A few other hands in the crowd had shot up as well. Guliford had asked for an assistant, and Huxley had just got volunteered. What made Jonah think this was a good idea? While trying to hide out from someone, you shouldn't try to get invited on stage. Huxley decided tomorrow he should get some new friends.

He fought to bring his hand down only to find Bennett clapping for "The hero of Mayburn!"

"You too?!" Huxley spat. Surely Bennett was smart enough to see how dumb this was.

Bennett motioned to the side entrance. Huxley followed his hand to see his father walking straight for him, his glare was cold and determined. Huxley's stomach twisted. The crowd began to notice and join the chorus. It grew through the audience until the magician couldn't ignore it anymore.

"What's that I hear? A hero you say, right here at my very own show! Well then, he simply must meet The Magnificent Guliford!"

That was all the prompting Huxley needed. He dashed to the stage. He had never once volunteered for this sort of thing. Under normal circumstances, he would have hated the whole notion. But being embarrassed on stage and getting to slip out the back seemed a far better alternative at the present moment. He didn't realize the steps were on the side of the stage and met a four-foot wall in front of him. The crowd picked him up to lift him on stage causing a sharp pain in his ribs. He had briefly forgotten about his wound.

Huxley righted himself and looked out at the enormous crowd. It didn't seem so big when he was in it.

Maybe I should have let my father catch me. He thought absently to himself.

He looked for the exit backstage when he was spun around by Guliford to face the audience. Guliford's face was red from exertion and perhaps the flames of a moment ago. He beamed at Huxley and said "So just what made you the HERO of Mayburn?! Perhaps you saved young maidens?" He paused and listened to the crowd's reaction. His eyes were raised so high, it pushed his hair back. A few girls squealed but no one else. He lowered his voice and adopted a mockingly grim growl, "Or perhaps you helped put out the fires brought on from the recent attack?!" He looked excitedly back to the crowd for various degrees of response. The crowd began to answer in a smattering of different voices when Guliford held out his palm firmly. "Shhhh, everyone, please, I must have silence, for I have divined the truth! Guliford the Magnificent is not only a teleporter and wrangler of wild animals but a seer of minds!" Huxley chuckled to himself. Now that was a stupid thing to say. No one can read minds. Every story about the Embers he ever heard had nothing to do with telepathy. Even if he could read his mind, Huxley wasn't totally sure what he did or why he was considered a hero. Guliford looked at him and mouthed the words, "just go with it," and dramatically ran to the other side of the stage.

Huxley scanned the audience looking for his father. He couldn't see him which probably wasn't a good thing. No doubt, he didn't want to make a scene. Huxley became motivated to be the best assistant ever and perhaps never leave the stage. Suddenly, Guliford declared, "Watch now as I plumb his innermost thoughts and mind! No secret is safe from me. Even now, I am peering into your notions and impulses." He made a big show of staring intensely at Huxley. Huxley had to admit, it was hard to look away. Huxley had the odd sense that Guliford wasn't just focused on the performance. He seemed focused on something else. Then Huxley felt a sudden pull from inside of him. It was like someone else's heartbeat was inside of him for just a second. Huxley was shocked. That was no mere trick. Something actually happened. Huxley gasped and Guliford snapped his hands back in a dramatic theatrical flair. Guliford gasped as well but Huxley wasn't sure anymore if it was for the audience's benefit or not. The magician waved his body around and breathed "yes, yes I see now! I see what he was hiding," he clicked his tongue and said *tsk tsk* "my friend, those are ladies you are having those thoughts about!" The younger teenagers in the crowd all whooped and laughed at Huxley. An embarrassing moment for sure but he was too worried about what had just happened to be upset about it. There would be time to be embarrassed later. The magician made a few more comments at his expense but Huxley wasn't listening. He rubbed his chest and then it happened again. The phantom heartbeat occurred, right in the middle of his chest. *Thu-thump* Huxley's mind forced an image to the surface. It was a page from the grimoire, a page that he had only briefly tried to decipher. There was a sketch of two men standing about the same distance away from each other in the same fashion as Huxley and Guilford stood now. But that was all he knew. Huxley realized he vastly underestimated Guliford. He was no ordinary magician. His quiet time in study had produced a new instinct in him. It wasn't panic, or fear but similar to how he had been trained in the militia. He knew a threat when he felt one. And sensing that, he usually would reach for his weapon that hung at his side. There was no weapon at his side though, so Huxley reached elsewhere. He had had enough of being scared and made a fool of. Perhaps Guliford would like a taste of his own medicine. His mind reached out, and then all of the lights and sounds faded. The magician was still hollering silly things, but his voice became muffled like he was underwater. The bright stage lanterns burned low, emitting far less light. With a shimmer, the swirling stars returned to Huxley's sight. Before him were an assortment of stars just like the ones he had seen during the battle. It was hard to determine how many, some had a more defined shape than others. They were all distinct, having their own vibration and color. One danced forward, the same he used to defend the wall.

"No!"

He was determined not to use that one. That was deadly, exceedingly deadly. He only wanted to surprise him. The moment he came to that conclusion, a different star flew right in front of him just inside arm's reach. Huxley snatched it out of the air. He held it in his hand, and felt the energy surging, an unbridled amount of potential just waiting to be released.

Well, he thought, the people did want a show.

Guliford was still doing his best to get more laughs out of the audience. And then as though he could feel Huxley's mood shift, he looked over his shoulder at his would-be assistant. Huxley flung his hands forward. A harmless crackling flew through the air emitting jarring pops accompanied by pinpricks of light. The Grimoire's section on weather patterns was most enlightening. At least, he was pretty sure it was about weather patterns. He had practiced this one before in his room and it seemed harmless enough. His ploy worked. Guliford the Magnificent leaped off of his feet and nearly fell to the ground. The crowd reacted immediately, cheering. Guliford, however, did no such thing. He glared at Huxley with eyes the size of dinner plates. The audience took it all in stride and probably thought it was part of the act. The two regarded each other for a moment before Guliford pushed down his astonishment. The reality of what had just happened slammed into Huxley.

How could he have acted so impulsively? What possessed him to lash out like that?

It was likely a miracle that he had been in control of that. The pages of the grimoire floated in his mind as though they were a part of him. It really had been second nature to reach for its knowledge. What kind of power did this book really contain? And how long would it be before Huxley kills someone again?

Guliford's face returned to normal, and the showman pretended like it was all part of the act. Huxley decided he had enough fun and likely needed to get away to avoid getting dragged back to his house by his father. He turned to leave the stage, but Guliford proclaimed "Ladies and gentlemen, a big hand for the Savior of Mayburn and Savior of you all!" Huxley paused and gave a courteous bow. He didn't feel like he had earned all the applause. He lowered his head and before he could look up, the floor dropped out from underneath him. A mechanical snap slammed the trap door back before he landed on a feather-filled mattress. The wind was knocked out of him, and his ribs screamed in pain. What was that about? He looked around alarmed, worried he was imprisoned. He wasn't. He was just underneath the stage where a large sign hung in front of him stating:

"Shhh! Or you will spoil it."

-M.G.

Huxley was annoyed now. He had enough of Guliford's silly magic tricks. He wasn't entirely sure he wasn't being mocked. Huxley stood up as steadily as his body would allow and made for what he hoped was an exit. The crowd cheered again, but the voices were now muffled. He had never been one for the spotlight. Luckily, he wouldn't have to navigate the crowd now. He found a door in the far corner of the room. Passing through it he found what he guessed was Guliford's dressing room. It was full of costumes and multitudes of fancy looking props. Huxley rolled his eyes and looked for an exit when a voice behind him spoke.

"And just how did you learn that little trick, young Ember?"

Surprised, Huxley turned already recognizing the voice. Guliford the Magnificent stood staring at him. Or more accurately, Guliford the curious looking. He had abandoned all of his stage drama and now just looked like a man in a ridiculous outfit waiting for an answer. Huxley squinted. There was something about Guliford that had changed. He seemed more familiar now, like someone Huxley had met before.

"What little trick? And I'm no Ember." Huxley lied weakly.

"It's been so long since I have spoken to another practitioner. It's a rare honor. It is good to meet you, Huxley. Did you really do what the stories say? Are you that powerful?" He pressed on, ignoring the lie.

"...I, uh-" Huxley began.

"What am I saying! Of course, you are. When our hearts twinned,

I could feel it. You really are a hero…" His gaze shifted away and then he spoke but almost as though to himself. "And I dropped him down a trapdoor. You must forgive me! Are you hurt? Injured?"

Huxley was holding his side. His hand had pressed against his newly aggravated wound. His hand had moved there almost unconsciously.

"Well yes, but it's from the battle. Not the door." he responded.

"Ah! I'm so sorry lad. I don't usually use that little trick, but I just knew I had to speak to you, and I couldn't let you just walk away. Please let me attend to it." He reached for Huxley's shirt, but Huxley pulled away.

"What?! No. I've not wanted any of this attention." Huxley moved for the door while saying, "I just want to go home and be screamed at by my mother, then confined to my bed for another month."

Guliford side-stepped in between Huxley and the door and with a pleading look in his eyes said,

"Let me take just a look! I can likely help you. I'm no Ember, but I can help with wounds. Bones are easy. It's your ribs, right? I could feel something there."

Huxley stopped not wanting to aggravate his wound any further. He was also curious. If Guliford could help it would be a huge burden lifted and maybe even worth all of the irritation he suffered. It's not like he would hurt it worse…right?

Huxley reluctantly sat down in what he guessed was Guliford's makeup chair.

Ok, Huxley, you're here. Just let the guy take a look, He thought.

He lifted his shirt and Guliford stared quizzically at it. As Guliford moved to put his hands on him, Huxley instinctually shied away.

"Do not worry, I will be quite careful."

He ran his fingers as promised over the bandages and slowly removed them. Huxley started to get a sense that Guliford was at least familiar with wounds although definitely not a doctor. Maybe he was militia-trained and knew field medicine.

Guliford looked for a moment and said "Shrapnel or a weapon? Shrapnel, right? Yeah, your ribs caught most of it. A few fractures. They did their job though and protected your vitals. How long has it been? Three weeks? Four?"

"Uhh, about four." He replied.

Guliford stood up and said, "just a moment" and walked across the room and began rummaging through a bag.

As he looked Huxley asked "What did you mean our hearts twinned?"

Casually ignoring him he returned with a book. He flipped through the pages with speed, finding the one he was searching for within seconds and ran his finger down the page. He spoke while he read but it only came out in half spoken phrases.

"...infections for all types...no....how to set a...no...identifying gangrene...no, ah! Here we are."

His expression hardened and he read silently now. Another moment passed and just as Huxley was about to ask what was going to happen Guliford snapped the book shut.

"No worries my young patient, Doctor Guliford, the amazing physician can help." A broad smile emerged on his face discomforting Huxley further. Huxley realized he was actually starting to miss the previous annoying versions of Guliford.

Guliford leaned back, snapped his hand forward, grabbed at nothing, then drew his hands back. His fists were balled up and he could see they were straining. He placed his hands suddenly on Huxley's ribs with more pressure than Huxley wanted. The now familiar pain coursed through his body and just as he was about to cry out, it ceased. A warm sensation radiated from Guliford's hands soothing Huxley's injuries. It was unlike anything Huxley had ever experienced before. It made its way through his ribs and then his chest, ending on the other side. It was like an internal massage. The whole thing lasted only briefly then Guliford released Huxley.

"That should help my friend."

"Wh-what did you just do?"

Guliford stared at Huxley flatly.

"Oh, come now, surely you recognized that?" Guliford responded.

"Recognize what? I've never seen that before." Huxley said.

"You've never seen Magnincy before? ... son, you used it on stage tonight. We can be plain with each other. We both have seen each other's ability. And the twinning made it incontrovertible. Now tell me, who taught you? Surely not an Ember. No, you never would have even come here if you studied with them. A local practitioner? Surely not Palithur?"

Huxley felt both exposed and relieved. For some reason, he felt more ok speaking to Guliford than he had with the Warden. Guliford didn't work for Danador. He wasn't even from here. Maybe he could help.

"No one taught me...I found a page from a book."

Guliford gasped. "You found a page from a Grimoire! Is that what you are telling me?!"

"...yes, *a page*, it fell out of an old book from the library." He decided to let Guliford's assumption that it was a grimoire play out before he revealed more.

"Well, that can explain it. A page from a grimoire is a powerful thing. How is your mind? Have you begun to slip?" His voice began to grow more frantic, "You must take extreme caution with it. Almost any piece of knowledge about reality itself could be inscribed on it! Literally anything..." He trailed off remembering something.

"Wait, did you almost shoot a bolt of lightning on stage tonight?! Was that what that was? Boy, you could have killed me and yourself, not to mention a good portion of the audience!"

Huxley held up his hand hoping to silence him. It worked, and Guliford stopped.

"I found a page that had lots of crazy talk on it. It outlined a lightning bolt, yes. But I have toyed with it for some time now. I have practiced it in my room."

"You toyed with Magnincy...in your room?" Guliford said each word thick with incredulity

"Well, yes..." Huxley responded.

"Do you know what you have? What you are capable of ... This is no mere stage trick."

"But, you-"

"What I do is the result of years of study and practice, and even then,

I employ minute amounts of Magnincy on stage for my own safety. One day, I won't be on my game and reach too deep..."

"Too deep?" Huxley asked.

Guliford stiffened again and said, "By the lost kinsman you really are uneducated, aren't you? You just found a page of magic tricks and started grabbing what you could!" His expression grew stern. It was a strange look from a man covered in makeup.

"Huxley, whatever you have read is the result of years or likely decades of study. Magnincy is the study and wielding of the truth of Magnadun itself! All around us," He motioned widely with his arms, "is what's possible and what simply is. If you study enough and comprehend enough it can be possible to reach out and take hold of that knowledge. To literally hold it in your hands you need a thorough understanding of it. To grab knowledge you aren't ready to accept will collapse your mind and throw you into madness! You mustn't ever do what you did tonight again. I trained for years only to be rejected from formal training with the masters. My knowledge is as a child's finger painting next to the master-piece of what the Embers make. And even then, it taxes me. The benefit of Magnincy is untold knowledge and the ability to wield it...its cost, however is your mind."

"Wait, so Embers all go crazy in time?"

"Not the good ones. But yes. Arrows and the quiver! That's what it is. Each arrow is the knowledge and the quiver is the stability of your mind. More knowledge, bigger arrows, more stability, bigger quiver. Do you understand?"

"Arrows and a quiver?" Huxley nodded as he repeated.

"Yes! If you have a modest understanding of, say, basic thermo-dynamics, as an example, you may be able to produce heat or even flames for a short period. You could call on that knowledge and use your under-standing of it for your own purposes. Lighting a fire, warming a room, or frightening a wild animal, for example. That may go well at first, but the more you use it without rest, it taxes your mind. The more thoroughly you understand something, the more you can call on its knowledge to wield but if you over-tax your mind it will break.

"How long does it take to fix?"

"Fix?! Depends entirely on how much was called on and how much was grabbed. Maybe a few minutes, hours, days, months, years or never. Most embers that over reach only have bouts of madness that last a handful of minutes. But in that time they are defenseless. An Ember is the most dangerous thing on the planet but a mad Ember can't do anything to protect himself. A trained mind will find its way back to stability after a time but you never know how long it will be for sure. It's like being shown every formula, every equation, every measurement all at once; all screaming for your attention. When your mind breaks, it isn't met with a void, but an overflow that drowns you in information. Never able to make sense of it, again." He stepped back to indicate he was finished. "...So, it's a curse," Huxley asked, sounding somewhat defeated.

"It's a gift from the stars themselves! It is only through knowledge gained after many hours of research does an Ember dare walk into its true power. When we were on stage, I saw that your soul has been kindled as mine has. We have seen the truth of our world and what it offers us. We will never be able to ignore it now. But a practitioner that overreaches will spend the rest of his days in madness. Now tell me...is that worth impressing your friends again?"

Huxley sank into his seat. He had been such a fool. Of course, he wasn't able to do this. He had stumbled upon a grimoire intended for someone else, likely another Ember, and read through it. How arrogant was he that he thought he could handle this kind of power? It was probably a miracle that he had made it this far. Potential Embers were taken as young children because they had the academic aptitude for handling this. He was tested long ago and passed over quickly. He remembered failing the exam before he even knew it was happening. It all made sense now. A warden visited his class and met with each student asking them strange questions. "These tools are at your disposal, how would you solve this problem?" or "Look over these sequences of numbers, what stands out?" No one from his class was taken. Only the one girl, Onders, from the year ahead of him ever tested well enough to be accepted. At first, he thought it was a mistake, like the Warden didn't realize he was speaking to children and not graduates. But there had been no mistake. That was how they searched for potential candidates for the college of Danador. How old had he been? Six or maybe seven. It baffled him then as it did now. His continued attempts to test after so many failures seemed infantile now. Perhaps Palithur was helping him by always discouraging it.

One question lingered. It needled at his thoughts.

But then how did I do what I did? He was far from a thorough understanding of anything academic. If it took hard work and patience to produce a flame, then how did he drive off so many on that night. He knew nothing about stars, in fact, the more he thought about it, he became suspicious it wasn't a star at all.

"...yes, I am certain that is the best course. Don't you agree?" Guliford asked, but Huxley had only just then realized he had become lost in his own thoughts. Guliford's instructions had turned into a lecture, one that sounded oddly familiar to the way Palithur would scold him. It seemed whenever someone started lecturing, Huxley's mind instinctually left for more interesting places.

"Uhh, agree? I suppose yes." He said reluctantly.

"Oh my! Wonderful, I will begin the paperwork immediately. I assume you are old enough to join? You look it. I haven't had a proper apprentice in years!" he exclaimed.

Huxley's voice caught in his throat, and he blurted out "Apprentice! To you?! I don't...I mean...well...what?!"

Guliford stopped and said, "Haven't you been listening? You need a guide and you are too old to be an Ember so you might as well train with me and I will show you how to be a great Magician."

Huxley blinked. Well, that was certainly a path he hadn't considered yet. Run away and join the circus, he thought with incredulity. Now THAT would be incredible for his mom to hear. *Well, mom, I don't want to run the shop or be a soldier or join the mining company, so circus it is!*

"I'm so sorry, my friends are waiting for me. They're probably wondering where I got off too."

"Oh, the two boys? They are right outside. My attendants found them and escorted them here. Pay no worry to them. Listen, what you possess is a strange and unique gift. The stars do not bestow on everyone their truth. Many study for years and years and never are granted what you have been given. You know enough to kill yourself or others without training. But I could help you hone what you have and give you a safe life; one that is quite fun at times. We travel all over Danador and Valdannon. We hope to reach all over Magnadun someday. You could be a part of it. You could have a place here with us." Guliford told him.

This time Huxley listened. To his surprise, he was considering it. It's true, he could hurt someone. And, at least, he would get some kind of training. It made all the sense in the world, which is why he didn't even understand why he blurted out:

"No."

"No?" Guliford said.

"Uh, Yes, no."

Guliford furrowed his brow and began to speak but Huxley beat him to it.

"It is a generous offer and perhaps I am a fool but I don't want to risk losing my mind any more than I already have. I would rather put all of this behind me and never think about it again."

"Oh, it's far too late for that my friend. You have glimpsed into what is possible. Your mind ached for more and you have been granted it. No one goes back to the way things were, not after you've experienced true Magnincy. It's wildly dangerous to remain untrained."

An idea occurred to Huxley and he said, "What about the college of Danador?"

"What about it?"

"What if I showed up there and tested again?"

"Oh, Huxley" he said soothingly, "...they have an extremely high bar for admittance. And even then, you are too far behind the others your age. You will never be an Ember."

Huxley deflated but pressed on with an ounce of hope. "Well, I could still be something inside the school. Right?"

Guliford stroked his beard and said "I...suppose you could...perhaps a researcher one day that would give all of his hard work to someone else to study further. A glorified note taker."

The notion of having a place with the Embers lit a spark in Huxley he had never known was truly there. He sat up straight. "You mean it?! I could actually work with them?"

"Haven't you been listening? I said you wouldn't do anything of import. Just researching abstract concepts and turning over everything to them."

"Working with the Arcane Flame in order to serve Embers would be the best thing in the world to me! And perhaps I could ascend higher than you think. Maybe I could even master some of what I read already."

Guliford was crestfallen, "There is never talking anyone out of it. You are the fourth young man who has had an inkling of potential and his imagination ran away with it. Don't you see? They want to use you with no care of what your wants are. If you came to work with me, you could be a part of something and have true freedom. They will never offer you more than that. They would even take that page of yours, the one from the grimoire. Working with the Arcane Flame requires total commitment."

Guliford then perked up and said, "I'll tell you what! Let's make a deal. You come and work for me for one year, I'll train you and show you the ropes of Magnincy. If at the end of the year you want to give it all up and go work for them, I'll let you go no strings attached."

"Why would you offer something like that with no strings? Why train me for a year just to risk me leaving?"

"Because I know you won't," Guliford said with a smile. "This life is truly fantastic. You can have the life you never knew you wanted." He stuck out his hand to shake.

But a muffled voice came through the wall. "Yeah Hux, go be a circus clown!" The voice belonged to Jonah. "Learn how to juggle and jump through rings of fire." He said laughing. A hard thud sounded and Jonah yelped in pain with a "shhh," from what Huxley was guessing, was Bennett.

Huxley pulled back his hand. "He does have a point; it doesn't seem to be me."

Guliford looked toward the wall then back to Huxley, "I understand, how about you take the night and think about it? We leave at seven in the morning, sharp. I won't wait for you. Go and think it over. If you decide to join our troupe then you may. If you wish to try for a life in the college, I will help as much as I can." Guliford stood and turned towards his vanity. He slowly lit the candles surrounding it. The light shone on his face revealing his age. His smile was gone but the makeup remained.

"Thank you for your offer, Guliford. I will think about it. It's just, my friends are waiting."

Guliford looked up at Huxley through the reflection. "Our lives are here and gone in moments. We could use those moments for discovery, smiles, hatred, or....you name it. The longer we wait to choose, the more we miss. I chose my moments. Make sure you are doing the same."

He looked back to the vanity and began taking off his makeup and Huxley walked out the door.

10

∽

Gates and Reminders

....the force to the product of the charges and has an inverse-square relation to the distance between them." - **Page 78 Excerpt from the Grimoire**

In the room right outside, waiting for him, were Jonah and Bennett, just like he was told. Jonah ran over and gave him a hug. Immediately realizing his mistake, he let go and apologized, "Oh jeez, sorry your rib! I don't want to hurt the new and amazing Huxley the magical!"

Huxley wasn't ready to explain what happened and just said "no, problem."

The boys walked out onto what was once a choked street. Now, barely a few dozen made up its inhabitants.

Jonah said "I haven't seen your father. Most of the fair is closing up and dispersing. He likely thinks we're gone. It should be safe enough."

"You ok?" Bennett asked with a probing look. His voice was really degrading now. It sounded dry like rocks being rubbed together.

"Yeah...well enough...did you guys hear all of that?" Huxley asked.

"You know we did. What an opportunity! This is the perfect solution for you right? You don't have to run a shop, you don't have to join the militia, you don't have to stay here! You get to leave and finally see some of the world. What's to turn down? Besides your horrendous ability to look comfortable on stage...honestly man, you just looked sweaty and awkward up there, like Bennett did the first time he talked to a girl."

"He makes a good point." Bennett croaked.

"Oh, come on, you weren't that sweaty," Jonah stated.

"No, shut up." He swallowed hard. "You know what I mean."

"Yeah, I do. It just doesn't seem like the thing I wanted." Huxley admitted.

The boys had reached the end of the downtown streets and turned to walk back home. But Bennett hesitated.

"What is it?" Huxley asked.

He looked around, swallowed again, and said "Ok, I have an idea..." He paused. "you're already in trouble, right?" Bennett said.

"Oh, man, I'm already excited for whatever you're about to say." Jonah chimed in.

Huxley just nodded, yes.

"So, staying out a bit later won't change anything right?" Bennett said.

"No, I guess not." Huxley said.

"Ok. Follow me, I want to show you something."

Jonah erupted with guesses as to where Bennett was taking them. All of them were wrong.

"We're going to set a fire!

"...No"

"Oh, how about heading out into the wilds!"

"Why?" Bennett criticized.

No wait, we're going to break into the armory and get some real sword fight training?"

"Shut up and just walk. We should probably be silent."

Huxley followed along. He would have been more curious, but Guliford's words had worked their way into his head. If he didn't choose his path soon, one would be chosen for him. Fate, it seemed, was a bad author, only giving the good stories to those willing to make hard choices.

They continued away from the middle of town. Mercifully, Jonah had listened for the most part and quieted down. Although "quieted down" for Jonah was still louder than most. He folded his hands and put them behind his head and sighed out loud. "Ok, I've figured it out. No more guessing, this is it."

Despite his annoyance. Bennett looked at Jonah as though asking him to go on. He was probably enjoying it more than he let on. You grow used to Jonah over time and even start to like him.

"It all makes sense if you think about it, making us walk alone, all late into the night. Taking us out and showing us a good time at the fair, always looking out for us, and now leading us to a secret location...yep it can't be anything else." He looked at Huxley and Bennett, took a deep breath and said, "It's obvious that you've fallen in love with us and can't choose between Hux and myself."

Bennett turned and walked away without a word, with Huxley close behind.

"What?! All the evidence points towards it! You ignored every girl tonight, always wanting to be around us instead. It's ok, my deep-set masculine features as well as my roguish wit are too much to handle." He called after them. "Hux's nice and all but he's too meek. It's me that is the catch! Hey, come back, I AM FLATTERED!" They had turned the corner and were getting out of sight. Jonah took off after them.

A grim destination awaited. One Huxley had tried hard not to think about.

The site of the battle.

Nothing had been cleaned up. The hole made in the wall was still sitting open and gaping. You could even see outside. Two guards were posted by the hole with rope tying it off. The smell of smoke lingered and Huxley could even see blood spray still on the ground. The boys stood and stared. It felt both a lifetime ago and like it just happened. Huxley had been in his first battle and it was over before it began. Then...then the thing happened.

Bennet stepped forward, turned and looked at Huxley. There had always been a nobility to Bennett, as though he had never been a boy, just a young soldier waiting to grow up. He was nearly always composed and ready for duty. When he looked at you, with those steely eyes, they demanded your attention.

He surveyed the rubble and said, "Just look at it...really look."

Huxley saw a terrible scar on his town, one that could have been worse. if not for him.

Bennett produced a canteen and drank deeply. When he was done, he winced and prepared to speak but Huxley interrupted, "You really don't have to. Just rest your throat, you've talked enough for tonight."

Bennett ignored him and said, "They have barely done anything. Mayburn is the last stop at the end of a long track. Apparently, we are of so little note that Danador couldn't dispatch anyone to help us. We serve a nation of vast strength and power, yet we aren't worth their protection. This tells you everything you need to know about what choice to make. I don't know what it takes to be an Ember, I don't know if Guliford was right or not. But I do know this...you drove them back Huxley. Whatever you did, whatever ability you accessed, you saved us all. I trained as hard as I could, never missed practice. I even practiced at home in my spare time. I am meant for this. But even if there were a hundred of me, we would have lost. I've kept running that day over and over in my head. They beat us fair and square. Thoroughly overwhelmed us. But one action from you and they turned tail and fled!"

He spit blood on the ground and growled in anger. "Damnation, there was FEAR in their eyes! You made those monsters feel *fear*. They barely even looked at me as an opponent..." His eyes had begun to water and he paused.

"Bennett I-" Huxley said

"No! Wait, just let me finish." He wiped the corners of his eyes and continued. "If they got in, we would all be dead. I can't think of a different outcome. That army came to kill. Kill us all. My family, yours, Jonah's. Everyone. But you stopped them. Hux, you're one of them."

"Who?"

"The Embers."

The words hung in the air like an actual ember floating up from a fire.

"You did something people write stories about. I was there, I saw every second. You did what seasoned warriors couldn't. You have Magnincy or whatever it is that they have. You may not know it, or be able to wield it as they do. But you have it. And you have to learn how to use it. Because one day, they will come back or if not them, someone else. The only ones who will protect Mayburn are people like us, because we love it. The Embers won't, but you could go and learn from them. Become one of them. Return here and become our guardian. You heard Guliford...you know it's possible."

Huxley started but caught himself. He had to think about this. It did get him more excited than he cared to admit.

Bennett refused to stop, "He offered you a nice life, but one that is far from here. Feel free to make your own choices and pursue what you feel is best. But as for me? I will guard this town. I will dedicate my life to ensuring what happened a month ago, never happens again. That job will be way easier if I have a best friend who can route an entire army. I already know you aren't going to join the circus. You can stop pretending to mull that over."

Huxley had to admit, Bennett was making a lot of sense.

"You aren't about making money and living a cushy life. That is the life of a performer. That has never been you. You care about people and learning. Your path has never been clear because you've never had a path. You were never going to be a soldier, a cobbler or anything else..."

He trailed off and to Huxley's surprise Bennett sniffed back some tears, not from pain, but sadness, Bennett looked over the destruction. He stared at it like it was his own personal failure. Maybe to Bennett, it was. He squared his shoulders and stood as a soldier would. He was right. Even if his chances were low or impossible to ever become a full-fledged Ember, practicing so he could pass the test was the best chance he would ever get.

Jonah was silent for once. He was at a loss. He walked slowly to stand beside Bennett and Huxley followed. The three boys stood in silent reverence. The moon pierced through the clouds revealing more details. Broken spears, splintered shields, and rubble, all tied together with crimson-stained earth. Jonah, in a whisper, spoke.

"Through knowledge and will he keeps madness at bay, his mind is our savior and our protector. Sundered lands be made whole again, may it be reclaimed..." Jonah had recited the benediction spoken in reverence for Ember Palithur. But he didn't speak it in triumph as usual but in melancholy. He continued looking out and said "Savior and protector...we know now that we can't rely on them. But we can rely on you Huxley. Our hero failed us...but you didn't. I don't know if they will ever erect a statue like his for you, but you deserve one. We know it, go show them that you deserve one too."

The three stood in silence, Huxley's eyes finally looked at the place where Captain Pilch fell. He had always been so focused on wanting to leave practice or escape attention he never really stopped to appreciate the captain. A good man died here, and lots more followed him.

"...I'll try," said Huxley in acceptance.

The somber moment evaporated. Jonah looked to Huxley with renewed enthusiasm.

"You are going to become an Ember! You are going to be the next hero of Danador."

"Hero!?" Huxley exclaimed.

"Well, ok well maybe not a proper hero...but maybe a passable one!"

Huxley blinked. There's no way he was making a joke. He didn't know about what his father had said. He was just being Jonah.

"...ok, fine, a passable Ember, let's say." Huxley replied.

There was nothing left to say, Huxley had decided to figure out the Grimoire and become an Ember of the Arcane Flame, now he just had to convince the people he'd been trying to convince all his life.

The boys parted ways after chatting the whole way back. Jonah detailed a list of Embers and what each one was known for. "...He splits weapons and armor in half," Jonah was saying, "You basically have to try and beat him naked."

"Ok, thanks Jonah. I'll be sure to watch out for that." Huxley told him.

———————————————————————————————————

The moment came for Huxley to face his parents. Yesterday, if he were in the same position, it may have frightened him. But the events of the night along with his newfound mission left him feeling different, confident. It was strange having a plan and a direction after going so long without one. He ran through the list of issues he might deal with but for some reason it filled him with determination rather than despair. It was as though the challenge fueled him. He made a mental checklist and before he was through, one thing became apparent. He knew his mother would not let him go so easily. She couldn't stop him...at least he didn't think she could...but he preferred not to have that fight. The only solution left, after much internal debate, was just to leave now. In the cover of darkness, he could slip back into his room, grab the Grimoire and a few essentials, plus a few clips he had, and get to the train. Hop on board with Guliford and then hope he can sneak out when the train gets to Danador. Not a bad plan, lots of holes, but for now it was his best option.

He snuck into his house with great care. It was nearing midnight and everyone would have been asleep for hours if they weren't waiting up for him. It appeared they weren't. Perhaps they forgave him and weren't too angry. It was a nice thought but history taught him that it couldn't be true. Huxley deftly walked through the hallways wincing after each squeak in the floorboards until he reached his room. The grimoire was just where he left it. He almost opened it, wanting to use some of the new information he had gained from Guliford. But now wasn't the time. He tucked it into his satchel and grabbed another small leather bag and stuffed in some clothes. It was hard to see with only the moon illuminating his room. He swiftly surveyed everything and grabbed stationary, pens and ink, and a traveling cloak. It was certainly not enough but it would have to do. He wavered. The stress of his actions and the flurry of new thoughts finally caught up and his body ached for sleep. The train wasn't going to leave until seven, if he slept now he could get a couple of good hours. But how would he wake up on time? No city bells to wake him up and he certainly didn't want his parents to find him. The veranda outside provided his answer again. He glanced upward and the stars filled the sky despite the moons dominating presence. *Am I just noticing them more or are they brighter?* He thought. Curling up just under his window he fell asleep.

Sleep came in fits. He never truly rested but how could he? After what felt like enough trying, Huxley climbed out his window for the second time that night and ran towards the train station.

Huxley dashed down an unfamiliar path. The sun was still asleep but was sure to awaken soon. It was silent save for his rapid footfalls and the hiss of gas lanterns. His satchel weighed on his shoulder and he could feel the Grimoire thumping against his side with each step. His thoughts screamed at him regarding all of the likely mistakes he was making. Responsibility, loyalty, family...he knew his actions in some way betrayed those things. He pushed away those thoughts and replaced them with the breached gates, bodies scattered around him, the Grimoire, and the vision of him wearing Ember's robes. If he was to protect his home, he would need to be drastic. A new feeling broke through, an emotion that bubbled up and gave strength to his muscles and focus to his mind. A newly awakened sense of purpose and adventure fueled him in a way he had never felt before. It was joy. Unbridled, giddy, wonderful joy. He was finally on a path he wanted to be on. Huxley Durant of Mayburn would be an Ember of the Arcane Flame, as long as it didn't cost him his sanity first.

He arrived at the station late at night. He hadn't bothered to check the clock when he left the house but he knew it was past midnight. The gates stood grand and imperial, towering over Huxley. The cold black steel that made up nearly everything in the station served as a reminder to all residents that they were a part of something far greater. Mayburn was the last in the line of a grand conquest from years ago and everything beyond it was untamed Fecundity. You could easily forget just how great of a nation Danador was, that is, unless you visited the train station. It was the lifeline of the town; without it they would be alone. It was spoken of with pride and reverence. The grand train line united everyone in the nation both physically but also in hope. Before it existed, travel and trade were synonymous with peril. The countryside was unpredictable. Who knew what could come crawling out of the wild verdure? Only a well-equipped band of travelers stood a chance, and even then...survival was questionable. But if you were on the train, you were not only safe but a part of something greater. It was the symbol of order and dominance over nature.

Huxley marveled at its sheer size and splendor. Even the gates were crafted to exude power and mastery. He had approached them before but never went inside. What business would a shoemaker's son have with something like the Grand Railways? Even now looking at its imposing gates, he felt he didn't belong here. That somehow the station knew he was a nobody with no business on the train. He reached down and let his fingers touch the Grimoire, almost like it was his train ticket, and in many ways it was. It was the means by which he could leave this town. He pulled his hand back out and was newly encouraged. He hadn't had a need for the Grand Railways before. Today, he did. In just a few hours he would be in Danador, the Capital of all things good and civilized. He shivered in excitement at the thought. He found the ticket booth. Or rather the heavy equipment entrance. Knowing this wasn't going to be a standard entry he opted to try for a gate that looked as though it had already received its cargo. People were already forming a deep line on the main entrance and Huxley didn't want to be the reason it took longer to get in. Huxley strode up to the glass and stood before it. An older man in his fifties glanced up from a ledger and narrowed his eyes at Huxley.

"Are you lost?" He asked.

"Me? Uh no, I'm here to join the circus." Huxley said.

Fool! Huxley scolded himself. You could have said something more clever than that!

"Joining the circus..." the attendant said back to him in a way that begged for more information.

Huxley regained his wits. "Well, an apprenticeship has been offered to me from the Magnificent Guliford, err, I mean, I earned it. And he told me to be here early and to not be late." He emphasized the last part to sound more official.

"So...you don't have a ticket?" He asked.

Huxley shook his head. "no."

The attendant set his jaw and gave a long groan. "I'll have to clear it with the station's Warden. Wait here." The attendant hopped down from his desk and disappeared into the back office. A spring of worry popped up in Huxley. *What if Guliford didn't put my name down? What if I can't contact him?* He thought. Then a voice from behind him made him jump in surprise.

"You've joined the circus huh? Well, now that is surprising."

Huxley knew who it was before he turned around.

Huxley swallowed hard and turned to meet his father. He opened his mouth, but his father cut him off.

"Son...I understand."

He what?! Huxley was certain he hadn't heard right.

His father saw his shock and went on.

"I do. I was young once too. I sought a different life than the one offered to me just as you are now. I wanted to go and experience all the big city had to offer before I settled down. I knew my parents would never let me, but I did so anyway."

"Dad, that's not-"

"Stop and listen," His father interrupted, "I know you son. Better than you think I do. Before you run away, please remember this." He stopped and searched for the right words. "Don't let it fool you."

Huxley blinked.

"I have seen how you pour over books about grand heroes and epic tales. I'm sure it feels like you can even be one sometimes. I'm not sure what your friends told you or what you think you can do now but I've heard the stories. Also, I bet old Palithur has spun you hundreds of tales of his exploits by now. I have seen you grow into a good young man with a wild imagination. You get these ideas in your head and it runs away from reality. Please don't lose yourself in a fantasy of what you want to be rather than what you are."

Huxley's face fell as he listened. He agreed, it was foolish to have got his hopes up but the implications his father made wounded him. He didn't want to hear the answer, but Huxley asked anyway.

"And what am I?" he asked weakly.

"You are...." he trailed off searching for the right word.

"....passable?" Huxley repeated quietly. It was a phrase he had heard way too often to ever forget.

His father looked surprised as he recalled what he had stated before. "Well...yes, but that's a good th-"

"Stop!" Huxley's emotions coiled up within him, "I've heard you say all of this already. Dad, I can wield Magnincy! I can train and come back and defend Mayburn as an Ember!" he blurted out.

His words hung in the air and sounded ridiculous in this context, but Huxley knew that it was the truth.

They both stood straighter, each not backing down. His father held back his emotions, but Huxley could tell he was getting frustrated.

Narrowing his eyes, Huxley's father began, and said "I'm sure you think you can do those thi-"

The air exploded with energy and light. An invisible force slammed him to the ground. In the span of a second, Huxley let his anger from the last few years boil over, and his father was the focus. He grabbed at the last thing he remembered before he spoke to Guliford and let it loose. Lightning. Not a whole bolt. That would have killed them both. But enough to make an impact. And it did its job. The outward force knocked one of the train station gates off its hinges, causing it to clatter to the ground. He stood looking at his fallen father with his ears ringing from the impact. When he spoke, his voice was muffled in his own ears, but he needed his father to hear this.

"I can wield it. It is mine to command! I have a long way to go, but I can do it. I will not let you or anyone else tell me what I can or cannot be from now on!"

It felt good to say, but right after he spoke the words, he knew he had overstepped. He really wasn't in command of it yet. Huxley knew he had to start saying it to believe it. If only for himself.

He turned to leave wanting to hide the tears welling in his eyes. That surprised him. How could a father not understand his own son so acutely? It was like he was incapable of hearing, really hearing his son.

Huxley had enough. He would show his father if he wouldn't listen. A voice called out to him, farther back than he thought. "...you'll need this."

His father wasn't quite up yet. Huxley saw that he had brought something for him. A rucksack. He held it out for Huxley to take. He considered leaving it, not wanting anything more from him. but something, perhaps survival instinct, told him to take it. He walked swiftly back and snatched it out of his hand. His father made a move to embrace him. but Huxley had already pulled back, not wanting his father to see his tears. Voice shaking, he said, "I will return, strong enough to defend this town."

His father now seeing his son perhaps in a different light said, "Just...return. Okay?"

So that's what he was afraid of. It occurred to Huxley that it might not be a disbelief in his abilities, but rather a fear that his abilities were real ... and with it, all the danger that would put him in. Huxley couldn't be certain if that was a true motivation or just something his mind made up to make himself feel better. It rang true though. These were the words of his mother being channeled in a desperate attempt to keep her son safe.

"Goodbye, dad."

Huxley climbed over the fallen gate not waiting for the attendant to get back and made his way into the station and out of Mayburn.

11

Luggage and Lies

"Analyzing two-dimensional projectile motion is done in two segments one along the horizontal axis and the other along the vertical..." -**Page 314** **Excerpt from the Grimoire**

The gates were nothing compared to the grandeur of the Grand Railway. The locomotive had engineers crawling all over it like ants on sugar. Several voices shouted orders and commands, but he couldn't tell who, if anyone, was in charge. The train waited impatiently, huffing as it was being boarded. Huge crates were being loaded by men and machines alike. Pulleys attached around the cargo pushed and pulled the hulking pieces into place. Around them a flurry of lavishly dressed passengers bustled to their cars, followed by children and attendants laboring with entire wardrobes worth of clothing.

No one paid any attention to him, which was just fine with Huxley. He knew entering without a ticket was foolish, but technically, he had been invited. It felt more like a clerical error than a lie. Plus, after what just happened with his dad, there was no turning back now.

What was it about arguing with family that always ended so much worse than with everyone else? Huxley pushed down the lump rising in his throat and focused on the task in front of him. He was inexperienced with trains, but anyone could tell it was preparing to leave and he needed to be on it. He hefted his packs, one on each shoulder, and scanned the cars looking for one that looked like a circus car.

It should be distinctive with loads of color and pictures of animals. This notion was only supported by pictures he'd seen in books.

Someone knocked into his shoulder causing him to fall to the floor spilling his bags. The grimoire slid just out of reach. Huxley scrambled to recover it. The offending person began making apologies, but Huxley wasn't listening. A few people stopped to watch. He could feel their eyes on him as he scooped up the Grimoire. He relaxed when he tucked it safely back into his sack. Huxley picked himself up off the ground to find a young woman with a playful smile. Her face was covered in dirt. The whites of her eyes shone brightly amongst all of the earth. A hand emerged from her green cloak offering assistance.

"Did I break your ears too? I said, "I'm sorry!"

Huxley blinked.

"Of course, I can hear you. I just wanted to clean my things up."

"Clearly," she said, rolling her eyes. "That book is really important to you, huh?"

"What? No, I just didn't want to make a mess. Why would you even ask?" Huxley posed the question trying to sound nonchalant.

"Just the way you dove after it, and ignored these." She motioned to a small bag of clips strewn about the ground.

"Oh, right of course!" He hastily grabbed the money. The girl just watched.

"You're pretty clumsy, you know."

"I'm what?" Huxley said exasperated. "You ran into me!"

"Well, of course, I did. But you went down so easily. Like a baby. Or no...like a pile of books. That seems to be more your thing. A tall, wavy pile of books. And you fall like them." Her eyes ran over the mess at her feet. "You better clean that up. It's like two hundred and ninety-seven clips, only outer rings. Weird, are you from here or something?" She was hard to keep up with, her thoughts jumped around and didn't seem to take counsel with each other. He eyed her again. She couldn't have been much older than Oakley, maybe by only a year or two. She spoke differently than anyone else her age that he had ever met. *What's a kid doing out here and this dirty?*

Huxley's eyebrows rose as he finished collecting his belongings and stuffed the money back into his bag. There was a note with it. He unfurled it.

"Son, I just wanted to tell you-"

It was a note from his father. He shoved it into the sack, he'd have to read it later.

"Well, you should sit with us. You're awkward, and you clearly aren't supposed to be here. And neither am I. So, we should sit together. We're in the back."

With that, she left abruptly. She moved so suddenly, darting between people, like she knew where everyone was going to be next.

Huxley stood for a moment trying to process it all. *Did she knock me down and then insult me for it...twice?*

The train blared an ear deafening howl that almost made Huxley fall again. It would have been the loudest thing he had ever heard if not for the explosion that had preceded the battle. His ears may have only just recovered from that. The crowds thinned as they filed into the cars. At each door sat a uniformed man punching their tickets. Huxley tried to figure out what to do. *Maybe I can say I lost it, or that I left it on the train, and I just need to grab it. No, that might work in a small-town railroad but this was the Grand Railway. There would be protocol.*

A pebble smacked him in the side of the head.

"Damn! I thought you would fall down again!"

It was the wild girl beckoning him to the end of the station. She was smiling and both her eyes and teeth showed comically in contrast to the rest of her filthy face. She was leaning out the back of the caboose, her green cloak billowing out in a rush of steam. Huxley's brow furrowed and he rubbed his head.

"Well? I said come sit with us. Besides, you don't have a ticket!" She shouted.

Now that was the loudest thing Huxley had ever heard. In a panic, he ran to her, if only to shut her up. A few people snickered at his obvious discomfort. The ticket punchers were too focused on their work to look up. He had assumed outing someone as a non-ticket owner would sound an alarm, but no alarm occurred. She kept shouting over the din of the station.

"I told you Bookpile, you can sit with us! And you don't need a ticket. Just don't get any ideas."

"My name isn't Bookpile," he stated through clenched teeth.

"Hah! Fine then what is it? Mine is Elatress." She said extending a hand for the second time to Huxley.

"I'm Huxley." He replied, this time taking it.

"Aww, I liked Bookpile more."

Elatress yanked Huxley into the caboose and slid the door shut.

Huxley had traded people for luggage. The caboose was empty of passengers except for himself and Elatress but bursting with bags and suitcases. Some parcels were stacked in orderly rows, others were tossed in at random. If there was a path somewhere underneath it all, Huxley couldn't discern it. Elatress slipped over and slid under everything as lithe as she had navigated the crowds. She disappeared almost instantly, but Huxley could still hear her moving. Her voice reached him through the mass of it all.

"Just push them out of the way. Hurry before the train starts moving. It gets really unorganized then."

"This is organized?" he responded, but he doubted she could hear him. He could barely hear himself. The luggage was absorbing so much sound. He knew he was in the back of the car, so the only option was to move forward.

"Come on, it's only a couple of feet Book Pi-, err Huxley"

Huxley didn't respond and shouldered his way through. After a few claustrophobic seconds, he emerged in the front of the car. There was a cleared section with a small sitting area. Elatress waited impatiently just outside of the jumbled mass. A strong tobacco smell replaced the aroma of leather. Sitting down on a seat nearby was a cloud of dark smoke with legs. From the gray cloud, a crimson spark shone out as a pipe being puffed.

"Wait!" a voice from the cloud commanded. "Don't move! You're in the perfect spot. Alright, try and catch it."

"No, he won't be able to!" Elatress protested.

"It's fine, it won't hurt." said the cloud.

There was a click of metal and from the other side of the train car, a contraption fired at Huxley. An object flew in a wide arc, it was a cage containing a little doll inside. At the height of the arc it shed its cage and flung the doll outward. It was flying right at Huxley's face. He recoiled defensively when a hand shot forward and grasped the projectile right before impact.

"Abernathy! He's a guest." Elatress stood holding the little doll.

"How did you snatch that so fast?" Huxley gasped.

"Well, that's a strange way to thank someone." She said in a mocking tone.

"Elatress is good at ballistics," A mustachioed face said as it emerged from the cloud.

"And he wasn't harmed." He waved his hand dismissively to Elatress. "Did you see? It deployed just as expected!"

"No...only expected by you!" Elatress pointed at Huxley. "Does he look like he expected that?"

Huxley clutched his bags, seriously doubting his decision to follow this girl.

"And it smells terrible here." She continued, "Look at your mess! It looks like your machine shop." She moved towards him and reached over his work-table and opened the window letting in the sounds of the train station. The cloud immediately dispersed, and Huxley could finally see the man holding the pipe. He was like Elatress, filthy, but not from dirt and earth. Rather, he was coated in soot and engine grease. It streaked his chin and cheeks leaving only clean rings around his eyes, likely from goggles. Though obscured by a thick mustache, Huxley could see his broad smile. The mustache was so wide and thick he wondered when it couldn't be counted as a mustache anymore and just part of a beard. But the ends were tapered to points making it clear this was his design. His eyes twinkled despite a lack of good lighting. They had a soft amber glow. The cleaner areas of his face revealed lines and wear befitting a man in his fifties, maybe older but it was hard to tell. Abernathy remained seated and motioned for them to join him.

"Come, have a seat. Who is our guest?" His hands flipped his pipe upside down emptying out the tobacco. Elatress watched and waited for him to put the pipe away.

"Come on, come on, I won't shoot at you again, boy." He promised as he waved Huxley over.

Huxley sat reluctantly as Elatress plopped down next to him. The chair was plusher than he anticipated. It reminded him of his favorite chair at the library. He sank a few inches, happy to be off his feet.

"Thank you. I don't exactly have a ticket, but I'm supposed to be here! I don't want you to get in trouble, Mister Abernathy. Huxley wondered if he got the name right. "Is that right?"

"Trouble." Abernathy echoed, as if fondly remembering something. A smirk crept onto his face. "No trouble here. I'm the Chief Engineer of this railway and I can let anyone I like ride with me. And yes, I am Abernathy. But I am far more interested in you. Did Elatress invite you onboard? Because if so, you are special indeed."

Huxley took a second and tried to reconcile the information he was given.

"The Chief Engineer rides in the caboose? I would have thought they rode upfront." He was puzzled and yet excited to speak to a real engineer. He had so many questions about the train. But this man wasn't fitting his expectations of a professional from Danador.

"Well, yes, but a man can only listen to others' questions about mundane topics for so long before he craves solitude. Well, as much as you can get on a train anyway." He said while glancing at Elatress.

"He's not special." Elatress stated flatly. "I just felt bad because I knocked him down."

Abernathy snorted in surprise.

"She knocked you down? You *really* must be special."

Huxley began a response, but was cut off.

"Ugh, Abernathy!" She blurted. "There was a lot of noise, and something threw my direction."

"Yeah. Him!" Abernathy said, pointing at Huxley.

"I'm sorry, but I'm confused. What happened?" Huxley asked.

"She never knocks something down unless she means to do so. Elatress is one of the nimblest people I know." Abernathy said with an encroaching smile.

"Well, I'm done with this chat. I'll be with Arktos!" Elatress declared and stomped out of the caboose.

Huxley watched the door slide shut and an awkward silence descended the room.

"I think she's upset." Huxley ventured.

"Oh, most certainly. The point remains, however. She wanted you to ride with us." Abernathy stated.

"Like I said, I'm here to meet up with someone. I really should go look for him." Huxley started to rise but suddenly, the train lurched forward. Abernathy reflexively ducked his head and threw his hands up in a defensive posture.

"Heads up. lad." He yelled. Three suitcases came loose from their perches and came crashing down. Most of them missed Huxley, but one smacked his arm on the way down. Abernathy chuckled.

"These quarters are tight and not particularly safe, but that's the price I pay."

Huxley just looked around and rubbed his arm.

"Give it a minute before you leave to find your friend. The train needs to settle."

Huxley had never heard of a train "settling," but he had also never rode on a train. Wanting to avoid more injuries, he decided to take the advice.

"First time riding with us?" Abernathy asked.

"First time riding anywhere really," Huxley responded while looking out the window fascinated with what he could see. He had rode in carriages being pulled by a small team of horses when traveling to the militia training grounds but that was nothing like this.

The train picked up speed and Huxley could feel the back-and-forth lurch become less frequent. It eventually smoothed out. The experience was more exciting than Huxley had expected. He had never moved at such speeds before.

Within moments, Mayburn had left his view. Worries faded away and a sense of discovery welled up inside of him. What new experiences lay ahead? Abernathy may have sensed that Huxley was taking it all in and obviously enjoying seeing the countryside for the first time. Abernathy kept quiet and let him watch.

In the distance, the sun had just peeked over the mountains and bathed the fields and forests with a tide of light. He knew from his lessons and experience just how dangerous outside the city walls could be. But at this moment, it looked as though nothing could have been more peaceful. Almost as though sensing his thoughts, his eyes focused on the harsh line of the Fecundity. He had never seen it so close. It stood imposingly on the border of civilization. Tangled and gnarled, a complete opposite to the order Danador was trying to create. The Fecundity waited right at the outskirts, teeming with life and energy. It crept outward, always eager to expand. To Huxley, it looked like a caged animal eagerly awaiting its next meal. Thankfully the train was moving further and further away from it. Somehow, the tracks had been laid through the Fecundity. He had read about the effort it took and what happened to those that pioneered that first trip.

Huxley shivered thinking about it and looked away from the window. Abernathy was fiddling with a contraption of some kind. It was a piece of whatever it was he shot at him earlier. Huxley could get a good look at him now that the smoke had fully cleared. His hands were calloused and dirty like his face. He worked rapidly holding pieces together with one hand while the other screwed pieces into place. It reminded Huxley of his father making shoes. He made delicate and precise movements that Huxley didn't expect from his bulky arms. Abernathy had a paunchy stomach but the rest of him was well-muscled. His head was beginning to bald, but his face made up for any losses on top. Both his hair and his mustache had a peculiar hue, there were strings of golden blonde accented through the bronze that made up the bulk. They wove like a river through a valley. Huxley hadn't seen anyone quite like him before. Both he and Elatress must be from Valdannon, he decided.

Abernathy was comfortable with the silence and Huxley didn't object. The pace of Abernathy's work created a calming resonance in the room when it mixed with the train wheels bumping over the track. A constant mechanical hum was everywhere. Not loud like an engine, but more like a stream falling over rocks.

After the morning he had, he was grateful for it. Huxley settled into his cozy seat and gazed out the window. The Fecundity mercifully faded from his vision but now something else approached. It was Mayburn's sister town, Galdor. It was the next leg of the trip. He didn't see the walls yet, but the signs were there. It would only be an hour or so. And that meant that Danador was only a half day away. The stress of approaching the college hadn't been present in his mind. He didn't fool himself into thinking it would be easy but he hadn't been worried about it because getting on the train was enough of a challenge. But now he realized the train may have been the easy part. He had better prepare. Huxley knew he couldn't practice Magnincy on the train. There was too high a risk of something going wrong. But he could always study and decipher more. Perhaps he could make some progress if he could just find a place to read.

Huxley looked up at his riding companion and wondered if this was a good place to study. It was quiet enough to concentrate but perhaps he didn't want his new friend to start asking questions about the book. No, it's probably best to keep it a secret for now. Huxley cleared his throat politely to get attention. It didn't work. He tried again and this time Abernathy looked up.

"I, uhh, have to go look for my friend now. Thank you for letting me onboard."

Abernathy nodded, looking eager to return to his work.

Huxley stood up and made for the door. When he slid it open, he froze. Wind rushed into the car and a rage of sound burst into his ears. He slammed it shut again. Silence reclaimed the room with only the chuckle of Abernathy filling it.

"Did it blow you back in? Don't worry my friend! It's all bluster. No one ever falls off, at least not since we put in the guard rails. Hang on tight and jump over confidently!" he joked. "Oh, also take this. If one of those wardens find you without a ticket they might throw you out at the next stop, or worse, make you listen to a lecture about rules and regulations. And let me tell you, they really like those."

Abernathy handed Huxley a card that read:

Abernathy DelaCourt

Owner/Proprietor of

The Gearbox ™ Inn/Tavern -Industrial District, Saintamo Street

Grand Craftsman and Lord Engineer of the Arcane Railways

and Savior of the Crag villages of Valdannon

Huxley read it over twice. Even Ember Palithur didn't have that kind of title. Perhaps Abernathy was far more important a person than he thought. Huxley thanked him again and left.

The advice he was given was sound. Getting to the other side wasn't difficult. The next car was luxurious, clean, and quiet. He looked around for a moment, seeing a few of the cars occupied by people he had seen clamoring to get on board. Now they were calmly sitting and sipping tea. His hopes of finding an empty car were dashed. Only one car had a single occupant. He was an older man quietly reading a newspaper. He was well dressed in a modern suit, which Huxley assumed was quite stylish. Huxley couldn't be sure because he had no idea what styles were popular in Danador. Huxley slid the door open. The man's eyes looked up at him. Huxley gave an awkward hand movement asking if it was ok if he sat. The man mumbled something and looked back down at his paper. Huxley took that as a yes. He sat near the window and once again marveled at the countryside flying by. Hoping not to get distracted, he tore his attention away and reached into his bag. The familiar feeling of the grimoire met his grip. He glanced as casually as he could at his silent roommate. He didn't seem to even care that Huxley was there. *Well, I suppose this is the most privacy I'm going to get,* Huxley thought. He pulled the ancient book out of his bag and placed it on his lap.

He propped it up on his knees so its contents would remain hidden. He undid the buckles and flipped it open. There was the familiar crack of the spine as the pages flipped open. Huxley was pleased that he was gaining a real familiarity with the book because he turned to the exact page he wanted.

"Electrons," he read silently to himself. Electrons were on the page that had information about lightning. The notes included other words that ended with "-ton and -tron" They affected lighting and gravity. He remembered this page when he was on stage with Guliford. He had produced a close approximation of lighting. Their connections were numerous. He wrote his notes outside of the pages.

There were at least three distinct styles of handwriting in the Grimoire. Huxley had surmised it was the original author, his student, and the latest was a mystery. The original author seemed obvious because each page started with his handwriting and introduced each category along with a brief summary and some data. It was enough of a working understanding to begin explaining. The second writer looked to have an apprentice-type understanding of the texts adding further research and obvious experience with the related fields. The third was strange. He could tell it was the same handwriting but its clarity shifted page to page. Sometimes it oozed finesse with pen flourishes and even drawings of effects. On other pages, it was written in haste, sloppy and confused. At first read, it unnerved Huxley. Now that he was familiar with it, he was beginning to understand. especially after the conversation with Guliford.

"Upon my death or madness..." Huxley repeated quietly as to not disturb his neighbor. Madness. This was the handwriting of a man who was losing his mind. A shiver of fear rippled through Huxley, and he nearly closed the book. But then he reminded himself that he was just reading and not practicing. He would wait for real practice when he was with the Embers and could be taught properly. This man was obviously a hermit of some kind and went mad being alone. That wouldn't happen to him...right?

He continued his work undisturbed for some time. His progress was steady and growing the longer he was left alone. The pages made more and more sense to him. Huxley could feel his confidence growing. The pictures were the easiest to remember. Huxley focused primarily on studying the original author's words. They were the most general and even lacked a thorough understanding of the topic, but it gave a solid starting point. He became fascinated with "bonds." He read that there were things so small, not even a magnifying glass could see them. These bonds made up all things living. They formed over time and were all different from one another. Another section was about energy. How it was made and how it passed through objects. There were laws at work that defined it. He read them over several times. Like the first time he read it, the words made sense to him, but all together, it was difficult to understand. He redoubled his efforts and wrote copious notes asking many questions he would like answered later.

"If energy passes and makes work or heat, can it make anything else?"

"Why can't energy be trapped and forever produce results?"

"How much energy could one thing produce?"

While he wrote, he felt a sense of belonging that he had never felt before. He was finally in his right place. The questions came so naturally to him. It frustrated him that he didn't have the answers, but the questions kept coming along with the realization that they might never be answered. On and on it went until he began to run low on paper. He needed to have at least a little paper for when he spoke with the Embers. So, he folded up a few empty sheets and put them away. At the bottom of his last sheet was room for three more questions.

So, he wrote:

How did the first author figure out this information?

What tools will I need to further the research? And perhaps the most important,

How can I avoid madness like the last author?

When he finished writing the last sentence the chill returned. If madness really was a legitimate outcome here, he had better make every effort to avoid it. Screaming and running through the streets while pausing to make insane notes in a book, filled him with dread. The idea made him so uncomfortable, he thought he would rather do battle again. At least in the heat of a fight, you could trust what you were seeing. Unlike madness which can have you seeing things that aren't actually there.

He shook away the thoughts and realized his fatigue. The sun's rays caught his eye and he squinted. *How long have I been reading?* He decided to ask the stylish gentleman what the hour was, but he was gone. Huxley must have been so engrossed in what he was doing, he didn't even notice the man leave. Fatigue had found him again and he felt his energy slipping away like sands in an hourglass. He cleaned up his notes and rebuckled the grimoire. After it was safely stowed in his bag, he closed his eyes. Sleep found him seconds later.

Huxley found himself standing on the beach again. He looked up and saw an innumerable number of stars. The sea reflected them like a mirror. Huxley approached the water and felt the waves flow around his toes. When it moved out, he felt himself sink a few inches into the sand. The warm water felt like he was slipping into a bath. It called out to him. He stepped forward and felt the water rise up around his ankles. The salt smelled crisp and there was a light breeze. He stopped and looked up into the sky and saw the stars again. They moved and swirled, more than ever before. Each one responded to his sight. The ocean warmed further, and he felt a tug as the waves rushed out again. He was startled to find he had walked out and was waist deep. "Keep walking". The words echoed in his head spoken by an unseen voice. He breathed deep and wanted to leap in. It would have been so comforting to feel completely immersed in the waves and brought out to sea. His legs tensed. He prepared to leap but was shaken awake.

"End of the line! Get off the train!" His traveling companion was nowhere to be found. This time a Warden stood in front of him. "We've reached Danador!" The Warden looked Huxley up and down and said "Head to the immigrant's bureau. Do not try to enter the city without proper paperwork."

"I'm not an immigrant." Huxley said in a daze.

But the Warden had gone, repeating his message to the rest of the train.

He brushed the sleep out of his eyes and looked outside. The lush countryside was now a train platform jam-packed full of people. Huxley took a step back feeling the gravity of what was to come. What was it he said about proper paperwork? His mind finally caught up and put some unsettling pieces together. His pocket still had Abernathy's card, but he doubted that counted as an invitation into the city. He increased his pace knowing it was possible to lose his chance to get in the city. He ran back through the doors to the caboose. Abernathy, Elatress and the luggage were gone. Huxley could hardly believe it was the same car he had been in just a few hours ago. It was swept clean and free of clutter. The small sitting area Abernathy had occupied was still there which confirmed he wasn't crazy. Not yet anyway.

Guliford! A spike of annoyance coursed through him for not remembering the magician sooner. Why hadn't he sought him out in the first place? Had the train intimidated him so much? He saw people filling out now. Guliford was probably one of them. He dashed back through the cars hoping to catch him. He searched one car after the next. Each one was basically the same. About eight rooms with space to hold four in each. If it was full, it would take time to search everyone's faces. But most of the passengers had already made their way off the train. He didn't know how many cars there were in total. Huxley hoped he had made his way through at least half. He didn't want to look foolish explaining to a Warden that he had been invited by Guiliford. His hopes were extinguished when he met the end of the passenger cars.

Huxley sat down, shoulders sagging and a lump rising in his throat. He fought back the feeling of failure. He took a deep breath. He would make his case to the Wardens, and he would find Guliford. The door slid open, and an older man walked in wearing a suit and holding a neatly folded newspaper tucked under his arm. It was the same man that had rode with Huxley silently for so many hours. He strode across the room and sat down in front of Huxley.

"You lied to me."

Huxley blinked in surprise.

"You said it was a page from a Grimoire. That looks like a complete life's work. You have the keys to the kingdom, and I doubt you even realize it. Well, at least, you lie well. A half-truth is harder to discern than a complete fabrication." The man sighed deeply and took a second to compose himself. "You studied for five hours and thirty two-minutes Huxley. Not bad by most scholars' benchmarks. But you will have to study eight hours a day as well as practice and research to stand a chance. If this was difficult for you, then there is no way you will last a week in college, even with someone's Grimoire to guide you."

Huxley gaped.

"G-Guliford?" He asked.

"The Amazing." He corrected. Everything about Guliford's face was different, even his eyes. This wasn't just stage makeup removed. This man's face was entirely different. The way he carried himself was alien; this man was quiet and reserved, barely a shadow of the over-the-top personality who he met in Mayburn.

Then his voice changed, it aged and dripped with contempt, "You aren't the fool I took you for afterall."

That voice...it was Ember Palithur's. Huxley studied the man in front of him. Was it Guliford pretending to be Palithur or the other way around? He sat back. He hadn't realized he'd been given pieces of a puzzle to solve but when they all slid into place, it horrified him. Could all three be the same man?

"Why didn't you say anything?" Questioned Huxley.

"I knew you'd be too stupid to see through my ruse. Why weren't you more careful," Palithur countered. "You read a grimoire right in front of me! Did you not consider that I might take it from you? How easy would that have been?

Huxley was on edge now. Could Palithur really stoop that low?

"I could have, but I didn't." Palithur added. "Don't be foolish enough to think you'll get the same treatment from any Embers inside the college. Ten years ago, that grimoire could have been my ticket back to prominence as an ember.

Huxley started. "So why didn't you take it?

"Being the Amazing Guliford is my sole indulgence left in life. No one is impressed by what Palithur has done, only with who he once was, and I can't be that man anymore. I'm Guliford now, a street magician that impresses the ignorant."

"Anymore?" Huxley inquired.

"Haven't you been listening! Magnincy takes a toll. If I fought...it would be my last fight. Had I helped at the wall, I'd be a raving madman now." Ember Palithur cringed at the thought. Magnincy sits at the edge of thought always begging to be utilized. When you get to my age, you best show restraint. You can fight it off eventually, but the time inbetween can be substantial...which is suicide in a battle."

"My friends could still be alive!" Huxley protested.

"I would have fallen into madness mid battle, and then the enemy would have taken us seriously instead," Palithur stated resolutely. "If you don't understand that, then I take it back. You are still a fool." His composure loosened.

"Why weren't more defenders called? More Embers?" Huxley demanded.

"If I had requested help, they would have removed me from my office and retired me. I..." His voice faltered. "I thought the guard was enough."

"Well, it wasn't!" Huxley had never felt so angry. Hearing the reason for his friends' death, their lack of a real protector. Pride had kept Palithur from asking for help?! He seethed at the idea of Palithur cowering in his office.

"I'm sorry." Palithur whispered. "I can't fix what happened, but I can offer you something...I can get you into the college."

Huxley perked up. Palithur owed him more than that, but it was a start.

"But know this before you accept. I was curious to see how long you would study. Study is everything to an Ember. I've seen that you have an aptitude, but that only gets you an interview. If you have weak study habits then not only will you fail, but Madness awaits you as it awaits most practitioners of Magnincy. Are you prepared for these demands?"

Huxley thought it over. The two shared a moment of quiet as the last statement was no idle threat. Huxley knew somehow that Palinthur was telling the truth. The image of the broken town wall and the blood spray flashed into his mind again. Huxley could not return untrained.

"...Yes." He said so quietly, he barely heard himself.

"Good," Palithur responded, "You will need this. I will await your return to Mayburn. And whoever left you that book...you should thank them."

He handed Huxley a rolled-up letter with a crimson wax seal emblazoned with a large "P". He stood up again and made to leave the train.

But I thought you always said I was too foolish and stupid to get in?" He blurted out.

"Oh, Huxley..." Palithur said looking down at him, his face softened, a slight ripple went through him revealing features that looked more like the magician he saw on stage.

"You are a sweet and trusting young man. That's the first thing you should deal with before you enter their world. Lies abound, learn how to identify them."

"Lies?" Huxley repeated back.

"You ask too many questions. I was once like you. Too curious for my own good. My curiosity got me shipped to Mayburn, the furthest town from the college. I've been trying to save you the disgrace that became of me. Be careful, Huxley. Always be on your guard."

Huxley couldn't believe what he was hearing. "Wait, you think you're protecting me?"

But Ember Palithur had disappeared around the corner.

Huxley blinked and tried to rationalize what the Ember had told him. Be careful?

He sat for a second thinking through what had just happened. Huxley looked back down at the letter he was given. The wax seal still radiated warmth. The "P" looked at him and he stared right back. He tried to bend a corner up to look inside. It pulled at the seal and he stopped immediately. Huxley stood to leave the train. He held the letter in his hands, fearful that the seal might break inside his bag. With the familiar weight of the Grimoire on his shoulder, and his letter of "acceptance" into the college, Huxley disembarked.

The train stations' imposing stature was nothing compared to Danador. Huxley had seen pictures and heard it described by travelers and teachers, but none of it captured the real thing. It struck him as soon as he stepped off the train. Waves of walls flowing inward, the largest standing at least a hundred feet straight up. It bore no marks and flew no banners, no flags, no adornments of any kind. It was just imperial gray blocks, fixed to one another, encapsulating Danador. He couldn't see over it. The only thing he could make out was identical walls but smaller and slightly higher up inside the city. Beyond those, was a grand tower in the middle of it all. Atop of it was a beacon of fire that shone even in daylight. Danador was laid out in a five-pointed star shape. Each point has access for trains. Only one ran regularly, and he just got off of it.

The mass chaos that preceded the trip was different and opposite of what it was now. The former passengers now moved in unison through a pathway to the entrance of the Danador offices. Huxley looked around to ask someone for information but found none. It seemed the only option was to join the lengthy line. He sighed with resignation, clenched his invitation in his hand and waited.

12

∾

Breath and Gates

"When fuel and oxygen react, heat and light energy are released creating heating energy. The mixture of both affects the size of combustion."
-Page 192 Excerpt from the Grimoire

From the depths of the Wilds a figure emerged. He took three long strides out of the forest and stationed himself. Blood stained and weary, Grubmush stared at Danador. He breathed in deeply, allowing his lungs to fill entirely and held it. He stretched his arms to the sky and pushed himself onto his toes. Finally, after a minute he released his breath. Another moment passed. Grubmush watched a train arrive in the distance. It had surely carried hundreds of fearful studiers and cowards. A flash of pity made its way through him, it melted and reformed into resolve. Fresh warm blood oozed onto his shirt. His stretch must have reopened the wound. It didn't pain him anymore, not since he learned what it meant. Grubmush looked down and saw that it made a nearly perfect circle with small lines leaking off to the side. It reminded him of the ring left on the bar when a mug was lifted that had overflowed with ale.

A hand gripped his shoulder, then another grabbed his ribcage, another his forearm. Twelve members of his cabal surrounded him. Grubmush looked at each of them as they took their places. Each was an excellent warrior, and each as worthy as he. But he had one thing they didn't: the gift of Faldurin. Many of his cabal had been the most bitter of enemies before he united them. Grubmush could feel even now how badly they still wished to destroy each other. It was him alone that held them together. It was Grubmush that gave them purpose. And now it was time to let them know what that purpose was.

The cabal shifted making equal space around Grubmush. A rhythm began. Their breathing aligned. Starting shallow, then building their harmonies, their voices grew deeper, and their breath drew as one. Their skin began to shift in hue. Veins bulged and appeared through their bodies. Vital sinews and muscles became outlined. Slowly and in great depth the breathing grew until one's voice cried out in rage. The first to touch Grubmush was the first to act. He produced a jagged dagger and plunged into the place his hand had once been. Grubmush didn't move, accepting the wound, keeping his breathing in sync. Then the next did the same. Each replacing his hand after the attack. Blood spurted onto their faces and hands. Still Grubmush remained. After all twelve took their turns, their breathing returned to normal, and they removed their hands.

Grumbush spat out blood and declared, "Unwounded and un-broken."

In unison they repeated, "Unwounded and unbroken."

The knife wounds closed around his body. One by one they left his side and walked back into the Wilds stopping at the tree line.

"Faldurin blesses all of us with strength and deeds. But she has given me focus. A focus that cannot be ignored."

The others nodded their heads or grunted in approval.

"I will enter this city without violence. I will teach them to focus as we have. They will see the truth of things through words and not deeds. It is not their way, but I will show them."

"And if not?" A voice from the trees asked.

"If they will not see with words, then they will see with deeds." Grubmush promised.

"We will prepare."

"I am confident you won't have to."

"We will prepare."

"Have faith in Faldurin's gifts. Her shadow reaches far and is unfailing. I am her chosen survivor."

This time silence from the trees.

"Give me three months to make them see."

His proposal was audacious enough, but the timeline was unheard of. The Cabal's faith was strong; however it was still new and untested.

"We will prepare..."

Grubmush huffed and turned his back on them. Looking over his clothes, what was once only blood stained had now become blood soaked and torn.

This won't do. Not for a proper ambassador. These people fear blood like the beasts. And torn clothing makes one seem unhinged. I am not unhinged, I am a priest of Faldurin, and truth will be preached. He thought.

Grubmush spotted a stream not too far away, he could stop and wash off the blood and sew up the holes before he entered Danador. He had to look his best if he was to gain converts and he had less than a season to get it done.

———————————————————————————————-

Huxley's face was beginning to sunburn. Even though the weather was turning cold, there were no clouds in the sky to give him respite. He squinted and tried to see how far away he was. The line moved forward consistently but slowly. His enthusiasm still beat strong in his chest but realizing that it may be dark before he gets in, worried him. Hours marched by and so did the line.

He had finally neared the offices. He had spent the majority of the time looking with fascination at the city. From what he could guess it looked to be made in ascending levels. He could see no houses, but those were likely too small to be seen over the wall. With each step the wall climbed higher and higher blocking his view, it even blocked out the sun before it set. There was a river that came out of the Fecundity that led to a part of the city he couldn't see. No boats floated in or out. The Fecundity wasn't overly close to Danador but certainly closer than he expected. The last hour he could only see a sheer unscalable stark gray wall. The difference in Danador's defenses and Mayburn's was astounding. Huxley didn't think a hundred fires and explosives could even dent this fortification. In Mayburn, it only took one.

A Warden demanded his attention.

"Well, boy? Which are you? Citizen, Immigrant, asylum seeker, traveler?"

He had been so lost in thought he hadn't noticed he had reached the front of the line. An auspicious table was before him, manned by a Warden whose uniform was exactly the same as the ones in Mayburn, even down to the same button placement. Huxley was impressed with the congruency. Only one thing stood out, the city insignia on their right shoulder. This was emblazoned with the city seal of Danador. A flaming pyre atop a vast spire. No doubt it was the Arcane Flame of Danador that he could see glowing from deep inside the city.

Surprised, Huxley scrambled to find his letter. The Warden continued while he looked.

"By the looks of it, immigrant. You will have to join the processing station to my right. Go there now and make room for citizens."

The man behind him stepped forward slightly pushing Huxley out of the way. The Warden began again asking about status. The man was ready and replied "Citizen" before the Warden could finish. He produced his papers, and he moved right along. The Warden stamped and wrote something on his papers, then handed them off to a lesser Warden.

Suddenly, Huxley remembered, I'm such a fool, he thought.

"I'm a student!" He called out.

The Warden had already begun processing the next one and stopped.

"Excuse me?" He responded, "A student?"

"Yes, I am a student at the college." Huxley tried to sound confident.

"The College of the Arcane Flame?" He questioned.

"Yes."

The Warden looked Huxley up and down then raised his chin, "Boy, the College doesn't have students, and even if they did, this is not how that works. You are obviously a liar. Just go join the other line."

Huxley pushed past the people who had moved in to replace him and smacked his letter from Guliford onto the Warden's desk.

"I am a student! I've been invited to come study here, Mister..." He scanned his uniform for some kind of personal identification but found none.

The Warden glared at him with growing irritation, then glanced at the paper. The wax seal looked right back at him. He snatched it and moved to open it but stopped right before the seal broke. He studied Huxley and his eyes narrowed.

"Where are you from?"

"Mayburn."

"And you say you are a student, and this is your invitation."

Huxley nodded his head.

"Just a moment, wait over here." He motioned to a spot behind the table.

Huxley moved obediently. Time crawled as Huxley's mind raced with concerns. What if the Wardens think I forged the letter? What if they break the seal and I can't use it again at the college? Where will I go if they don't let me in the city? I can't get back on the train! No, he wouldn't let his thoughts focus on the negative. He was in the only place he could have been with the only line available.

A moment later the Warden came back with two more of his kind. Both wore the same uniform but seemed to be of higher rank somehow. Huxley had no idea how they kept it all straight. Their uniforms signified nothing to show who was above who.

"Hello young man, my name is Warden Adams, this is my associate Gendry." He motioned to the man standing next to him. He didn't move. "And you say you are with the College?

"Yes, I spoke with Ember Palithur in Mayburn and he thought I would be a great fit there."

"... The Ember Palithur you say?"

"The P on my letter stands for Palithur I think."

"Just a moment, we will of course need to read this." He responded.

The two Wardens left Huxley alone again. He was unfamiliar with such bureaucracy. All cities must have some in order to function, but when he looked around and took it all in it amazed him. There must have been dozens of Wardens all stamping, writing, and filing papers. They reminded him of a clock, each having a place and moving with precision and purpose. He was the only thing slowing down his section. One Warden returned this time.

"We grant you provisional access to the city for twenty-four hours."

"One day?" Huxley stammered.

"Correct, we cannot be sure if this is a forgery or not."

Huxley straightened in anger, but the Warden continued.

"You will proceed directly to the college and deliver your letter. If you are telling the truth, the Embers will handle your arrangements. If you are lying, then I really don't know what will happen. To my knowledge no one has ever tried forgery for fear of reprisal. Either way, the matter will be dealt with efficiently. Welcome to Danador."

The Warden ended his warning with a firm handshake. Huxley gulped. This was not the welcome he had expected. His letter was handed back to him unopened. Then, he was given another document stamped in triplicate. Huxley didn't understand all of the information on it except the part in red. It said "PROVISIONAL". He didn't feel good about entering the city under these circumstances but at least he was permitted inside.

The gates to the city did not reflect the grandeur of the wall. There were two gates for those on foot, and a larger entrance in the middle for carriages and horses. A few Wardens were posted near the entrances; they eyed everyone who entered, but no one was questioned. He bet that most people who might sneak in didn't do it through the front gates.

Danador laid out before him utterly resplendent. Huxley's jaw dropped when he finally looked around. Hundreds, perhaps thousands of people walked the streets in front of him. It made the Kinship Revival Festival in Mayburn seem trivial like an intimate gathering of friends. A long straight road cut through the middle of the city leading directly inward. The main road was littered with every color of the rainbow. Bright signs of yellow and green practically screamed at him. A booth draped with azure curtains enthroned a citrus merchant. A red and cyan lined booth had stacks of hats. Everyone; merchants, shoppers, and gawkers, were all adorned in gold-tinged robes and jewelry. It couldn't be real. Certainly, this was a special market day with dignitaries from afar that caused everyone to wear such fine clothing. The wealth that dominated the main market street hid the truth though. On either side were stacks of houses piled on top of each other. It was random and chaotic. The houses were all made from different materials. The bottom-most had to be made of stone or they could never have supported the weight. The higher the houses climbed, the more subjective they became. Some connected via precarious bridges made of thin metal and ropes. Tenuous ladders littered the structures made of similarly found materials. How many people are living this way? He breathed in deeply and began to choke just looking at it. No one else seemed to share his discomfort. The loosely put together houses were of no concern to their residents. They navigated it easily, knowing what would support their full weight and what wouldn't. There was a rhythm to the movement, no one seemed to be in the other's way while moving shoulder to shoulder. It was impressive. When Mayburn gets busy it shuts down whole sections of the city. But Danador was not Mayburn. He had to keep reminding himself of that fact. *Don't gawk.* He chided himself.

Huxley's attention left the strange houses for the spectacle in front of him. He was right about the city being laid out in levels; there were three more significant segments of the city inside of the sprawling outer circle of Dandador that he was in. Huxley had read about these kinds of layouts before. When a city is planned it can have defined sections like these. It makes for easier control of a population. All of the engineering here looked to be based around control. You would never have to guess what part of the city you were in. A simple glance up showed what level you were on. And the main road could not be confused with any other. It was the most heavily trafficked and maintained. Everywhere beyond it was left up to the inhabitants.

The sun had fully set now and the street lamps burned to life. The flickering light brought an interesting glow to the vendors Huxley passed.

Now each jewel caught firelight and sparkled. On any other day Huxley would have loved to spend time just browsing the goods in this market. There was so much he had never seen before. The opposite of the goods on display at the kinship festival. These looked authentic, and even well crafted. But it would have to wait. He wasn't sure how long it would take to get to the college from the city gates, but having a time limit of twenty four hours hastened his steps. It was even easier to see the college at night. The beacon of fire atop the tower was impossible to mistake. Its firelight reached all parts of the city, it seemed. He made for the main road when a young man approached him with purpose in his eyes.

"Huxley Durant from Mayburn? Hopeful applicant to the College of the Arcane Flame?" He asked in a way that wasn't really a question.

Huxley saw the young man was a Warden, the youngest he had ever seen. As though knowing he didn't look the part, the young Warden explained.

"I am Warden Jefferies Sapleen. Junior city officiant and escort to new residents. I am fully trained and able to perform my duties."

True to his word, he wore an identical uniform to the one Huxley had seen earlier. Huxley tried to guess his age. He was likely only eighteen. A few wisps of growth on his face showed he had been trying to grow facial hair without much success. The young man was sweating profusely for such a chilly night. His cheeks were flushed. Warden Jefferies shook Huxley's hand vigorously.

"Escort to new residents?" Huxley asked.

"Yes, or in your case, day visitors."

"I don't think I need an escort. I can see my destination from here." Huxley said.

Jefferies looked to the college then back to Huxley.

"Of course, you can. It's not about finding it. Every city guest is required to have an escort. Now come along."

Huxley didn't see how having an escort would be a bad thing. Jefferies it turned out was the excitable type. Every building they came across interrupted his previous explanation. He wanted to make sure Huxley knew the history of everything he looked at all while keeping a brisk pace. Despite his frantic energy, Huxley was happy to hear more about the city.

"The street vendors in Danador Commons are the most diverse you will find anywhere in the world. Hence all the smells." He sniffed dramatically then gasped as though it was the best thing he had ever inhaled.

"But the smells alone aren't the best part. Danador commons is a testament to the working man. When the land got too crowded, they built up rather than expand outside the protection of the walls. Who would ever leave Danador? It is the best city in the best province in the world. And it's the safest city too. Did you know it's the safest? Not only that, but it's the richest both in knowledge and in wealth. We allow all manner of people to come into the commons. While they aren't citizens, they are contributing members of Danador. Would you like to become a citizen some day? Of course, you would! Where else would you live? Valdannon? And do what? Paint all day and sing songs while not actually making anything useful? Hah! Don't get me wrong, they are fine people, but their art is nothing compared to the knowledge of the Embers. The Embers' contributions to science, engineering, and all forms of higher thinking are beyond compare. Their feats are the stuff of legends. And we get to live next to them and directly serve them. My instructor once assisted an Ember five times!" He said the last part with great emphasis. "He even called on him by name the last two times."

Jefferies stopped in order to let the impact of what he just said impress Huxley.

When the moment caught up to him, Huxley managed an "Oh wow! He learned his name?"

It wasn't his most sincere compliment, but he didn't know what else to say.

Undeterred, Jefferies went on. "Of course, I wasn't there, but I have heard about each of the five experiences and how he was allowed to serve."

"...allowed to serve?" Huxley repeated for clarification. He realized how little he knew about how to behave around the Embers.

"Well yes, Wardens serve the Embers in all capacities they deem fit."

"And what about day guests?" Huxley said.

The young warden stifled a laugh and searched for the right words. Then it came to him.

"The Embers have specific needs that are only trusted to the Wardens. You won't be asked to do anything like that. It wouldn't be appropriate, do not worry."

That only added to Huxley's questions, but Jefferies continued talking about the city. Jefferies' thoughts were scattered and difficult to follow. He continued prattling until they reached a gate. Huxley's legs ached. He realized they must have walked further than he thought. Danador was far larger than it appeared on the outside.

These second gates were less intimidating than the first ones.

"Get your second rung clips ready." Jefferies said.

"Second rung? I only have outer clips. I haven't seen a two-rung clip in months." Huxley said.

"In months? Why don't you convert them? Everyone needs a few of every size." Jefferies said.

"Not in Mayburn. We mainly just use outer clips. It's easier." Huxley countered.

"Easier? What could be better than the Embers' design. Core rung is one hundred, three rung is fifty, two rung is ten and outer clips are one. You clip together to make a whole coin. Each whole coin adds up to one hundred sixty-one. Count your whole coins in multiples of one hundred sixty-one!"

"I've never actually seen a whole coin before." Huxley said embarrassed.

"Never?" Jefferies gaped.

"Outer is usually just what we use."

Jefferies smiled hoping to dispel the awkward air that crept in and said "Well, prepare to see your first whole coin then. You'll need one to get to the college." And Jefferies produced one. He plunked it into Huxley's hand like it was nothing. The design was smart. A small inner coin of gold was clipped into place inside the next largest, a coin that shone of silver. And that clipped into a larger one that surrounded it with a composite of various flecks of gold and silver metals giving it an interesting dark look.

And last was the outer rings which were a combination of steel and iron. When all combined together, they showed the basic outline of Danador though it was rounded on the outside instead of pointed. Huxley studied it and marveled at the design. It was amazingly efficient and simple to count. He could keep large sums of money in just a few coins that fit together. He slipped it into his pocket and searched for Jefferies to thank him, but he had left to discuss entrance with the door Wardens. The gates appeared to double as a community hub. Advertisements and news littered the walls. Deals from the vendors covered most of the area along with housing vacancies. There was a portion that was clearly the official section. It sported three sheets. One was a large sign-up for work in the industrial section that was totally filled out with an additional sheet added to the bottom with more names scrawled on it. The next was a frightening "Wanted" poster with an image of a man in black robes and a strange mask holding bubbling flasks. The mask had a long beak that curved out like a toucan, but vacant of color. Its eyes were wide and empty. It read:

Beware! A crazed former doctor from the Wilds lurks just outside the walls seeking to poison wayward travelers. Wanted for six counts of murder and fourteen counts of forced madness via poisoning. Dead or Alive, 300 full clips.

A shiver ran up Huxley's spine.

"This guy lurks outside the city walls!" Huxley asked once Jeffries had returned.

Warden Jefferies responded cheerfully, "We hope he is. He has been seen inside this very ring of the city. Security is more lax here. Just about anyone can get in if they are motivated enough. I wouldn't worry about him though. No one gets into the inner city without being a citizen or having special credentials, which you have." He beamed at the last part.

"Which brings us to the backbone of Danador, the industrial ring." He stood with an outstretched hand presenting the gate to the second rung of the city.

They passed expediently through the gates, having a Warden escort allowed for that. Huxley and Warden Jefferies made their way through the second part of the city. It was as Jefferies said, a place of industry, but it didn't hum with life like Huxley thought it would. Towering buildings covered in soot and rust lined every street. Some of them were brimming with energy, with workers shouting and hustling about. Others looked dark and vacant, a few seemed barely able to hold their own walls up; a hard kick might take them down. The air was thicker and smelled acrid with only brief moments of sweet respite. A few bakeries and pubs dotted the streets. The smell of bread or beer was a welcome change to whatever was being produced in the factories.

Jefferies continued with history lessons the entire walk. Normally Huxley would have been interested, but the more they traveled, the closer his destination came. The excitement of actually being in Danador faded and he was trying to prepare for a face-to-face greeting with an Ember. He began reviewing his knowledge gained from the Grimoire and organizing his thoughts. He wanted to impress them right away. But how should he do that? This wasn't a magic show. He wouldn't put on a performance like Guliford. Surely that wouldn't be expected. Huxley worried that it might be a written exam. His stomach twisted at the thought. Exams had never gone well for him. Whether he studied or not, the anxiety and expectations set around them always made him unable to focus.

"...and that's why this district is so fascinating, but our town center is where Danador really shines!" Jefferies finished his thought looking expectantly at Huxley. Huxley smiled and nodded as though he had been listening the whole time. They made their way through the industrial district far faster than the rung before. Less foot traffic and mundane buildings made for a shorter journey. If Danador was laid out in rings like shown on the clips, the doors were exponentially closer with each ring.

Passing through the third rung gates felt like stepping into the maw of a beast. Danador was truly encircling him now. His wonder had evaporated and now he just felt woefully unprepared. The third rung of Danador was exactly what Huxley had expected. Clean and efficiently laid out, every building had an obvious purpose. There was a market like the first ring, with no more similarities than that. There was no shouting or climbing over each other. Orderly queues and polite conversation dominated the atmosphere. It reminded him of a library. In fact, that was the first building he saw. He stopped walking just to marvel at it. It rose three stories high and was packed with rows of books. He pressed his face against the window, mouth agape, in wonder. The rows were just wide enough for maybe two people shoulder to shoulder. Ladders were at the end of every row on a track that could slide up and down. Huxley tried to see the back wall of the library but couldn't. Mayburn's library wasn't a tenth as big as Danador's. A few readers looked up at the boy making face prints on the window. He couldn't help it. It was the best building he had ever seen! A thought struck him. Embers are probably here! He looked around hoping to see one. He had only been around one in his life, but now that he was so close to the college, there were probably at least two or three in the library. His eyes darted around, searching. He furrowed his brow when Jefferies tapped on his shoulder.

"Please do not walk away from me. I am your attendant and responsible for you."

"Oh, I didn't, I just had to see this place." Huxley said.

Jeffereies looked at the library then back at him.

"Surely you don't want to stop and check out a book?" He stated flatly. Huxley's face lit up.

"Could I?" He said in almost a yell. He wasn't hiding his enthusiasm well.

Jefferies cringed and whispered to Huxley, "No, that is a right that citizens have. You are a temporary guest, and might I remind you that twenty-four hours are now twenty-two hours. If you have business with the college, I suggest you settle it and not gawk at books."

Huxley sighed and realized he probably embarrassed himself. And Warden Jefferies was right, he had to make good use of his time.

Jefferies recovered and said, "Now then, I will leave you at the final gate. It has been wonderful showing you our city. I hope you gain admittance to the college. I hear their exams are quite thorough." His eyes flicked upward. "Although it seems they are closed now, check with the guard."

"Closed?" Huxley asked but Warden Jefferies was already walking away.

Huxley stood in the immense shadow of Danador's College of the Arcane Flame. Compared to every other building in the city, this one stood apart. The stone-work looked ancient, chipped and weathered. Despite this, it showed no signs of weakness. Were it not for the roaring fire atop its spire, Huxley would not have been able to see the top because of the night sky. The luminous peak shone so brightly, it seemed like the stars wouldn't approach it. He was sure it was merely a trick of the light, but all the same it looked strange. He finally looked away from its tremendous size and searched for an entrance.

The guard that Jefferies had referred to was like no other Huxley had ever seen before. Catching every glimmer of light stood an armor-clad knight that reminded him of children's story books. Similar to the beacon so high above, this guardian stood shining in the darkness of his post. It was no surprise that the college wouldn't just have a lobby he could march into and request an audience. But an armored guard? Did the most powerful Embers on the planet really need guards? *I've come too far to let this stop me. And besides, I have an invitation.* His own thoughts were weak next to the task before him. A singular gate awaited with a slot for his small golden central clip. Exhausting each one at each gate left him with just it. Dropping it with a plunk, a hollow metallic echo answered back. No mechanism to determine if it was authentic or not. Perhaps no one dared to try and cheat the city at this level. He swung open the gate and entered. The knight didn't seem to be in the business of invitations. Huxley steeled himself, straightened his posture and began his approach carefully doing his best to look confident.

He failed.

The moment his foot crossed the boundary of Danador's final rung to the courtyard of the college the knight shifted. Not violently or with shock, but with purpose. Huxley walked straight forward not wanting to look any worse than he already did. The closer he got, the more this knight came into focus. He stood taller than almost any man Huxley had ever met before, besides for the man-beasts that attacked Mayburn. He wore no sword or shield, but rather gripped an imposing halberd that was taller than the knight by a foot or more. The brilliance of his armor and weapon were not as perfectly immaculate as Huxley first thought. Dark black speckles of dirt in spray patterns across the breastplate became visible as he approached. The guard was clean shaved, dark hair pulled back in a top bun. His eyes were even darker than his hair and they were intensely focused on Huxley's every move.

"The College is off limits. Turn around and go home." It wasn't a threat, but a command. He had never heard anyone speak in that tone before. It seemed almost otherworldly and oddly feminine.

Huxley's limbs began to shake and instinctually his eyes saw the dancing stars come into view. This time he had gained a clearer understanding of each one's purpose. Far from perfect but some of the fog had lifted. He shook away the idea of a fight believing he wasn't ready, when a thought occurred.

Perhaps this is my first test! The Wardens must have notified the Embers of my arrival. This knight-guard might be an illusion or is presenting me with a riddle. Of course! Wizards in stories were known to protect their gates with all manner of trickery.

He reached into his pocket and produced the invitation still emblazoned with a "P" and held it out for his first test. In one motion, the knight-guard sliced the invitation in half causing Huxley to yelp.

"The College is off limits! Turn around and go home."

This time, Huxley was close enough to see that this was, in fact, not a young man, but a woman. Her features were lean and angular, a mirror to the discipline of her movements. Her face betrayed no emotion except the seriousness of her command.

Okay, this illusion is a dangerous one.

Huxley still held one half of his invitation in his hand but felt ridiculous holding onto it. He froze not knowing what to do when his Magnincy showed itself again. Knowing he might be in trouble he reached for a combustion-based star. It flew to his hand eager to be used. The moment it touched his grip, something cold and sharp touched his neck. The Knight-Guard had placed the edge of her halberd against his throat. The thump of his pulse pressed against the blade. His skin separated slightly against its touch.

"I won't tell you again." She said truthfully.

Her dark eyed gaze bore into Huxley. The dirt sprayed across her armor came into clearer view. It was not dirt at all but dried blood.

Maybe this isn't a test. Huxley surmised.

He gulped, adding another slight cut akin to a shaving nick to his neck. He dared to look away and locate his missing half of his invitation on the ground. If he left here without it, this whole trip would have been a waste. Huxley couldn't let that happen. Magnincy bounced around in his hand begging to be used. Pages from the Grimoire opened themselves in his mind, but the halberd remained, the sting of its edge ready. Huxley leaned backwards hoping the blade didn't follow. Mercifully it did not. I can't kill this guard and get my throat cut. That would be a bad first impression for sure.

"I will leave now, but I need to pick up my invitation. Can I please reach down and grab it?"

She shifted abruptly and shot her bladed staff into the mud snagging the invitation, and somehow not doing additional damage to it. She moved it toward his hands. Now having two halves of the invitation, one clearly dirtier than the other, Huxley felt it was time to go. He got the feeling she wasn't going to answer his questions, so he nodded in thanks. He couldn't tell if she returned it or not. If she had it was imperceptible. He took it as a good sign that he wouldn't be killed if he turned his back on her. He stepped backwards and left feeling her watching him the whole way out of the courtyard. Huxley's body shook from the stress and intensity of what had just occurred. *I need to sit down.* Just outside the college he found a street corner and plopped down.

When his heart rate finally slowed and his adrenaline abated, exhaustion hit him. The shops around him were closing down for the evening. Huxley needed to figure something out. He wouldn't try again at the College, that was for sure. He liked his neck too much. Warden Jefferies was long gone and everyone that might be helpful were evaporating from the streets. Perhaps he could find a street corner to sleep on or an alcove, just for the night. He might be able to afford a night at an inn, but he hadn't seen one since he arrived. A sobering thought hit him.

What if I have to walk back to the first rung and stay on one of those shanties?

He imagined himself trying to climb up to the top. It was almost as frightening as facing that Knight-Guard again...almost. Surely a city of this size had to have an inn. Then he remembered. He dug into his bag and found the card, pulled it out and read it in triumph. "Abernathy DelaCourt, Owner/operator of the Gearbox INN and tavern!"

How could he have forgotten? He still had enough time to go there and get some sleep. He would come back in the morning and find someone that could help him. Huxley picked himself off the street corner and made for the Gearbox.

13

Stew and Furs

"...the autumn months cause Ursus to consume large quantities. Sometimes in excess of 90 pounds of food a day. In contrast, the post hibernation months the intake is reduced to around 8,000 calories a day." - **Page 444 Excerpt from the Grimoire**

A single flake of snow fell from the clouds and drifted downward to land on Huxley's nose. Huxley instinctually pulled his coat tighter around him, hoping he would find his destination soon so he could be warm again. The streets of Danador were asleep as if the whole city just shut down after hours. A few residents still hustled here and there, but for the most part, it was silent. Mayburn was similar but he always thought it was just because of how small his town was. Memories of Mayburn invaded his thoughts, and Huxley suddenly felt quite alone. The gas lamps that lined the streets made a soft hiss that was a pleasant reminder of home. He felt far away from there now, from his friends, and from the comfort of his own bed. It wasn't the wrong choice to board the train to Danador, but at the moment, he wasn't sure he was up to the task that lay before him.

He wandered aimlessly in search of the Gearbox. It's been said that it is hard to get lost in Danador but Huxley was starting to feel that wasn't true. He couldn't find Saintamo Street. The card stated it was in the Industrial District which seemed simple enough. There were only two rungs to the industry sector and while the city was arranged in a circular fashion, it would be more accurate to think of the layout as a five-pointed star. Each area had five distinct points. Each point had an entrance with railroad tracks that led to other smaller cities outside. After the world was reshaped, Danador restructured itself almost like Magnadun had. First, a large section of the wall was removed, which the river now occupied. Refitting a landlocked city into a port was difficult. The Embers, of course, guarded the port and always protected the city from threats, but they couldn't be everywhere all the time. The trains and the river had become necessary for safe travel since the Fecundity took over. Traveling on foot outside of the city was more than dangerous, it was guaranteed death. With the new train routes, it became possible to populate cities outside of Danador again. No one could be absolutely sure how the rest of the world coped. It was presumed that they suffered similar challenges. Walking around Danador, Huxley thought that perhaps such straight lines and demarcations existed so that if another shift happened, they could pinpoint the change. It's what he would have done if he was designing a city.

His eyes were drawn to the surrounding wall of the Industrial District. He felt like he was going in circles. His eyes looked upward as they usually did, hoping that the stars would be able to provide a sense of comfort, but the light pollution from the lamps made it too difficult. Only a few exceptional stars were able to break through.

"You will never see them here, Bookpile," a voice called out from a nearby alleyway.

The voice was so calm it didn't startle Huxley, but it was unexpected.

"Elatress?" Huxley asked into the darkness.

She didn't answer except with another question, "How many times are you going to pass by us tonight? You've made three loops of the district."

"Well, it's difficult when the streets aren't properly labeled and there is no sign indicating where the Gearbox is."

She emerged out of the alleyway and stood before him. The flicker of the lanterns peeled away the shadow surrounding her and for the first time, he saw her face clearly. "Of course they are and of course there is," she told him bluntly.

He stared into her dark eyes, searching for answers. He sensed a restless energy that burned beneath her exterior. Elatress had wide, nearly black eyes that had an intensity to them like they were waiting for an opportunity. She was really just a kid in many ways, but the way she spoke and carried herself suggested otherwise. What was once mud-caked skin was now visible, her small, delicate features were accentuated by an enigmatic twist at the corner of her mouth. Her hood was still up making it impossible to see her hair. She reminded Huxley of a kitten that would bite if you got too close. She turned from him and moved towards a nearby building, as though she was a dancer in mid-routine, each step planned and meticulous.

Elatress swung open a dark wooden door that emitted a low creek. She held it, waiting for Huxley to follow. "Welcome to the Gearbox," she stated in a welcoming tone.

Emerging from the alley and following her, Arktos lumbered across the road bumping into Huxley and leaving a smudge of mud on his trousers. The appearance of the bear startled Huxley. He had not sensed its presence. How it had managed to get so close without him realizing, was disturbing. The bear shoved himself through the door catching his midsection on the sides, but the momentum was enough to see him through.

Before Huxley could ask, Elatress said "That's Arktos. He lives here. Don't frighten him."

Huxley choked on his words. "Me? Frighten him?!"

"Yes." She said flatly with only a hint of annoyance. "And please come in now, we aren't open and I don't want customers."

Huxley looked left and right at the barren streets. The impossibility of customers right now seemed lost on her. He came in all the same, glad to have finally made it to his destination. As he stepped inside, he tried to study her in short glimpses, wishing he knew more about this girl, wondering if she would ever confide in him.

The Gearbox Inn and Tavern was a disaster. A dozen lanterns littered the room but only three still burned. It was darker here than outside. As his eyes adjusted, he saw an enormous hearth with dying cinders. Several long tables meant for ten or more filled the main room with several smaller sitting areas along the walls, likely designed for more intimate discussions. Spices and hops saturated the wood and the walls, leaving lingering bouquets of both. Half-drunk tankards and bowls of stew littered the room. A man still holding on to both lay passed out in the corner. A game he had never seen before was set up on two of the tables. It had little catapults on either side with lined sections of a city wall. Its parts and pieces were scattered about.

"Busy night?" Huxley inquired.

"The usual," Elatress shrugged while making her way into the back-room. "Have a seat at the bar, I'll get you some dinner." She called out from the serving window.

Huxley's hunger won out over his concerns about the cleanliness of the establishment. He just hoped the food was hot. Arktos had disappeared again. How could such a huge animal be so stealthy? All the doorways were smaller than the entrance. If he had trouble before, he surely couldn't get through any of these. It was then that he noticed the staircase leading to a second floor. It was tucked at the far end of the tavern and was probably where the guest rooms were. The flutter of the lanterns continued to impede Huxley's vision. Elatress could be heard from, what Huxley guessed, was the kitchen. His bar stool creaked as he sat down. He plopped his bag with the Grimoire inside of it down on the next stool. Huxley took out the two halves of the invitation and laid them down in front of him. He moved the two pieces together, reforming it. The cut was so clean it looked like it had been done with scissors, straight down the middle in a line, one-half dirty, the other still clean. He could read it now, the wax seal having been broken.

This boy shows signs of-

A steaming bowl of stew plopped in front of him right on top of the letter. Bubbling brown liquid with all types of vegetables and meat swam inside.

"Hey!" Huxley protested, but Elatress was already back through the swinging doors.

His nostrils eagerly took in the mouthwatering aroma. He made no effort to wait for it to cool off.

"I hope you like it. It's Arktos's favorite, and mine too." She called from the back. "Abernathy always keeps at least a gallon or two ready for new guests. He says, "start them with the light stuff to strengthen their gut for real meals." She reiterated the statement in an overly deep voice that was, at best, a loose impersonation of Abernathy.

Between mouthfuls, Huxley said, "This isn't the real stuff?"

Elatress' head popped up in the kitchen window. Her hood was pulled down and her dark eyes were now shrouded by her deep brunette hair, both of which contrasted sharply with her skin. "His real stew will kill you. It started as a beer we called the Cleanser, but nobody ordered it so he had to make it into a stew."

Huxley had a question about how beer becomes stew and if that was even possible. With his initial hunger sated, he slowed his mouthfuls so as not to come off as a starving animal. His eyes had finally adjusted to the dim light and the full view of the establishment known as the Gearbox came into clear view. It was still certainly messy but it looked like it was mainly from the night's business. Overall the corners and small nooks were well-kept, plush cushions lined each seat. It even had a few tapestries on the wall, one depicted an Ember emitting a bright light pushing back darkness and the horrible shadow creatures contained within. Huxley recognized this immediately. Everyone knew this story. It was told to him when he was just a toddler. "The Arcane Flame holding back the darkness and showing the way." The other tapestries were far more complex. Huxley hadn't seen them before. Like the first one, it seemed to have a religious structure. It was difficult to even discern the characters and movements. There were no clear lines or ideas. What kind of art was this? It was a whirlpool of colors in one spot, and many different ones feeding into it. The colors made a knot surrounding the whirlpool. In the low light, it was too difficult to make out much more. It reminded him of the symbol in the grimoire.

Just then, the bar vibrated, shaking the remainder of his stew. He grabbed onto his bowl not wanting it to spill. And for the second time in the same night, Arktos appeared unexpectedly. His enormous mass climbed out from under the bar and settled in front of him. The brown bear sat unmoving excluding only his nose. It sniffed the air fiercely following an invisible scent that pointed right at Huxley's dinner. Huxley realized this apex predator, possibly the biggest animal he has ever seen, wanted his bowl of stew. He let go of the bowl slowly and scooted his bar stool backward. Arktos made for the stew immediately. His entire head eclipsed the bowl but stopped just short. He seemed to restrain himself with a monumental effort. His breath made tiny waves in the broth as the bear looked up at Huxley, eyes pleading ... *was he asking for permission?* Huxley looked to Elatress for help but she was nowhere to be seen. Arktos made a grunt while waiting. A large drop of saliva ran down his teeth and climbed over his gums. It hung on his lip, then free fell down into Huxley's bowl. The bear made another grunt followed by a low growl. It was definitely asking him. Huxley nodded his head, yes and in an instant, the stew was gone. A monstrous tongue scooped it all up and swallowed it, then licked the bowl. Arktos hummed in happiness which shook the bar again. A door swung open and Elatress surveyed the situation. She saw a terrified guest with a giant bear licking its chops.

"Arktos! The stew isn't for you. It never is! Stop stealing from people. Get to bed. It's late!" She demanded.

Arktos huffed in annoyance and glanced at Huxley before giving in to Elatress and somehow shoving his enormous body back underneath the bar. Huxley listened to the rubbing of fur and annoyed grunts as he got himself comfortable. Once he settled down, he almost immediately began snoring.

Elatress picked up the bowl and apologized to Huxley. "I'd like to say that he never does this but that would be a lie. I don't know if he's ever really been full. That bear is a great friend, probably the best friend

I've ever known, but he will steal your food and watch you starve if you let him."

Huxley tried to lessen the tension, "Well, I'm told bears are not good at sharing."

"Oh?" she perked up excitedly, "And who told you that? Do you know much about bears?"

A smile crossed his face fleetingly. It was odd to him that she didn't pick up his sarcasm. He chuckled "No, I just...don't worry about it. I didn't really hear that. I just made it up." He averted his eyes until she went back to her work.

Their conversation transitioned into an awkward silence. He put the letter away, resolving to read it later. The silence ended when Elatress asked "That sure is a big book you have in your bag. Do you always carry it around trains and towns? No one carries a book that size...except maybe the Embers."

Huxley choked on his own breath in surprise.

"How did-"

Then the bar rattled again.

Huxley looked to Arktos but the bear was still asleep.

"No, Arktos doesn't shake the bar like that. That's Abernathy." Elatress indicated.

"Abernathy?" Huxley shifted on his barstool. From what he had guessed was a storage room, a metal door from a basement entryway squeaked open and clanged against the floor. A plume of smoke puffed out followed by Abernathy. Is he always covered in soot? Abernathy pulled himself up from the ladder and dragged his feet over the floor. He sat with a thump next to Huxley and took a second to clear out the acrid vapor from the rest of his lungs. Elatress plunked an enormous stein of clear liquid in front of him. He huffed a rough "Thank you" and drank it down in nearly one gulp. His mustache soaked a good amount of what was intended for his mouth. It dripped onto the floor after running down the ends. He looked precisely the same as he had on the train, covered in soot and grease stains all over his arms.

Abernathy continued to drip onto the bar and finally said "So you found us, huh? Well, if you haven't been welcomed already, welcome to the Gearbox, Inn, and Tavern." Abernathy waved a brawny hand. "We specialize in the finest food and drink in all of Danador and provide the coziest rooms outside of your own home." He smiled broadly revealing teeth that lost a few companions. "Well, most of the time anyway." He added as a disclaimer.

He shifted in his stool to face Huxley more directly. "I would have thought you would be sleeping in a dormitory, studying day and night with the Embers by now. What happened?"

"Well nothing 'happened but that is the problem. I was turned away at the gate by the most frightening woman I have ever met." Huxley responded.

Abernathy and Elatress shared a look.

"Oh my," he said, "You met the Butcher of Valdannon."

Huxley blinked and said, "Butcher?"

"That's what people call her. She is one of the few immigrants from Valdannon who has a real job in the government here. She and her band are given special assignments, usually hunting down enemies of the state that the Embers don't have time for." he explained.

"Then why is she guarding a gate?" He asked.

Abernathy began to speak but was cut off. "She isn't so tough, you know. Not even a real butcher. She's just an overgrown muscle head like the rest. I could bring her down easily! She thinks her armor covers up her weak spots but they don't. In fact, it just makes them easier to see!" Elatress issued these declarations with an overzealous enthusiasm born of a child's whim.

Abernathy raised a flattened hand to Elatress' eye level. She noticed it and seemed to remember something. He slowly lowered his hand to rest on the bar. When it laid flat, she was calm again.

"I'm sure you could, dear, but that's not a concern of ours, is it?"

"No," she muttered. Her face dark and impassive.

"It's probably time for rest now." His voice was hard and insistent.

She breathed a heavy sigh of frustration and lowered her head resolutely. Elatress walked away making almost no noise. She slipped down into the room that Abernathy had come from without a sound.

Huxley let his eyes shift to Abernathy. "Did you hypnotize her?!" Huxley accused without hiding any of the alarm in his voice.

Abernathy uttered a deep low chuckle. "Hypnotize! Hah, if I could do that, my troubles would be over. She just needs help calming down sometimes. She has many capabilities, but unfortunately they aren't all nice. It's best to always stay ahead of them."

Huxley had many more questions about what that meant but wasn't certain he really wanted to know the answers.

"Ryla the Butcher of Valdannon, is a title given to inspire fear, I think. She is actually a delightful woman, if you ever get to speak with her off duty."

Huxley had no intention of finding out for himself and decided to take his word for it. He shifted uncomfortably in his seat. His stomach rumbled, demanding attention. What was it that Elatress had called this stew? The Cleanser?

Abernathy didn't seem to notice. "I certainly know what it's like arriving in a big city with nothing but a dream and the clothes on my back. You are welcome to stay here until you get situated"

Huxley pushed down the discomfort bubbling in his stomach. "Stay here? Oh no, I just want to stay for the night. I only have twenty four hours, well, now twenty hours to gain admittance into the college of the Arcane Flame."

Abernathy rolled his eyes and said, "Those Wardens love their rules and restrictions. I swear, if they had their way, breathing would be regulated." He laughed mainly to himself and went on, "well, the Gearbox still operates with little of either." He stated the matter with pride but Huxley wasn't sure the complete absence of rules was a good thing.

"If it's twenty hours, feel free to spend eight of them asleep here." Abernathy offered. "Here's your room key." He produced a brass key with flecks of black from his pocket. The blade and teeth of it were irregular. They jutted out in a few different directions. They didn't just point up and down as he had seen before. He placed it in front of Huxley and said, "your room is on the corner of the second floor. It even has a view." His eyebrows raised while saying the last part. Huxley couldn't imagine a view in the Industrial District but picked up the key with a "thanks" anyway.

Abernathy got up and began to walk away, dragging his feet. Huxley knew the conversation was over but he needed to know one more thing.

"You've been so kind to me...the train and now the room." He let the obvious question hang in the air.

Abernathy didn't stop. He kept walking and replied over his shoulder.

"She likes you. That's rare enough. I like seeing her happy."

"Oh. Well, I'm glad she likes me then." Huxley responded but the old man was already through the door leaving Huxley alone with a giant bear snoring at his feet.

Huxley found himself alone in the Gearbox. He grabbed his things and walked upstairs to find his room right where Abernathy told him it would be. The upstairs hallway looked out over the dining room and bar he had just occupied. His key clicked into the lock and it popped open without having to turn it. He was too tired to wonder how such a mechanism worked. He made a mental note to ask later and entered his room. When the door opened he heard a click of a mechanical button and a gas lamp sparked on. The flame illuminated the room evenly. It didn't flicker like the outdoor lamps on the streets. Huxley tossed his things on the bed and made right for the privy. After a few minutes, he emerged relieved. The room was surprisingly spacious. It sat in the corner of the building with two windows looking out. A bed large enough for two lay waiting to be slept in. It had a large fur comforter from an animal Huxley couldn't recognize. There was a desk and wardrobe as well as a chest at the foot of the bed. It had another lock and key similar to the one he used for his room. He sat down hoping to finally read his invitation and study the Grimoire before bed. He made it halfway through his letter and his eyes began to struggle, but he forced himself to read it all.

The boy shows signs of Magnincy. Not only that, but it's possible his skill already exceeds my own. He is at a high risk of madness and may have had a tutor he hasn't told me about. Huxley would perhaps be an asset to the college of the Arcane flame. Please consider him for admittance. Note, this is my fourth possible student of aptitude I have sent. I expect our relationship to be elevated as a result of all the good I have done for the college. -Palithur

"High risk of madness?" Huxley whispered to himself.

He didn't feel like he was going mad. But the idea alarmed him.

Perhaps I shouldn't have read this. Now I might not be able to sleep at all and tomorrow could be the most important interview of my life!

No, he said, *I have to start dealing with the harsh truths of what I hope to encounter. If madness is something to contend with, then I need more information about how to do that.*

He reread the note. Nearly every line had him asking questions. "I exceed his skill? How would he know?" He answered his own question about the tutor, "I have a Grimoire...that is a kind of a tutor." Huxley wondered why he would note that he has sent students already. He knew about Onders, the star pupil who Palithur told everyone about. Perhaps, he might meet some of the others. Huxley wandered over to the corner window and looked out. Just as he thought, sheer stone walls limited his view on both sides providing only a sliver in between. Technically, it was a view though and Huxley saw that the snow had picked up. Several flakes touched the window and melted. He shivered, suddenly remembering how cold it was outside and was just glad it didn't encroach through the window.

Huxley walked over to his bed and climbed into the furs. They were warmer than he anticipated. Heat seemed to radiate from them as though the animal was still there. He tried reaching for his bag to study but couldn't bring himself to release any heat. This was perhaps the most snug he had ever felt. He wondered if this was what baby animals felt like in a den surrounded by their siblings. Through great physical effort, he forced himself to reach out and switch off the light. He crawled back in, and a contented sigh escaped his lips before he passed out.

14

Marble and Stone

"Atmospheric differentials cause pressure to accrue and distribute. As the pressure moves it creates climatological changes." - **Page 152 Excerpt from the Grimoire**

The sun rushed through his window demanding a start to the day. He was awake before he opened his eyes. The only thing in the world that could have got him out of that bed was admittance to the College. And because of that, he pulled off the blanket. He crawled out and sluggishly started to get dressed. Opening his bags, he searched for the right outfit. His imagination was flooded with excitement over entering college and what his first day might be like, although it was tempered slightly by his anxiety. Almost nothing had gone the way he had hoped so far. He started to fret about all the ways today could go wrong. Pausing his search, he glanced at the mirror. It helped to calm him for a moment at least.

You can't control how the day will go. Just do your best, trust in yourself, and don't kill anyone with Magnincy. He thought it over and decided that motto needed work. He was so worried about things out of his control, he forgot about everything in his control. *You can at least try to have the appearance of a student.*

He took a few extra minutes to dress properly instead of rushing out the door in case that could make a difference. The twenty-four-hour time limit needled him. He knew there was plenty of time to get back to the college and gain admittance. But the idea of being thrown out was worrisome.

He changed into a clean button-up shirt and carefully tucked it in. The slacks could have fit better, but they were free of wrinkles. Adjusting the suspenders, and straightening his green vest completed his ensemble. He rarely wore a vest, but it didn't hurt to try and look your best. He fidgeted with it a bit, trying to make sure it fit as it was supposed to. His search for his tie was fruitless. Of course, he forgot the tie. It was probably for the best, he never really got the hang of tying it properly. Huxley slung his bag containing his Grimoire over his shoulder. He looked at himself again in the mirror presenting himself for inspection. His long hair was a mess. He tried pushing it back but it would need a comb and some effort. After five minutes, it was loosely tied back in a ponytail.

Everything looked right, except for one nagging thought. The Grimoire. Why do I feel like I shouldn't bring it? The nagging persisted. There was a useful trunk lying at the feet of his bed. Palithur's warning lingered in his mind as well. Choosing to heed it, Huxley locked his Grimoire away. Better to let them think I've been properly trained.

With two halves of his invitation in hand, Huxley left his room. At the bottom of the stairs he glanced around and everything looked precisely the same as the night before, except now, a golden ray of the sun brought out new shades of color which gave the establishment some much-needed warmth. Abernathy and Elatress were nowhere to be seen. He peeked behind the bar and saw Arktos still fast asleep. Good. On the bar was a note that said, "Good luck -El", and an apple sat next to it. He made short work of his breakfast and exited the Gearbox.

Finding the college was no trouble except now he didn't have a Warden as a guide. A few people were being let into the inner rungs depositing their three-fourth full clips to Wardens. Did people pay that much every day just to get through the gates? Huxley would have to spend months of his income just to walk into the inner rung to say nothing of having anything left to spend there. That was probably why the college didn't receive many visitors; to even enter you needed a substantial amount of clips. The Wardens saw him and tapped their clipboards reminding him of how much time was left. He swore he had certainly not forgotten and they let him pass.

The gates of the College of the Arcane Flame were still intimidating in the daylight, but far less without Ryla the Butcher of Valdannon standing guard. He pressed his fingers to his neck where his scratch had scabbed up from his encounter with her.

"I guess this means it's open now." He stated aloud.

The doors to the college lay before him. They lacked the pomp he thought they might have, just being slightly larger than average doors. They had the insignia of the college carved into them. He swung them open and entered. A chilly wind escaped and a sprawling marble floor made up most of what was to be seen. It shone brilliantly and forced him to squint. A single desk was situated at the other side of the marble sea and he made for it. Each footfall echoed through the chamber and reverberated in the rafters. He shrunk in embarrassment at the racket he was making. His eyes adjusted and he looked to see if there was anyone else around but there was only the scribe seated at the desk before him.

The scribe was busily writing. Huxley took a seat before him. The man noticed Huxley and finished his sentence with a flourish. He was quite a bit older than Huxley. His nose was long and followed his quills movements. Eyebrows stretched out from his head almost as long as his nose. He wore simple robes but still looked official, like a warden, but without the accompanying buttons and rank insignias. The scribe placed his feathered pen into the inkwell and blew onto his work. He held the paper up and read it over. His face scrunched up when he noticed a flaw. It caused the lines on his face to deepen into gulches.

"Were you the one making all that racket?" He accused, but showed a hint of a smile.

"I wouldn't call..." He stopped, realizing it best not to start with a disagreement. "I'm sorry, I didn't realize the floor would be so loud"

"It wasn't the floor that was loud. It has been quite silent for hours.

It was only when you showed up that things went awry. Walk quieter next time."

"Ok..quieter next time, then."

The Scribe appraised him critically.

"How are you going to do that? If you lost any weight, you'd probably die."

Huxley blinked.

"Umm, I said I would step softer."

The Scribe's face scrunched even deeper than before. The lines on his face were like a maze that covered every inch of it.

"What business do you have with us?" He asked.

Huxley thrust his invitation forward holding it up to the Scribe. The man stared. "Oh, a letter...for me?"

"No, it's for entrance to the College."

The Scribe laughed. It was like a forceful wind coming out of his nose more than a laugh though. Eyebrow raised, he leaned forward and cast a shadow over Huxley's invitation.

"Entrance...to the college?" He repeated back like it was a punchline to a joke.

Huxley nodded his head..

Amused, the Scribe read over the two halves of the letter, lining them up on his desk. "Palithur sent you, huh, or is it Guliford now?" He barked a laugh this time.

Huxley again nodded his head yes.

He studied Huxley's face, trying to make sense of everything. "Entrance into the College of the Arcane Flame isn't done like this. There are lots of problems with your story. If I get up from my chair and go find an Ember, and some part of your story is untrue or falsified..." He trailed off. "Are you sure this is what you want?"

Huxley gulped. He summoned his courage and spoke, "Yes."

"Very well, then. My name is Walters, and I serve the College in every way I can. I suppose today, instead of clerical work, I am a messenger. Have a seat boy, I will be back soon."

Walters got up and walked around his desk to open equally unassuming doors for such a large institution.

It was at that moment that Huxley glimpsed it.

A colossal library lay behind those doors. It was like nothing he had ever seen before and he had only seen a small part from the lobby. He could feel his eyes expanding trying to drink in what the remainder might look like. Huxley saw vast rows of books and numerous men clad in robes all studying. They were Embers! Probably researchers or their assistants. Nothing was more Arcane than the work they do. He was so close now. He could have shouted and they would have heard him. The reality of his situation set in. Likely, in a few minutes, he would actually speak with one. Huxley experienced a new feeling that greatly confused him. He was telling the truth, but even to him, it sounded like a lie. Would the Embers really be able to tell the truth from a lie, as Palithur said? They can do a whole lot of other things. Why not?

He forced himself to sit and try to look casual. He crossed his legs and leaned back to stretch his arms wide on the back of the bench where he was seated. He straightened his vest and looked at the empty space where a tie should have been.

Ok, he thought, *you're not in your living room after a long day. You're a serious student and you need to make that obvious.*

He fiddled with his seating arrangement in a vain attempt to get comfortable. It was an impossible task. He gave up trying when someone entered. It was a young man about his age. He had robes on like the Embers but they were worn and tattered, especially on the knees and elbows. They exchanged looks. The young man carried a large wooden bowl full of water that was overflowing with suds. He poured an amount on the floor and began scrubbing.

"Oh, am I in your way?" Huxley asked.

"Hmm? No, no, I'll work around you. I can come back later if you would like." The robed man said. His voice had a docility to it. It sounded like it belonged to someone far older.

"You don't need to do that. I'm just waiting..." Huxley couldn't help the next part. "...I might be a new research assistant!" A smile spread over his face as the idea took hold.

"Me, too." He answered back now deep into his chore.

"You're...a research assistant?" Huxley asked dreadfully.

"Oh, yes," he said, "I'm on a short list to be considered to study under a researcher in the next few years..."

The more information he gained, the less he wanted. Huxley didn't continue his line of questions and no more conversation was offered back.

Many minutes passed, far more than Huxley expected. Deliberations were probably good, he decided. That at least meant there was a discussion and not outright refusal. *Or maybe they're deciding what unnatural creature to turn me into.* Huxley smiled at his own joke. Deep down, he wasn't truly sure he was kidding though.

Finally, the door creaked open. Walters came back in and sat at his desk. The familiar quill scratches resumed, albeit with a hastened pace. Huxley's excitement battled his dread for dominance. Before there could be a winner, the quill snapped down against the desk.

"Ok," he breathed out. "Follow me". The scribe walked back through the doors.

Realizing that could only mean him, Huxley jumped up and raced after him, stepping through the doors of the College of the Arcane Flame.

The two walked silently together through the library. Huxley tried hard not to giggle. That was certainly something Embers didn't do.

I am inside a dream. This is the kind of library that Kings keep. If I had all the years of my life to be left alone to read, I couldn't get through a quarter of this; and I bet I wouldn't understand half of that! If only Agnes could see this!

Doors encircled the library leading to corridors. Where those corridors went, he had no idea. A staircase sprawled upward, so high that Huxley assumed it ended at the burning beacon on top of the tower itself. Perhaps every room was connected directly to the library. The entire tower looked to be a library packed with books similar to the Grimoire.

They were all different shapes and sizes, if he put the Grimoire into this room, it would not stand out.

His tour ended abruptly at another doorway, identical to the last two. *Did every door look the same here?*

Walters looked as if he was about to leave without further instruction but then gave a slight gesture of his wrist suggesting that Huxley should enter.

Huxley heard a voice from inside.

Ok, Huxley, he thought to himself, *time to-*

The voice bellowed beyond the door.

"You are disturbing my work. Enter now or leave!"

Huxley did as instructed. Inside, was an office that could have been mistaken for another library, but in disarray. Stacks of books were balanced on top of each other and more books lined the room. There wasn't a chair for him to sit in. Just as he expected, a fully robed Ember of the Arcane Flame sat before him taking notes. Huxley foolishly chanced a glance at what he was writing. The notes looked like a page from a Grimoire! He could not make out the structure he was sketching. There were connected points and the word "Astronomy" written above it. It was outside his depth. Huxley got the impression interruptions were a serious offense, so he forced himself to look away and waited. His invitation lay on the desk, next to a nameplate with the title:

Ember Maddox,

High Researcher of the Lost and Forgotten

He approached slowly hoping to convey respect. It was remarkably stuffy in the office, probably from too many musty old books and a lack of open windows. Huxley felt like he couldn't get a deep breath. He neared the desk and his throat constricted tighter. He kept his breathing under control but had a hard time keeping calm.

"Palithur is a joke and so are you. Prove yourself! Demonstrate some ability. But remember the research in this room is more valuable than all of Mayburn. If you damage anything, you won't leave this room alive."

Huxley's throat tightened further.

"Yes sir", he squeaked.

The stacks of books seemed to lean in closer, threatening to topple over at any second. Huxley wasted no time.

Some ability, he thought, ok, good. *He just wants to know if I can use Magnincy.*

He focused and the stars floated within his grasp, again. The pages of the Grimoire opened in his mind and they turned to page one fifty two.

Low and high air pressures... He thought that's what makes wind. *Interesting. I could try to summon a gust in here..but that would surely get me killed. Maybe just this for now.*

Huxley reached out and grabbed a star. It jumped around in his hand, begging to release its full potential. The idea was certainly fun but Huxley did not want to be killed today. Instead, he restricted it greatly and allowed a nice breeze from his hands to blow his hair up. To his surprise, it did exactly what he asked it to. *Controlling Magnincy was less burdensome if you asked less of it,* He noted.

The wind swirled around his hair for a minute and dissipated. His lungs thanked him for the brief respite but found themselves constricted again a few seconds later. Huxley, satisfied with himself, smiled expectantly at Chief Researcher Maddox.

Maddox hadn't stopped writing. He hadn't even looked up. The only indication that Maddox had seen Huxley's demonstration was that he reached forward and held down his paper.

Huxley cleared his throat and said, "Well? That was "some ability". Did I do it right? I chose a section of climatology just now."

Maddox looked up. His face was nonplussed. "How old are you?" He asked.

"Nearly twenty-one" Huxley responded.

"My assistant is twenty-two. She mastered climatology at eight. You are thirteen years behind her. If that is all the knowledge you have gained in your time on Magnadun then-"

"I can do way more! You told me not to mess up your books." Huxley blurted out.

Maddox sighed. "You've wasted enough of the College's time. You have obviously reached for something higher and that could be useful to us. You may go see my assistant Onders in the Magnincy Arena if you wish to demonstrate more thoroughly. If she deems you fit for service we will find something for you to do here."

"Something to do? I'm here to become an Ember!" Huxley stated with all the defiance he could muster. He knew he was overstating himself but his indignance at his treatment spilled out.

Maddox's hands flashed forward. He flicked his hands open and the air drained from Huxley's lungs. Huxley tried to breathe in but the atmosphere turned into a vacuum. When he opened his mouth, his breath was pulled out rather than in. His eyes went wide and he began to flail.

"You will find oxygen outside if you wish for some," Maddox said while gesturing to the door.

Huxley instinctively threw himself towards the door. He would have gasped but didn't have the air for even that. Mercifully, the door was only a dozen feet from where he stood. He sprinted. His sight darkened at the edges and crept inward. His lungs felt like dried-out raisins. He collapsed to the ground but maintained consciousness. *Don't die on this office floor, Huxley.* He demanded of himself.

Forcing his limbs forward, he crossed a threshold and air filled his lungs again. He fell to the ground gasping and trying not to cough louder than he already was. Some force closed the door behind him while he lay sprawled on the ground trying to recover.

Huxley sat dumbfounded. Embers had never had a reputation for being friendly, but that seemed like a real attempt at his life. And for what? Asking for attention? He tried to slow his heart down, but his body was still in shock. Maddox's door sat next to him daring him to knock and try again. Just the thought made him breathe a little deeper.

Well my first meeting with an Ember didn't go as well as I'd hoped...but maybe his assistant is the talkative type. He reasoned.

Huxley stood himself up and made sure he wasn't lightheaded anymore. *Wait...did he say a Magnincy Arena...like a gladiatorial arena?* The thought excited him. To think about Embers dueling each other while crowds cheered wildly. Huxley smiled at the thought but then realized he was going to be standing in it soon. The color drained from his cheeks and he said, "Am I going to have to duel someone?!"

Huxley wrestled with that and looked for what could be an arena. He found himself on the outskirts of the library. The whole tower was bathed in warm candlelight. This place had no gas-fed lanterns like everywhere else, just the old candle lamps. In fact, the whole tower was lined with beautifully ornate black metal lanterns. Each had a bright white candle that cast ambient light far into the room. He finally had a moment to take in the library. It stretched high, containing tower shelves of books and various scrolls that looked far older than anything he thought possible. The first floor had solid stone floors with a smattering of carpets. Above was a complicated, interconnected network of short bridges and ladders leading higher than he could see. Spiral staircases littered the floor reaching multiple levels above them. Iron bridges connected the sides and alcoves jutting off, providing space to read and take notes. He couldn't see the names of the sections, like in a traditional library or even a librarian to help find them. Of course, there had to be a structure or a system of filing. Huxley just didn't recognize it yet.

The silence was palpable, broken only by the sounds of pages turning and robes swishing. As though responding to his thoughts, a young-robed woman put down her book, careful to save her place, and approached Huxley. At first glance, she appeared the same age as Huxley but her face was sharp and lined with a serious scrutiny, one not found in people her age. She had long black hair that had a tendency to veil part of her face. Her eyes ran all over Huxley, measuring him. Huxley sensed fatigue in her. It was something she was trying hard to hide. It reminded him of his father after a long day.

Huxley finally made the connection, she was Palithur's first apprentice! "You're from Mayburn too! Palithur has told me all about you!"

Her eyes narrowed on him and a shadow of dislike crept onto her face, "I am Onders, apprentice to Maddox, an Ember of the Arcane Flame and Chief Researcher of the Lost and Forgotten. I provide him assistance and research into antiquity as well as anything else he requires. Today that appears to be...*you.*" Her words dripped with contempt, "Do you wish for more of the college's time in assessing your abilities?" Despite her fatigued appearance, she spoke directly and moved the same.

"Yes, I am supposed to go to the arena with you."

"Indeed. Follow me then."

The pair walked wordlessly through the library. Huxley tamped down his normal curiosity and tried to look like he wasn't impressed or scared. Things hadn't gone well so far. He felt like he made some kind of mistake already but couldn't figure out what it was. Onders led Huxley to a door that had no ornate finish or carvings. It was a metal door with rivets around the sides, with just bare hints of rust that crept in from the corners. They walked through it and soon the warm light of the library left and was replaced with the cold glow of stone hallways that descended lower. Lichen glowed in the cracks and corners, the light was minimal but it was enough to navigate. Huxley felt like they were walking underground now. The College's enormous tower must need a substantial substructure to hold it up. He was now getting a glimpse of that. Their steps echoed down the hallway announcing their entrance. Spiraling down, it curved like the tower's library, as the pair descended ever deeper. Glowing lichen wasn't entirely new to Huxley. He had seen bits of it before. Never this much though, and never this concentrated. The glow deepened and grew as they progressed.

He couldn't hold it in any longer. "There are no torches here, so obviously they must have planned on the glowing lichen, right? How did they nurture it?" His voice echoed and was louder than he anticipated. Unfazed, Onders answered, "Lichenology is one of the innumerable areas of study that more than a few Embers have mastered."

"But...how?"

"Knowledge gained is through study. Do well in the arena and you may just learn one day." Onders had stopped and gestured to the black air.

The arena opened in front of them. They must have entered it a while ago, it was just so large, Huxley hadn't noticed. Onders placed her hand on a gray block on the wall and it glowed blue at her touch. The light woke up the other blocks and they all lit up around Onders. Now the chamber came into view as the blocks continued to wake, climbing up the walls and floor. It looked to be roughly the same size as the library. The only difference was, water dropped from the ceiling.

Onders stood before Huxley and said "In a moment I will open the gate. Step out into the middle of the arena. Show me whatever you deem appropriate for the college to evaluate. Should you do well enough, we may consider you further. Lose control of what you summon and I will kill you. Do you agree?"

Huxley shivered but not from the frigid room they were in.

"Kill me?" Huxley repeated.

"Do you agree?" Onders repeated.

Huxley thought again of the blood sprayed on the wall, his friends in a pile bleeding around him, *This is the only way,* He conceded.

"I agree."

"To the arena then."

15

Bubbles and Silver

"Composite liquid film in lieu of nuclei and diffusion will cause the film to last indefinitely. Pressure applied will strain the creation, but with ample amounts of stability added it could hold up to extreme forces."
-Excerpt from page 198 (theories annex) from the Grimoire

Onders gestured towards a gate that may have been iron. The blue glow of the rocks didn't illuminate enough for Huxley to tell. Huxley approached the gate and prepared himself. He turned to ask a question but Onders was gone. A mechanism engaged and lifted the gate haltingly. Huxley now worried he hadn't asked enough questions about what he may face here. His mind showed him a handful of pages that were well-studied. A few were still muddled, like seeing through fog. Feeling uncertain, he elected to go on the defensive. So far, his time studying was far greater than his time in practice. Experimenting was dangerous in any area but now, he had no choice. The few things he had already wielded seemed of no use now. Time to try something new. He didn't know much about shielding but perhaps a malleable bubble would work well enough. His knowledge of malleable things and coagulants seemed the right choice. He reached out and grabbed a star that best represented his idea. He asked for a shield against harm. That was really broad and he wished he could be more specific but with his limited time utilizing Magnincy, he thought it would work. He released the star and the knowledge proved sufficient as a bubble formed around him. It distorted his view making hard lines look wavy. It wasn't enough of a distortion to throw him off though. The bubble undulated as he stepped forward. Huxley felt it pull at his knowledge of natural elements. The gate fully opened and beckoned him forward.

The meek young Ember hopeful stepped forward. The arena was empty of obvious threats. No wild animals or warriors charged at him. The space was large enough for a few combatants. The ground was weathered and looked older than the rest of the stones that surrounded it. An enormous drain sat in the direct center, Huxley didn't want to know why it was necessary.

He tried to look courageous but failed.

High up in the stands, Onders spoke.

"You have only a few minutes to demonstrate your abilities. Go on, then."

"Am I going to fight anyone?" Huxley asked.

"Like who?" Onders replied.

"Well, it's an arena right? Surely there is something to fight in here?"

"Oh, there is, but the arena is for Embers, Huxley. If I were to release even one it would consume you instantly. I just want to see what you are capable of producing. Go on then." As she spoke that last sentence, Huxley finally found her up in the stands. She was sitting further away than seemed appropriate for observing someone's abilities.

Huxley relaxed. At least I won't be stabbed or eaten today, he thought to himself. Huxley summoned every star he could think of. They swooshed down in front of him begging to be drawn on. He had nearly selected his first one, when Onders asked, "Is that a defensive bubble? I don't understand, why not something that would actually work like a barrier of some kind. Does it help you float or..." She was at a loss for words.

"It's an experiment. I think it works as well as a wall. Less rigid. It may absorb and deflect better than a straight block." He explained.

Onder's nose wrinkled as she clarified, "An experiment? Here? Now? You would toy with madness so casually?"

Huxley didn't know what to say. "I learned it from my old militia captain. It's about flow and strength."

"Ok, then," Onders said, betraying the barest hint of interest. "Continue."

With his defense setup, Huxley then grabbed at fire and lightning. He wanted to make an impression. He held the knowledge of fire in his left hand and the chaotic speed and energy of lightning in his right. Both were extremely active and didn't like being held. They were meant to be free. So, he released them.

A column of fire roared out and a crackle of lightning shot, the glowing rock illumination was like a firefly compared to the sun. The effect was immediate for both. The lightning however was gone as fast as it came. The flames having nothing but rock for fuel also went out but lingered for a few seconds. Huxley's hair flew backwards and his ears rang, interestingly, he didn't feel the heat like he had before. The bubble must have blocked the heat or absorbed it.

Dang, I really am experimenting. I have no idea how that worked.

The bubble in response, tore apart like paper.

Ok, he thought, *it can absorb heat before it is destroyed. At least at this level. I should study that more for sure.*

He glanced up at his judge, Huxley had lost some of his night vision because of the flashes but he could see her silhouette. She sat unmoving. Huxley felt he should continue. He considered what he'd try next. Movement and pushing? He knew a lot about that. When his thoughts moved to those subjects the stars reacted swirling into his grasp. He reached out and grabbed one. As he had studied friction recently, it seemed the right choice. The science of friction floated in his hands. He knew less about this...but what he wanted was the opposite. So perhaps if he asked it to do the opposite of what came naturally to it, that would work? Friction felt tight and rigid, like the soul of a stubborn attitude. Friction was a new part of the grimoire he had only begun studying.

He noticed a loose amount of rocks and pebbles on the ground near him. He released his hand and the friction discharged from them. They shuddered but didn't move. Huxley kicked them and they flew out in all directions. A few struck him as well. Gravity still worked the same on them but it was like all the bonds had been removed from the bunch so one kick was enough to send them flying. He smiled and noted the opposite might work to keep them all together.

But his thoughts were interrupted as Onders sighed. "Are you through with your warm-up? At least, I hope that's what this is. These elements are a child's level of understanding. Fit for soft-minded crowds like your magician friend or clowns of the same ilk. What we do here is far more...*advanced*. Is that the best you have for us?"

Huxley's heart sank. Anyone else would have been incredibly impressed. He thought for a moment. *Ok, what is the best thing that I know? What would truly impress her?* He knew the answer already but dreaded it. He only used it once and it hurt so many people.

"Fine, then," Onders said while standing up and heading for a doorway. "I grade you beginner statu-"

"Wait!" Huxley yelled up into the stands. "I have one last thing to show you."

"No, you had your chance. And I have wasted nearly thirty minutes of research time with you. Follow me out."

"No!" Huxley shouted, surprising even himself.

Onders disappeared from view and instantly appeared in front of him. The air cracked and a plum of purple smoke grew from her robes. Something pushed Huxley backwards. An unseen force.

"You forget your place," Her voice was cold and violent. "Right now, you are walking out of here with your life and nothing more. Shout at me one more time like the uneducated whelp you are and you won't see Mayburn again."

Huxley looked away frightened but couldn't help himself. "I can do far more, and I have learned so much. Please, just one more try."

Onders snorted derisively and shifted backwards. "You are woefully unworried about your own life."

When Onders moved, Huxley finally saw what had pushed him.

"I can break your defense."

"You...*what?*" Onders replied, not trying to hide the condescension in her voice.

"I see it now. You have angular-like netting. It absorbs like mine but is more rigid. It's a matrix of smaller rigid shields to form a whole. I can beat that." Huxley explained.

Onders' pale face turned crimson. Her whole body tensed up and she said, "I dare you to try. This netting as you put it is the most perfect way to block incoming forces and has withstood far more than you could ever hope to produce." She spun and walked to the center of the arena. "Very well, then, your desperation will be your end. If you manage to break my defense then I won't kill you for wasting my time."

Now that Onders had moved a distance away from Huxley, it revealed her full network. Huxley had indeed been right. It was a pattern of hexagons that floated in front of her. Semi-translucent, it was difficult to see from far away or looking straight on. But at an angle, he noticed how the light refracted around it. Huxley knew what to do, or at least he hoped he knew. He resummoned his bubble. It pulled again at his knowledge, making him briefly unsteady. This marked the most Magnincy he had ever used before. If he didn't win here, that would be the end. His mind was feeling taxed by the draw he was undertaking.

Onders noticed and laughed at his effort. "Having trouble keeping your thoughts clear? A wicked smile plastered on her face. She was enjoying herself. This was a person who enjoyed playing games. It was possible that she was drawing this out because she liked the distraction. Her threats and air of superiority were so unlike the young girl that had left Mayburn. She was enjoying threatening him. In some terrible way, Huxley realized this seemed to be a trait that appeared common among all Embers.

Huxley steadied himself. "Alright Onders, here's what saved my life once, and it's going to do it again."

The other stars left and only one remained. It danced in the air looking lost for a moment then found its path. Floating to just outside of his reach. He stepped forward grasping once again for it. When he reached his furthest and could go no further, it floated into his hand. As he held it, he felt no pull on his knowledge like the others. It was just as before, smooth like a river stone but rippled outwardly. His mind remained sharp and he saw what he had to do. Onders was in the middle of the room surrounded by the four pillars. Huxley lobbed it high into the air in an arc. He leaped behind one of the stone pillars and braced himself.

The star exploded in all directions releasing a tide of sound. There was a scream and a thud as Onders slammed to the ground. The star shot in thousands of directions, all at once, releasing spears of bright light. Huxley's defensive bubble exploded again and the pillar he was hiding behind fell into rubble.

He leapt up feeling shaky, and found Onders on her back, glassy-eyed. The other three pillars remained but had become more porous as a result of the attack. Onder's shield was gone. She carefully pulled herself back to her feet. Huxley felt a surge of joy. Onders looked angry enough to kill. He had done it! Surely that was impressive enough to gain him entrance.

Suddenly, Huxley's mind shut down and he was no longer in control of his own thoughts. A vaguely familiar voice spoke to him, one he couldn't remember hearing before but still was somehow familiar. Like it came from his own brain, it said "Reach." When it released his mind, Huxley's eyes closed and he collapsed onto the floor.

Huxley stood at the sea once more. He had walked rather far out this time. He looked up into the night sky where the cosmos was laid bare. It had never been so clear before. All of the answers to his insatiable curiosity were out there. But the water...the warm ocean water pulled him ever deeper. The more he looked, the more the two joined at the horizon. In fact, the longer he stared, the more he couldn't tell which was which, the water became the stars and the stars, the ocean. Who could tell the difference? Just as he was about to slip away into the current, he felt something pull him back. His own body instinctively reacted. Was it fear? No, it was purpose. Now was not the time for resting. He had just done something good. What was it? He felt like he was in the middle of something, but was just placed into the ocean at night. *Purpose*...he felt it again. The ocean-pull lessened and his mind cleared. I have to....do....something....he thought so slowly. It was like trying to sprint in deep, thick mud. The familiar voice returned "Keep reaching, keep searching, you are so close to me...." The voice faded and Huxley awoke. He jerked his arms only to find himself bound to a bed.

—————————————————————————————————-

Walters stooped over Huxley and put away his smelling salts.

"He's waking up." He said over his shoulder. A conversation halted behind him.

"What is this for?" Huxley demanded.

Walters looked him over, studying him. "Can't say for sure, but he seems alright."

Onders shoved him out of the way. "Of course, he's not! See! Madness has taken over. Let me end him!"

Huxley's former opponent produced a silver hooked blade from her robes. The prison torches reflected off of it sharply. Huxley jerked wildly at his restraints as the dagger drew near.

"I think he has his senses, young master," Walters said to Onders. It was enough to make her stop advancing. She still held the knife firmly and far too close for Huxley's liking.

"What's your name?" Onders demanded.

"Uhh, Huxley?"

"Where are you?" She went on.

"The college of-"

"How big is that door? In centimeters."

Huxley looked at it trying to think of a smart guess but couldn't. He kept glancing at the knife.

"How could I know that?"

"Ugh, what are the compounds of this blade?" Her face twisted with annoyance.

"I read about that once...hang on let me think."

"No, silence. You're unworthy of-"

"I broke your defense!" Huxley interrupted her.

She straightened and shot a side glance at Walters who didn't react. "No, you lashed out in a foolhardy attempt to-"

He cut her off again, "foolhardy maybe, but I *did* break your defense."

Onders' composure melted and she made for Huxley.

"That's enough girl! He is clearly fine and you have wasted enough of your research time." A voice said from outside of Huxley's view.

Onders held Huxley's gaze as she sheathed her weapon. Her eyebrows shook in anger but she held whatever argument she had inside and left the cell.

Walters whistled and ran his fingers through his thin white hair and released Huxley from his bindings. "I thought I'd have to mop you up after that. What did you do to her in there?"

Huxley didn't respond. He was too alarmed to make sense of the situation.

He lowered his voice and said "That little jerk is the most insufferable of all the Embers around here...thanks."

"Thanks?!" Huxley blurted.

"Yeah, no one talks like that to..." He leaned down to unfasten his restraints and continued "...well, to anyone around here. I bet she'll really hate you now."

Huxley rubbed his wrists and sat up.

Walters continued, "Well, gather your things and follow me, I will take you to your room."

"Wait, so am I in? Did I pass?"

"Not for me to say, I just need to show you to your room. But for what it's worth, I'd say you did. We haven't had a new trainee in some time. It's like the Embers lost interest."

Walters beckoned Huxley to follow. If Huxley had been turned around in the tower before, he was absolutely lost now. He just trusted that Walters was taking him to the right place. The journey to his room was far less exciting than he had hoped for. Huxley wished to have one more glimpse at the library before bed, but the corridors they navigated were only dimly lit by lichen and the stone walls all looked the same. Walters just seemed to know which way to go. Huxley secretly hoped to learn the layout of the college quickly. It would be so embarrassing to have to admit he was lost. Periodically, a robed individual would pass by without notice or even a glance. After a quarter-hour, they arrived at a door that could have been the same exact one they left from. Walters opened it for him and revealed a small dorm room. It had a bed, privy and wooden desk with a few half-spent candles surrounding it. The bed was disheveled, and Huxley didn't dare check the privy. The difference from the room he last stayed in was substantial.

"...This one seems occupied." He said out loud.

"Hmm? Oh no, not anymore...he's gone now. You can make use of it for the night. You have a meeting in the morning. Be ready for it." Walters said.

Huxley perked up. "A meeting? Like with an entry committee? Or an admissions counselor!"

"Sure, yeah an admissions counselor." Walters chuckled, "See you at dawn."

"But it's still early. What should I do for the rest of the night?"

"What any good Ember would do. Study." And he motioned to a small collection of books under the bed. The door shut behind him and Huxley was left alone. Huxley hurried over to the books and began reading the titles. There were a few science books and some children's stories. He couldn't help but be disappointed. He was hoping for an ancient tome that would unlock at least some of the mysteries of the Grimoire. He felt foolish thinking that a book that valuable would be stuffed under a bed. Valuable or not, he didn't want to waste the few hours he might have left, so he read. To his surprise, much of the information was already beneath his understanding. He had had so little access to science books that he assumed he still didn't grasp the fundamentals, but perhaps the Grimoire had taught him more than he thought. His weariness caught up with him and he tried to sleep. The bed matched the room in its comfort. He knew he shouldn't have been disappointed. It was, after all, the exact place he wanted to be. But he couldn't help but compare it to the incredible bed he had experienced the night before. He instinctively looked for a window so that he could see the stars, but the walls held no such luxury. He drifted off to sleep.

16

Fuel and Coal

"Crystallization occurs when water molecules attach to pollen or dust in the air during sub freezing temperatures. The patterns are symmetrical as they run on the predetermined spaces of the..." **-Excerpt from Page 101 of the Grimoire**

The ocean and stars in his dreams were not a shock. In fact, this time he expected it. Off in the water he could make something out. It floated at the top of the ocean or it was hanging low from the stars. He only saw it because it was the one singularly dark place. No stars, no lapping waves. Just darkness. Was something out there? He reached outward and felt like it was reaching back when he thrashed awake. His sandy brown hair was soaked and clung to him. The cold stone floor was a shock as well.

But that was nothing compared to his realization that two Embers were present in his room. Were they just watching him sleep? Huxley got to his feet and regarded the men before him. The first had his hood low with only a skinny pointed chin for proof someone was in there. And the second's hood wasn't up at all, with a fleshy face and a balding head leaving nothing but horse-shoe pattern growth on the sides. . Seated behind them was a warden, with a pen, and inkwell at the ready, writing in a page full of notes.

"Good morning Huxley. Let's get started", the first said in a nasally voice. "Where did you learn to harness Magnincy?" Their presence and frankness threw Huxley off balance. He was still recovering from his dream.

He tried looking for his clothes when the warden barked, "Answer him!"

Huxley yelped in surprise and offered "Uhh Gulifo-"

"An obvious lie." The bald Ember denoted.

Huxley gulped and sat down on his bed. He was immediately thrown back up by an unseen force that made him stand.

"You've read this somewhere. We suspect you are either the foolish thief we've been looking for or foolish enough to have bought it from the thief, so which fool are you?"

Huxley blinked not knowing what to do or say.

"The knowledge you displayed took more than talent and careful study to acquire. You have neither of those. We will ask again." The pointy chinned Ember said, "Tell another lie, and it will be your last. Where is the Grimoire?"

"The Grimoire?" Huxley repeated. Their expressions perked up at the mere mention of it from him.

Huxley felt closed in on all sides. How had he been so foolish to believe he could pass himself off as one of them? Of course, they would see right through him. Now he would have to tell the truth. Somehow they knew everything already. He wouldn't dare lie again, but the truth would mean...well he didn't know what the truth would mean but they didn't seem to be the forgiving sort. It was then that another voice joined the room. One that he had heard the night before. *Run* it urged.

The idea was appealing to him at that moment, but he was still firmly in the grip of the Embers.

"Run where?" He squeaked.

Anywhere. It responded.

The embers shifted uncomfortably. "He hears him," The bald one said to the other, not bothering to lower his voice.

"Very well boy, you will be made to serve the Arcane Flame as fuel then."

"Fuel?"

"Everyone serves...some more useful than others. Your mind will be the fuel that allows others to grow brighter."

Huxley had made a lot of brash choices in his life up to this point. But none was more ill-advised than what he did next. He didn't know what the Ember meant by being fuel. But his explanation chilled him to his core.

Huxley seized Magnincy and attacked.

————————————————————————————————————

Huxley lay in a crumpled heap in the snow. The cold was leaching into his joints. Only his racing heart was keeping his will alive and thoughts of submitting to the freezing temperature at bay. Smoke rose from the tattered remains of his clothes. He was waking from a dream, a crazy one, where he actually attacked, not one, but two Embers. Suddenly, his stomach convulsed. He sat upright and wretched into the snow. Dinner mixed with blood. He finished, wiped his mouth, and got up. He tried recalling the last few minutes. How did he get out here? Wasn't he just deep inside the college...and then didn't he just have an awful confrontation...

A grim thought occurred, "It wasn't a dream..."

The sudden reality of his actions was sinking in and his stomach gave a repeat performance. Luckily, it was quite empty. His body shook and his head swam. His hopes were beginning to dissolve in front of him. What could he possibly salvage now...now that...he strained trying to remember what happened.

But when he tried, his mind exploded with thousands of other voices, each demanding his attention. Suddenly, his eyes became aware of everything around him; each snowflake's trajectory, its weight against gravity accounting for wind resistance and collision pathways with other flakes as well as the current temperature. The building's architectural requirements, load-bearing capacity, and composition of rock and stone mixed with mortar. His pile of vomit on the ground, the number of proteins, carbohydrates and lipids from dinner mixed with his blood. He could see how they separated and formed together. Then his own rhythmic breathing focused him on the oxygen entering his body, and he could even make sense of where it was being distributed amongst his red blood cells. All of this plus thousands of piles of coded letters inundated his waking mind. It demanded. No, screamed for his attention, flooding into his eyes and his brain, filling it like a hose filling a thimble. He reached his capacity instantly and then pleaded for clarity to anyone who could hear him. His legs flew into action before he asked them to. He ran blindly into the night, closing his eyes tightly trying to block out the information. It merely changed the subject. Suddenly, a hardened composition of fifty percent carbon, forty-one percent oxygen, and six percent hydrogen impacted his occipital lobe. It took him off his feet and the shock caused him to stop screaming, his throat now raw from the overuse of it.

"Shut up Bookpile...or I guess, Bloody Vomit Scream Pile...you're scaring Arktos!"

Huxley looked up and saw a young woman covered in microorganisms on her face, along with various degrees of decomposing plant matter. Her cloaked figure standing above him held a wooden-handled hatchet with a carnivorous mammal from the Ursidae family. The urisde's composition was in flux unlike everything else, and the figure's own swirling mind was of two different makeups. In fact, hers was as well. An impossibility that must be a mistake. As he grappled with this, and the rest of his incoming information, he felt himself being dragged by incisors and a few canines. The pounds per square inch was not sufficient enough to harm his epidermis but might give a mild contusion.

Occasionally a "shh", or, "You are actually sounding like a book right now Bookpile," worked its way into his ears.

After what seemed like hours the voices and information dulled and then retreated. By the time he was aware of his surroundings again, he sighed deeply. He was in his room at the Gearbox. The sun came in through the window and thankfully no statistics told him about the makeup of the window, the air, or the sunbeam. All was quiet. He lay still for a long time, happy in the silence. He tried to think about nothing...which proved unsuccessful, but he felt like only thinking about one thing at a time was just as good as nothing. Huxley stretched and felt his hand hit a basin full of warm water next to his bed. It had a few rung-out rags next to it. He climbed out of bed carefully, still not totally trusting his own body to work properly. Thankfully it did as he asked it to. He found himself dressed in underwear and smelling ripe. Other than some scrapes and bruises, he didn't seem to be badly injured. He fingered his old rib injury and marveled again at how it was healing. He made his way to the trunk and checked for the grimoire. It sat safely inside and hopefully it would stay that way.

He picked it up and cradled it in his arms and he thought about the note, *Upon my death or madness, deliver this Grimoire to its heir.* A bit of the haze of yesterday was lifting and he remembered the Embers asking about it. Was it really theirs? Was the grimoire stolen and accidentally left for Huxley to find? Or was he really its heir? His heart sank at the notion, of course, he couldn't be its heir. How could he be? The simpler explanation was that it was stolen from them with this note already in it. Its true owner was someone destined to unlock its knowledge; someone who probably wasn't mystified by its contents. He'd always wanted to be an Ember, to be someone who people looked up to and respected, instead of a failure of a student, soldier, and everything else. Was this journey of his just one last ditch effort to try and be somebody before he settled into adult life...had his boyish dreams got him into real danger? Then he saw it again. The blood, the cries of pain, and the look of utter savagery. If Huxley hadn't been there, Mayburn might not exist. The thought comforted him marginally. He might not be a hero on a journey, but he certainly had a mission to accomplish. He decided that he didn't care if he was the heir or not, it had come to him and he would use it to save his town. If the college wouldn't have him, he'd just have to learn by himself.

Just then, he heard the door downstairs open and boots clomp into the Gearbox. He couldn't make out their voices, but it didn't seem like customers stopping by for a friendly visit. Huxley pressed his ear close to the bottom of the door to try and hear when a wall panel slid open with a metallic clink. A chute of silver, rust and soot sat exposed in his room.

Engraved on the inside was the message "Slide down". Huxley didn't like the look of it and decided not to listen to the message. It was probably just a malfunction, he was more worried that the rest of the walls were hiding chutes. He cast a suspicious eye around his room when a familiar voice slank under the door.

"You will not prevent me." It commanded.

He could hear pleading objections from Abernathy and could only vaguely make out the conversation. Words like "Guests" "Privacy" and "Stew" could only keep the figures occupied for so long. The boots began to move with purpose. They were fanning out, searching the building. He could hear them getting nearer. Huxley's jaw clenched at the sounds of footfalls on the stairs. Who were they looking for? He remembered that he had attacked someone...not just someone...Embers. Suddenly, he recognized the voice. It wasn't just a guard's voice. It was Ryla the Butcher of Valdannon. The boots stopped at each door on the second floor. How many doors before his room at the top of the stairs? One? Two? He couldn't remember. The voices were closer now and he could hear shouts of outrage from guests. Suddenly, the open pipe seemed quite inviting. Huxley made for it as the guards' shadows lined the bottom of his door. He put a hand inside when smoke billowed out and hit him in the face. He did his best to suppress a choke and coughing fit. It was like coal dust was being poured down his throat. The handle to the door began to twist but it was locked. The guards rattled it back and forth before a boot crashed into the door, making Huxley jump. He weighed his options and climbed into the pipe, right as he was about to let himself slide down into the darkness, he remembered...*the Grimoire*...he grabbed the sides of the pipe before he free-fell and flung himself back out. The boots kicked four or five more times and the door began to crack. Abernathy's voice rose up asking them to give him a moment so he could find the key; it was a fine cedar door and breaking it wasn't necessary. His pleas didn't slow the assault. Huxley seized the Grimoire off the bed and left everything else. The door was splintered now. He leapt into the pipe feet first and slid down just as the door gave way. Huxley's body hit a lever on the way down swinging the panel shut.

Black coals surrounded him, and for a moment he felt a warm sense of relief. But that warmness was merely him reaching the bottom of the coal pile to find some that were still quite hot. He yelped and clambered to get off the pile as fast as he could, spilling onto the ground and clutching the Grimoire tightly to keep it safe. The room he was in was too dark to make out much. Trying to catch his breath he heard, voices emanating from his room. The metal of the chute gave their voices a tinny resonance but it was easier to understand than the muffled voices through his locked door.

"We know the boy was here, Norun. Our agreement is becoming difficult to keep. He is a thief and an enemy of the city. Ryla will find him, and we can't be held in breach of contract for what she does to him. The Embers have commanded it." One of them said.

"He stayed here a day ago and went off to join your school!" Abernathy avowed. "I hope he got in. Frankly, he was overly strange, loved talking about measurements and figures. I know you folks are always looking for recruits, so I didn't think anything of it." Abernathy stated coolly.

"Just remember your position here, Norun, if we find out you lied..."

"Of course, I'll inform you right away if I find out anything," He reassured, "How about in the meantime, I pack you up with another case for your troubles."

The voices moved away from the room, too far to hear anymore. After a few more minutes they left, and a moment later, Elatress's voice called down from the pipe, "hey Bookpile...you didn't get stuck did you?"

"No." He answered back.

A few minutes later an imposing metal door above him swung open with a screech and light and fresh air flooded the room. Able to see now, Huxley spotted a staircase leading up. Abernathy appeared at the top of the stairs and slowly made his way down with Elatress behind him. He patted Huxley down attempting to remove some of the soot. "The Embers, The Wardens, *and* The Butcher....now what did you do to win all of that attention?"

———————————————————————————————-

Ryla marched towards her destination. Seething at the loss of her quarry, she gripped her halberd in frustration. Her armor clinked to the rhythm of her steps. Abernathy had clearly been hiding something. But she had never been any good at discerning people's words. Lies and truth were so closely related to each other, how could you ever see one and not the other? To Ryla everything was partially a lie and partially true, the trick was seeing how much of each was present. Hunting had never been her talent either, she longed to be finished with it. Who this kid was and the book he stole did not matter to her. She reminded herself why she was doing this and it strengthened her resolve.

She was flanked by city guards that walked in discord from one another. Who knows if they were even aware how out of sync they were. The racket gave her a headache. She modeled a perfect cadence step for them to follow but they were either too ignorant or just didn't care. But they were nothing compared to the Warden that accompanied her. That wreck of a man walked so discordantly, it shocked her that he could remain upright. It was more like each step was catching him from falling down. What was worse was that no one besides herself seemed to notice. The frustration caused her to start seeing a new landscape. One that she had envisioned many times, screams were a part of it, but the painting was more about screaming silence. A silence that was so serene and beautiful; a silence that cried out for her to create it. She put it out of her mind, not now. Soon she would paint, and soon everyone would know her brilliance. A smirk formed as she thought of the term they'd given her.

The Butcher.

She would trade anything to be as precise and elegant as a butcher, but that meant something else here. Here in Danador, it referred to some moron hacking at dead animals. But in Valdannon, a true butcher could arrange cuts so lithe and precise you'd think the meat had been born that way. The title of butcher in Valdannon was the mark of a true artisan and sculptor of reality. The difference was like night and day here; she quietly enjoyed the complement of her nickname while being keenly aware they meant something else. They passed by a wanted poster that always made Ryla happy. The poster was everywhere now, it depicted a man with a large mask with a nose that curved like a bird's. It was strangely beautiful, shocking and bold, it demanded attention. It wouldn't stand out in her homeland but it did here. It was still dreadfully vacant of color. She imagined him with tinged green and yellow, or perhaps a purple base with long red streaks. She felt her anger subsiding, now that she could imagine something else worth doing. Finding him would be wonderful right now, the red streaks occurred to her again but in swathes, splayed out in every direction. She continued musing until she arrived back at the Warden's office. He shuffled out in his maddening gait, he managed to walk much like the rabble she'd been assigned to.

"Success?" He asked with a weak smile.

"None." She responded.

"Was he lying? How did he seem?" He responded.

"Nearly everything people say is partially a lie. What would be different about what he said?" She retorted.

Just then the other Warden, subservient to the one she encountered, now stepped forward and cleared his throat with an intentioned cough.

The Wardens regarded each other and did a formal acknowledgment of each other's rank. The higher one dismissed the guards and turned to her. "Very well, we appreciate your time Butc-uhh Ryla of Valdannon. We will handle it from here, dismissed."

Ryla longed for just that order but couldn't help herself, she was too curious, and asked "Warden, if he really is an Ember in training, why send me and not fully trained Embers? Would I even be a match for him?"

The Warden reached for her hand, grasping it firmly and said.

"You? Oh Ryla, I have yet to meet anyone who would be your match. And I pray you never find them in our city. No, we sent you to intimidate them. He is likely a coward at his core and will run home. We cannot allow it, of course. He knows too much. And of course, our Embers were attacked. That can't go unpunished. If word got out, there would be blood in the streets. But until he is found, we needn't pull the Embers from their studies. We deployed you instead."

Ryla appreciated what he said, it was after all, part of her job here. Chasing some boy through the streets was hardly fitting for her ability but it was better than standing guard. Far better. She again remembered why she was here.

"Only a few weeks now before your big moment, huh?"

"Yes," she admitted, "When I will prove to Danador I am far more than a Butcher."

"Far more, indeed." He released her hand and began discussing events with his fellow Warden, they both smiled when he showed that Abernathy had given them an extra barrel of his brew. They slowly moved it into their offices and remained there. Ryla turned back to the snowy streets becoming once again bored by the constant white and gray...

This city really could use a dash of color.

17

∽

Legs and Machines

"The flow of Magnadun reaches all who live on it. Those that see what is, what could be, who they are, and what is around them. Especially those that are burdened with seeing even more than that." **-Page 2 Excerpt from the Grimoire**

Holding a steaming mug of...something...Huxley sat on a broken-in couch. Its worn leather stretched and creaked as he got comfortable. The hearth was stoked to a steady flame by Abernathy. Huxley told the story of his time disembarking the train until now. It had only been a day, but a lot happened.

They sat for a time in silence as Abernathy considered what Huxley told him. His reaction so far had surprised Huxley in that he didn't seem surprised at all.

Elatress followed along with "Oohs" and "Ahhs," but he felt like she was more making fun of him than empathizing. Recalling the events was difficult. When he finally finished telling them what happened, his drink was cool enough to sip. Before he could bring the cup to his mouth, Abernathy got up. He walked over and gave Huxley a hug that reminded Huxley of Captain Pilch. The hug wasn't expected, but greatly needed. He hadn't fully thought through what had occurred to him over the last day. Kindness right now was as welcome as a thick blanket on a cold night.

When Abernathy released him, he felt better. Abernathy raised his eyebrow at Elatress and she hugged him as well. It was awkward but Huxley didn't mind. As long as Arktos didn't get up and try, he'd be happy. Abernathy sat tapping his leg making a "tink", "tink" sound each time. When it struck Huxley as odd, he finally looked at it. His real leg was replaced by a metallic one. A fake leg wasn't the most uncommon thing, but he had never seen one of this make! It seemed to function exactly as his original one had. The engineering alone on it was unheard of. Huxley had questions he didn't feel were appropriate to ask. In fact, Huxley had many questions, of course, not fully understanding why things transpired as they did. But, he doubted Abernathy would know.

He also realized Abernathy may not be ready to seriously house a fugitive. He started to wring his hands at the thought. Could he really survive long as a fugitive? He surely couldn't ask anyone to help him. That would only endanger them as well.

What other options did he have now...he couldn't try to squeak out an existence in the Fecundity...and he definitely couldn't go back home. They would watch there for sure. He felt foolish even trying to strategize a path for himself. If he wasn't out of his depth before, he certainly was now.

He finally took a sip from his mug. It was spiced tea of some kind, and unexpectedly pleasant, Huxley had braced for something stronger. He got the feeling Abernathy only brewed stuff that could either kill you or bring you back to life. He took another sip and sighed as he looked up at the two tapestries again. He ignored the one he had seen before of the Arcane Flame holding back the darkness. The strange one was a whirlpool of colors and shapes. He remembered his thoughts from the last time he saw it. It reminded him of an idea forming in someone's head. The tapestry looked different in this light. He couldn't remember if it was as well-lit last time but this time it was. The colors were more true and the lines sharper. With only fire light, it was difficult to see the whole picture as it was meant to be. Then a depression caught his eye beyond the tapestry. It was covering up a section of wall that was storing something metallic.

Finally, Abernathy spoke.

"Huxley, you may have guessed by now, but Elatress and I are no-"

"And Arktos," She interrupted.

"Hmm? Oh, yes, of course, Elatress and I and Arktos are not true supporters of Danador."

A "hmph" came from under the bar.

"In fact" he went on, "We may even be labeled as enemies of the state if certain activities were brought to light."

He paused as if to arrange his next words carefully.

But Huxley interrupted. "They called you Norun".

Abernathy sighed and said "Yes they did. That's because I am one."

Huxley gasped and stammered, "You! You can't be. The Norun are the reason the world broke, they tried to destroy the planet, or control it...and they all died in the attempt. Now only their ghosts stalk the scorched remains of their cities." Huxley trailed off realizing how ridiculous he probably sounded.

Abernathy chuckled and said, "Well, that accounts for the loss of my leg but the rest is..." He winced and said, "I don't want to lie to you...many of the stories you've likely heard are true. My people, and by extension myself, are responsible for much of the world's larger problems. We certainly had a hand in it."

He gestured armistice trying to calm Huxley's immediate reaction and said, "I assure you, I am quite safe and am no boogeyman. And I really don't want to overburden you with more information. For now, let me just say, I am not the Ember's friend, and neither is Elatress OR Arktoss."

She nodded in confirmation.

"You two are...criminals?" Huxley asked.

"According to them, yes," Elatress interjected.

The frankness of her answer gave him pause. Huxley had still hoped that maybe there was a pathway that could lead to some form of forgiveness from the Embers. The longer he stayed here, the longer that felt further from possible.

"And now" he went on, "It seems you are on the other end of their wrath as well. That is why I believe we can help each other out."

Abernathy was right, this new information was burdensome to his mind. He felt like he had just come out of a fog and now he was getting all new problems to deal with.

Sensing his hesitation, Abernathy stated, "For now though let's focus on you. Are you sure you're feeling well? What you went through shatters most Ember's minds. It's ok, if you're having trouble, just tell me so I know what to expect."

Huxley blinked a few times. He wondered if what happened to him was the madness that Guliford told him about. He remembered screaming, flailing, and raving lunacy. Huxley realized he had never actually seen a "mad" person before, but last night, he probably qualified.

But what had happened to him was understandable. It was like seeing everything that could be learned all at once. Or like all of the contents of a library poured into his head and he had to make sense of it. It was enough to make anyone lose touch with reality for a moment. He certainly didn't feel mad now.

If anything he was feeling pretty good, at least, physically.

"Are you handy with machinery?" Abernathy asked.

"Machines, like, am I good with hammer and nails? I am a pretty good cobbler." He said.

"Uhh, yeah hammer and nails' ' Abernathy repeated. "Good. How about this Hux? You stay here for a week, free of charge, help me with some projects downstairs, and we will keep you out of sight and make sure your head is clear. During that time, you can ask me all the Norun boogeyman questions you'd like. If at the end of that week you want to leave, then by all means do. If you want to stay and get involved with what Elatress and I are up to, then we would welcome you."

He stuck out his hand waiting for Huxley.

"A week of work and at the end, I can leave?"

"If you'd like."

The crackle of the fireplace and the low snoring sounds of Arktos were the only things to be heard.

Huxley considered his situation: head out to the streets and perhaps be found by Ryla or take a gamble with these two.

They were certainly strange, but Huxley did have a good feeling about them. And there was the opportunity to meet and talk to a real Norun, two in fact, if Elatress was one as well. Huxley did hear they traveled in packs like roving predators. Huxley shook his hand not having close to a better option.

"Can I also practice some?" He asked.

"Magnincy! Here?" Elatress blurted out. She shifted in her seat and said "Not inside, we have enough trouble keeping the building together."

"Together?" He repeated.

"Yeah, Bookpile. It gets loud and shifty here."

"She's right, it does." Abernathy huffed and said, "Perhaps you should take a week off and rest your mind." He said gently.

"Take time off? I heard, in order to be good at this, you need constant practice."

"That does seem to be true, but you just put your mind back together. You went mad you know, I'd say that warrants a good rest." Abernathy smiled faintly.

"So it was madness?" Huxley felt a bulge in the pit of his stomach.

"Yes." Elatress and Abernathy said in unison.

"How? I've done Magnincy before and I never freaked out like that." Huxley protested.

Elatress leaned forward and said, "All Embers go crazy, it's not right to wield that kind of power. You just have a head start. You'll turn into a crazy young man rather than a crazy old man."

Huxley started but Abernathy spoke up and said "Uhhh, well, that's not necessarily true. The way Embers do things does produce amazing results, but they also push themselves incredibly hard. It isn't too surprising that it causes their minds to fracture. That's why we are so concerned for you."

"I did get better though," Huxley said.

"That's true, you did. And far faster than I've heard they can." It takes

Embers days to heal. Maybe the first madness is easier, but progressive bouts get harder. I don't know."

"First and hopefully last," Huxley said.

"Hopefully," said Elatress. "But not likely," she quipped. "About as likely as me quieting my own or Abernathy–"

"Ahh, that's enough El", Abernathy interjected.

Huxley blinked and looked at both of them finally saying "You two as well?"

"I don't suffer madness." Elatress said, "Madness is not knowing what's happening. I know what's happening."

Not addressing her, Abernathy stood up and said. "You're in good company, is what we're trying to say, Huxley. All of the children of Magnadun can draw from her power, but it can leave lasting impacts if not approached carefully. As I said before, I will answer any questions you have. But first, we need to get the Gearbox ready. It's almost time for the lunch rush. Elatress, you're host and server. I'll cook...and Huxley, you're on the dishes."

"Dishes?" Huxley frowned.

"Yeah, Bookpile, scrap anything that has big chunks into Arktos's trough. Try and sneak in a few vegetables, he needs it."

Arktos protested weakly with a long, low whimper.

"You DO! You only eat meat and gristle. A carrot won't kill you! Got that Bookpile? Meat and carrots."

Abernathy got up and made for the kitchen. As Huxley moved to follow, his stomach gurgled in alarm. The spiced tea had made its way through him swiftly. He ran for the bathroom. After what felt like an embarrassingly long time, he finally emerged. He really had to stop drinking here. Huxley heard hissing pans and bubbling pots from the kitchen. Elatress was behind the counter and tossed him an apron.

"Welcome to the Gearbox, junior employee Huxley. Pay is low and the hours are bad, but we won't try and kill you. And that's a unique benefit only we offer. I'll see you after the rush."

She began cleaning the bar and paused. She looked at the door and yelled through the kitchen window. "Doc workers! Six of them, cod stew would be my bet."

"Cod stew" Abernathy repeated back.

Huxley looked at the door and six men in overalls and wool sweaters came in. Huxley shot a look at Elatress, "Like he said, you're in good company, now get to work!"

———————————————————————————————————-

Three hours went by and Huxley's hands had become deeply pruned from constant submersion in dishwater. It was nice to focus on scrubbing plates and placing them on a rack. It struck him as oddly therapeutic. There was nothing difficult about it. Just keep up, scrub hard and place it neatly. He repeated the process and found himself relaxing. He was actually disappointed when Elatress said it was the last plate. Maybe it was because he was good at it. The only thing he'd accomplished in the past few days was being confused and frustrated and almost getting himself killed.

Abernathy thanked him for his work and told him he had a two-hour break before the dinner crowd came in. Elatress had already left with Arktos. He got the sense that mid-afternoon was a great time to relax. Huxley dried off his hands, went to his room to change, sat at his desk and opened the Grimoire. It was the first time he had read it since meeting the Embers. He flipped through the pages. It felt different. Learning that it may have been stolen made him feel like he had broken into someone else's diary. That had always been true to some degree, he never truly felt like it was his. Nevertheless, he had been given the opportunity and he took it. He didn't feel like a thief but he didn't feel honest about it either. Maybe he should give it back, shove it in a bag and drop it on their doorstep. Then maybe they would just leave him alone. He shook his head "no" at the thought. He had done too much, seen too much and told them too much. Like or it not, he was an enemy of the Embers. His only real hope now was to find the real thief and clear his name, which seemed highly unlikely. The other option was to hide out long enough for everything to blow over. He liked the second idea more but felt the outcome was just wishful thinking. A smell caught his nose and Huxley shut the book, deciding it was time for a bath. It had been a while since he had cleaned himself properly. Maybe after a long soak, he would have an idea of what to do.

He had no such luck. He was without any real plan, the schedule Abernathy put him on was arduous. Elatress wasn't kidding when she said the hours were bad. Early mornings in the machine shop along with hard afternoons and late nights helping in the kitchen. It did afford one amazing thing that made the hard work worth it. Huxley got to help out in Abernathy's machine shop. Under the Gearbox tavern and inn was an actual gearbox. His naming of the tavern wasn't a fun way to appeal to the industry workers of the city. There was a large subterranean work-shop that Abernathy used to build all manner of things. Huxley was limited in his ability to help or even understand what he was working on, but he was happy for the opportunity to watch. Chief Engineer was an understatement for his title. Machinery whirled and spun to life around him, and Abernathy did the same. While he worked, he would become so engrossed, he would sometimes talk to the project. Most of his efforts seemed to be on smaller parts of larger machines. Joints to something that needed to rotate three hundred and sixty degrees, pistons that were firing too slowly, interlocking gears that ground. Mostly steam powered with some making use of coal instead. The most puzzling thing was, Huxley could not tell where the power sources were. It was easy enough to see that they ran on something, but Abernathy never lit a burner or powered it on via his own machinery. He always placed them, when finished, next to the entrance of the Gearbox. Elatress would sometimes take them out or they would just get picked up by someone else. The door would simply open, a man would stick his head in and tip his cap and grab the item. Huxley was so impressed with Abernathy's work that he had neglected his side of the agreement for the first two days. He hadn't asked him any questions about the Norun. Huxley certainly wanted to, it was just that the more he thought about them, the more ridiculous the stories became. Clearly Abernathy was no monster, nor had he come from a long line of them. Questions begged to be asked, but Abernathy was so focused that it never felt like a good time.

On the third day at the Gearbox, he finally asked.

"So how far north is Norun?"

"In miles? Around fifteen hundred. You can make it in a few months on foot."

"Do monstrous beasts really live there?"

"Yes, but they're here too, in the Wilds. The ones up north are more suited for the cold."

"Is it true that the Norun are the reason the world changed?"

"We believe so, yes."

"What happened?"

"Now that I don't know. In fact, it's a lot of the reason why I'm here."

"What was that thing that you shot at me on the train? The caged doll?"

Abernathy laughed, "It's part of a game that Elatress and I made, but also a prototype for something bigger."

"A game?" Huxley asked.

"Yeah, Ballistics and Bureaucrats, the game can be won by either. You fling barbarians, fire, or plague into the opponent's city with catapults. Then your bureaucratic responses limit the damage. You have to outlast, outfire and out-plan your opponent. It's a work in progress," Then he remembered something, "that's also a trademarked name and game."

"Trademarked?"

"Yeah, like the Gearbox, trademarked. Everyone will copy my ideas otherwise. Like Horace, he wouldn't be in business at all if it wasn't for him stealing from me."

"Horace?"

"Yeah, Horace."

"What other things can your metal leg do?" He asked.

Abernathy stopped working and stood up, he looked affronted as he removed his goggles, "What other things does it do?" He asked incredulously.

"Yeah, like, hold extra tools, or conceal weapons, or double as a communications device?"

Abernathy clunked his leg hard onto the floor and said, "Do you know how hard it is to replace a whole piece of your body, and not only replace it but have it be able to keep perfect balance with you? Most people ram a peg into what's left of a stump leg and call it a replacement. Mine is perfectly suited to match my old one in every way! It doesn't need anything else. It keeps me upright. And that should amaze you!" Clearly, this was a touchy subject for him.

"Sorry, I had just assumed since so many other things around here aren't what they seem..."

Abernathy just huffed in annoyance and muttered "I'd like to see you make a better one."

Undeterred, Huxley kept his questions going for as long as Abernathy would allow. He allowed it for quite some time. Abernathy, Huxley found out, was well-traveled. He was in fact from the north of Magnadun and was one of the Norun people, but he had also circled most of Magnadun. Huxley hadn't met any foreigners before besides a few from Valdannon. He'd heard stories of people from the west, and only rumors of the ocean folk, but the Norun were the real mystery. People chatted about the others beyond the Fecundity but no one ever really knew. His friends and family loved to tell stories around the dinner table or late at night but he'd never thought much of it was true. Abernathy could be feeding Huxley stories that couldn't be substantiated, but something about Abernathy made Huxley believe. Perhaps it was the authority with which he spoke or his demeanor; he had always heard a good bartender was easy to talk to.

Finally, Huxley asked, "Do the Norun use Magnincy, like the Embers do?"

"No", he answered, "we are far more powerful and far more useful."

Huxley's eyes went wide.

"How can that possibly be? MORE powerful than an Ember? I haven't seen you do anything besides be smart." Huxley accused.

Abernathy put his tools down and looked at Huxley. His amber eyes met Huxley's. They still shone brightly even in the basement.

"I said, I wouldn't lie to you." Abernathy declared.

Abernathy closed his eyes and began to hum. His face relaxed and became impassive. His hum grew louder. It was slow and dull, devoid of rhythm. He pressed his palms together in what looked like a form of prayer. After a moment passed, all of the machinery stopped at once. The air reverberated and shook Huxley's insides. All motion in the room stopped. The machinery hung lifeless, almost sagged like a tired guard propped up on his spear. Elatress came bursting through the door and rushed over to Abernathy. He faltered and lost his balance. Elatress slid on the floor to grab him before he hit the ground. Huxley gasped and ran over to him as well.

"You...you can run this whole place!?" He surprised himself with how loud he yelled.

"Give him a second, Bookpile!" Elatress protested.

She sat him up and patted him down.

"What happened? Did the bell ring?" It's way too early for that." She asked.

"No, no not that. Just showing Huxley that Magnincy is universal."

"You could have just told him"

"I really don't think I would have believed him," Huxley said, amazed.

Elatress shot him a look. "Are you happy now?"

Huxley didn't have a response. Happy? How about shocked, bewildered, amazed and frightened? If one Norun could run all of these machines with Magnincy...

"So you're like the Embers." Huxley tried to clarify.

"Well, it's more accurate to say the Embers are like me." He stated carefully. "I'll have to rest now."

Elatress and Huxley helped him up but instead of going upstairs. Elatress guided him through a small side door near the furnace. Huxley stopped following as he got the impression it was a private room. He heard a bell chime several times. The hum of each ding danced through the air and diminished into silence.

Elatress came out a few minutes later. She motioned for him to follow her out. The workshop struck him as eerily quiet after seeing it in full operation. The silence creeped him out, like the machines themselves were more than just "off", but that the life had been taken out of them. Huxley shivered thinking about it.

His schedule said they were supposed to get ready for lunch, but Elatress pulled a sign out that read "Closed" and hung it in the front door. When she latched the door, Arktos stirred awake. He shifted his weight to roll out from under the bar and made his way to the fireplace. He plopped down half on the couch and half on the floor.

"No lunch today?" Huxley asked.

"Probably not for a few days," Elatress replied

Huxley swallowed hard. "Is he going to be alright?

"Oh, he'll be alright. He goes for a few days at a time like that, then crashes. It's inconsistent for business but I enjoy the breaks. It doesn't bother me at all. I can leave..." She narrowed her eyes at Huxley and added "...and no one's going to tell him right?"

"Uhh, of course not."

"Good now, help me with this." She was trying to lift the massive stew pot. It was just beginning to bubble and smelled quite nice. Huxley lifted it with her. She brought it over to the hearth beside Arktos and gently sat it next to him. She said, "Eat up." but it was hardly necessary. His entire head had entered the cauldron before she began to speak. Arktos devoured the meal that was meant for over a dozen people. Elatress sat down next to him and stroked his fur. She hummed a song too quiet for Huxley to make out, especially with the noshing of Arktos.

Suddenly, her eyes flickered and she said, "Hey, want to go to a great place to practice?"

"Practice? Magnincy?" He asked.

"Yeah, you have to get better right? You're probably terrible at it after having gone crazy before. And I need some exercise. I'll show you a great place."

"But...I can't leave the Gearbox, I'm a fugitive, remember? I need to stay out of sight."

"No one will see us," she admonished him, "I do it all the time."

He did feel pretty cooped up at the moment, and it was true he did want to see more of the city but his fear of getting caught took priority.

Perhaps sensing his hesitance, she switched tactics and said, "Don't you want to stretch your legs and move a little? It's a few miles. Can you walk that far?"

"A few miles...of course I can." He affirmed.

"I sometimes ask because you book readers never move around much. I never know what you can and can't do.

Huxley pushed down his instinct that she was insulting him. He was getting the feeling that Elatress was just honest all of the time, no matter what. If nothing else, he could prove to her that he regularly completed five-mile loops in the Mayburn guard. He raced upstairs to get the Grimoire and met her back downstairs in only a few minutes. She had already changed and had her green cloak wrapped around her.

"Do you wear that everywhere you go?"

"No, only when I don't want to be seen or when I'm going to the wilds." She responded, "And we're doing both. You'd better bring a snack."

As if to abbreviate the point, Arktos let out a burp that shook the pot he'd been eating from causing it to reverberate like a bell.

18

Sewers and Pools

"Apis mellifera utilize hexagonal architecture to maximize the number of cells and minimize gaps making the structure both rigid and flexible."
-Page 419 Excerpt from the Grimoire

A half hour later, Huxley's feet were caked with what he hoped was just mud and his legs burned. Elatress and Arktos led the way through a sewer pipe that stretched on into the darkness. She moved confidently in the darkness. Huxley's vision was limited and he feared if he lost track of them, he'd be lost down there indefinitely. Periodically, sunlight would streak into the tunnels giving him a vague ability to track his progress; it mainly just served to allow him not to smash into a wall. Fortunately, Arktos was so loud that he was impossible to lose.

She would stop when the tunnel had a fork and wait for him to catch up.

"You said you could handle this." Her voice echoed softly.

"When you asked if I could walk a few miles, I thought you meant, *a few miles.*"

"This is a few."

"A few dozen you mean?"

She rolled her eyes and said "Barely one dozen round trip. That's what the snack was for. I know it's slower in the sewers but we don't run into people down here. It's a far better way to travel."

Huxley doubted that, but didn't feel he was in a position to argue. Ryla was up there along with the Embers and probably a bunch of Wardens on the lookout for him.

"And" she added, "we don't have to stop at all of those checkpoints."

"Yeah", Huxley conceded, "that is nice. What are all of those for anyway? Is it just about collecting clips or are the people dangerous?"

"That's probably more of an Abernathy question. He's always talking about the good sort of folk and the bad sort of folk. I can't really tell the difference. I really would like to know how to tell someday. It would be helpful."

Huxley heard a squelch of toes in the water and debris. He noticed that Elatress didn't have shoes on. "Oh, Elatress...uhh are you sure you don't want to put on some shoes?"

"Rarely, I can't see a thing otherwise."

As though anticipating more questions, Elatress flicked some of whatever was on her feet at Huxley and he recoiled violently trying to dodge.

"Come on Bookpile, we're almost out."

Huxley left it alone for now and traveled on as instructed. They walked all through the undercity slowing only under larger spillways to avoid detection. Elatress pointed out various things along the way, like the market square, and even the library he had seen before. It was all rather academic because he had no real way of seeing anything other than a few people and a small section of a building. But their mode of travel didn't offer much in the way of visibility. Eventually, they arrived at an opening in the pipes. It seemed hundreds of them were all cut off and pouring into a pool. In the center of that was a whirlpool pulling everything down. Huxley guessed before she said it. "That's the way out?"

"Yup."

Suddenly, Huxley's drive left him. "Can we go back, I don't want to practice anymore. My Grimoire will get wet."

"What's a Grimoire?" she asked.

"My big book." He amended.

"Well…use what it teaches you to make it so that you don't get wet."

He wasn't sure if she was joking or not, but it wasn't a bad idea.

"How long will we have to swim?"

"No swimming. It just pulls you in and spits you out."

"Well, how long does that take?"

"I've never counted. I just hold my breath. Arktos can do it, and he's always out of breath."

The giant bear was panting and looking for a place to sit.

Then an idea occurred to Huxley…what if his bubble defense actually trapped air in. He might have made a way to have at least a few extra breaths. Maybe, he could even try to take the hexagonal shapes he saw from Onders into account. He had even read about them recently. The idea worried him, what if he gets it wrong? No, he thought, he came out to practice. If he was going to survive, it was going to involve risks. Better now, than in front of an Ember. He told Elatress, "ok," and to give him a minute. He flipped through the Grimoire hoping to find what he had read about it. It still wasn't deciphered properly and he chastised himself for not doing a better job at it. Now, he could only hope for a mathematics page to be useful. It was one of the most difficult sections. Math is built on itself so you have to master the basics before you can do anything advanced. After a few pages, it abandoned numbers altogether and used letters. He wondered if adding the letters together would form words and that's how spelling got started. It didn't look like it. All of the formulas were either "X, Y, A, or B." You can't spell a lot with that. Stopping to think of what to try next, a voice next to him said "Try Zoology."

"Ok, I guess", he responded.

"Ok, I guess, what?" Elatress asked.

"For…" Huxley remembered where he had heard that voice, and it wasn't Elatress'. He slammed the book shut and looked around. Elatress, startled by his reaction said "What, what?! You found a new subject to read about?"

"I…no." He shook his head. This was the third time he heard something when no one else had. Perhaps madness was sneaking in faster than he thought. Next thing he knew, he would start seeing things. Then another voice came echoing down the pipes. This one was definitely not in his head. All three of them perked up. Arktos even got to his feet. It was a vaguely familiar voice that Huxley couldn't quite place. It seemed to be coming from miles away but they could still make it out. "Hear the feathered good news... and be glad, for violence...love and loss...talons of purity...clearness...and that's...hear me..." It lost some of its resonance periodically. It had clearly traveled some way.

"The feathered good news?" Huxley repeated.

"That's from the market square. I think this sewer connects to that one." She said pointing to a pipe spilling into the pool to their right. " It doesn't get a lot of use so it has less to absorb sound. A bunch of religious nutcases gather there sometimes. No need to be scared."

"Can they hear us?" He asked in a whisper.

"Us?" She laughed. "Even if they did, who would care about sewer voices? Now finish your reading."

He thought better of having a debate about it and let it drop. Curiosity had gotten the better of him, and he flipped to Zoology. It was mainly the anatomy of various creatures observed in the Fecundity. One sketch did catch his eye. Honey Bees, or rather honey bees if they were five times larger and fiercely territorial. The kind of bee it was illustrating looked large enough to kill a man. It had a harpoon shaped stinger and mandibles that could crush bone. But that wasn't what caught his eye. It was their honeycomb. It looked almost identical to Onder's defense, and was exactly what Huxley had been looking for. He scanned the page. "Drone behavior... mating habits...hierarchy...feeding habits...ah! Hive structure! Here we go." Elatress let out a, "Yipee," that dripped with sarcasm.

"Make fun all you want, but I see what she did and I think I can combine our ideas. Watch."

He reached out in his mind for Magnincy again, and like before the stars appeared before him. He reached and combined his bubble with the honeycomb structure. He felt the two pulling together into something new. They swirled in his hands. He didn't feel a pull on his mind as before. The knowledge was rooted and fresh. "Come closer you two." Arktos and Elatress listened and moved in. He took a sharp breath and released it. A grid snapped into structure around him. It formed a sphere centered on his chest and surrounded him in a ten-foot diameter. The three of them were thrust into the air with a jolt. The sphere encircled them and suspended Huxley in mid-air while Elatress and Arktos were pressed together on the bottom. "Whoops' ' Huxley said, "Looks like I focused on myself. Good thing I had you guys close in around me."

"Or else what?"

"Not sure...maybe you'd just be repelled...maybe you'd be-" The implications were troubling so he stopped.

Elatress looked up at Huxley floating above her. "Ok, you made your thing. Now what?"

Huxley leaned towards the pool and the bubble grid rolled underneath him. Still suspending him in place, he pushed it further. Elatress and Arktos cried out as they began rolling as well. It splashed into the water but held. Huxley gave a whoop of happiness and his heart leaped. The implications of combining ideas filled him with a joy he hadn't felt in some time. How much was there to discover? He suddenly and clearly understood the ferocity with which the Embers chose to study. If you could combine scientific ideas and construct them together...the limits might be endless to what he could do.

The three of them and their orb began to spin in the middle of the pool. Slowly, at first, and then swiftly picking up speed. Huxley's happiness tempered when he realized they were sinking. The water line rose only a few inches at first but rapidly increased. The honeycomb flexed under the water pressure and the bubble's film bulged inward. Elatress and Arktos were frozen in place.

"Uhh, hang on everyone." He said.

"To what?!" Elatress said more alarmed than Huxley had expected.

Arktoss gave a mixed growl and whimper.

"Anything, I guess." And Elatress grabbed onto Huxley's leg. Water enveloped the rest of the sphere and they were sucked under. Huxley marveled at the clarity. He could see underwater! The rush of the current propelled them. The tunnel curved suddenly to the left and Elatress yanked hard on his leg causing Huxley to cry out. "Ouch! Let go!"

"Definitely not!" She said, digging her nails in deeper. She was now fully hanging off the bottom and in doing so threw Huxley off balance. The sphere started spinning slowly at first then faster and faster. Elatress and Arktos tried to stay upright but that was a constantly shifting target.

The pressure began to greatly stress his shield. A mixture of joy and worry swirled through Huxley. On one hand, this was the best shield he had made by a huge margin. On the other, what if it collapsed and water smashed into them? By chance it lasted long enough. Elatress had been correct, it was a short trip. Their strange underwater vessel breached the surface shooting a few feet out of the water and splashing back down. They bumped up against a dock frightening a fisherman and causing him to yelp. Huxley released the defensive bubble and he splashed into the water. He reflexively grabbed at his Grimoire and tried to keep it over his head. The freezing water shocked his muscles and he nearly dropped it. Panic kept him from totally submerging and he managed to keep the Grimoire above the surface. Arktos was already pulling himself up onto the dock. Elatress pursed her lips together and said, "You should certainly practice more. That was the worst boat ride I've ever been on."

19

∽

45° and Mushrooms

"Singular fungal subterranean growth in small threads are called mycelium. These reach in a rough three hundred and sixty degree pattern causing a ring." -Page 432 Excerpt from the Grimoire

The docks shifted under foot and Huxley tried to steady himself. His legs shook from the cold but his body had grown quite warm from the extended hike and intensity of his newly discovered ability. Elatress just hugged Arktos until she emerged warmed, Huxley elected to just be chilly and keep moving.

The trio had arrived in the section missing from Danador, aptly named, The Forty-Five. It was an odd angled removal from the city that occurred during the shift. Why it happened to this portion of the city, was an enigma. The precision was so odd, it made the angle seem rather mundane. Cities have cracked under earthquakes or shifting tides or even man-made borders. But this was something entirely different. It was a precise removal of forty-five degrees. It was the subject of deep fascination within the Embers community and terror to the local population. When the world shifted and the Fecundity appeared, it took forty-five degrees out of the center of Danador. Exposing the inside of the city as well as letting in disastrous floods. The first few days were chaotic. After some order was reestablished, rumors swirled about why this section, in particular, had disappeared. Was it an unknown god's wrath or some experiment gone wrong? It affected the entire area around the College of the Arcane Flame but luckily stopped short of damaging the building. Most of the population believed it was Magnincy gone terribly awry but others surmised it was the work of conniving Norun. The only truth was that no one knew.

Time marched on, and like all strange things, the event became familiar and even accepted. At first, it was a place of tourism; not only was it an interesting cross-section of the city, but under the water, on a clear night, you could see a rainbow of coral growth with multitudes of seaweed and kelp. Usually, only oceans could contain that type of life, but just like the Fecundity, nature had gone wild. The forty-five experienced explosive overnight growth, inconsistent with the rest of the natural world. When the world was reshaped, it brought with it the most fertile areas for growth ever known. It didn't seem like anything could die naturally out there.

Because of its total lack of infrastructure, eventually, the Forty-Five became a place for outcasts. As the Wardens reestablished borders and gates, reentering the city from the Forty-Five became difficult. The Forty-Five became an island of strapped-together boats, barges, docks and whatever would float. It was hard to tell what was solid ground and what was floating debris. Perhaps, there wasn't even really that much of a difference. The residents of the forty-five made a crude type of living and enjoyed more freedom than anywhere else in Danador. Wardens rarely, if ever, visited there. No guards patrolled it. Law and order were more like an agreed-upon social contract, the rules to which no one knew for sure unless you lived there. Elatress had indeed known a great place to practice. Inside here, an explosion would barely lift an eyebrow. Huxley strapped the Grimoire tight to his side and kept a tight grip on it. The longer he walked within the Forty-Five, the less he became concerned about book theft. Their bartering system was based on survival needs: food, clean water, and clothing. He doubted anyone would try and grab a musty, old book. Elatress was more at home here than he had ever seen before. Everywhere else, she kept a reservation to her movement. Here she and Arktos walked freely, as though a young woman sporting two hand axes and traveling with a bear was of no note at all. Huxley had been so concerned with not being seen, he didn't take the time to look around properly. She took him through broken walls, under pieces of metal and through cracks, wandering through living spaces, stores and back into the water on occasion. There were absolutely no street signs. Navigating was impossible by traditional means. Everything was so transient, Huxley suspected nothing was permanent enough to warrant a signpost.

They hopped hull to hull for a time and eventually found themselves on a boat full of people. It didn't have a crew but it certainly was meant for travel rather than a part of the flotilla. They were waiting for more passengers when Elatress ducked suddenly and lifted her hood to conceal her face. Huxley instinctually followed her lead and peaked at what made her flinch. A Warden was making his way by them, a huge stack of papers under his arm and sneer permanently affixed to his face. He paused at a dock poll, placed the papers down and drew. He nailed it up and left without even a look around. It was another wanted poster, the one with BEWARE written on it above a picture of the crazed doctor. Huxley tried not to look interested in it but things were starting to make sense to him. Forced madness was what he had been threatened with at the college. Forced madness, was what was written on the poster. He couldn't quite read the rest and didn't want to draw closer as that might show interest. Before long, more travelers hopped onto the boat and they pushed off. No sails or oars, it just caught stream and gently floated downriver. It was interesting to see this part of the city. It was like a textbook cross-section and illustration of the inner workings. He could see the outer rung, the industrial district and the inner rung. Each one was so distinct from the other, it reminded Huxley of a layered cake with different flavors. The outer was thick with colors and sound, the Industrial was gray and sullen, and the inner was lightest with a few sharp angles and some rich color.

Not five minutes into their trip, their boat slid to a stop on a shore. Elatress and Arktos leaped off and made straight for the Fecundity. Huxley followed but stopped at the tree line and looked up at the overgrowth.

His body froze at the prospect of entering. "You didn't say it was in the Fecundity. I've never been there before."

She huffed from inside the tree line and called back "We've been in the Wilds ever since we left the pipe."

"What?!"

"The Forty-Five is the wilds. The predatory fish under those waters could skeletonize us in seconds and the fire coral's venom could kill us outright. Lethal for sure."

Huxley blinked and was cut off before he could voice a complaint.

"Don't worry, they don't like the taste of bear."

Arktos made a "Hmph" sound to confirm.

"Oh good," he said, "I was worried about Arktos."

She reached her hand out and grabbed his.

"Stop worrying. I lived here for years before Abernathy found me. You're safe with me."

Gripping his hand tight, she pulled him further into the wilds.

"You know it's more accurate to call it the Fecundity."

"Well it's more accurate to call you lots of names other than Bookpile but I just go with what works. It's the Wilds....that's what it is. Now hurry before something catches our scent."

The Fecundity was dense, hot, and wet, it even resisted the cold winds settling in for the winter. Only a few feet in, he felt like he was in another world. Branches snapped and crunched under his feet, He couldn't find a clear path forward. Each step brought a new host of sounds. Elatress and Arktos were a different matter. They moved here like fish through a stream. Little leaps, side steps, and ducking under the considerable growth. It was like they saw a path he didn't. After a short but laborious trip, they reached their destination. True to her word there was a rare opening in the flora. They emerged into a gap filled with fungi instead of plants. It circled the area in what Elatress called "Fairy circles". Huxley didn't see any fairies but he did like the area. It felt secluded enough and he immediately pulled out his grimoire. He settled on the ground and began reading more about honeycombs as he absent-mindedly drew hexagons in the dirt.

Hours passed, and the sun hung low in the sky. Arktos had shifted his way over and settled behind him providing him with a bit of warmth and a place to lie back when his back needed a break from being hunched over. At first, Elatress excitedly ran about the circle, digging her toes into various places and following it up with "oohs and ahhs". Eventually, she started throwing her hatchets around. Mercifully, she kept them flying away from Huxley, but he couldn't help but feel like she was sizing him up periodically. She even made the claim she could throw the hatchet and brush the handle across his cheek without hurting him. He didn't challenge her. The idea of perfecting his defensive bubble was becoming increasingly important. He scribbled notes of his discovery about combining the two together. He hadn't seen any other notes about it. Adding information to the Grimoire felt strangely wrong in a way, like scribbling in his parent's ledgers or stealing some religious text and drawing in it. It was kind of sacred to him. Not religious exactly, but it felt like the Grimoire was something above him and he had no business altering it. The writing had become familiar to him at this point and it contained many levels of notes, so clearly he wasn't the first to deem note taking necessary. There was the immaculately written original text, then the second author's follow-up questions and answers, then a third scrawling that read like answers, but he couldn't make sense of them. A sense of pride eventually won out as he added his note to the honeycomb area in the Apis section of Zoology. He even added a footnote linking it to the mathematics section of minimal surface area that led to him making a bubble. Elatress sighed, dramatically. When it didn't get Huxley's attention, she did it again. She tried several more times but Huxley was too deep in concentration. Suddenly, a hatchet blade struck the ground in front of him, cratering dirt that landed on the grimoire. Huxley jumped in surprise but all Elatress said was, "Good, I thought you fell asleep. Where's the lightning?"

"Lightning?" Huxley repeated.

"Yeah, that's what you Embers do, right?" She asked.

"I'm not an Ember yet, and maybe...real lightning seems far too advanced. I can make electrical discharges." He offered.

"Bookpile...that's lightning."

"The wattage is entirely different."

Sensing her dissatisfaction with that answer, he snatched some floating stars in front of him and released them out of his hand with a snap and a hiss. Arktos jumped awake from the sound but closed his eyes again.

"That was more like a firecracker," she criticized.

"Well, any more than that, and I could kill us all. One time, I unleashed it on a stage, and I couldn't control it very well."

"Aww, you care about us?" She teased.

"I certainly do enough to not get on your bad side. Now please don't throw any more hatchets at me, or I will hit you with lightning."

"REALLY?!" She said with entirely too much excitement for Huxley's liking.

"No," He stated flatly, greatly deflating her. She had already recovered her hatchet and was readying it.

"I get the impression you are disappointed with my practice time."

"You can say that again, I thought I was going to see all sorts of spells."

"They aren't spells. Magnincy is science in motion and mastery of it. And to accomplish that, study is the best method."

"Fine, then I'm going to go get dinner."

"Dinner?" Huxley looked up at the sky and realized it was growing late. "How late can we stay out here?"

"As long as we want...there aren't guards or anyone to come looking for us. Abernathy will be out for a while and even if not, he doesn't know about this place."

Huxley didn't feel good about leaving Abernathy, but he didn't know much about how they did things yet. Maybe it was fine.

He looked up at her to find she had already left. Arktos leapt up, realizing the same thing, and chased after her. Dinner did sound good. He tried not to think about what she thought would be dinner out here. With the fading sun, his eyes strained trying to read. He began to close the Grimoire but a thought occurred and a star floated over to him. The electromagnetic spectrum could be bound up in bulbs. Light bulbs weren't common, but he'd seen them made. It was vibrating wavelengths of electromagnetic radiation. If he bound it in a thin bulb he could make light. He'd have to feed it constantly to maintain the output. The complexity of it was perhaps something he could manage. As he considered the mechanics of it, he realized a far simpler solution. He mentally chided himself for greatly overthinking how to create a light source. He gathered a few twigs and dried out moss and looked up fire in the Grimoire. "Rapid oxidation," he repeated out loud. He reread it a few times and gave it a try. He grabbed the star associated with it and released it into the fuel. It sparked to life and began burning. Soon enough he had a humble crackling fire. It felt like the first time he had fixed a shoe for his dad. He sighed contentedly as it warmed him and provided the light he needed.

He thought about the defensive bubble and how that drew far less from him than before. Other times he used Magnincy, it had taxed his mind greatly. Was it getting more familiar and thus easier? Perhaps the time difference between reading it and recalling it was a factor as well. Even now, the fire he just made was nearly effortless. He scribbled his questions down to not forget them and warmed his hands as the cold settled around him. The stars of Magnincy swirled around him now, some asking to be grasped and the others dancing out of reach. Dismissing them was far easier now. They used to appear at random or when he was in distress but now he could keep them ready for whenever.

He was making progress.

Maybe not the kind he wanted from a formal education, but twice today, he had moments of significance in his understanding. Perhaps becoming an Ember wasn't altogether impossible, and maybe, if he truly mastered the bulk of the grimoire, they would readmit him...but probably after trying to kill him first.

The darkness finally pushed the remaining sunshine under the ridge of the horizon and Huxley was greeted by twinkling stars. The moon was nowhere to be seen and the cosmos shone brighter in its absence. Huxley's light source was now a full-fledged campfire that hissed and snapped. He laid down with his arms crossed behind his head to form a makeshift pillow. He tried to align his Magnincy stars with the stars in the night sky, craning his head to see if they would match. No luck. Soon Elatress and Arktos came back carrying...something.

"What is that?! Huxley raised an eyebrow trying to see what it was that Elatress dumped next to the fire. "I think it used to be a deer." She laid its body out and began skinning it.

"Used to be?"

"The Wilds turned it vicious...they all turn that way out here."

"A vicious deer?

Elatress stopped skinning and looked at the lifeless face of the animal. "Not sure if he was...like deep inside...but they all turn this way if they eat and live here."

For once, Huxley understood her. The Fecundity were ever-changing and ever-growing but never seemed to stray from within its borders. It should have aggressively expanded but it seemed to have an agreement to stay within its own lands. The Fecundity may have agreed to these terms but the inhabitants didn't. Anything originating from here grew severe and violent. Hunters, prey, and everything in between seemed to possess at least some killer instinct. Huxley's appetite started to vanish at the site of Elatress's bloody work, but also at the thought of eating something from here. Even though they were less than a few hundred feet from a path, he suddenly felt surrounded. Huxley glanced around furtively. It felt like each branch and rock were closing in around him like the jaws of the very predators he worried about.

"It's getting late," he said, a slight shake to his voice that betrayed his true feelings.

Elatress gave a long sigh. She put down the flank she was working on and said "Huxley". There was a sweetness to his name, he hadn't heard before. In fact, she spoke his real name so rarely that it rang foreign altogether.

"You do know that I'm from here? And there is nothing to fear from this place? Huxley's nod was a little too quick to be genuine. "Or from me." She added.

He had not known that for sure. He certainly had suspected that she wasn't from Danador.

"Yes...of course, I know that," he stated carefully. "You were born here?"

"I think so. Memories of the Wilds and Arktos go back as far back as I can remember. Except, sometimes I dream that I lived on a farm, not in the Wilds. Strange dreams. A farm that grew gold and boys brought me presents." Her eyes wandered away with the thoughts. Arktos waddled up and rubbed his scalp under her palm. He hummed a soft melody to her and forced his head back and forth under her palm. Her eyes returned to lucidity and she apologized.

"No, it's ok," Huxley said, "Sometimes I feel like my mind drifts away too. Like the day gets so full, I can't really have my own thoughts, or my own feelings, without everything else demanding attention. Have you ever been to Mayburn?" He asked, suddenly.

"No, only around its borders." She replied.

"Well, I can't say that it's so fantastic that you need to visit there, but there is a spot on my roof outside my bedroom that is about the best place I can think of. It's quiet, not too much light and you can see deep into the night sky. I can feel myself coming back in those moments." He shifted and looked at her, "Does that ever happen to you?"

"The stars? They're great and all, but I don't usually look at them." She sank into Arktos' side as he nestled into a deep sleep. "I find more fascinating things the other way; in the ground and around me. I do know the feeling you're describing, that's Arktos." She lovingly patted him.

"Arktos?"

"Yeah, when I feel myself coming undone, you know? I just nuzzle into him and I'm home again in my mind. Doesn't that happen to you? Doesn't petting an animal just restore your calm?"

"Restore?" He laughed. Since meeting Arktos, the bear had done everything except restore his calm. It was more like he was a lumbering mound of stress. It wasn't that Huxley didn't like Arktos, but...well, he was a bear. Even a docile one is still a bear deep down, right? It hunted and had instincts like any other predator.

"No, not quite. Although, I think he's great." He lied, but only to protect her feelings. He was getting the distinct impression that Arktos understood everything he said, a little too much for his liking.

"Well, if the stars do it for me and Arktos does it for you, then I guess you and I are both in a good place. Elatress sighed in agreement, and her eyes drifted away to a new thought she wasn't sharing. Something startled her. Suddenly, she stated, "You're right Huxley. It's late. We should go."

"But what about the deer? We can't just leave it." He argued.

"Oh, don't worry about that. There are three hungry onlookers right now that won't believe their luck when we leave." She said, making no effort to point them out.

Huxley noticed shifting branches near the tree line and wondered how dangerous they were.

"They're not that big," as if reading his thoughts. "About the same size as Arktos."

Huxley stared hoping that she was joking.

"We can go now."

Huxley snatched up his belongings and followed.

The return journey from the Wilds was without incident. There wasn't a boat to take them back to the flotilla so Elatress took a different route. It was a little slower but Huxley didn't mind. He was feeling strangely peaceful. It had been a really productive day. The new revelations about Magnincy and the Grimoire were by far the greater achievement but he also felt like he was a little closer to understanding the city. They followed the shoreline to the sides of the flotilla and saw more wanted posters of the Mad Doctor. Huxley was glancing again at the strange cross-section of the city when Elatress spoke up, "Well it's not all bad, at least they made your hair look good." Huxley raised an eyebrow and turned to see what she meant. Next to the old wanted posters was a new, freshly inked, one. It featured Huxley's face. Elatress was right. They managed to get the hair right.

20

∾

Parties and Dates

"Strigidae's hunting patterns vary, most do so nocturnally and utilizing various tactics such as perch and pounce or quartering flight...some few species run along the ground in lieu of flight." **-Page 414, Excerpt from the Grimoire**

Beware! *Crazed former student from Mayburn at large within Danador looking to rob and attack citizens. Wanted for theft and attempted murder of an Ember via Magnincy. If seen DO NOT approach, alert a Warden or guard immediately. Ten Full Clips for information that leads to his capture.*

"Well, you're a proper fugitive now, Bookpile. Ooo also a big Lecture Hall debate is coming up." Elatress read on past his wanted poster of upcoming events. Though none of it was nearly as interesting.

Returning to the underground sewers was easier than exiting them. He still didn't like this mode of travel, but it didn't require any clips and they didn't meet any guards. His legs hadn't quite recovered from the journey, holding back their progress. Elatress didn't give him any grief about it and even walked beside him for stretches of time. She was strange, but good company. She was always lost in thought and gazing at random points around them. She walked precisely and gracefully, like a dancer performing a routine. The fluidity of her movement drew Huxley's attention often. He was fascinated by the mundane tasks she would perform like cleaning a bartop or walking through a sewer. It was all done as if choreographed on a stage with an audience watching. In contrast, her thoughts and speech were haphazard and stunted. She rarely offered anything but the truth without tact. Huxley had no trouble believing she was expressing herself as best she could, but it seemed that she preferred not to speak unless she needed to convey the exact information she needed to. If he had just met her, he would probably think that she was perhaps mad or at least touched by it. But madness didn't operate like she did unless it was a whole different breed from what he was used to. They walked through the early night until just before midnight, Elatress told him they'd arrived. The ladder they'd climbed down hours earlier was waiting for them.

"Do you always know where you are?" He exclaimed, amazed that she had made sense of the sewers in near pitch blackness.

"Do you never know where you are?" She countered as she ascended the ladder two at a time.

He turned to figure out how Arktos was getting up there but Arktos had wandered off again. He decided he didn't want to follow a giant bear down a sewer, so he followed Elatress up. They emerged into the Gearbox dry storage room and Elatress immediately stepped out. Huxley however was struck by what he saw beyond the door.

The Gearbox was alive; Alive with people, with energy, and with sound. Lamps were lit, the fire roared, and a musician pounded on a drum with strange attachments Huxley had never seen before. Cymbals clanged and an airy flute hummed from some corner of the Gearbox. Laughing, singing and all known expletives and exclamations reverberated in the rafters. It all hit Huxley like a bucket of warm water poured into a chilly bath. The Gearbox was having an extremely late-night party and Abernethy was in the middle of it all. He was ripping off hunks of roast pig and slapping them on empty plates, whether the customer asked for it or not. His enormous mustache brushed the meat periodically and was soaked in juices. Abernathy's face was flushed and his smile pushed his eyebrows so high, they nearly touched his hairline. Like always, the aroma of the spices and seasonings grabbed hold of Huxley's nose and held it hostage. Elatress leapt to work clearing plates and tankards. Huxley's legs ached at the prospect of doing dishes, and his stomach practically screamed at him to go get a plate. He reasoned that he couldn't wash dishes on an empty stomach. Elatress whispered something into Abernathy's ear as she passed him. Abernathy excused himself for a moment. No one seemed to mind as he darted into the kitchen. Bursting in, Abernathy grabbed Huxley and hugged him, seizing him so forcefully that it stopped Huxley from breathing.

"So glad you're here! I want to introduce you to many fine folks and a few not-so-fine, hah!"

He released him from his grip and Huxley gasped saying, "I can't! I'm a fugitive, remember? These people could recognize me. There's even a poster out!"

Abernethy's kind amber eyes held so much joy that it felt bad even disagreeing with him. It was like he was trying to rob him of his happiness.

"Ah, you misunderstand, these people are not just any rabble off the streets. I've invited all of them, just like I invited you. They are revolutionaries, pirates, smugglers, swindlers, alchemists, gamblers, and forgers."

Before he had time to raise all of the problems with what Abernathy just told him, he was pushed through the door.

"No work for you tonight lad, just have some fun, meet some people and maybe for the first time since you got to Danador, enjoy yourself!"

What fun meant for Abernathy was different than what Huxley, and possibly most people, thought it was. Huxley struggled with the concept of fun as he was given drinks that stank of engine grease and hops, slapped so hard on the back his eyes watered, and half-told stories that barely had a point and always ended with uproarious laughter. After being spilled on, spit on and shoved around the room for what felt like hours, he needed a break. He made for the kitchen door a handful of times, each time being blocked by someone grabbing his shoulder, spinning him around and forcing a story on him.

Abernathy was always one person adjacent to him and always felt like he needed to hear the story being told. Escape wasn't an option. He was too easy to grab. He decided instead to find a booth and make himself a smaller target. A defensible location from all of the fun. He found a near-empty plate, flicked the gristle, fat and all other accumulated juices onto the ground. He filled it with the biggest beef flank he could find and surrounded it with veggies and potatoes. Shoving his way through the crowd, he finally made it to a booth. His clothes were nearly soaked from beer, sweat and whatever else clung to him as he plopped down into his seat. He neatly arranged the plate and fixed some of the carrots that had nearly rolled off. Then a voice from his worst nightmare cut like a blade through the commotion around him.

"By her razor talons, steel beak and feathered goodness, I knew you'd find me", a gruff voice said. "I am Grubmush of the Kilikans and priest of Faldurin. We finally meet!"

Huxley glanced up from his plate. There was no mistaking that voice. Even sitting, he loomed taller than Huxley stood. Clothed in furs, feathers and bones mixed with some kind of contemporary but blood stained shirt, sat an old enemy he had nearly forgotten about. A crazed smile split his face, showing teeth that were intended to be a smile but looked too animalistic for that. His shoulders stretched so wide they took up two seats and his face sported a beard that may have never known the touch of a razor. It was arranged into three long braided tails that swung back and forth as he spoke. He stretched his arms open wide revealing dozens if not hundreds of scars. It was impossible to find a stretch of skin unbroken at some point in time.

Huxley's chest constricted in his lungs. He gasped and it wasn't from the spiced beef. He instinctively reached for Magnincy. He didn't care much about what he grabbed, anything would do.

Abernathy threw himself half onto the table and yelled "Now, now lads! No fighting in the Gearbox, especially on a night like this!"

Huxley stood up in his seat and grabbed at two particularly nasty pieces of Magnincy he had been reading over and pulled his arms back ready to release.

Abernathy pleaded, "PLEASE Huxley! He's a guest." Saying the last part like it was enough.

"THIS GUEST KILLED MY FRIENDS AND ATTACKED MAY-BURN!"

"Well, specifically," The Grubmush argued, "I was just there. I had advised against attacking and was compelled to follow my chief. It was *you* that wounded *me*, actually. And I await your further wrath!"

The man-creature closed his eyes and turned his palms skyward. His breath came in huge huffs like he was preparing to plunge into a frigid river.

"Deliver your vengeance upon me so that I may endure." Huxley wondered who he was talking to. He seemed to be speaking more to the sky than to Huxley.

Hate and rage swelled within Huxley. Abernathy's pleading eyes held him back. Seeing him here brought forth questions that Abernathy needed to answer fast.

His rage and curiosity battled. If he killed Grubmush, he wouldn't get the answers to his questions but allowing him to live meant that he could kill again. As always, the ever-growing and unceasing part of his brain demanded the questions be answered first.

Grubmush's hands ripped open the shirt he wore in one fluid motion revealing a gnarled torso twisted with wounds and dried gore. There was one round, clean spot in the bottom right of his torso. It was a perfect circle of skin, unwounded, untorn, and undefiled by what was likely a lifetime of fighting.

HUFF "Because your wrath is as hers, *HUFF* holy, righteous and clean! *HUFF* Your wrath brings gifts from heaven *HUFF* that fix the broken and heal the wounded.*HUFF* Your wrath is the key to *HUFF* salvation unto her feathered wings, Fald-*HUFF*-urin is our great god and you are her Prophet."

"Madness," Huxley spat, "You have no idea who I am. Have you gone mad?"

His wide smile broadened as he said, "Is it possible that *HUFF* like me, you don't know of her mark on your life? *HUFF* When you attacked me and gave me the *HUFF*clarity and instruction of pain I knew she had picked you. *HUFF* How else could we have been brought together? *HUFF* How could you produce her power unless you were her servant?"*HUFF*

Whatever Huxley was about to do next, Abernathy jumped to intervene.

"Ok, then, good to know, see you for tomorrow's sermon, Grubmush." He then turned to the rest of the bar and said "Party's over! Same time next week though."

Grubmush didn't move and resumed his position waiting for Huxley's attack. His smile lessened, confusion creeping into his eyes. *HUFF*"I will accept anything you offer me as her Prophet." *HUFF*

Even though it pained him, he had run through the night of the attack a few times in his head during Grubmush's confused speech. He remembered now. Grubmush was the one who called for the fight to end, and he was clean of blood. But then he was hit by the star. How this man survived being eviscerated was shocking. He should be dead.

But of all the scenarios Huxley had thought about, this one had never even entered his mind. Worship? Like a religion? It was a religion he certainly had never heard of before.

Finally, hearing the quiet desperation in Abernathy's voice, Huxley banished the stars and relaxed his mind. He finally chanced a glance away from the creature and saw that the room had cleared. Behind Abernathy, loomed Arktos. It was difficult to make Abernathy look small in any way, and Grubmush was larger still, but both of them seemed like children compared to Arktos. He had never seen the bear on his hind legs before. His body stretched so high it looked like it might brush the ceiling. His prodigious paws hung at his side with claws that matched looking like spearheads.

Suddenly, Grubmush remembered something. He clapped his hands and buttoned his shirt. He even changed his voice to sound like an impression of a warden. "Clearly, I have offended my host with sub-texts of violence. I had no intention of violence, that is not the way of

Danador and is therefore not mine. I hope I haven't offended you or your business"

A voice spoke from behind Grubmush's seat. "No, of course not. Prophets, blood rituals and sacrifices are a normal part of the Gearbox's nightly activities." Elatress appeared and reattached her hatchets to her belt loops. "We love it when things get tense around here."

"I have been told threats of physical violence are not the norm in your city." Grubmush said, "And under threat of expulsion, I have agreed to those terms. "

"Yes, that is the rule of the city. And it's the rules of the Gearbox too, especially on a night like this. Thank you for coming, I'll get your things." Abernathy said as he turned to move around Arktos and hurried off.

"Your bear is a violation of city codes." Grubmush pointed out.

"He's not my bear," Elatress stated.

His eyebrows raised as though learning something new and said nothing further. Standing up, he paused to collect his things and turned to Huxley, "Please come and hear my sermon tomorrow morning at the market square. I can explain further to you if you don't understand. Ignorance of her true nature will not save even the strongest."

Huxley's hands shook. He didn't manage a response. The ludicrous idea of inviting him to what sounded like a religious service left him feeling cold. He could only see the blood-spattered walls, Pilch dead, and Bennett being savaged for the crime of defending his home. Now, this creature wished for peace?!

Abernathy showed Grubmush out and Huxley waited for the door to shut. Once the latch clicked, Huxley collapsed into a chair. His anger and fear had driven out all the rest of his emotions. They returned with a vengeance. He blinked tears from his eyes which dripped onto his pants.

"I'm sorry to have upset you so badly, I didn't realize you knew him," Abernathy confessed.

"Knew him?" Huxley stated mirthlessly, "He travels with murderers."

Elatress began rubbing his shoulders to try to calm him down. His body finally stopped shaking and his heart slowed down. "I think it's time I told you two everything."

The three sat and talked all through the night. Mostly, just Huxley spoke. He told them about his upbringing, his time with the guard, and eventually his discovery of the Grimoire. He mentioned his struggles with understanding what is written on the pages and his fear of being caught with it, and of course, his battle with Grubmush's people, and the wounds inflicted. Most importantly, he told them about the responsibility he placed on himself and the intense burden of protecting his hometown.

They were a good audience and listened without interrupting. Huxley had expected they would have had more questions or surprised reactions. None came, in fact, besides an infrequent nod of understanding, or the rare clarifying question, they listened intently. Halfway through, Huxley realized he hadn't really gone through everything succinctly. He really had come a long way in a relatively short time.

The morning had arrived at some point during his conclusion. When Huxley finally finished, the trio stirred from their chairs and stretched deep. Exhaustion sat thick within the Gearbox and they decided on sleep. Work would have to wait for at least a few hours.

A small device screeched at Huxley next to his bed. It stirred him awake until it went back to sleep like Huxley wished he could have done. The strange device also awoke the anger and protest of his body. Running through the sewers, pushing himself in Magnincy, nearly attacking a man-creature and staying up all night had a way of exhausting a guy. His legs were cramped and sore from hiking. He slid out of bed, careful to not put weight on his legs too soon. Barely keeping himself steady, he looked around in a daze for his clothes. Then the device screeched again at him. He hadn't heard many animals die, certainly not painfully, but the noise could have matched any cry of pain. He ignored the cramps in his legs and fumbled to silence the device when he heard the true source of the screech. It wasn't from his bedside. It was from downstairs in the Gearbox. His hearing came into focus more and he pressed his ear against the door. Muffled screams of outrage were the best he could piece together. In a flash, he threw his clothes on, but only enough to protect his dignity.He tried to clear his mind enough to summon Magnincy, before throwing open the door and charging down the stairs..

"If you like him so much, why don't YOU go out with HIM!"

"Me?! You're going out tonight. It's part of our deal!"

"The last one you sent me out with talked the whole time. THE WHOLE TIME!"

"THAT'S WHAT HAPPENS ON DATES! PEOPLE TALK!"

Elatress was out of breath and with cheeks flushed so dark the red was turning purple. Not to be outmatched, Abernathy was finding his own shade of red and purple. They paused to catch their breath and resumed as soon as they could. Abernathy used the time to light his pipe, probably hoping it would calm him down. He gave three succinct puffs to get it lit and started back in but was cut off by Elatress.

"They can't fight! They certainly can't find a-"

"All of that is irrelevant!"

"Irrelevant? A man who can't fight!"

"Not on a date, we're looking for a nice boy, who isn't violent!"

"Fighting isn't violent!"

Abernathy was taken aback. His thoughts regrouped, but she assaulted him again.

"I should be able to choose who I go on dates with and what outfits I wear." She seized a dress off the table and shook it at Abernathy. "THIS IS RIDICULOUS!" The last part was nearly inaudible, her words becoming jumbled while combining with the volume she was producing.

Abernathy held his hands up pleadingly like he was approaching an animal caught in a snare, trying to soothe it.

"Remember? We tried that before, you didn't pick anybody and lied to me and a bunch of people. All of the boys showed up to different places looking for you. And where were you actually?"

"In the wilds!" They said at the same time.

"It's better there," she said.

"It's rage and violence incarnate, it's not better than an evening with a boy."

"It's SO much better than an evening with a boy."

She noticed Huxley looking down from the second floor and her face lit up. She instantly decided on a different tactic.

"Huxley, that's right! He chaperoned a date I went on last night, Abernathy! He was like a big brother to me. He made sure that the young man watched himself and everything. So there's my one for the week!" She crossed her arms in a way that signified the conversation was won.

Abernathy turned around and looked up at Huxley, eyebrow raised, and said, "A date?"

"Uhh" was all Huxley managed when Elatress started nodding her head furiously at him.

"Yes, some kid showed up and I took them on a long stroll, a boat ride, toured the markets and we had dinner together."

Abernathy took a long look at Huxley, probably trying to judge whether to believe a single word. After some time he said "Is that true Hux? Did she really go on a date with a boy?"

"Sorta" He lied.

"Sorta?" Abernathy repeated, boring deep into Huxley. Behind him, Elatress nodded her head, desperately communicating to just agree.

"Yeah, I suppose," Huxley affirmed.

Abernathy sighed, expelling a cloud of pipe smoke, he nearly disappeared into it. Gave a *harumph* and said, "The dress isn't ridiculous. It's modern and made particularly for you." His voice had lowered considerably signaling he had given up this fight but still had a minor stake in one last point.

"I don't care about...wait...made particular?" She asked, curiously.

"Yeah, I had them include hidden slings for your hatchets."

Elatress' eyes betrayed her interest, despite her anger. She looked again, inspecting the waist area, and checking for hidden slings. When she found them, she rolled her eyes and said "Of course, it has those, who could wear such a thing and not be armed?"

"Most people." Abernathy's face contorted.

"Well, most people are prey." Elatress shot back.

"You certainly aren't." Abernathy pointed out. They embraced each other, Elatress still holding the dress.

"The laces are stupid."

"I'll have them removed."

"Throw the whole thing away while you're at it."

Huxley hoped that this was the end of the fight. He was a little concerned that he lied to Abernathy. It was only then that he noticed someone sitting at the end of the bar, shifting uncomfortably. The young man had lowered his shoulders looking to make himself smaller. He had a bouquet of flowers, held limply at his sides.

"Sooo....no date tonight?" He asked, meekly.

Elatress made no response and left for the kitchen. Abernathy said "Ahh, seems like we had a scheduling conflict. Can we try again next week?"

Looking eager to run from the Gearbox and never come back, he said, "If she actually wants to...I suppose we can talk about it."

Abernathy nodded and the boy fled.

Huxley, only now, got a good look at him, he was about Huxley's size but dressed immaculately. Huxley had never seen a suit like that before. It stood out starkly inside the Gearbox, everything inside was various degrees of stained and soiled. His suit, however, was free of blemish, with a carefully folded pocket square that matched the roses. Huxley's guess was that it wasn't by mistake. And a pocket watch that grabbed every light and reflected it back, bringing attention like a fire at night. In fact, Huxley mused, he even looked a bit like Huxley in his bearing, look and demeanor. The only difference was his face was rounder and quite red. Was it embarrassment? Huxley couldn't tell.

A blast of cold air filled the Gearbox when the would-be suitor opened the door to leave. Snow rushed in as though trying to escape the cold. A two-horse carriage waited outside, the coach poised with whip in hand, ready to depart. He shook his head, "No," when the driver began to hop down to help him in. Before he turned to close the door behind him, he called out to Abernathy, "We can try again next week!" Abernathy just waved and hurried over to help him push the door closed. Finally, with a click of the lock, they were alone again. Abernathy dumped himself onto a barstool looking deflated. Huxley wanted to hide back in his room and busy himself with whatever he could come up with to avoid the awkwardness, but he felt like he owed Abernathy an explanation. He still felt quite lost with what that was all about, but that didn't stop him from taking a seat on the stool next to Abernathy.

Abernathy sat half holding the dress and half holding a dark drink he had poured for himself. He twisted a few of the ribbons that she had disliked so much. "I'm trying with her...I know she doesn't like this, I don't really either. I just don't know what to do to help her."

Huxley winced as he blurted, "Help her?" Huxley knew their relationship was complicated and he didn't want to ask personal questions, but questions came more naturally to Huxley than breathing lately, and it wasn't the first time he'd asked a question he shouldn't have.

"Help her with all of it," Abernathy replied, placing the dress down and waving his hand in the air. "It's probably stupid but I thought helping her to do normal things that girls her age do, like going on dates, would make her remember who she was. When I found her she was kind of like you, lost and confused. I guess once you're a dad, you never really retire from that job. You start seeing all young people in that light."

And if Huxley had made a mistake before in asking a personal question about Elatress, he was about to make a right and true error. He knew how dumb it was, but his questions always won it seemed.

"You're a dad?"

Abernathy's chin shook and he sobbed. Not a loud whimpering cry, but a deep, heart-clenched sob, the kind where your stomach convulses and your heart feels empty. Huxley knew that feeling. It was like your body is trying to fill in that emptiness with whatever it can find, so it sobs drawing air. Abernathy's whole body heaved, tears soaking his cheeks, mustache and the dress in his lap.

"I'm so sorry," Huxley said, realizing in horror what that reaction may have meant.

Seeing his retreat, Abernathy explained, "No, no, it's not anything like that. They are just far away, and I miss them...greatly." His voice cracked near the end.

Huxley's curiosity had again, pushed too far. Abernathy drained the rest of his drink. The dark liquid disappeared faster than it had been poured. He regained some of his composure, clapped a hand over Huxley's shoulder and said, "I'll hopefully be able to see them soon. Magnadun is in more danger than you know Hux. I, like you, am here trying to gain more information on how to help my home." He glanced up at the door Elatress had disappeared behind, "As is Elatress, in her own way." He added. "In fact, that's why I put together this whole place." He swept his hands out wide towards the Gearbox, "I noticed before long that here in Danador there are more pilgrims than any other place I have been. Something calls them here. They left their homes, which takes great bravery and sacrifice, in hopes of getting what they need here." He shifted in his seat and faced Huxley.

"You see, the Norun people are, in fact, special and quite different as I expect all peoples of Magnadun are. We are helpers. Everywhere you go, you will find helpers, segments of the population that want to be of service and make others' lives better. But for the Norun, it's our way. We go about it differently, but all of us are bent toward it. It compels us, drives us, and sustains us. It sounds nice at first but an obsession of any kind has its pitfalls. When Magnadun first changed and we found ourselves with new neighbors, we knew we had to act and help. Bands and troops of our best were sent out to all corners of Magnadun. We realized two things swiftly; first, people needed our help far more than we anticipated, and second," He paused to find the right word, thought carefully and said, "Helpers get taken advantage of."

"Advantage?" Huxley pressed.

"Yes, when we left to help, some might say rescue, it left us undefended. And those who define helping differently than I, moved in." He shuddered and continued, "They shut us out and did vile things in the name of help."

Huxley's mind asked no less than ten questions but on occasion, he also didn't wish for an answer.

"That is why I asked Grubmush here last night."

Huxley blinked. He had figured he invited him here because he looked like he could use a hot meal, not because he had an agenda.

Abernathy went on, "I, like you, have use of Magnincy, but it isn't the same as yours. It has its uses. You saw that I can power machinery and it helps me with those efforts. He leaned back and swung his metal leg back and forth." He wrapped it with two knuckles and said "I'm a great engineer but a power source that small just for a leg is a challenge and a half. I power it with Magnincy."

Now Huxley had so many questions they got jammed up in his mouth. It reminded him of two people trying to walk through a door at the same time. He had been waiting for an opportunity to ask about what he'd seen in the machine shop a few days ago. But before he made sense of what to ask first, Abernathy broke in and laughed, "Haha, if THAT surprised you, wait until you hear what everyone else in Norun can do!"

"Norun has Embers?!" Huxley shouted, louder than he intended.

Abernathy laughed again, but dismissively.

"Embers? Hah. No, no Embers. Embers are your people. Everyone here was from all walks of Magnadun, all five convergences, Danador, Valdannon, Norun, Sumine, and Dathu. All of them draw on Magnincy. Your people draw on it via learned sciences, math, physics, biology, but it isn't the same for everyone else."

"But theirs is far weaker," Huxley said. "They may have use of it, but I've never seen anyone who can do what the Embers do. It's not the same, they're wielding a shadow of what true Magnincy is." Huxley worried he was sounding dismissive but it was true, wasn't it? He'd seen some small things, even from Abernathy and Elatress that were impressive but nowhere near the same level as an Ember. Embers broke through the Wilds itself. An unhindered Ember could bring down a building and scorch a town. He'd experienced their power firsthand and doubted they were going full force.

"Oh, it's the same alright. In fact, I'd argue that Danadorians have great power but their weakness is the time it takes to master the arts of their Magnincy. And they make it so much more difficult than it needs to be." He huffed in annoyance, "They don't even share their information with each other. Instead, they jealously guard it and only teach others when it directly benefits them." He sighed, "they could be so much more."

"Who's the strongest then?" Huxley asked. What Abernathy was stating just seemed too difficult to believe.

"Strongest?" Abernathy questioned as though he'd never heard that before. "I can't know that for sure. Certainly, the Embers, if given another fifty or so years to recover their artifacts. I think Valdannon could give them a run for their money, Sumine is the most scattered and likely has the least interest in being the strongest of anything. And you've seen what Dathu can do. My people, well, it's tough to make a helper ever want to stop helping you, so fighting isn't our way. Though no one escapes conflict and when we're forced into a corner...it gets ugly."

"Why are the Embers only more powerful if they recover artifacts? What artifacts? How do you know all this?" Huxley demanded.

"And THAT!" He slapped his real leg in excitement, "Is the real reason I'm here! I was sent to help Danador, but I realized they needed very little once I got here. Why is it that Danador retained its strength of Magnincy while the rest of Magnadun seemed to become extremely limited in their use?" He paused, his voice sobered some and went on, "The answer is obviously intertwined with the world reshaping. I expect an Ember went mad, like truly, utterly and bewilderingly mad. The kind of madness that makes crazy seem reasonable. Who else and why else would you dice up the whole planet and change it?"

Huxley turned serious, "You think the Embers did that?! Why does everyone believe the Norun were to blame?"

"If you were an Ember, wouldn't you blame it on someone else? And if not an Ember, who else then? God? The Kindler of thought? Or was it a random cosmic occurrence? All evidence points to the Embers. They reached far too deep into Magnincy and grabbed a hold of something no man could wield. Their boasting of their great powers and abilities is impressive to the masses but to me...I think they're tragically underplaying what they are truly capable of. They treat the destruction of vegetation and animals as some great feat. A grand light show and dramatic explosions are great for stories but their true power is greater than that." His voice turned cold. "It can shape worlds. And if The Kindler is still nearby he should fear their power."

A chilling silence fell over the pair, cold and heavy like the blanket of snow that was falling outside. Despite the ever-present roaring hearth of the Gearbox, Huxley shivered. A question birthed from the cold within him found its way to his throat.

"Are you going to try and kill them? The Embers, I mean?"

"I mean to stop them."

"Stop as in..."

Abernathy got up from his stool and walked over to the tapestry Huxley had noticed his first night. He swung it outward revealing a suit of armor. Not like a knight with heavy plates and big shields, it looked like a machine that fit around a man, but it was missing its right leg. It then dawned on Huxley that it matched his mechanical leg. It had gears, pulleys and latches that looked like his machine shop but formed in the fashion of a suit. The workings were lost on Huxley. He had never seen anything like it before. This armor could do any number of things. If he hadn't known Abernathy, and seen it, he would have guessed it was an art piece that he didn't get the meaning of.

"We were once like them, before the reknitting of the world. The Norun society grew at ten times the speed of Danador. We measured that based on your technology and discoveries. We attribute our swifter evolution to ready power sources that you likely lacked. The Norun at full connection with the cosmos could give any Ember a true and proper fight, and if I do say so myself, have far more societal application for his efforts. But now it's like someone is choking our air as we gasp for breath. We once drew so deeply of Magnincy, it was like drinking water, natural, entwined in us. Now I can barely run my own workshop, and even then...it takes a lot out of me. You've seen it."

Huxley nodded his head remembering all too well Abernathy drawing back the machine's power. How they all hung lifeless afterwards, how quickly Abernathy passed out. It reminded Huxley of when he first used Magnincy.

"I expect every other part of Magnadun is the same. From the stories, I've heard, and the tales told, their powers and greatest practitioners were like the Embers. They were capable of great feats or perhaps greater. But when the world reknit, it stemmed the flow. Magnincy was choked off from the rest of the world...except your people. And that Huxley is why I think the answers are inside that tower. Guarded by the Embers to preserve their hold on power and cut it off from the rest of us." He shook his head bitterly and went on, "And now they assert they are the dominant practitioners?" Abernathy grunted distastefully. "No, Magnadun and its people are all meant to share in the light of the stars. The cosmos lights our way and we were kindled to follow that path."

Huxley scrunched his nose and said "Abernathy, that sounded almost religious."

"Hmm oh?" His bearing shifted. He loosened and said, "Yeah I guess, never had much time for religion. I figure what's true is true, and if it's true, I believe it and if it's not, I'll figure it out. Religion has its place, but it sure does like to present truth as lies and lies as truth."

Before Huxley could ask for the obvious clarification, Abernathy picked up the dress, smoothed out the wrinkles and said, "Well, I think after the all-nighter we had last night and today's not looking much better. We should get some work done." Huxley deflated knowing the conversation had ended. "Ok, need help in the workshop?"

"No, I need to work on some special projects that require skilled hands, no offense. And after sleeping all day, I will definitely be up all night. It's a rare opportunity to get some work done on my more...off-brand projects. It will be quiet tonight. I expect Elatress is gone until dawn. Whenever she's in a mood like that she and Arktos slip away. You could get some study done."

Huxley perked up. He had been wanting to look more into a few of the ideas that were wriggling around in the back of his head. "You're right!" He said excitedly. "But...I agreed to help you for my stay here. I can't just study."

"That's true, you can't, but I think you should. Maybe take a few days by yourself."

"A few days?" He asked incredulously.

Abernathy paused thoughtfully and said, "I think the heat is turning up to find you." He produced another BEWARE! Poster. "For a wanted man, we haven't done our best work to keep you hidden. Sneaking out with Elatress is probably fine, but being on the main floor could lead to...leaks. Do you understand?"

"I thought you said we could trust everyone here?"

"That's true, we can, but we can't trust them not to make mistakes."

Huxley gulped. Abernathy had a point. There were a lot of faces that have seen his lately. And the idea of an Ember or Ryla showing up in the Gearbox asking questions or worse, finding him, caused him to shift in his seat. "Besides, I've never known an Ember that didn't want more time to study!" Abernathy added consolingly.

"I'm not an Ember though."

"Oh Huxley," his gaze met his. His amber eyes glowed. He smiled again, though it was mainly hidden by his considerable whiskers. "You've been an Ember for a while now. Have you not been listening? Anyone who wields Magnincy as you do is one....at least in my book."

No one had actually called him an Ember before. Huxley's chest swelled. Abernathy might have just wanted to encourage him, but it didn't matter. Being called an Ember relit Huxley's drive. He got up right away and made for the stairs eager to have the unbroken time ahead of him. Halfway up, he heard Abernathy call to him. "Oh, Ember Huxley?"

He stopped, smiled and looked at him.

"Please don't try and reshape the world or anything like that...just study? Let's keep it quiet..."

"Of...of course," Huxley replied.

21

Questions and Lectures

"Drag and lift are the primary concerns in relation to the subject. Considerations for flow as in its laminar or turbulence will determine outcomes." **-Page 154 Excerpt from the Grimoire**

High up on the second floor of the Gearbox Huxley studied, deep below Abernathy worked, and somewhere in the city Elatress and Arktos sat alone but always together. The three did just those things until the sun rose again. The snow had finally stopped falling but had accomplished its job of blanketing Danador. Only the burning fire atop the tower of the College of Danador repelled the cold. It sat burning brightly as a beacon to all. Huxley could see the glow of it over the skyline. It was an ever-present reminder. Sometimes it helped drive him; other times not. The beacon towered so high, it constantly symbolized how much more he had to go before he could lay claim to be an Ember. Despite this, Huxley began to enjoy his studies for the first time in his life. It was as slow as ever because translating the Grimoire was still difficult and he still did not know much of what it was telling him. The rhythm of the work became familiar though and that familiarity brought comfort. He was happy knowing he was making progress, however, the end goal still seemed far out of reach. At this rate, it would take years before he could return to Mayburn.

A week had passed, but it felt far longer at the Gearbox. Huxley noted that it was a few days past his agreed-upon stay. Abernathy didn't seem to mind and Huxley was in no rush to leave. Their goals seemed to have aligned. He felt like he was in a flow for the first time in his life. Time passed away and didn't seem to hold the same restrictions it once had. When he was deep in study, huge sections of the day would pass. He'd miss meals entirely or neglect to leave his room unless he was forced to. His room became his safe haven. He enjoyed the Gearbox, well enough, but it was almost always full of people. He hadn't been eager to attend another party. Elatress stopped by at odd hours, sometimes to bring a snack, sometimes to bring him food when he forgot to eat. She was a nice reminder of home, she grew to remind him of his little sister Oakley even more than she already had. A few times she'd climbed through the window much to the protest of Arktos who waited outside and was quite offended he'd been left behind. One night, she'd brought a dried-out skull and showed it to him with excitement. "It's the deer from the night we went into the Wilds! Picked clean and left to dry out, probably as a thank you for the free meal." It was frustrating to be pulled out of study to look at a skull. He viewed his research as the most important way to spend his time, but whenever Elatress stopped by, there was usually a discussion about something important to her. She had become less foreign to him. Her mannerisms were still odd, especially to people who didn't know her, but they were quite endearing actually. At first, he suspected that she was touched by madness herself, but if she was, he couldn't detect it. It was exciting to have a conversation with someone where you could never really predict what was going to be said. With her, it was like discovering a new depth of her mind each time they spoke. He suspected it was similar for her. He seemed safe to her. It was probably something she hadn't ex-perienced much based on her deep understanding of survival and nature. He wasn't going to be a threat to her and always tried to listen. It was sad, but he figured he might be the only one who's ever really treated her in such a way. Even Abernathy was more of a father than a friend.

When another week passed, Huxley found the flow of study to be stagnating. His sleep was regular but the dreams of the stars and ocean remained with a singular island off in the distance. It was impossible to make out details but it called to him still. He was growing frustrated. The grimoire had unlocked a great deal for him, especially since getting to Danador. but he'd felt like he ran out of keys for the rest of the locks. Why couldn't he understand more of what it was trying to teach? Physics was the most puzzling as its language was both his own but of math. It spoke in formulas that he hadn't studied. He memorized the layout of them and what they were supposed to be but had no idea how they applied. Biology was challenging as well, the human body, and all bodies for that matter, had layers and layers of systems in place to keep it healthy and growing. Knowing and studying even one of those systems could take years of effort to properly grapple with. There was one section just labeled "Theoretical" and it seemed to be confused with itself. Huxley all but skipped it. Astronomy had been perhaps his best subject. He attributed it to a base desire to know the stars better and heavily suspected Magnincy's similar look to be of no coincidence. So he spent most of his time there, with breaks into environmental science. Elatress was able to add a few notes for him. The growth of trees and animals was something of a specialty for her. He wondered who had taught her but she'd only laugh when asked. Formal schooling seemed to be absolutely ludicrous to her. His own notes had turned into more questions than facts after a time. The Grimoire wasn't for questions to be written but for answers to them.

On his sixteenth night at the Gearbox, Huxley tried understanding physics again. His irritation grew steadily but it ceased when Elatress tapped on his window. She had never bothered to tap before, it was strange that she did so now. He closed the Grimoire and walked over to open it. The cold blew in and fought for its place among the warmth of his room. A glance showed that no one was there. Had he imagined it? It didn't sound like it could have been anything else. Shrugging his shoulders, he gave up when another knock came but this time it was on his forehead. He yelped and rubbed it while looking for whatever hit him. It felt like someone squarely flicked him. It reminded him of something Jonah would do when he got too engrossed in reading. Suddenly, he spotted her. A girl stood on the opposite roof, eyes blazing even in the dark. Her hair stood unnaturally still in the winds of winter and her hands grasped tightly around something he couldn't see.

"That was for breaking my defense." Onders' voice whispered as though right into his ear.

Huxley reflexively jumped back and summoned Magnincy. They'd finally found him! Embers were probably surrounding the house and Ryla was likely downstairs. He couldn't think of what to summon. His mind had flooded with too many ideas but Onders' voice spoke again and broke his train of thought. "Oh, relax Huxley, I've known you were here since you left the College." She whispered again.

"You what?" He demanded.

"Can I come in?" She asked.

"No!"

"You really want to talk to me out here Huxley? Calm down."

"NO!"

"If I wanted you dead, you'd be dead already. Calm down!"

Huxley didn't respond. He didn't think she was totally right, but it would be foolish to underestimate her. She had been training most of her life.

"I think we can help each other." Onders admitted, "Can I come in?" She repeated.

"If you try anything, I'll fight back, and I've learned a lot since we last talked." Huxley threatened.

Her lips pursed and said mockingly "Yes, in the two weeks since we met last, I'm sure you've advanced considerably. Would you like to advance more? That's why I'm here. I can help you."

Huxley really didn't think it was a good idea to let her in, but if she knew he was here what leverage did he have? She could go tell all the Embers and Wardens, and that would bring a world of trouble to his friends. "Fine, give me a minute to clean up." She didn't respond but he assumed she heard him. He closed the blinds as calmly as he could then dashed to hide the Grimoire. Not having a better place, he locked it in the chest at the foot of the bed. It would have to do for now. He cleaned up a few other items and returned to the window. She had left the rooftop and now waited just outside his room. She was floating above the ground, with only purple smoke wisps swirling from under her cloak. "You can fly!" Huxley exclaimed.

She gave him a flat look and said, "You really don't know much do you?" Not waiting for further permission, she stepped in. A heat radiated from her that pushed Huxley back a few paces. It dissipated when her feet touched the ground. She casually looked around and said, "It's unbelievable that your room is nicer than mine."

"Abernathy worked hard to make it, and I'd like to keep it nice. So, let's not wreck it. What do you want?" Huxley asked.

"An exchange." She said, her eyes still casting about the room. Shedding her casual demeanor, the old one he had met weeks ago crept back in.

"Of what?" He asked.

"Information. I want to know how you beat me and in exchange, I'll answer one of the many questions you have."

"How do you know I have questions? Maybe I have it all figured out." He gambled.

A smile twisted on her lips, "No formal training, no grimoire, no talent. And yet you somehow got one over on me. You've learned something and it allowed you to blunder into an ability you can't hope to control for long. You're probably scared and desperate, which is what led you to the College and to lash out at me. Then you attacked Embers. Everything about you should be screaming with questions. It's the one trait everyone who has touched magnincy shares."

She was overwhelmingly right. They both knew it.

Huxley decided on a dangerous tactic. She held all the advantages here except for one crucial mistake. She assumed he didn't have a grimoire. For whatever reason, she judged that part wrong. He could use this information but he needed time to figure out how.

Onders stepped closer and said, "I've got a few questions, as I'm sure you do. Answer mine and I will help you with my considerable knowledge."

She wasn't the teacher he had hoped for, but she might be one he needs.

"You want to know how I beat you?" He asked.

"Yes, but don't try to answer that now. I doubt you really know how you did it."

Huxley was affronted but tried not to show it. The Embers had so far universally underestimated him and that could still be useful. She went on, "My life here has been difficult, though I have enormous natural talent and hard-won knowledge. The Embers still keep me from true knowledge, the kind they jealousy horde while I reread old tomes with principles read hundreds of times before. I think you've stumbled upon something ancient and rare. If I can learn it from you, it might give me the advantage I need to earn their respect."

"That's really terrible." He responded. "I'm sorry it's been that way."

"You, what?" Her smile had disappeared and now only indignation spilled out. "You live poor in clips and knowledge, being hunted and maligned, and you feel sorry for me?" She rubbed her head as though dealing with him was something she had to endure. She exhaled in frustration and shook her head. "Do you want to do this or not? I am offering something here, a genuine exchange. I could just turn you in, you know? You'd be dead or driven mad by the end of the evening."

"Well, when you put it that way..." He said sarcastically, but she did not pick up on it.

"Good. I propose one question a night from both parties. I ask mine and you ask yours. We will answer in good faith and be done. When I have gotten what I need, we will part ways."

"Won't you just turn me in then?" He accused.

"No," She snapped, "try not to be stupid. If you waste my time, I will stop coming here. This is an opportunity for both of us to get ahead."

Maybe, she was right. He was beginning to think he had also underestimated her.

"Ok, one question a night. I can agree to that. I know Embers can tell if you're lying, but how am I going to know if you are?" He studied her closely to see her reaction.

"I am not an Ember, and they can't tell. They are ok with people thinking that though. Truth in belief is not a hard fact in which Magnincy is made of. Telling the truth is often circumstantial at best and impossible at worst. Ok, now my question."

"Wait! That wasn't my question!" Huxley said, suddenly alarmed.

"I just emphasized not wasting my time and gave you valuable information someone would pay many clips to know. Either that was your question, or you're wasting my time. Choose."

There was no joke to her tone. "Ok, that was my question."

"Good then answer this," She paused to make sure she had his full attention. "When did you start dreaming of the Ocean and Stars?"

He blinked, *That's what she wants to know?* He thought.

"Answer!" She demanded.

"Just after I used Magnincy for the first time."

She hummed to herself and clicked her tongue. "Ok, then, I will see you tomorrow. Leave the window open." She turned to leave and Huxley followed her and asked, "That's really all you wanted to know?"

"I'll answer that tomorrow."

"No! That's not my question." He corrected himself.

She laughed to herself and stepped out the window supported by some unseen force. The moon, now half full, cast a pale light onto her. And for the first time, Huxley noticed how truly beautiful she was. He had been so flustered every time they spoke before, he hadn't noticed. He remembered her hair tightly bound before but now it flowed in loose waves, black as the night sky. The lantern light from below and the moonlight from above shimmered off her face. She glowed so radiantly that he wished that she would never cover herself again with a hood. Huxley knew how dangerous she was, but he couldn't help himself at that moment. He involuntarily stepped closer to her, as though he was being commanded by an outside force. She leaned back into the window, inside of his grasp, and her breath collided with his in the cold air that now filled the room. The mist of it joining together. "I am happy we came to an arrangement. Stay alive so I can learn more from you." Then a snap and puff of purple smoke replaced where she had been and Onders was gone.

"Me too," Huxley said to the darkness.

He stood alone. The cold didn't bother him at all.

————————————————————————————————

It took him some time to get to sleep. He should have been alarmed at being in close contact with Onders but her offer was too good. One question might not be a lot, but if he asked the right one, it could reveal loads about the Grimoire. That night his dreams returned to the confusing landscapes of oceans and stars. Onders and the warden asking about them confirmed a suspicion he had. It wasn't just a dream. It was something that all who touched Magnincy shared. He stood only ankle-deep in the water. It still beckoned him outward and now a voice repeated, "Reach," and only that.

Huxley slept well past noon. The device that normally awoke him, did not sound. He stirred, exhausted from his late night when the odor of a fugitive rose out of his shirt. It found his nose quite unprepared. How many days had he been studying and not worrying about his hygiene? He started doing the math but hated the answer he was forming. That may have been why Onders was so eager to leave. Banishing the thought, he decided it was irrelevant. He stripped his clothes which he would likely have to resort to burning to deal with the smell.

He drew a bath and hopped into the tub. The heat permeated every part of him. He felt himself relaxing more than he wanted. He'd likely far overslept and left Elatress and Abernathy short-handed. But the warmth and quiet made a strong argument to not worry about it. The quiet didn't last long. He was still in the Gearbox after all. Quiet was a distant relative who only visited at odd hours and definitely came unannounced. Oddly, it wasn't shouts or outrage. It was stuffy and angry. The muffled voices slipped under his door and made their way into the bathroom with him. He could make out Abernathy's voice. Was there ever a conversation in the Gearbox that he wasn't a part of? Curiosity drew him out of his bath sooner than he would have liked. He wrapped himself in a towel and made for the door. He leaned low to try to hear better but remained ready to run should the tube open again for an escape. The thought of sliding naked down that tube into smoldering coals did not appeal to him. In fact, it was downright terrifying. Already the relaxation of his bath was falling away into memory. That Gearbox's door shut with a thud while he sat dreading his options. He exhaled in relief, there would be no naked tube-sliding. He got dressed as briskly as he could, threw his hair into a loose ponytail and made for the door. He flung it open to find Elatress waiting. She was cleaner than normal, perhaps having had a bath herself. Only one small twig was tangled in her hair. Her outfit was an approximation of a dress, at least by her standards. It was more like a traveler's garb with a little frill around the waist. She had her forest-coloured cloak clasped around her as always. He yelped in surprise as she grabbed his arm. She smiled, and Huxley realized he had never really seen her smile...not like that. She was excited, more excited than he'd ever seen her.

"We get to go! Finally, it's here!" She shoved a traveling cloak that had been left by a patron into Huxley's hands. She whispered, "Put this on, it will help you blend in." Her voice resumed its normal volume and she said, "The Lecture Hall! For ONCE something is happening and I want to go!" Abernathy began to shout from downstairs but was cut off sharply by Elatress. "It's a date! She proclaimed. I rescheduled with what's-his-name and he said, yes! Totally a romantic date with snuggling and dinner and dancing and all of that garbage. A date to the Lecture Hall! Right, Huxley?" She squeezed his arm so tight he winced. "RIGHT?"

"Yes..." Her eyes bored into his as he fumbled to figure out what was happening. "And I am the..." her head nodded as he found the word, "...chaperone.

Abernathy's stare was telling. "Yes, a fugitive heading out...to a Lecture...that will surely be crowded..." Abernathy didn't have to say anything more. His point was made.

Huxley's eyes widened. Each part of what Abernathy stated gave him ascending spikes of anxiety.

"If I can hide Arktos, I can hide you." She said.

"Really?!" Huxley asked in surprise.

Yes, I took him last year and barely anyone saw him despite the fact that he's huge. You're so much smaller, practically tiny."

"Tiny!" Huxley protested but her fingers just dug deeper.

Abernathy tilted his head to one side, "he is right...running around at night in sparsely packed areas, is one thing. But sneaking into the Lecture Hall is another. Are you taking the sewers again?"

She huffed and said, "Well, of course not! You don't take sewers to go on a date. Besides, Rence, or Rowan or whatever can't handle that."

"That's never mattered to you before." He protested, "And his name is Reince!"

Undeterred, she went on, "Well, it does now. We are taking a few rooftops, then in through the wardens' tents and then under the bleachers."

"The War-" Huxley began.

She squeezed again, stopping his argument.

Abernathy gave a "harumph" that she took as approval.

"Exit strategy?" He inquired.

She shook a string of vials dangling from her belt, they clinked together sounding like rain. Abernathy gave another "Harumph".

"Great, we will be back before dinner starts...well, maybe a while afterwards."

She practically yanked Huxley out the door as he clasped his cloak around his shoulders. Arktos climbed out from under the bar moving once again faster than he should be able to for his size. He blocked the door and bellowed. Elatress looked her companion up and down, rubbed the top of his head and pressed her forehead against his. "You know why." She whispered to him. His eyes turned sorrowful and just gave a soft *harumph* back that sounded like he was doing an Abernathy impression. He moved out of the way, albeit far slower than he got there.

Abernathy glanced suspiciously, "Aren't you waiting for your date? Isn't he going to pick you up?"

"No, Bookpile's taking me to his house!"

And she pulled Huxley out the door.

The duo hurried down the side streets, sloshing through a deep accumulation of snow. Huxley had been so curious to go to a Lecture Hall in Danador that he had neglected to ask an obvious question, "Elatress, why do you want to go to a Lecture? It strikes me as a thing you wouldn't care about."

"Hah! I forgot you don't know about Danador at all. It's only housed in a Lecture Hall. There is no actual guy talking about something he learned in a book." She stopped walking and said, "I bet that's really disappointing to you."

Huxley stopped as well and said, "I guess, but if not a lecture, then what?"

"A battle!"

"In a Lecture Hall?"

"Where else would it be?"

He didn't know of any suitable place for a battle, but that didn't mean the location of a lecture hall made any more sense. She huffed and said, "It's big, empty, and easy to watch. Now come on! Or we will be late!"

———————————————————————————————

The icy streets of Danador were empty. Barring a smattering of people who either didn't trust their stores to remain unguarded or like them, were just plain late. This much snow, slush and ice on the ground did little to deter foot traffic. Huxley doubted even a blizzard would slow this city down but the day of a Lecture was apparently enough to grind it to a halt. The pair walked so hurriedly, it might have been a jog.

True to her word, their path led them over rooftops and through back channels. There were alleys through the industrial district with only one rooftop jump, to avoid a two-man guard patrol. Then, they moved onward to the first rung. Elatress led him to an edge about twenty feet high. It was a long drop. The wall before them was sheer, so climbing up there would be difficult as well as dangerous especially if they were caught. The tiers of the city led upwards as you went into it, so naturally, it was like going downhill to leave. You just usually didn't notice as much going upward.

She pointed at a hole in a storage shed behind the main road. Little bits of red were visible through the snow-covered roof. The hole was obscured with a piece of fabric presumably to keep animals out but Huxley doubted it worked. "Jump through the hole, there is a hammock set up to catch us."

"How do you know it's there?"

"The same way I know where most things are." Sensing his fear, she said, "It's not as high as it looks, watch." She stepped off the side and fell. The snow from her boots showed a light flutter trailing after her. She tore through the fabric, ripping it away, and instead of a thud, Huxley heard almost nothing. She exited the door to the shed and motioned him to do the same. He judged the distance and his own ability to hit a small hole. His mind ran through all of the probabilities and what would likely happen if he missed. The conclusion being, his head busted open against the roof that he was definitely going to hit. She motioned again, growing annoyed. Huxley took a step back. The wind blew the loose bits of his hair in front of his eyes. He tried tying it back but it was too hard to get it together. He wished it would stop so he could think.

Suddenly, a page from the Grimoire flashed in his mind. *Meteorology.* "Hang on a second." He called down to her.

Wind was too difficult to control directly, if he dared try it would take far too much out of him. It was connected to so much, he'd have to call on huge amounts of Magnincy. But for a moment, he might be able to get it to go his way. Just for a moment. He closed his eyes to try and remember his studies. Meteorology, pressure, flow, heat and cold reacting, all producing movement. He grabbed what he could of those elements, they swirled and protested at being held. He gripped them tight and dashed for the edge. The second his foot left the ground he threw as hard as he could directly underneath him. A huge gust roared to life and smashed upward underneath him, and for one glorious second, he was being carried by the wind. Then the snow caught up, it blasted every exposed inch of his skin like tiny needles. He yelped and flailed, losing his balance and began to falter. The zephyr that had been summoned weakened as it released its strength in all different directions. Huxley dropped and slammed into the ground with a "flump." He slowly opened his eyes as though keeping them shut would have protected his body in some way. Shockingly, he felt ok, more than ok, actually, kind of exhilarated. He smiled despite how ridiculous he looked flopping through the air like that. It had worked to some degree. Balancing on the wind seemed to be enormously difficult. An image of the word *Aerodynamics* came to his mind. He couldn't recall any information about that section of the Grimoire. It probably had something to do with what happened. He'd have to look into it, tonight. Elatress appeared next to him and pulled him out of the snow bank he had lodged himself in.

"You're more than lucky Bookpile. Do you know what you could have hit underneath all of this?"

Huxley blinked and said, "Do you know what I could have hit?"

"Yes. You wouldn't be walking right now if you did."

He brushed as much snow as he could off himself. It had lodged itself into every available space. "How do you always know? How do you know where things are all the time? Or where people are? Is it part of your Magnincy?" When he finished cleaning himself off, he looked up at her. She met his eyes and really searched them. He didn't know what she was looking for but he had never seen her look this way at him before. It was piercing and uncomfortable.

"It is my Magnincy." She said with her head downturned.

All of a sudden her countenance shifted again and she said, "For a smart guy you sure do miss a lot. Have you ever met a Suminen?"

Huxley gaped at her. "You're Suminen?!"

"Sorta." She answered.

"Sorta?" He repeated.

"Yes." And Elatress resumed the journey not feeling the need to clarify.

Elatress and Huxley made their way through the empty market and found the Lecture hall just off the main road. The front entrance was packed with people trying to get in. Elatress brought him to a nearby building that looked on the verge of collapse.

"Ok, up we go." There was a ladder up the side that stood broken halfway up. It was held together through a mixture of rope and what looked like puddy. It swayed and creaked in the wind. He hesitated and she said, "Don't summon a tornado or something to get yourself up there. Just climb."

He had considered something in line with Magnincy, though not a tornado. How would that even work? It would definitely be in the field of Meteorology, perhaps if he could mix-

She snapped her fingers, near his face, breaking him out of his thoughts.

"Huxley! Stop. Climb." She spoke each word as though he would have trouble understanding.

He did as instructed, not wanting her to get any more annoyed with him. She had been right to trust the ladder. It held strong, and before he knew it, they were on a rooftop amid a thick blanket of snow. The crowd was quite loud now, though the snow was absorbing lots of the ambient noise.

"One last thing and we're inside the security."

"Wait, really? It's that easy?"

"For me, yes, but you…"

One more jump lay before him. Apparently, you could get to all sorts of places inside Danador if you didn't have the clips by just jumping and climbing. The well-secured Rung entrances were not as effective as he thought. Despite a good idea of using a more directed form of wind to lessen his fall, he listened to Elatress this time and jumped where she told him to. He didn't have to hit such a small mark as last time. He fell into a snowbank for the second time and when he pulled himself out, a tunnel lay before him. It channeled the noise from the crowd directly into his ears.

The Lecture was about to start.

22

∽

Art and Rage

"...integrated action of many cells need to be involved. A biological cascade follows in an automated process the body does instinctually. The cytokines do their work signaling others to begin repairing tissue." - Page 410 Excerpt from the Grimoire

The Lecture Hall wasn't as large as he thought it would be. In his mind, he had imagined scores of seats packing thousands of people together. Instead, it was more like an auditorium that had been retrofitted to house more seats so it fully encircled the building. Then Huxley spotted it. A sheer cut in the stonework, an unmistakable mark of the Forty-Five. It hadn't been totally cut but it likely lost most of its backside making it not an ideal place to teach or preach or whatever this place was originally used for. It didn't match the opulence and sheer scope of the rest of the city. The arena likely wasn't built with housing the whole city in mind, and definitely not for battles. Danador didn't strike Huxley as the kind of place for things like that. Displays of violence and needless bloodshed were not something he was taught was prized by the erudite learner. He doubted it was even largely approved of by the Embers.

But here it stood, despite it all. No combatants had entered yet, but a man was taking a position in the middle of the arena. Huxley excitedly looked for a place to sit but felt a tug from Elatress. "No seats for us Bookpile, this is the only clear look we will get." She motioned him to follow, and he did. It was exciting to see some action that wasn't going to be directed at him for once. He needed to think about something else besides the Grimoire, dishes and being attacked, for a little while.

She led him into a service closest in a small tunnel headed underneath the arena. It was dark inside and cramped. They nearly didn't have room for the both of them. The only light was a single beam of sun sneaking in through a section of crumbled wall that was losing its battle with time.

"It should be around here somewhere," Elatress said. Huxley took a moment to loosen his travel cloak. Right as he removed it from his shoulders, Elatress' boot smashed into his face. Rubble soon fell around him as well, narrowly missing his new boot-printed head. He cried out in surprise and pain. Dust spun wildly around and Huxley waved his hands trying to dissipate all of the particles. The sunlight caught each one and he had to squint as it filled the room with light and dust. Elatress had left the room, and Huxley behind. He looked around for her and saw her head poke out from the crumbled bit of wall.

"Did you use me as a ladder?" He admonished incredulously.

"More like a staircase"

"You could have asked." He spat not keeping his annoyance hidden.

"You would have argued. It's over now. Come on up." She held both arms down to him in offering.

Huxley wiped the dust off himself, looked around the room and sighed. "We have to watch through cracks don't we?"

"Well, don't blame me!" She said pointedly. "I'm not a fugitive. Abernathy said to keep you hidden. This is the way to do it. Besides, it's actually a good view."

Huxley doubted that greatly, but resigned himself. He moved to the wall and looked for something to help him up.

"Don't you dare use Magnincy in here!" She barked.

"I wasn't going to." He lied. He could probably affect the air inside here far easier than outside with all of those other elements. With the particles in the air swirling and finding peace again from being disturbed, he thought it'd be an excellent place to try.

The roar of the crowd intensified and it shook him out of his thoughts. He took her help and she pulled him up, rather easier than he expected. They climbed through a few dozen feet of rubble and debris. They were no longer inside but on a cliff underneath the newly constructed seating of the arena. He could see the whole of the Forty-Five underneath him. He moved to look how far down when Elatress grabbed his hand.

"It's not stable." She said.

"Where?" He asked, surveying the ground around him.

"Everywhere. More falls each day. Best to stick close to the wall."

She climbed on well-chosen spots and settled next to a gash in the rock. She patted the section next to her and Huxley followed to take his seat.

"Now you see why Arktos couldn't come. He'd have caved in this whole section."

It did turn out to be a pretty great view. They had missed some sort of pre-show with a display of skills in combat and were just now introducing the main combatants. Their seats were no good for hearing what was happening. Huxley strained to hear. Elatress rolled her eyes and said, "I'll explain, Danador allows a battle here once a year for everyone who's brave enough to enter. The rules are, the last person standing is the winner. You can quit by running back into your chamber or by dying."

"Dying is quitting?" Huxley asked.

"No, it's dying." Elatress said and went on, "You can use whatever weapons you can bring so long as it won't hurt the audience. If you win, you are granted a request from the city. It's not without limits, but you can get a lot from them. Most people just request Clips but some request something more audacious. It varies person to person. That's basically it. I guess it's frowned on to murder your opponent after they've been beaten but it happens regularly. Any questions?"

Huxley just blinked and said "Someone's going to die down there?"

Elatress just shook her head yes and looked out onto the make-shift arena.

The Hall was similar to Huxley's trial ground within the College of the Arcane Flame. Pillars, rubble, and sand made up most of it. But there were platforms and pieces of wall from some other buildings attached. It may have been from the very place he now sat. There were a few places to hide but not for long. Tactically, you could gain the high ground in the middle but be greatly exposed on all sides.

Eight gates surrounded the arena with four already opened. The four that were out already were checking their gear and swinging their weapons nervously. The first he saw was a bald man in leather studded armor. He had a small buckler shield and a spear in hand. He hopped back and forth, jutting it forward. The next was a stoic soldier that dressed as the city guard did. His armor was adorned with slightly different colors, Huxley thought he recognized them from another leg of Danador's reach, Hammersnow Point perhaps. He held a two-handed hammer meant for war with several knives strapped around his belt. His equipment looked largely ceremonial. He must be representing his town both in presence and effect. A few streaks of blue and silver lined his outfit and he even had stripes down the side of his face. Huxley glanced at Elatress, who shrugged.

Then a bowman caught Huxley's eye, his quiver wasn't quite full. Huxley looked closely and counted seven arrows with the eighth already knocked. Elatress jabbed Huxley's ribs and said, "Ooohhh, I love him! Gavin is from Ladrona, out east. He always brings the exact amount of arrows for the combatants involved."

"So, he's boasting? Like those are all he will need?" Huxley inquired. He wasn't sure if he should be impressed or scared for the man.

"You could say that, if boasting is being correct, then, yes."

"It's not-"

She jabbed him again and pointed at the next one. "I don't believe it! He actually came back!"

In contrast to everyone else stood a man who nervously fiddled with a device in his hand. Huxley was reminded of the same device employed in the battle at Mayburn. Some kind of explosive projectile cannon but smaller, able to be held and directed. A bespectacled face scrunched up in tight concentration. His pencil-thin mustache twitched in annoyance as he fiddled with his cannon. Precision tools hung on all sides of his belt, most were aligned neatly in front of his waist but in contrast a huge blood-splattered wrench dangled behind him. "Horace is Abernathy's biggest rival. Abernathy would hate it if he won!" She smiled at the last part as if it would be the funniest thing if he did.

"Is he any good?" Huxley questioned.

"If he did his math right, then yes. But Abernathy says he's too sloppy to ever get it right."

Just then the announcer quieted the crowd. He held his hands outward and lowered them slowly. A hush fell in anticipation. As though seizing the opportunity, an unsettling bellow came rushing from the fifth gate. It was a noise Huxley couldn't forget and one that he had sadly heard before. Animalistic, and primal, it was as if all sense had left and only instinct remained. Huxley shivered as he recognized the warrior resting on a three-pronged Trident, a weapon that was meant for gutting huge animals. The crowd, instead of cheering, as they had for the others shrieked in surprise, and small pockets even laughed. Standing naked as the day he was born, stood Grubmush. Panting hard, he looked like a farm dog does after collapsing in exhausting heat. His veins bulged and his muscles gleamed in sweat. The beard on his face was tied in the same way it had been that night at the Gearbox, in three long braided prongs that matched his trident. The rest of his body hair was a tangled nest, both dense and long, covering nearly all of himself. His face, arms and the rest of his body was gnarled and chewed up. It was a grotesque display of what a lifetime of violence begets. Huxley gulped in fear. Having some connection with this man was troubling. He shifted uncomfortably and so did Elatress.

"Why is he naked?!" She asked as though Huxley would know what brought on such bizarre behavior.

"I'm nearly positive that is the craziest person I have ever met, and I've met some crazy people."

"Is it a boast, like the archer?" She thought out loud.

"I doubt they have much in common in terms of thought lines," Huxley responded.

The rest of the combatants looked just as dumbfounded.

The man he had encountered at the Gearbox was a stranger compared to the feral beast in the Lecture Hall. This person was much more like the kind he remembered from Mayburn. Grubmush flailed about jeering his competitors and taunting the crowd. He began making a type of salute with his hands in a motion that no one understood. Huxley guessed it had something to do with the mad ramblings of his religion. Grubmush's hands jutted in violent gestures and leaped a few times. The announcer tried to move on and bring out the next competitor, but when the gate opened, no one came out. A roar of laughter bathed the Lecture Hall, mocking whoever was inside but Huxley felt like he was the only one who had any common sense. The seventh gate opened and a slight framed woman stepped out wielding two small daggers. She had forgone armor in exchange for tight-fitting clothing. Not a scrape of errant fabric or hair hung loose. She stepped delicately and kept her eyes on Grubmush. She made no attempt to get the crowd going, just kept her eyes locked on him. She was probably wise to do so, Huxley thought.

"Llias," Elatress said in a whisper. "I thought she had left."

"Is she Suminen, like you?"

"No, she's from Danador, but not like you."

Finally, the last gate opened. A full reflection of the sun emerged, each plate of her armor caught a new shade of light and shone out. Silver and polished as though ready for war or a regal portrait, Ryla The Butcher of Valdannon emerged, still holding the same blade that had threatened Huxley. It was a glaive that stood nearly as tall as her. The tip of it shone as her armor had. Elatress made an involuntary squeak of excitement.

She said, "By the lost and the found! Finally! I've only encountered her a few times, and she moves like no one else I've ever seen." Her words came pouring out of her barely stopping to connect sentences. "You can tell a lot, like a LOT by someone's gait, and stance. People walk in patterns and are predictable. Not random and crazy like Grubmush, that's still predictable, in an unpredictable way, you know? Ryla's every step is in rhythm, in a pattern." She paused, her voice caught in her throat. It even cracked when she said, "it's beautiful."

"Her walk?!" Huxley asked in surprise.

"No, all of her." She said seriously, "She is art in motion." Elatress clasped her hands together and pressed them in her chest. Her eyes looked over at Grubmush and narrowed. "He had better not hurt her."

Huxley wasn't sure they were even safe this close to Grubmush. He was beginning to lose patience. Unable to contain his energy, his pacing turned to jogging in a circle. The rest of the fighters took their places, knocked their arrows, readied their weapons, and hefted their shields. Horace reexamined his weapons and spun a few gears within it. Nodding in approval of his weapon, he holstered it and took his pipe out of his mouth, emptied the cinders and tobacco onto the ground with a tap of his boot, pocketed it and unholstered his weapon again.

The announcer hurried into a safe room just outside and began a countdown. All of which was lost on Huxley as the crowd was screaming in excitement only to be outmatched by Grubmush's war cry.

They all moved at once. They must have heard the announcer say, "Go," because Huxley certainly hadn't. Grubmush tore off, kicking the ground as he sprinted, straight forward to the middle of the arena. He cleared the steps in seconds and leapt off the top. For a moment time stood still, Huxley's brain trying to take in a starkly naked Grubmush in full display of hundreds of people. Wailing in madness, he was finally let off the leash of civility. Howling and heaving his trident over his head, he landed with a crunch onto the first man Huxley had seen. His spear and buckler clattered to the floor. Grubmush stepped off and slammed his trident down on him a few more times, spraying bits of the man upward. Huxley gasped. It was almost exactly what had happened in Mayburn. He winced at the sight and looked away. Ryla had also made for the middle but at a leisurely walk...or was she strolling? Either way, she seemed totally unconcerned with the shocking violence that had just occurred. Llias had disappeared from Huxley's view. Two arrows flew through the air and caught Grubmush in the back. They stuck deep and knocked him to the ground. Horace had taken a wide sweeping stance brandishing his weapon to limited effect. No one knew what it could do but knew it certainly did something. Gavin re-notched and aimed at Horace. Horace leveled his weapon and it exploded. Not in his hands but forward, outward. His cannon worked, perhaps even as intended. Something small ripped through Gavin's right arm, so small that Huxley hadn't seen it. A projectile of some kind. His ears rang and when that faded it was replaced with Gavin's screams of agony. Horace had a wide, and satisfied smile. He gestured triumph to the audience and presented his weapon. He couldn't quite make out what was being said but it looked as though he was in the market now barking his wares. He turned a few gears within, which spun and clicked into place. He leveled it again at Gavin but the archer had retreated to his entrance clutching his wounded arm.

"Aww, he forfeited!" Elatress said disappointed.

"He's missing a good bit of his arm...and he's an archer." Huxley pointed out.

"He still has another arm. That other guy dropped his spear." Elatress offered as a possible solution. Huxley rolled his eyes and saw that Ryla had found the exact middle of the Lecture hall. Somewhat elevated, her armor refracted every available light source. She stood and waited. Not even following the movements of the others, she presented herself as a target, it seemed. Her challenge was obvious. She was in the middle of the arena, with no possibility of not seeing her. She shone like the College's tower at midnight. What was she planning?

Horace tried to find a new target. The Knight of Hammersnow had engaged with Llias. One of her daggers stuck out of his side. He flung his hammer into her. He had been aiming for her head but only caught her shoulder. It was enough to crumple her to the ground. She wasn't dead but likely out of the fight. Satisfied, he looked up only to find Grubmush barreling towards him, arrows sticking out of his back. He readied his hammer hoping to finish the job that Gavin started when another explosion erupted through the air. Grubmush skidded to a halt. His rage passed and he looked...astonished. A bloody hole in his chest was now visible which hadn't been there a moment before. He poked a finger into it, with a look of disbelief that melted into a smile. He nodded acknowledging that yes there was a hole in his chest. The Knight took the opportunity and swung his massive hammer for Grubmush's head. Grubmush whipped his head out of the way, still fingering the hole in his chest. The Knight lost his footing, having expected to catch Grubmush unaware. Grubmush surged forward and grabbed the man's head with his huge paw-like hand. The Knight of Hammersnow yelled something in protest but it was muffled. Grubmush met his eyes, his rage now returning. Grubmush buried the man head-first into the dirt. Llias hopped up from the ground grasping one dagger.

"A feint! She is so devious!" Elatress exclaimed.

Llias snuck up and stabbed the dagger into Grubmush's side. She smiled wickedly and tried to push it deeper as he howled. Grubmush dropped his hand to grab the dagger. Llias released and stumbled backwards, her confidence fading. She looked around for a weapon, finding none, she made a break for her gate. Grubmush ran her down before she got halfway. His trident found the middle of her back. She wasn't faking this time. His howls of rage returned.

Horace fiddled with his weapon, he spun a few more gears but desperation now streaked over his face. Grubmush was looking to see if his opponent was still alive. His body was twitching so Grubmush kicked it a few times. Horace grabbed for a tool on his belt but dropped it, adrenaline causing his hands to shake too much for such precision. He fumbled on the ground to try and grab it. The confidence he showed earlier, had disappeared. In desperation, he reached for the wrench that flopped around on a hook, pulled it free and readied himself ... Only to find Grubmush had not come after him. Grubmush had left. Seizing the opportunity, Horace ran for his gate signaling his forfeiture. The gate shut and he stared back through the bars glad that he had escaped with his life.

Grubmush now stood looking up at Ryla. His trident hung at his side. He yanked the two arrows free. His face betrayed no pain in the process. Huxley thought he might not have felt it at all. He had read that adrenaline and rage can be a sort of pain duller in the right circumstances. The crowd quieted and the announcer said, "Two remain, Ryla the Butcher of Valdannon and Grubmush of Kilika." The pair regarded each other, Ryla finally shifting her stance from a parade rest to holding her blade in a wide arch. She held it up and Grubmush lifted his trident. The pair exchanged a sentence or two, but it was impossible for Huxley to hear what. Murder filled his eyes and a bellow issued forth from his lungs as Grubmush rushed her.

———————————————————————————————————

Ryla couldn't call this her best work, but it was her most creatively satisfying. Her brush hadn't touched paint yet but she directed the piece all the same. A good work of art is said to have always been there; it was just the job of the artist to make it visible to everyone else. This day held many pieces that could have made great art, but they wouldn't be true to her spirit, or her nature. Ryla had pushed down her impulses for a little over a year now. To restrict an artist is a crime, not just against them but against the world for the loss of their art. Ryla had chosen this day and this place to show Danador and her people what mastery of Magnincy really looked like. That animal that prowled on her canvas was serving his part. She cringed at his erratic movements and base instincts. His work was akin to a child's finger painting, certainly not of Valdannon's children. He roared and carried on dousing the sides of her work with nonsensical spatter and debris. It didn't matter. It would all serve her vision in the end. She had seen it in a dream. Now was the time to create her masterpiece. She relished the idea of finally dipping her brush into the deepest sanguine. Color pulsed out of him now, through arrow wounds, scrapes and cuts. A little even dribbled from his mouth. No doubt, he bit his own tongue in his mad thrashing about. Ryla readied her brush and prepared to paint. Let all who are here this day witness her artistic talent.

———————————————————————————————————

Huxley and Elatress didn't speak and just watched enraptured. Huxley didn't even know who he wanted to win the exchange. Both had threatened his life and he'd be fine if both were out of his life. He would know soon enough.

Ryla waited at the top of the steps in the middle of the lecture hall. Grubmush put a foot on the bottom and shot upward at a full sprint. Making it to the top in a flash, he did a side hop to leap off a piece of rubble and ascended high into the air. It looked like he could have cleared seven feet straight up. His trident tips struck downward and plunged itself into Ryla. Huxley and Elatress gasped along with the crowd, but soon all screamed in amazement. Ryla had side-stepped it! The weapon must have missed her by inches! For a brief moment, the pair stood nearly face to face, one passive with the other's grim satisfaction melting away. Rylas' glaive handle struck Grubmush in the nose, breaking it. The crunch echoed and Grubmush stumbled backward. Ryla leveled the glaive's blade and stabbed it forward at his chest. He dodged backward but not far enough and the glaive found its mark. It sank only a few inches. She pulled it out and slung droplets of blood around her. The pair now regarded each other. Grubmush felt his nose and righted it with another crunch. He blew some blood out of it to clear his airways. Huxley wondered how Grubmush even stayed on at this point. He was more than broken, he had a huge gash in his side and arrow wounds on his back. Grubmush lifted his trident once more but adopted a different stance. Obviously, Ryla was ready for another frontal assault. Grubmush grunted. It was clearly how he worked himself up for a fight. Before he got the chance, it was Ryla who moved first. Raising her glaive high she spun in a circle above her head. It spun so fast Huxley couldn't track its movement. Grubmush did not retreat. He advanced as well. He held his trident horizontally in a defensive stance and squatted low, perhaps hoping to get underneath her offense. In a flash of light, she sliced him again with a low thin cut that splayed blood outward, producing a fine red mist that hung in the air like a cloud. Grubmush retreated again and fingered his new wound. He pushed the newly opened skin back together as an animal might. Grubmush resumed his original stance of trident held high over his head but instead of rushing her, he hurled it at her. The crowd gasped and Ryla's face for the briefest second showed surprise. The pronged weapon tore through the air. Ryla caught the middle handle with the tip of her blade and knocked it skyward. Grubmush dashed immediately at her and Ryla now found herself facing the oncoming naked man. He was a fool to think this would have worked against her, he'd only exposed himself more. Perhaps, he thought she wouldn't have been able to recover her defense in time. He was wrong. She sank her glaive deep into Grubmush's gut, but his momentum was too great. She fell backwards but kept her grip on her weapon. Her back hit the ground, which also propped the glaive up, skewering Grubmush in the air like a kebab. Grubmush, unaffected by the horrendous wound, grabbed the handle and pulled himself downward. He didn't even cry out in pain. It was like this was his plan the whole time. He slid through and down the handle, landing on top of Ryla. His hands gripped her throat and it began to crush. She tried to gasp but couldn't even get that out. Grubush was killing her. Huxley could see it in his eyes. That wasn't anger or rage, it was death. He'd only seen that look once before. It caused him to shiver. His body reacted before he could stop it. Huxley began to summon the stars again. Maybe if he could lob it near them, he could stop this madness. Elatress saw Huxley shoot his hands forward, summoning Magnincy and she grabbed his arm. "No, Huxley! There are people everywhere. You'll be caught AND you may hurt someone. You're not practiced enough! They signed up for this. They knew what they were doing." Huxley didn't release but held the star in his hands. She was right. of course. There were lots of ways this could have turned out worse than it already had.

Ryla was slowly losing consciousness and had begun to go limp. She stopped flailing, her arms fell to the ground. The roar of the crowd and screams around her quieted. Her eyes became only narrow slits.

This was the end of the Butcher.

Huxley could only watch as her eyes closed. Almost immediately they reopened again, changed. They were drained of color, her iris now fully black and surrounded by white. Even in this moment of panic and fear, she managed to banish it and regain composure. She stopped trying to push him off of her. He was locked in like a dog on a scrap of meat. Instead. she reached around him and pulled her glaive the rest of the way through. It slipped out rather easily. Flipped it up and pointed the glaive downward. She rammed it into his back only a blade length and sliced outward bringing blood, gore and sinew with it. He didn't let go immediately. A few seconds passed before he seemed to register he had been opened up. Finally, his grip broke and his eyes fluttered. Ryla shoved him off her and staggered to her feet. She rubbed her throat now red and dirt-stained, already bruising. She coughed and gasped, recovering herself.

Hefting herself up on her glaive, she stood over her opponent. Grubmush lay unconscious in a heap next to her. The sight nearly made Huxley sick, fortunately, it was far enough away to not see the details. The crowd remained in stunned silence, then slowly, one at a time, a few in the crowd began to cheer. Then, like a damn bursting, they all did. The announcer was saying something but it was pointless. She used her glaive to keep her steady and moved for the center of the Hall where she had fought Grumbmush first. The battlefield had truly taken on a bizarre kind of symmetry, chaotic and jumbled on the outside but with broad movements and lines in the middle. It reminded Huxley of a kind of painting. Ryla took her time ascending the steps. The only thing fierce about her now was her smile. It was dawning on her that she had won. Ryla the Butcher of Valdannon, had won the battle of the lecture hall.

Huxley was pleased for her. He wasn't sure what she'd request for her reward and, now, more than ever, he was still frightened of her hunting him down...but he was pleased anyway. Anyone that could come out of that on two feet had earned whatever was coming to them. The crowd quieted as she made her way to the top of the stairs to formally accept the title. The announcer could now be heard but Huxley didn't pay attention. He had never seen so many skilled fighters in one place. Tragically a few had died, not all of them though. Most surprising was Horace. What was that device he used? He remembered a similar one in Mayburn. Abernathy may want to know about it.

Finally, Ryla had made her way to the top. She gave a faint wave of her hand that was more an acknowledgement of her win. Everyone had waved or tried to engage the audience in some way but she seemed wholly unconcerned with their presence. Ryla laid down her Glaive carefully on the ground and waved more earnestly. Her bright smile was a deep contrast to her red and black throat. It was nearly the same wound that Bennett had, but if it was bothering her, she was ignoring it. It was hard to know for sure but it even looked like tears were forming in the corners of her eyes. Huxley got the impression this was a rare showing of emotion, despite it being in public.

The clapping faded suddenly and gasps replaced it. Ryla picked up that something wasn't right. She looked side to side to see what was the matter. Behind her stood Grubmush. Screams burst out but it was too late. He had snuck up the back along the rocks and grabbed one that fit right into his hand. He brought it down onto the back of her head. The thud of it punctuated the action like an exclamation mark.

Ryla dropped.

Her armor clattered with the rest of her, and Grubmush stepped into the spot that she last occupied. Huxley gapped. How could this man be standing? The answer was clear, though he couldn't make sense of it. Of the numerous wounds Grubmush had, the two that Ryla made were the worst. It appeared that she had taken out most of his midsection, just one of her strikes was lethal on its own but Grubmush had received two. But there he stood, in defiance of logic and what Huxley had assumed was proper biology. His left hand was clutching the larger wound and holding the larger parts of his gut together. His right hand dropped the rock. He raised his right hand to the sky in triumph. His roar, noticeably weaker than it had been at the beginning of the battle, issued forth. It was somehow more intimidating. Huxley had once totally impaled this man, and now Ryla had disemboweled him, and yet he lived! The question asked itself, almost free of Huxley's impulse to ask. "What would it take to kill this man?" Or worse, "Can he be killed?"

The crowd didn't cheer, most sat in dumbfounded silence. They were likely wondering the same thing Huxley was. It was Elatress who then asked a question that was more upsetting. She surveyed his wounds, and what he had done, and said simply, "Maybe he's right about his religion..." which was a deeply worrying thing all on its own. Religion had been a universally disliked aspect of life that only the desperate or ignorant clung to as a means to feel better about reality. Before he thought further on it, she continued, "but if he is, then you might be like a priest or prophet or something like that....what did he call you at the Gearbox, again?"

Huxley remembered all too well, "A Prophet" Huxley breathed in resignation.

"That's right! What messages do you bring, oh, great Prophet?" She teased.

He hated the idea of being associated with Grubmush, but having a place within his belief system was as bad, if not worse.

Elatress didn't wait. She stood up, and mocking a ceremony, bent low in a bow sweeping her arms out, "Well, come on Prophet Bookpile! The crowds will soon spill into the streets and it will be harder to move unless you want to go back into the sewers." A wicked smile formed and she said in a tone of reverence "No, Prophet of the Wilds should ever have DIRTY FEET!" She threw her hands to her chest as though scandalized.

"Oh no!" He glared, "Do NOT call me that. It's not funny."

"I disagree, Prophetpile."

23

∽

Immigrants and Fugitives

"Reach is a universal trait amongst inheritors. It is one of the only qualities that is so amongst the inhabitants of Magnadun. Though it is equal it is not always fair based on a myriad of outside factors." **-Page 7 Excerpt from the Grimoire**

Testing acid and explosive-based weaponry was always tricky at night. It invited too many questions. During the day, however, the sounds were far more commonplace. Abernathy's boots trudged through the snow but the sound of his footfalls were drowned out by the mechanical whirr of his device. Between the buildings and riding on the wind, voices whispering had replaced shouts of excitement. The Lecture Hall was a good distance away but it was hard to ignore when in session. It provided an ideal time for testing. So much attention was drawn by the fighting, the noises he generated wouldn't be too out of the ordinary. Blending in was key in Danador. This was normally an impossible feat for a man like Abernathy. Standing at his height, and at his size, and with his jovial personality, Abernathy attracted attention. His mustache had been too freshly washed and not dried well enough. It had taken on icicles at the points. Add a near-complete exoskeleton chemical pod thrower and, well, he was a downright spectacle. Assembling it in secret would be a waste if people put the pieces together regarding what he was up to. It helped that even he didn't totally know what he was doing, that was one of the greatest advantages of building like he did. Schematics and plans only gave away your goals; building by feel and imagination was far more exciting. He had finally found both a good mixture for the rapid breakdown of organic and inorganic compounds and a way to contain explosives that ignite only when intended. Both discoveries had cost him dearly. His eyebrows, more than a few times, had paid that price. His changing method needed work. It operated but *rapid* was hardly the word he'd use. The containment pods had also finally reached sufficient tensile strength to crack upon impact and not engagement. He shuddered remembering the day none of them left the barrel intact. But not today, he smirked at the thought.

To think even right now, Horace was trying to showcase lead propulsion. It was an already well-mapped idea that only did one thing well. He could throw nearly any substance he wished with near-pinpoint accuracy. He felt bad for Horace, in a way, he was a fine enough engineer, especially for the crazed space he'd been forced to learn and invent in. But his ambitions muddied his judgment, greatly. If he survives the Lecture Hall, and IF his device works as intended, he will be a lucky man. His workshop will see an influx in orders that may cut into Abernathy's own bottom line. His eyebrows furrowed but Abernathy stopped and reminded himself that while Horace was a competitor, he wasn't an enemy. He was a pilgrim on a mission like so many who come here, and like so many other pilgrims, had lost his way. No, Horace was far from an enemy, just a man who needed guidance like the rest of the children in Danador. It served as a stark and even grim reminder of his own pilgrimage, of what brought him here. The weight of his device now made itself fully felt by Abernathy, as was the weight of his burden. "The Norun help," he said so quietly it may as well have been a thought. It was their responsibility, it was his task, and he could not fail.

His burden had been lighter lately at seeing the growth and good nature of Huxley. In fact, Huxley had rekindled much that was dark within Abernathy for the hope of the Ember's future. One bright young boy wouldn't be enough to change a whole people, but perhaps it could be the start. It comforted him greatly that Elatress had seemed to enjoy his company. Sometimes he felt like she barely tolerated himself and that she only liked the bear. He knew, of course, that they were lying about being on a date. Romance was a totally foreign concept for her. But that was the point of trying to draw it out. Hoping to awaken the more human aspects of her was a challenge. Part of him was happy he didn't have young people shacking up in the Gearbox. That brought all kinds of headaches he didn't want to deal with.

He remembered the lies he told to his own parents in order to sneak away with his girlfriend. The two of them would stay up late sharing every thought, hope, dream and ambition. Nothing was out of reach for them. She lit his soul like no one ever had. The ache that he felt from being so far away from her returned, but his smile didn't fade. He couldn't stop smiling when thinking of her, even if it hurt.

Suddenly, Abernathy noticed two city guards posted outside the Gearbox to deny anyone entrance. His signage had been so clear, he thought irritably. The Gearbox was closed Wednesdays. The only ones bold enough to show would be at best Wardens, or at worst, an Ember. They had a nasty habit of appearing at random and asking questions. He managed to duck down an alley before the guards saw him coming. Yanking his rapid-release pressure valve for his exoskeleton and it hissed sharply. He closed his eyes and drew back in the life that existed around him. "Hmm, about eighty percent. Not bad." He stated aloud as he climbed out. Abernathy pushed the exoskeleton against the wall and found some nearby trash to pile around it. It would do for an hour or so. Hopefully, no one stumbled upon it. It couldn't operate without him but fools can still do damage.

He emerged onto the main road and waved at the guards. They nodded slightly but did nothing else to acknowledge him.

"Hungry boys? I can get a stew on. Or maybe something harder for this cold?" He offered in passing. He said it mainly as a joke because he knew they couldn't accept alcohol even if they wanted to. But if you came to the Gearbox, you were getting offered food and drink, that was just the way of things. They predictably didn't respond but one's eyes softened a degree which felt like a win.

Inside, stood two Wardens with an Ember, no wait, two Embers. They nearly never traveled together. His hearth had been snuffed out and a rare chill had made its way inside. It felt wrong, like shivering at the beach. The Embers stood near the now dead fire and had been discussing something. They quieted upon his entrance. The Wardens sat at the bar with papers out like always, probably to show him some new addition to a clause or paragraph that he needed to initial. He dropped his jovial spirit. He knew it only upset them. Embers were temperamental on most occasions and violent the rest of the time. "Evening gentlemen...can I get you-"

"We are here to discuss our agreement as well as your citizenship status."

Abernathy raised his eyebrows and said, "Well, then I certainly need a drink."

————————————————————————————————————-

The return trip from the Lecture Hall had gone without incident, Huxley tried to stop Elatress, but she only teased him more. It went like that the whole way. Both of them were avoiding talking about the implications of the fight. Perhaps the most surprising was the prize requested by Grubmush. When the shock and insanity of the end of the battle settled, the Warden in charge had granted Grubmush's request. Grubmush declared that when he was fully healed, he wished to have a mandatory attendance sermon. It was a bold request, for sure, but Grubmush was absolutely nothing, if not bold. Huxley had actually thought it was going to be something far, far stranger. Everyone had to go to a church service by this crazy person? Sure it would be weird, and even alarming, but at least it wasn't to turn over control of the city to him or burn all the books in the libraries. They never would have granted such a request, Elatress said, it was usually clips, or for the Wardens to change a rule that favored their business over another. It was always far less exciting than the battle. This was the first time in the Lecture Hall's history that a lecture was actually going to happen in the Lecture Hall.

Huxley would have been worried, but he was nearly certain he wouldn't have to attend. It was one of the benefits of being a fugitive. Perhaps soon, he would be ready to try and speak to the Embers again. Maybe they had forgotten about him or maybe stopped caring altogether. If he couldn't gain admission to the college, then not being hunted anymore would be a nice second prize. The idea was dashed, as he passed another wanted poster of him. It had the same weird warning and the same lies. The clips prize had been upped, drastically. The bounty on his head was not nearly as much as the amount on his companion's poster. The Plague Doctor was gaining in status, it seemed. Huxley wondered what his actual crimes were. Was he just as innocent as Huxley? Although to be fair, Huxley did attack an Ember. He winced at the memory.

They had avoided the larger crowds by exiting swiftly. It made travel expeditious. They took the same route back except for climbing back up the wall that Huxley had tried to float down. Elatress had shown him a rickety ladder that was loosely nailed together by bits of wood. It was dangerous, but he didn't want to risk more Magnincy. When they were about a block away, Elatress altered their path and brought them up to the rooftops. He had stopped questioning her, it seemed erratic at first but traveling with Elatress was like traveling with a living map. She always knew the right path and always knew what to avoid. She said it had something to do with her Magnincy. Huxley didn't think "Cartography" was a subject in the Grimoire though "Navigation" certainly was, being able to summon maps would be nice. Elatress' Magnincy appeared to work entirely differently. Huxley doubted she studied much of anything. Her knowledge was so innate, instinctual. It was almost as if nothing surprised her. He was glad that they were becoming friends. He definitely didn't want to be her enemy. Just then, her hand found its way to his chest and stopped him in his tracks. Huxley lost his train of thought and looked around for what had alarmed her. Her gaze was fixed on the Gearbox roof.

"Stop moving Huxley. There's a lot of people inside we don't want to meet."

"Is Abernathy in trouble?" Huxley asked.

"Hang on." She said and she flicked off her boots. She stood barefoot on the rooftop, her toes contracting back and forth as though looking for a grip beneath the grimy snow. She refocused on the Gearbox and said, "No, but the movement is…" She searched for the right word, "Slow but tense. Likely Wardens…maybe an Ember, they are hard to detect."

Huxley suddenly had a realization. "Wait really? They're hard for you to see?"

"Sometimes…yeah." She said annoyed.

A satisfied smile plastered on Huxley's face and he crossed his arms. "So…that's why you ran into me at the train station. You couldn't see me." He accused.

Elatress stiffened.

Huxley laughed to himself, "heh, heh yeah, that's it! You were dodging through the crowd like you do but you didn't realize a bona fide Ember was in your midst."

She didn't rise to the bait. He was obviously trying to mess with her. Admittedly, it was bad timing on Huxley's part as she was trying to assess if they were in danger or not. But he couldn't help himself.

She remained silent for a moment and said "I ran into you because you're awkward and strange in crowds."

"No. you just said -- "

"Fine", she confessed "I hadn't been around someone like you before. I didn't know how to read you, yet, but now I do, so it won't happen *again.*"

Huxley, reached forward to try and playfully push her only to have his wrist smacked by the broadside of her hatchet.

"Ouch!" He yelped.

"As I said, it won't happen again. Now, seriously, shut up. Your stupid jokes have given me a good idea about how to look. I see them now."

"An Ember is in there?" Huxley asked.

"No, not an Ember, there are three Embers. Two inside and one behind us, but you know her."

Onders and Huxley gasped.

"That's quite impressive," Onders remarked.

"Yeah, ok, you two do your late-night talk. I'll go check on Abernathy."

———————————————————————————————-

Abernathy poured drinks for the wardens seated at the bar and was about to offer some to the Embers by the hearth, but the Wardens shook their heads silently. Unless they were addressing you, common folk would be wise not to venture anything. Besides, the rumors were that they were reading your minds anyway. Abernathy knew the difference between rumors and fact regarding Embers and he didn't even understand them as much as he'd like to. He pulled up a stool and said, "You know, I have a proper office space if you'd like..."

The taller of the two wardens held up his hand stopping him and said, "No, this won't take long." He then held out his hand to shake which Abernathy took. Abernathy's people didn't shake hands. The custom always made him smile. It was so...distant as a means of greeting another person, but the Danadorians liked it that way, he supposed.

"Very well, let's talk about our agreement and my citizenship status." He said in a way that mirrored their tone. He was just trying to sound professional. Not many people would accuse him of being overly professional. To Abernathy, formalities always seemed like lying about who a person was.

"It has come to our attention that you have been harboring the fugitive, Huxley Durant of Mayburn, in this establishment for some time now."

"Oh my," Abernathy said in what was definitely a mocking tone, now. The Warden didn't respond to it. "And by the many stipulations of our agreement, as well as your tricky status as a citizen of this city, you are in violation of multiple areas of law. We stopped counting at twelve. You likely know where the stolen property of the Embers is. The Gearbox will be condemned and gutted for parts, and you will be publicly executed along with that filthy beast you keep in here."

Abernathy took a long slow swig of his drink. They were right of course, but even in Danador there were rules, and you still needed evidence. He finished with a pronounced "Gahhh" and whipped the froth from his mustache.

"So some crackpot saw the wanted posters and is trying to collect. By taking advantage of an easy target like a vulnerable immigrant who has a lot to lose. Is that it? Surely, this person has credible evidence or is it just their own account?"

"We don't owe you that, only if it comes to trial."

"If? It sounds like you boys made up your minds already. I know a damn good lawyer, she will-"

The Warden smiled placatingly at Abernathy.

"We don't wish these outcomes. All we want is a new deal with you."

It was then that Abernathy's throat constricted. Like it had dried out, even though it had been seconds since he last drank. The Embers had made their way to the bar now, looming behind the Wardens. Abernathy recognized one. He had seen him before but couldn't place where. The Embers weren't much for wandering the streets, preferring to be sequestered inside their tower for weeks, or months at a time. But this one would go on walks; maybe once a week. He never spoke to anyone, just wandered here and there. His only defining feature was his pointed jaw and sallow cheeks. The other was someone Abernathy only knew by reputation. The Chief Researcher of the Lost and Forgotten, Maddox, only left the tower when it was something important. He was the tip of the spear when it came to quelling the wilds or anything that needed an absolute response. Behind them stood a third shorter Ember, his face was round and young but he held it with the same heir of importance as the other two.

"We will finish this discussion."

———————————————————————————————————————-

Elatress disappeared down the wall. Onders and Huxley regarded each other. She was wearing her ever-present dark purple cloak. Its cloth was bespeckled by white snow. It looked like the night sky, with bright stars all over it. It's trademark light purple smoke escaping its edges. His chest tightened at seeing her, both in fear, but also excitement. He always learned so much when he was around her.

"Is he in danger?" Huxley asked.

"Is that your question? You do remember our arrangement right?" She chided.

His eyes narrowed, "You know, we could get a lot more done without this rigidity? Why just one? Why make it so difficult? That's not my question, by the way, you don't have to answer it. But you should."

Annoyed, Onders conveyed, "Answers are the most valuable thing in Magnadun. Every dumb animal has questions. It is answers that empower us. The more answers you have, the more power you have over others. Give them away freely and-"

He interrupted her, "And everyone lives better! It doesn't have to be like this!"

"Better? The uneducated would roam the streets flinging Magnincy at one another. It would be true and utter madness. They can't be trusted with its use." Onders rebutted.

"Is this why you aren't an Ember yet? They keep you to only a little bit of knowledge a day? To make sure you don't try to kill someone when they beat your defense?"

Her face flickered with the barest sign of anger. "It's simpler than that..." She considered her answer for a moment and then said, "No. No more free answers. Ask your question."

"But-"

Her voice broke in frustration, "I don't want to debate every time we talk! Just answer my questions and ask yours!"

"Fine." Huxley relented.

The two faced each other, gusts of wind and snow their only companions. A moment passed while they reoriented their thoughts. Huxley tried to banish his emotions with only a pitiful amount of success. If he truly only had one question to ask, he couldn't mess up like last time. He got the sense Onders was getting more from this deal than he was.

They both spoke at the same time, and neither heard what the other had to say. "You go first." Onders offered.

"Why do I have dreams of the ocean and the stars?" Huxley asked.

"You don't know!?" She said mockingly

Huxley set his jaw, and asked, "Is that your question?"

Her eyes narrowed. Huxley followed up with, "Please answer as per our agreement."

"Of course," she looked at him from a different angle, like a curious animal encountering a new sound. Then she looked skyward and said, "Your question is speculative even amongst the Embers, but I will give you our best answer." She sorted through some information in her mind and chose a response. "We believe the stars and oceans of our dreams, our Magnincy and the sky are all there to speak to us."

Huxley blinked, indicating that he obviously didn't follow. Onders went on, "When an Ember first touches Magnincy they have a dream of the ocean and the stars. It is our sacred flame kindling within us for the first time. And like all flames it illuminates what was once dark. When they summon it, they see it splayed before them. And then in everyday life their brain orients to seeing stars...everywhere. We believe it is Magnincy communicating with us. There is disagreement on what that communication is, but I believe it is the creator of Magnadun."

"Creator! Like an actual God?" Huxley asked with urgency.

"What? No, remember, I said don't be stupid." Onders criticized. "Ok, that was your question."

"Wait! Just answer-"

"No! Haven't you figured out that answers lead to more questions? If I answer your next one, it will just lead to others. It's time for mine. Ask your question tomorrow." Onders told him firmly.

Huxley pushed down his bubbling emotions. It was harder than perhaps anything he had ever done. Her answer broke open so many more possibilities. Choosing a follow-up might be impossible. His mind was at work with this new information when he felt a Magnincy flick again on his forehead. "Well?" She asked.

"What?" He answered.

"Weren't you listening? I asked, 'What has your study schedule been like since your battle on the wall?" She repeated.

"That's your question? My study habits?" He asked incredulously.

She nodded. He knew he couldn't reveal that he was studying a Grimoire but wondered what he could be studying if not that.

"It's inconsistent." He said truthfully. "After the fight, I mainly just recovered. I practiced what little I knew and had pieced together through library books and observing Palithur. But really, I rested. Then here, I have been working hard at the Gearbox and running around with Elatress."

"Rested? Running around?" Her face drained of interest.

"Yes." He said matter of fact.

"Fine. Thank you. I will see you tomorrow." She turned to leave and he stated, "You know you can just enter through the main door like everyone else. You don't have to slip through my window."

"No, I need to keep our meetings unknown to everyone." She confided bitterly.

"Well, now Elatress knows, and she will likely tell Abernathy. But he would never say anything."

"Are you sure?" She challenged, her voice betraying more anxiety than he would have expected.

"Uhh, as sure as I can be."

"Fine then." She rescinded and left in another blink and puff of purple smoke.

Huxley turned back to the Gearbox to see what was happening, but there was no change. He waited for Elatress to come back. After what felt like hours, the sun had barely moved, and finally, Elatress returned and said they could go in. She insisted on using another pipe that seemed a lot like the one hidden in his bedroom wall. How many pipes leave the Gearbox? Huxley wondered absently. If it didn't send him to a smoldering coal pile, it was rather mundane by comparison. This pipe didn't lead to coal but had just as much soot. Once they dusted themselves off, they made their way to the bar. They found Abernathy hunched over paperwork, pipe in one hand puffing like a train and a forgotten glass of beer that was covered in condensation. His mustache rustled back and forth as he read over the document. Arktos lurched out of his sleep and shuffled towards Elatress. He made a low rumbling coo of affection and nearly stood on both hind legs but it turned into little hops instead. Elatress jumped into him and the two embraced.

Abernathy stopped and looked at the trio. "Any incidents?" Huxley wasn't sure who he was asking but Elatress responded from deep within an Arktos hug, "MMmmppphhh"

"Good", he responded.

Huxley felt like that was the right response.

"Were Embers here?" Huxley asked, feeling guilty that Abernathy may be in trouble on his account.

"Three of them, which is the most that have ever visited. No one can resist the Gearbox's spirits." Abernathy smiled but his eyes didn't match. They were heavy with uncharacteristic concern.

Elatress hadn't emerged from her bear hug yet, so Huxley sat down next to Abernathy. Abernathy clapped him on the shoulder and asked, "How did Horace do?"

"Horace?" Huxley looked at him surprised, "You want to talk about the Lecture Hall instead of what happened here?"

"Of course, my boy. All that happened here was paperwork. Who won? Tell me a story. Let me restart the fire and we can pour ourselves a drink."

Elatress emerged with a contented smile, and wandered behind the bar, grabbed three mugs, filled them and handed them out.

"Oh, uhh, ok." Huxley hesitated, sensing Abernathy was shielding him from something.

Before he could ask, Abernathy remembered something and rushed outside. He returned holding a bizarre system that looked like a weapon or armor or both. He placed it inside his large metal door that led downstairs to his shop and returned to the couch.

The three of them told the story of what happened in great detail and with enthusiasm. He was especially excited to hear Huxley summoned wind, something Elatress was fast to point out hadn't worked, but he was impressed all the same. Abernathy listened diligently once they started talking about his rival and asked all kinds of questions about his tool belt. Neither of them bothered to remember those details, much to Abernathy's disappointment. When they got to the part where Grubmush lived through two mortal wounds and not only did not die but managed to win the tournament, Abernathy was unsurprised. Elatress and Huxley shared a look as if to confirm they had conveyed the information correctly. They had. Abernathy was just better traveled and knew more about Grubmush. "Well, yeah of course he lived...He's from Dathu. Do you know what it takes to actually kill one of them? It's not easy."

"Wait...they're all like that?!" Huxley exclaimed. A second later his face winced and his stomach rumbled. Elatress patted him on the back, "You ok, Bookpile?"

"Yeah, my drink is just getting settled, I guess."

Ignoring them Abernathy rubbed his chin. "Well, I don't know about all of them, but their Magnincy is potent and unpredictable. If one wields it, then yeah, they could live through most wounds provided they have enough rage or time to heal. Rage is an effective shield to death...for them." He added.

Huxley had a mountain of questions based on what Abernathy just said. Magnincy wasn't raging feelings or swirling emotions, it was studied knowledge. It was peering deep into what was true of the world. But then he thought about Elatress and some of the wild things he'd seen from her. Perhaps, he didn't know as much as he thought about the true nature of Magnincy. Maybe his abilities were just one small part of a larger whole. It was then that the tapestry high up on the Gearbox wall drew his attention again, with its whirlpool of colors. If someone had attempted to paint what an idea might look like, that's the notion it conjured in Huxley's mind. He had thought that the first time he saw it, but now it seemed different.

Abernathy got up and dropped documents onto the table in front of them. "Let's talk about new legal arrangements then. This news has helped me understand a few clauses, and I've already signed the damned things so I might as well know what's happening."

"You signed without reading!?" Elatress stammered, and adopted a mock Abernathy voice, "Ooohh, look at me, I'm super smart and never sign things until I've read every word of every clause. That's what a smart person does!"

Abernathy didn't respond. He just let her finish her mockery and resumed explaining.

"As an immigrant, I don't have the same rights as a citizen, and as an immigrant from Norun, even less so. The original agreement said I had to agree to heavy taxes for all sales as well as brewing personal barrels for the wardens. An easy trade to make. However, it also binds me to total transparency regarding my business endeavors and whatever I build in my machine shoppe, I have to make known to them. That part has been, *lax,* lately." He cleared his throat and stated, "But they have no proof of that, and there's a good bit about no fomenting insurrection or sedition against the state." He glanced at Huxley and said "like harboring fugitives''.

"Oh, Abernathy. I'm so sorry. Did they see me?" Huxley asked, face contrite.

"Actually they have nothing except a well-founded suspicion. It's Arktos that got us into actionable trouble."

Arktos grunted from under the bar. "Turns out enough people have complained about having a bear inside a metropolitan area."

Elatress shot out of her seat but Abernathy held his hand up to her and declared, "But I've made arrangements to ease their worries about bears and fugitives."

Elatress, slowly, sat back down.

"I need to do three things." He continued

"First?" Her voice betrayed an unsettling fear. Huxley figured she was waiting for a terrible restriction on Arktos.

"First," Abernathy said in an overly calm voice, trying to soothe her. "I need to agree to allow a deep and thorough search of the Gearbox to ascertain all of my resources and projects."

"Pfft, they'll never find everything. Go on," she said.

"Second, I can't be here for a few days while they conduct their search. They don't want me interfering, which is rather smart of them, actually."

"Third?"

"And third wasn't so interesting until you told me about the Lecture Hall."

"Oh?" Huxley asked.

"Yes, apparently they want me to reserve one room from now on for foreign diplomats or religious missionaries."

"Missionaries like..." As the words left Huxley's mouth, he figured out what that meant.

"Is Grubmush coming to stay with us!?" Elatress squealed in delight.

Abernathy took a long swallow of beer, burped and said "He will be here soon, apparently they don't want to take care of him while he's recovering and they really don't want to leave him out on the streets. I expect they think they're punishing me without saying it. The truth is, I'm eager to get to know someone from Dathu."

Huxley sat back in his seat. *Why can't I escape this man?* As his mind reeled at not only having to see him again, but having to share a roof, and probably help take care of him as well. The man that was a part of the worst attack on his people he'd ever known. He tried to remain calm.

Abernathy's face scrunched and said "Well, it's a bit more than that. There's a fourth thing in the papers."

"Fourth" Huxley and Elatress inquired in unison.

"The inspection of the Gearbox is in four days and while that's happening we all need to be gone. They didn't want us wandering around the city so they've given us an assignment. We are to assemble whoever is brave enough to come, and we need to travel to the Wilds to find the man from all the wanted posters." He paused to dig through the papers and produced the "Beware!" poster of the Plague Doctor. It lay on the table now staring at the trio. "We need to bring him to the Embers."

Huxley and Elatress exhausted themselves questioning Abernathy. Abernathy had answered them as best he could but the truth was he was uncertain about much of it. Their best guess was that the Embers were hoping both fugitives would kill one another. But how were they so certain Abernathy knew where Huxley was and that he would be willing to fight? And they hadn't even asked about the Grimoire. Huxley hoped that meant they were losing interest in him.

Mercifully, the Embers had given Abernathy a little bit of knowledge to help arm himself. The name "Plague Doctor" wasn't quite accurate. It was more of a dramatic title intended to scare people. He had acquired enough knowledge to qualify and call himself a doctor. His expertise was herbal remedies mainly but he had some skills outside of that. He operated mainly in the lower rung of Danador. The people there had benefited from him for quite some time. But when he stopped getting new patients, he started introducing things into the water supply to keep people sick. He held some power in Magnincy but nowhere near the level of an Ember, and subsequently beneath their notice. He did however give no small amount of trouble to the Wardens, which was why Ryla had been tasked with finding him. She could deal with him in a more permanent way. Regrettably, he fled the city before she was able to look for him, so they put her on guard duty until they heard from him again. But now he has taken up residence outside the city and people are starting to get sick again. They believe that he is poisoning the river feeding the Forty-Five. The Wardens explained that it had taxed their medical staff taking care of so many non-citizens and the cost was becoming too much, so he must be stopped.

"I need you to deliver this for me El." Abernathy handed Elatress a rolled-up letter. She looked at it and read "Ryla?"

"Yeah, I'm asking her to come with us. She may want to be a part of this. Besides, she's great in a fight."

"Well, so am I," Elatress told him flatly.

"Of course, you are. Just please deliver it. The more the merrier on this expedition, I think."

Elatress left without more arguments.

Abernathy began walking downstairs, "I'm going to get a few items together that we may need. I suggest you study that Grimoire, Huxley, and for all of our sakes please bring it with you. We are certainly going to need it. I get the impression this isn't some cantankerous Doctor trying to drum up business...this will be something else entirely."

24

Games and Harmonies

*"Vibrations in the particles of matter produce disruptions in the air by the energy released. Frequencies vary but can be organized to create a resonance, imbuing the listener to ascribe meaning as they see fit." -***Page 117 Excerpt from the Grimoire**

Huxley accepted the advice and did exactly that. He studied well into the night. Occasionally, he heard bangs and crashes downstairs but nothing Abernathy couldn't handle. Huxley tried to read up on poisons, but found the Grimoire lacking useful material. He added his notes about wind, in low-pressure, and low-temperature areas. It wasn't noted in an academic sense but it was more like the results of his experiments. He felt embarrassed by his notations expecting that anyone who read what he wrote would laugh at him, but Huxley was hoping no one else would ever read it.

The few days passed without issue, except for the nightly visits from Onders. Huxley had wanted to expand on his original questions but worried they would only lead to more as Onders had warned. He decided to fill in a few gaps in his understanding instead. This deal was proving helpful to Huxley. Onders seemed to be answering in good faith. Her questions were not as he expected. She focused mainly on who he was as a person, and where and how he grew up. It wasn't the kind of questions meant to grow closer as friends. She was searching for something in his story. On the night before they were to leave, she arrived earlier than was her habit. Something was different about her. She was less rigid. Was she relaxing?

She stepped into his room and perhaps for the first time. her smile held true warmth. "I have news." She said.

"Oh?" Huxley asked, trying not to sound overly interested but probably failing miserably.

"Yes." She took off her cloak for the first time and laid it down on his bed. "But first, can you show me that game downstairs...what was it called again?"

"Ballistic and Bureaucrats?"

She snapped her fingers and said, "Yes!"

Huxley clarified, "You want to go downstairs? But..."

"That's part of the news. It's fine. Now show me this game."

"Ok...Elatress will be glad to."

A few minutes later, Elatress had finished explaining the rules. She had eagerly tried showing Huxley a few times but he hadn't shown much interest. Onders was diligently paying attention, while Huxley was distracted. Both the girls grew annoyed when he would pause Elatress to ask questions about something she had just explained.

"Bookpile! We're not even to the advanced rules yet! Pay attention."

"Yeah, Bookpile!" Onders joked.

Huxley couldn't get over how uncomfortable this made him feel. Onders and Elatress learning and explaining the rules of a game. It was too weird. Elatress was hardly acting any differently at all. Maybe she was just happy to have someone to play her game with. Shouldn't she be on guard when an Ember was in the building? The three of them were the only inhabitants that night. The Gearbox was closed and Abernathy was hard at work downstairs.

The two played four matches of Ballistics and Bureaucrats. Like Abernathy, Onders focused more on the swift response and delegation than pelting the other city. It was easy to overshoot with the catapults.

It required a lighter hand than you would expect. Huxley remembered, less than fondly, of nearly being hit with those little barbarians coming out of their cages. Like so many things Abernathy made, it was probably more complicated than it needed to be. But the more he watched, the more genius he recognized. At the height of the arc, the little metal cage released a little ragdoll in the shape of a barbarian. If they tried to send just the doll it would have terrible aerodynamics and wouldn't be nearly as precise as in the cage. You could also send fires or poison over the city, which were displayed by tokens associated with their colors. It was far more complicated than anything Huxley had ever played. He tried his hand at Noble Assassin once, but he got buried in the rules.

Elatress won the first two games easily, then, Onders won the third by a slim margin. Elatress bristled when Onders explained to her that preventative fire maintenance had all but ensured her attacks were useless outside of barbarians. Mid game, the barbarians were weakest and poison was the go-to move. Elatress must have been wanting Onders to do well initially because the fourth game was over quickly. Within three turns, she had cut off Onders' supply chain and killed all of her workers.

The pair nodded in respect. Elatress turned to the side and spoke to herself as she sometimes did and said, "No, I am inside and having a nice conversation with friends." She turned back to Onders and told her that was the most fun she'd had in a long time.

"Me too. Huxley can be a bit of a bore." Onders admitted.

"Don't even get me started on Bookpile." Elatress said, "Hey, Bookpile, want to do something fun?" She made a mocking voice and said, "No...I want to read and stare out the window looking at the night sky while breathing heavily."

The two laughed together. Huxley's feelings weren't hurt, exactly. He wasn't emotionally present enough for that. He kept thinking that he was having a bad dream with these two cracking jokes at his expense. Finally, Onders got up saying she had to leave.

"We aren't asking questions?" Huxley asked as she made for his room.

"No...I think we will have enough time for that soon." Onders replied.

"Wait...what do you mean?" His heart leapt at what that could mean.

Clearly, she had reported back to the Embers and deemed him worthy of readmittance. She was always his tester! Maybe this was it. This was his test! Why else would they let him escape, and then send her to ask him questions? It all made sense. The Embers didn't have a straightforward entry process because they needed to be sure of someone before admittance. Soon Onders and Huxley would spend their days together studying and researching Magnincy as colleagues. No more sneaking around in the cold, no more worrying about getting caught, no more insane people showing up at his home. He broke into a wide grin. He felt stupid for not having put the pieces together sooner but his happiness edged out his embarrassment.

Onders raised an eyebrow and said, "You're happier than I thought you'd be."

"Well, I've wanted this my whole life!"

"What? To trudge through the snow looking for a mad doctor?"

"I-what?"

"I'm accompanying you to get the mad doctor. We will have time to ask each other more questions over the next few days." Her face softened, realizing she may have given him the wrong impression.

Crestfallen, he nodded. "Right...no of course. I'm just happy to have more time for questions."

She cocked her head in confusion but did not pursue it further.

Onders nodded to Elatress and left. Huxley hung back and helped Elatress clean up. After he was sure Onders had left, he went up to his room.

Only to find Onders had waited for him at the window sill. Her purple cloak reattached, it fluttered inward towards him. For the first time his room felt cold, the window must have been open for sometime. An accumulation of snow had made its way past the threshold. It now clung to Onder's back and a few lucky flakes made their way to the floor before melting.

"Onders, what's wrong? Did you forget something"

A beat passed and she finally murmured "In a way...yes."

"Oh, ok." Huxley was at a loss for what it could be. She had already spent much more of the night here than he was expecting. Predicting Onders had proven impossible.

She looked now directly into his eyes and approached. Huxley tensed not forgetting the last time she approached so aggressively. It was an attempt to kill him. She closed the distance and stood within arms length. "I...uh..." she stammered. Her breath was becoming deeper as she internally struggled. She was searching for a word or an emotion. Huxley had no guess at what it could be. Was she upset? What could he have done now to make her angry?

Finally, she settled on it and regained her composure. "The last few visits have been...nice."

"...nice?" Huxley repeated.

"Yes." She leaned in closer.

The snow, the cold, the confusion was all lost into the recesses of his mind now. He still wasn't sure what she wanted to say, he gave up trying and waited patiently albeit awkwardly. Her face came so close to his, like she was going to whisper a secret.

"You are cute, but so foolish."

Huxley blinked but before he could respond she grabbed him, threw herself into his embrace and kissed him.

The two lingered in the moment, Huxley was shocked, but did not tear himself away. He no longer felt his room chilly in the slightest.

Finally, she stepped back. Onders seemed more surprised than Huxley.

"Yes it has been nice." She said, her old tone of having to explain things to him returned.

Huxley couldn't respond, utterly bewildered he took a step towards her. She recoiled as though she had broken a law, or sullied a sacred space. She disappeared out the window in her usual puff of purple smoke leaving Huxley alone with the cold of winter. Staring after her, he repeated, "Cute...but foolish."

Huxley read the Grimoire but no information made its way to his brain. What had just happened? The more he thought about it, the more his confusion grew. Onders went from trying to kill him, to unhappily spending time with him to joking and now a kiss? If she was trying to tell him something, he had clearly missed it. He focused again on his studies but everytime he began reading he saw her face, felt her close, and then...he shook his head. This was a distraction no matter how much he enjoyed it. Everyone was relying on him to understand this book and he had to make it happen.

Despite his desire to live in the College, and study there, the Gearbox was beginning to grow more comfortable to him like a new home. It made him feel strange that tomorrow, Wardens would be searching the place. They would be pulling up boards and putting their hands all over everything. It felt wrong, like allowing burglars to come into your home. And all based on a suspicion they had no evidence for. They wielded so much power over Abernathy, and yet he endured it all without much complaint. His life's work was about to get rifled through by people who didn't understand it. How could he endure that? Huxley imagined what it would be like if someone found the Grimoire and flipped through it laughing at what he wrote while doodling and tearing out pages. Would he be able to control himself? The uncomfortable thought made him shiver. It was such a violating thought to have someone else even holding the Grimoire, to say nothing of robbing it from him for good.

The Grimoire was his now.

He wasn't sure if he was the intended Heir or not, but it came to him all the same and no one was going to take it away.

———————————————————————————————-

Finally, his brain let him sleep but didn't get much before being awoken by a queer, rhythmic humming. It was a sweet-sounding melody. Mechanical lurches and late-night arguments downstairs were the normal things to wake a person up at the Gearbox. Singing wasn't usual, and certainly not singing that sounded like this. He couldn't make it out, but it sounded beautiful, like the crashing of waves or the wind through a tall field of grass. He couldn't quite call it music, but there was a rhythm and resonance that made its way into every part of Huxley. It gave him energy, his mind awoke far faster than it had before, even faster than when he awoke to alarm bells in Mayburn. That was because of panic. This felt different. It was peaceful like his mind and body were communicating more clearly. It felt like blocks that he didn't know he had were loosened. Relieved of them, he could finally feel like he was always meant to.

It drew him out of bed. He had to find its source. He threw on clothes and stuck his head out his door. The sound was less in the hallway overlooking the Gearbox. It was still there but diminished. He moved back into his room and searched. Huxley found the pipe that he had once used for an escape to be the source of the sound. While it had certainly elevated his senses and body, he still had enough of his mind to not to slide down it again. But he knew where it led. He walked as fast as he could without running, worrying that the commotion would upset the rhythm. He walked past Elatress' room. The light wasn't on, but that didn't mean much. She could be awake in there, or out for a midnight walk, or right behind him. He followed the sound all the way downstairs and to the workshop door. When he grabbed it, he could feel the door vibrating. The presence of his hand made it still again but the air continued to vibrate. He opened the metallic door carefully, fully aware of how hard he was pushing. The door squeaked like always but he had muted it as best he could. The rhythm pulsed outward and led him down.

Huxley followed it growing more aware of his body, every muscle, every tendon, his own breath sounded otherworldly to him now. It filled his body with heightened awareness. It would have normally frightened him, but the rhythms made it seem more than natural, like parts of him had been asleep for years and were finally waking up.

The uneven flicker of firelight wrapped around the corner leading to the place Abernathy had once retreated. When he drew back his Magnincy, and the machines lost their life. The crackle of the hearth now joined the hum that drew deeper. He could tell now that it was Abernathy, he was humming down here alone in this room.

No, Huxley thought, not alone.

There were other voices, at least two, maybe three or more. Their voices harmonized with each other and sang out. Placing each foot slowly in front of the other, he crept down the hallway. It may be an intrusion, in fact, he was sure it was, but he was drawn to it all the same.

Relying on the fact that he would be forgiven, hopefully, Huxley snuck into the room.

It was cramped, lit only by a fireplace. A few bookshelves in the corner and a red worn couch with rips and stuffing spilling out was occupied by Abernathy. Above the fire was a golden bell, much larger than one that could be found in a store to get a shopkeeper's attention. It wasn't particularly reflective but it did draw one's attention immediately. The bell was the focal point of the room, and Huxley suspected the source of the rhythm. It still emitted invisible waves and a low hum that was matched by Abernathy. The two were in sync. Huxley didn't approach further despite wanting to. Even with the deep draw of whatever this sensation was, the overwhelming feeling that he was intruding on something private, kept him at bay.

The bell eventually went still again and Abernathy reached forward with a soft-headed hammer and rapped it on the bottom, causing it to chime. He sat back and Huxley heard him make a long "hmmmmmm" that pitched up and down until he matched the bell. That was when the resonance commenced again. Huxley had never felt anything like this. He had to brace himself against the wall. It washed through every part of him. It wasn't frightening but it was exceedingly strange. The aura in the room was overwhelming and yet he was drawn to more of it. His worries and anxieties regarding the future and even ones about becoming an Ember melted away. Then it hit him. This felt like his dreams with the ocean. The closer he got to Abernathy, the more it felt like when he was in the ocean looking at the stars. Like he was about to reach the island he had slowly been wading towards. How were they connected? He may finally get some answers.

The bell's ring lingered for some time at a steady pulse. Right when he expected it to fade the room flashed bright gold. Huxley shielded his eyes but it was everywhere. He peaked between his fingers and saw three bright orbs, they had materialized in the room near Abernathy. They pulsed brighter and brighter, and with each pulse, they began taking shape, arms, legs...they were forming into bodies of light. Two shorter ones about the size of children and one adult. It was then that

Abernathy's body shimmered with golden light and fell into sync with the others. The hum returned and the four seemed to be communicating, though it was certainly not a spoken language.

Now totally certain he was intruding on something intimate, Huxley pulled himself out of the room. It proved far more difficult than it should have been, but the pulse, or hum or whatever it was, pulled him inward. The further away he walked, the more he regretted it. It's like his instincts had been hijacked by something else entirely. Even the stones that made up the hallway protested in the way they stung his hands. The cold bit into his flesh. He even began to feel his muscles tremble. His breath grew sharp and his body broke out in cold sweats. It was like his body or mind or...maybe soul...needed to be back in that room. Panic was beginning to set in when all of the sudden the strange feeling was ripped away. He regained his senses and felt normal again. His body ached for the feeling to return but also glad that it was gone. How could these two things be true at the same time? The contradiction made his head woozy. Abernathy's hand gripped his shoulder and spun Huxley to face him. A warm, flushed face, half hidden by a mustache, with amber eyes that welled up in tears, held Huxley's gaze. A white handprint was rapidly fading from his left cheek. It looked like a fresh burn that was healing before his eyes.

Huxley didn't know what to say and stumbled for an apology. "You uh...sing...very well Abernathy. I'm so sorry to have intruded."

He didn't respond immediately. Whatever had affected Huxley had done the same to Abernathy as well. Only, he seemed to be glowing, not like a firefly, but in his manner and demeanor. It reminded Huxley of a long-neglected flower that had finally been watered. Everything about him radiated like Huxley hadn't seen before. His amber eyes blazed within, so much so, they appeared as golden as the silhouettes he saw.

"It wasn't singing, I was in harmony with...those that I love. I wish you hadn't entered though. In the future, please refrain. My resonance was cut short. It will be some time before I can properly find the frequency again." A sense of loss punctuated his words. It was a tone Huxley hadn't heard before. It cut him deeply. Through his bumbling curiosity, he messed up some kind of ritual that was important to Abernathy. The color drained from his face as the implication of who "those that I love" might have been. He searched for the right combination of words that might constitute a real apology, but everything came up woefully short. Not one to twist the knife however, Abernathy just patted him again on the shoulder and muttered

"S' alright lad. No harm done."

Huxley blinked trying to allow himself to be forgiven. The whole ordeal of the last few minutes had been so emotional; from deep interest, and fascination to a dizzying high of discovery, then humiliation. Huxley had never wanted to ask a question more about what he had seen but knew deep down that he shouldn't ask. It was a difficult position for someone like him. He found his curiosity had driven most of the de-cisions in his life now. He gulped knowing how badly this was going to keep him up at night, both the curiosity and the shame of his intrusion.

He gave a short "thanks" and left as fast as he could without sprinting. When he reached the top of the stairs, he turned back to Abernathy once more to try and offer a sincere look of contrition to try and offload some of his regret. But Abernathy had already walked back into his small room. As he closed the door to the workshop, he heard the bell chime again.

———————————————————————————————————————-

Huxley didn't sleep the rest of the night, just as predicted. His brain wouldn't let him. After an hour of trying, he did what any hopeful Ember would do, he studied. But even then, the pit that grew in his stomach had gotten quite comfortable there. Studying was impossible, though a section on something called "covalent bonds" did look interesting. It made things stick together. Huxley was curious. Nothing permanent took root in his head though, he made a note of it and vowed to return to it later. As full as he had felt early, now he was equally as empty. His curiosity wouldn't stop, it hammered him over and over with questions. It was maddening. Soon he found he was writing down his questions and writing his own answers. It was a fraction more comforting.

So he wrote on.

His questions led him to a chart of sorts. It was similar to the primer he had made to understand the Grimoire, only this one was his own creation. He drew a crude map of what he knew of Magnadun, mostly from maps he had seen in school or in the Warden's office. He made categories from each group and began writing what he knew about them. It *always is hard separating the rumors from truth,* he thought with a smirk. A few moments later, his smile bled away as frustration set in. The closest was Valdannon. He had only met a few in Mayburn but he couldn't say he learned anything. He only knew, for sure, their train of thought was almost categorically different from his own. They saw art everywhere and in everything. That wasn't a judgment call, it was absolutely true. The only outlier was Ryla, who had barely spoken to him. She didn't seem like an artist at all. It made sense, how could a whole people group be one thing only? She was a warrior for sure, and she never painted, unless you counted the...

Suddenly, Huxley gasped and dropped his pen. What he watched in the Lecture Hall... was her art. The splays of blood, the flick of her weapon, and the arrangement. It was a macabre painting of some kind, only with blood instead of ink. Was her Magnincy art like the rest of Valdannon but she painted with violence? Huxley gulped and tried to move along without spending too much time on that memory. He didn't want to see her ever again, let alone during battle. He shook away the thoughts and made more notes. "Ok, the people of Valdannon use Magnincy in some way that involves art." He wrote as he spoke it. He added questions he didn't know the answers to yet.

"If their Magnincy is the same as mine, how come Embers seem to be so much more potent in their abilities? Is Danador truly superior or is there more to it that I'm unaware of? And if madness is the cost of our overuse, then what is their cost?" He wrote down a few more thoughts about it but none that burned as much as those. He moved along to the next group he had encountered, the Wild people of Dathu. He had thought that Magnincy was not part of Grubmush and his clan, but the last few days had greatly changed that opinion. Grubmush was capable of physical feats that some might call super-human. He could leap with the strength of a storybook character. It was terrifying, to witness someone capable of such a thing. He also appeared tireless, which couldn't possibly be true. Even if it was, some things the Embers did were far more spectacular. He made notes that asked about strength and endurance limits, and the ability to heal. At least two mortal wounds were struck in rapid succession and he managed to not only survive, but got back on his feet. Huxley wrote and underlined "Physical" because his astonishing traits were all physical. He swelled up in excitement. This had the feeling of a breakthrough. The Dathu must draw on Magnincy as well. It's the only thing that made sense. Their Magnincy affected their physical bodies. It would explain their instinct driven nature and dislike for weakness. In the, "do they suffer from madness category", Huxley just wrote a question mark. How could anyone get more mad than Grubmush? Perhaps he was already deep into madness which would account for just about every word he said. He shuddered to think that there could be a version of him even crazier than the one he knew. Finally, he wrote down *Sumine*. Elatress had told him a few helpful things. She always knew where she was going and where other people were. How far and how much detail was communicated, he didn't know. She had a handle on most buildings she was in, although she needed concentration to see further than that. What was she seeing when she used Magnincy? And why did he, for some reason, throw it off?

That's when it clicked, "external" he said. The pieces were falling into place, it was making sense.

"Ok, Grubmush's people are internally focused and gain great use of their physical bodies: Internally. Elatresses is the opposite, hers is nearly entirely outwardly focused: Externally. It was too similar to be a coincidence. Next Ryla's people saw art everywhere and made art out of almost anything. His own people saw art as a passing dalliance, at best. Danadorians looked almost constantly at the science behind everything. Were those two things opposites as well? Huxley's handwriting suffered because of the speed at which he was trying to write down his thoughts. He finally settled on, "If art is what things could be, then is science what things truly are?" He would need to talk to someone from Valdannon, not Ryla, but anyone else. Perhaps that was the next question for Onders. Huxley's curiosity was almost always driven by discovering more about how the world truly is. He knew there were invisible forces at work that governed Magnadun, and he had naturally assumed it was Magnincy. Of course, it was mastery of knowledge that led to the Embers defeating the Fecundity. This was done without the help of anyone else. But perhaps the other people wielded in ways that were outside of his grasp. Just like his curiosity, perhaps their curiosities lead them down far different paths.

He looked over his notes and felt like he had put some puzzle pieces in place, except for one glaring hole. The Norun. They were the fifth group of people and he knew the least about them. And if the other four had opposites, what was the Norun's opposite? Was there a sixth group of people even the Embers didn't know about or weren't mentioning?

He filled up most of the section of the Norun with question marks and half-thoughts. It was odd that he felt so comfortable talking to Abernathy, and he was likely his best source of information. But Huxley hadn't pursued his questions because it felt both intrusive and unearned.

His unceasing curiosity, like always, pushed down the rest of his emotions. The familiarity of questioning things calmed him enough to grab another hour or so of sleep.

He dreamed again of the stars and the ocean. This time, the island was illuminating. He was fully immersed in the water now and he swam forward. The stars and ocean encircled him as he reached his fingertips towards his goal. The voice was emanating from there. "So close now Huxley, just a little further!"

25

❧

Guests and Travels

"In regards to those who Reach into what could be, they are a special case. Magnincy flows through them but embeds within their works. It can be woven into their crafts, their words or in some small cases their actions...they are dangerous to underestimate." **-Page 14 Excerpt from the Grimoire**

A loud rapping at his door shook him awake. He had fallen asleep on his Grimoire, and globs of drool dotted the pages. He chastised himself for treating the book so badly. Rubbing the sleep out of his eyes, he stood and stretched. His back and waist shot spikes of pain through his body, apparently sleeping hunched over wasn't the best choice. Commotion pushed its way under the door. Getting awakened by surprise had become the norm the last few days. And it usually meant trouble. Opening his door a sliver, he peeked out. He couldn't quite see downstairs but could make out enough. Abernathy was shouting and perhaps Elatress was there, along with another vaguely familiar voice.

"Well, I certainly can't lift him! Just leave him here." The feminine voice said.

"He will bleed all over my best table!" Abernathy protested.

"Oh, you'd prefer the stairs to have blood then? Face it, this guy isn't going anywhere." She huffed.

That certainly wasn't Elatress, and it definitely wasn't a Warden. Huxley stepped out onto the balcony overlooking the scene.

Abernathy stood rubbing his chin, his hand impossible to see underneath his mustache. The woman standing next to him had a bandaged head and stood a few inches taller than Abernathy. She rested her weight on a glaive.

It was Ryla.

Out of her shining armor and into something more common, she and Abernathy looked over a bloody body. She had a loose-fitting tunic and tight trousers that stopped just past her knees. She was nearly a match for Abernathy in how muscular they both were, though she didn't have his paunch. Her leather boots weren't made for battle but for travel. Without looking up she said, "Maybe your out-of-tempo young Ember friend can find a way to get him upstairs." She turned to Huxley and Huxley's heart froze. "How about it? You know enough to lift people?"

Taken aback, he only stammered. How did she know he was there? Abernathy hadn't reacted, so that made Huxley feel a bit calmer. He clearly trusted her. It was only then that he noticed what, or rather, who, they were talking about. A bandaged and badly wounded Grubmush lay on the table. Dried blood caked his body, so much so that Huxley wondered how he could have any left. But after two encounters, and armed with his new theory about the Dathu, Huxley assumed Grubmush could pull off yet another miraculous recovery.

Finally, he answered. "Uhh, probably." Hoping to not have to actually do it.

"Don't bother the lad with this. He has enough to worry about." Abernathy intervened. He could probably bring down the whole place if he wanted to. He doesn't need to tax himself lifting people. We will just load him into the cart outside."

Huxley swelled upon hearing how Abernathy had such a high opinion of his capabilities. As much as he liked the compliment, taking down a whole building was way outside what he thought he could do.

"I can help lift him." Huxley offered.

"Wait, we're taking him with us?!" She stated, incredulously. "How are we supposed to look for a madman and take care of a madman, simultaneously!" She pointed at Grubmush.

Abernathy pressed a finger to his lips and said, "Shh, don't call him that. He's far from mad."

"By who's definition?!"

"By mine" And he added, "And let's keep him from getting angry."

She rolled her eyes and said, "He can't even hear us, look at him." She gave a light punch to his shoulder. "He's hibernating or something. I heard they do that."

As though to confirm it, Grubmush laid there quite dormant-looking. His chest was breathing but so shallow it appeared he wasn't breathing at all.

Abernathy shook his head in agreement, "It does seem that way. Well, that will make things easier. I wasn't looking forward to someone howling in pain all day and night."

Elatress appeared next to Huxley, having apparently been sleeping late. She yawned and muttered, "Ooo, Ryla's ok! Good, I was hoping to meet her. But what is she doing here?"

Abernathy looked at the pair of them and said "Elatress...you've overslept. You delivered this note to her last night. This is Ryla the...uhh..." He stopped realizing, he didn't know her last name. She waved it off and said "Just Ryla's is fine."

"How can you not remember that you delivered this to her?"

Elatress just blinked and said, "No, not her. I gave it to the Ember outside."

Huxley tensed up immediately. "Outside the Gearbox." Huxley asked?

"Ah, so she is here," Abernathy stated without any alarm in his voice. "Don't worry everyone, she will wait outside. When the Wardens delivered Grubmush this morning, they said she would be escorting us. Apparently, trust is low at the moment, and they want us watched more closely." He clapped his hands together and said, "Elatress you pack enough food for a few days. Huxley, you get yourself as disguised as possible. You will travel in the wagon with Grubmush and will pretend to be attending to him."

"Like a nurse or something?" Huxley asked. He was appalled and failed miserably to hide it. Abernathy either didn't hear the question or ignored him. "I will drive the horses. Ryla, you are our guide. You've been through these Wilds before."

Elatress coughed. "I can be the guide. Who knows the Wilds better than me?"

"Of course, you can El, but you have a different job. You and Arktos are our scouts." She perked up immediately, suddenly fine with this plan. "Scouting for what?"

"A white flower with red spots." He answered.

"Flowers?"

"Yes," Abernathy said with hesitation. "It turns out this Mad Doctor has remained so well hidden because his home is surrounded by extremely poisonous flowers. The kind that seizes up your lungs and turns your blood thick, or so I'm told anyway."

"Oh yes! I've seen those before." Elatress jumped a little.

"You sound excited?" Huxley asked.

"Wouldn't you be? I finally get to know where they grow. I can get their pollen and..." She trailed off looking up at the two and said, "leave it alone because it's probably dangerous." Abernathy replied with a flat stare. Huxley would have given it more thought, but he was too busy working through the rest of the plan. He had to travel with an Ember and pretend to be a nurse...to Grubmush. His acting skills were nonexistent matched only by his medical skill. If the Ember caught him, he'd be dead, and if Grubmush woke up, he might just kill him all the same.

Abernathy saw his downturned face and said, "Nah, cheer up. I've made some breathing masks that filter out most poisons and, besides, you've already met this Ember. The Wardens told me she's the one who tested you...Onders...right?"

Huxley gasped, "Yeah...Onders..I remember her." Suddenly, he remembered their talk from the night before and chided himself. Onders, Grubmush and Ryla, together, out in the middle of nowhere, with him. Huxley's mind imagined all sorts of ways he might not make it back from this trip.

———————————————————————————————-

How many people could want to kill a guy in one city, Huxley wondered. He was pretty sure Onders was the least likely to kill him, but he was dreading facing her again. Ryla had threatened to cut his throat once, and Grubmush was...Grubmush, though it seemed he currently associated Huxley with part of his religion, which didn't make Huxley feel any safer.

Huxley, Abernathy and Elatress all stole a moment away to discuss things. Huxley explained to Abernathy the agreement he had made with Onders. At first, Abernathy was annoyed at not being told about an Ember frequenting so often, but his annoyance subsided when Elatress said she had been monitoring her. If Elatress was comfortable with her, then Abernathy was, it appeared. He still warned Huxley against getting close with an Ember, they tend to be single-minded. If she had wanted the Grimoire once, she likely still did. If one tactic hadn't worked, she was likely trying another. Huxley didn't want to believe it, but all the evidence, so far, pointed that way. He had wanted so badly to have an ally like Onders. She was someone who knew real information, someone who was like him, someone whose smile was earned and not given..."

"Are you blushing, Bookpile?" Elatress interjected.

"What?! No! I'm just concentrating on what to do." He said.

"Yeah, ok, you're definitely concentrating, but not on that."

Abernathy waved his hand saying "Ok, enough. Huxley, please focus here."

"I. AM. FOCUSED!" He said over pronouncing, letting his embarrassment slip.

Abernathy chuckled but let it be. He shifted his attention to Ryla as he continued to converse with Huxley. "El and I will start loading up for our trip. It will likely be a few minutes before we're ready. It would be best if you spent a few minutes with Ryla. She won't try and hurt you this time."

"Is that a promise?" Huxley asked.

"Hah! No, I can't do that. But if you don't provoke her, she shouldn't hurt you.

That sounded fair enough to Huxley so he agreed. Satisfied, Abernathy and Elatress began packing.

Huxley found Ryla standing over Grubmush who was still splayed out on the table.

She didn't speak as he approached. He was always so bad at starting conversations. He needed Jonah for that. Ryla didn't seem like a chatty person. She stood now rigid, gripping her weapon with only her eyes in motion. Her breathing was steady but betrayed only a hint of emotion like she was working to keep it in check.

"I got into the College." Huxley ventured. "Well, not in, but into it. The building I mean, not admission. I'm still working on that part. Are you still working there? As a guard?"

She didn't respond.

Huxley thought for a minute and figured he could try another tactic. He probably shouldn't bring up the battle, or the time she almost caught him in the Gearbox. What his curiosity wanted to know was, why wasn't she trying to capture him now?

"I uh-"

"Please, stop." She uttered, Her voice was far softer than he remembered.

"Oh, sorry."

"What is it about walking and speaking and everything else that is so difficult for you people?" She asked.

Huxley blinked and shook his head, not certain what she was referring to.

"You stumble your way through your day," Ryla explained, her voice growing stronger, "walking without falling, amazingly, out of sync with the entire world. You assemble words in your mouth and let them spill out like a waterfall, and still expect people to understand you. It's maddening!"

He felt like he needed to respond but could barely follow her meaning. She didn't need him to, she kept on talking.

"Then a giant lumbering oaf like this," She gestured to Grubmush, "Comes stomping around, never even approaching what might be considered a rhythm." She breathed in heavily, as though preparing herself for something distasteful. "And he manages to *beat me*."

"Oh," Huxley said as he began to understand. Ryla wasn't mad at him, at least, not like he had worried she would be.

"You can calm down. Try to lower your heartbeat and breath. It's chaotic. I am not here for Danador or on their behalf. They released me from duty. Now I am just Ryla of Valdannon." She sniffed, her nose scrunching up and said, "As though I was ever a butcher."

"I never thought you were," Huxley stated sheepishly.

"You were terrified, like a rabbit in a wide-open field." She shot back, waving her hand dismissively. "But something changed within you. You've stabilized a good deal since our first meeting. You're a more put-together person." She faced him now, "What has changed? People, especially your kind, don't normally achieve that."

He tried to answer her truthfully, but even he didn't quite know.

She stepped at an odd angle and pivoted her foot downward and lowered her knee. She cocked her head and smiled. Huxley turned to see what she was looking at.

"There it is. Turmoil in the Gearbox. Mid-winter. Mind-only canvas." Her pupils sank in deep, widening, nearly drinking in the entirety of their white borders. She stood up straight, sniffed and stated, "I didn't ask your permission but I promise I will not paint it. Good and genuine turmoil is such a rare sight in Danador. Are you sure you are from here?"

Huxley felt like something stranger happened than what actually did. *Did she just name a mental image after me?*

"Yes." He said, the slight hesitation in his voice betraying his confusion.

"Strange," She contemplated, "Turmoil is a trait of my people. Danadorians are always so straight-minded. Nothing to mull over. That is probably the source of my first confusion with you."

She nodded to herself and turned to him placatingly, "Huxley, I hope you can understand I was under command outside of my own ability to refuse. I hold no malice towards you. I needed something badly from the men who control this city so I sold my services. They have released me so I no longer have any compulsion to apprehend you."

"Did you get it?" He asked. "The thing you were after?"

"In a manner of speaking. Wardens are not the easiest to deal with. They talk in doublespeak and always want to shake hands! I'm sure you've noticed."

"Very much. Come to think of it, no one tries to shake hands as often as they do. It's probably one of the many rules they follow."

"Indeed," Ryla replied with disdain.

A silence fell on the pair until Abernathy came back. An order had been arranged.

Elatress and Abernathy passed back and forth bits of information as Huxley stayed within the Gearbox and Onders remained outside. Onders was behaving strangely. She would only say that they were being watched but offered no more information. They had decided that while they were within the city to act as normal, which meant keeping Huxley out of sight. The Embers and Wardens may indeed know he was here but they were playing a larger game now. A game where they couldn't see all the pieces. Huxley agreed to remain hidden until Danador was far away to not provoke anyone, and Onders merely nodded her head when asked. She was the biggest wild card out of the bunch. Huxley trusted her to a small degree but agreed with Abernathy that the whole escapade was becoming suspicious. Something wasn't right.

It worried Abernathy about what the Embers and Wardens hoped to find while they were gone. He had plenty of illegal things inside but nothing he didn't think he could talk his way out of. If they were searching for the Grimoire, they would know that Huxley wouldn't be stupid enough to leave it to be found. So why all of this? They were out of time and out of options. The plan was to go through with what was asked of them while attempting to keep the Grimoire and Huxley hidden. Keeping Huxley hidden would be easy enough but keeping the book away from Onders would be far more difficult. It remained the singular thing he hadn't been honest with her about.

An hour later they were ready. Elatress and Arktos left before they did. It was still dawn and they could scout ahead and keep Arktos from being seen by too many eyes. They would wait just outside of Danador.

Huxley helped fashion a stretcher and the four of them, through great effort, loaded Grubmush into the wagon. His massive body took up half the space, the rest was supplies and a small stool for Huxley. Onders was outside waiting. She didn't even look at them, her nose buried in what looked to be a similar book to Huxley's grimoire. It was smaller than his and without the pages already full but it held the same buckles and no title. Perhaps it was her personal Grimoire. He desperately wanted to read it but knew he would never get the chance. Like his own, he wasn't eager to show it to others. It contained so many of his own thoughts now that it felt more and more like his own private collection. The other authors' notes and his were in agreement. Huxley felt like, ultimately, it was a good thing. He removed his own Grimoire and held it in his hands. The weight of it once felt so heavy, now it was far lighter and familiar. He shoved it under Grubmush's bed, betting that should Onders come in and look around, she wouldn't be interested in getting overly close to the Dathu. As he shoved the book under, he heard Grubmush moan. Not a painful one but one of waking up.

"Great", Huxley thought to himself idly. He hadn't regained consciousness yet. but it wouldn't be long from now.

The wagon lurched into motion. Abernathy clicked for the horses to begin moving and the stirrups snapped tight. Grubmush hadn't moved but his eyes were fluttering and his breathing became irregular. Maybe he'd wake up in a confused fit and attack everyone.

The roads of Danador had been relatively smooth but soon gave way to roads pitted with pot-holes. The train was the primary means of travel now, so traveling by road became arduous. All efforts went into keeping the tracks clear while the roads fell into disrepair. To make matters worse, the snow was over a foot thick in some sections. Folk who couldn't afford the train still used the roads, making them at least packed down in stretches, but it wasn't what anyone would call comfortable. They exited the city just before the sun crested the horizon. Huxley had hoped that maybe it would cause some of the snow to melt, but judging by the gusts of wind, he doubted it.

Regarding Embers, their guess had been right so far. Onders seemed to think of everyone as a burden, or at best servants. It was a complete contrast to her light-hearted demeanor just a few hours ago while playing Ballistics and Bureaucrats with Elatress. Onders kept to herself and walked alone, removed from the group. Huxley thought it strange but wasn't in a position to argue. He didn't dare use his time to study the Grimoire. If he was caught with it out, he wouldn't be able to deny it. He wondered if all of them, collectively, could defeat Onders if a fight occurred. The idea made him shudder.

As Huxley contemplated Onder's new behavior, he realized just how wrong he could be. What did he really know about her anyway? She was plucked out of her home at a young age, showing great aptitude for Magnincy. She had been at the College ever since and was easy to provoke. She was certainly more powerful than he was but he had managed to surprise her and technically win a fight once. And now she was seeking information from him. Then he remembered the way her cheeks flushed when she was winning a game, either against him or Elatress. It was a key detail. The way her eyes shone with deep interest and calculation. She really liked to win.

Elatress and Arktos reappeared almost immediately after leaving the city, and Ryla rode upfront with Abernathy. Onders wandered close a few times. He could hear her traveling off the path. Maybe she was looking for something.

He could hear Abernathy trying to make polite conversation with Onders. She didn't seem keen on it though. She would answer a direct question but that was about all. she wouldn't offer anything else. Finally, he shifted tactics and decided to be direct. That held a certain respect from Embers, Huxley had learned. They don't bandy words often.

"So, this is a big important job that requires the involvement of Embers, but they don't send them. Just one apprentice and a bunch of foreigners...why?"

She took a moment but finally answered, "Because we are expendable and because it is the right time."

Ryla, who had been silent so far, said, "Speak for yourself."

Onders didn't respond to her and kept on, "Our informants have reported that his hideout is surrounded by the white flowers with red spots, whose spores kill you within minutes once inhaled. Normally flowers cannot flourish in the winter months but something he has done allows them to anyway. Fresh snow fell last night. He is defenseless. The spores will have a hard time finding their way into the air. However, I still believe we will make use of your breathing device Norun. Ridiculous, that you would use such a device to merely protect your lungs from ash and fumes from metal working. It has so many applications."

"Uh oh, you brought up his favorite thing," Elatress said.

Abernathy guffawed a deep hearty laugh and said, "You've figured out some applications, have you? Please tell me what you have thought of!" His delight was soaked into each word. If someone didn't know him well, it would have sounded like sarcasm but Huxley heard it for what it was. The engineer was a man who loved that kind of talk and wanted to hear far more.

It was a restrained jubilation.

Onders may have taken it sarcastically because she refused any more of his questions. Each time he asked, his excitement lessened, having realized he overplayed his hand.

"Pollutants of all kinds?"

"Fumes and exhaust?"

"Perhaps everyday use for the third-rung workers?"

"When sleeping for more steady breathing?"

All went unanswered.

He finally gave up muttering, "No real engineers in this city."

26

Healing and Flowers

"Subatomically the notion is plausible in photons and even then, in informational settings only. For matter to move instantaneously is not a known science." **-Page 349 Excerpt from the Grimoire**

After an hour of travel, Huxley felt himself settling in. Elatress and Arktos left again to scout ahead. Huxley expected she hated how slow the wagon moved and he wondered how long it would be before they got to the Mad Doctor. He felt like they had traveled far enough for him to come out and stretch his legs. He looked around through the open flaps. All he saw were snow and trees. Periodically Abernathy would state loudly where they were. Huxley expected this was for his benefit but Huxley wasn't familiar enough with the area to really know what anything meant. His only real travel had been with Elatress, and he certainly couldn't find that place again. Another hour passed and all of Abernathy's polite questions ceased. Huxley had forgotten Ryla was there. This was not the lively travel party he would have thought it would have been. Was that boredom that was creeping into him now? Impossible, surrounded by danger and heading to worse, how could he feel that way? He knew it would be short-lived so he accepted it and even tried to relax. He propped his head against a crate of supplies and looked over at

Grubmush. Besides that sound he had made after they settled him, the Dathu had been silent as the grave. Gnarled flesh and a lifetime of scars littered his torso and every piece of exposed skin. What kind of life had he lived that gave him so many injuries? Huxley had maybe two or three real scars, one from playing too close to some rocks a few years ago and one from carelessly cutting up fruit in his hand. And even then there was a world of difference between his scars and Grubmush's. He doubted that Grubmush would even consider his scars real. It was then that he noticed Grubmush's eyes open and turned to stare at him.

Huxley's body tensed, but he didn't move. He felt like he was cornered by a coiled snake and one mistake would cause it to strike. Grubmush's eyes were bloodshot and tense, although that was always true. They bore into Huxley with an interest that was sure to be followed up by action. But none came. The pair held each other's gaze and regarded each other. Grubmush's breath changed first and he filled his lungs with a similar animalistic huff that Huxley had heard a few times before. But this was different. It was tight, and controlled, like some new variation of his heavy breathing.

Grubmush winced and moved his right arm, testing it, at first, for responsiveness. Each digit seemed to do as it was asked. Satisfied, he moved on to the next. He kept his back flat against the mat and felt his torso. Barely above a whisper, he made slight "mmhmm" acknowledgements to himself. It was like he was checking to see how much of him there was left. The self-diagnostic went on for a few minutes, each finger feeling between his ribs and over his chest. Finally, he drew in his deepest breath yet and felt his gored mid-section. He lifted his bandages and felt along the lines of each wound. Huxley cringed, not being able to tear himself away from the horrid spectacle. He hated this sight but feared Grubmush too much to look away. The wounds were clean, as though surgically made. Blood was still seeping and staining everything around it, but it was not as bad as Huxley had prepared for. It was certainly not the same as the wound he had received only twenty-four hours ago. It had healed greatly. Grubmush then sighed contentedly, pulled his fingers out of his wounds and held his right hand out towards Huxley. What was he reaching for?

Huxley's instincts and judgment had a brief but violent war. To grab a hand offered was natural, but there were so many reasons not to. His fear of upsetting the man won and he tried to appear like he wasn't frightened. His yelp betrayed him as Grubmush's hand closed around his own and tightened to pull him closer. The wild man stunk of dried blood and sweat, perhaps many weeks' worth. He pulled Huxley close and croaked, "Did she live?"

Huxley pushed his panic down and kept his composure. "Who?" Suddenly, it dawned on him. "Oh, Ryla?"

Grubmush's hand tightened some more, proving he was capable of crushing bone if he wanted to.

"Uhh, yes, she seems ok, actually."

"Ahh, good." Grubmush sighed. "I have never received such a savage beating like that before...except maybe from you. Danador contains many skilled fighters." With that, he closed his eyes again and slipped back into sleep. It was another minute before his hand slacked and he let go of Huxley.

"Is he going to be trouble?" Onders demanded.

She had stuck her head into the back of the wagon. Her hand filled with an unknown Magnincy begging to be released.

Huxley feigned bravery and said, "No, he's docile for now."

Without another word, the tent flap closed and Onders disappeared. Huxley hadn't felt the wagon stop in all the commotion. He heard the heavy labored breathing of Arktos before the bear crashed through the leaves and branches of a nearby tree line, which meant Elatress had returned. "We've arrived," she informed everyone.

Huxley listened intently. "I don't see anything." he heard Onders state.

"She's right." Ryla commented, "Look, it's already starting."

Huxley heard a few kicks from someone removing snow from the ground.

"Are these the flowers that protect his home?" Ryla asked.

"This is where they begin," Elatress confirmed.

"Then the corruption has grown. We are more than a mile or two away from where we should be." Onders stated, voice filled with contempt.

Onders began issuing orders. "Show us the rest of the way. Abernathy, dispense the breathing apparatuses, Ryla you follow from a distance. He may already know we are here and try a rear attack. Abernathy, you and Huxley will attend me. We can dispense with the rouse. No more Wardens watch us here."

Huxley gulped, *attend her*?

The rest of the group said nothing in response to her commands, seemingly resigned to following her orders.

The wagon raised a few inches as he heard Abernathy's boots hit the snow. "Uhh, what about Grubmush? Shouldn't someone stay with him in case he wakes up?"

Onders chuckled out, "Oh, no, no, no it is my sincerest wish that he does wake up while we're out here and the great oaf will wander off. We will be free of his moronic wishes and have the beast out of the city. We could only be so lucky. No, absolutely not. Huxley will attend me."

Onders spoke with new authority, Huxley thought, like the kind you would hear from a young child given his first responsibilities. They would take it so seriously and put on an heir of importance and walk around with their chest puffed out. The wagon flap opened again and Onders took another look at Grubmush. A sneer curled around her lips as she regarded him. She gave the barest hand gesture for Huxley to exit.

He tried to appear casual, and to whatever extent he was successful, he may never know, but he tried anyhow. Ryla, Abernathy and Elatress grew tense. Onder's actions were the source of the concern. They all were fiddling with their masks, adjusting straps, and stealing glances that betrayed their true thoughts. They may have a problem, not with Grumbush, or even the Doctor, but with this Ember.

Within a few moments, they were on their way. Huxley remained a few paces behind Onders not wanting to tempt fate. He had managed to stuff the Grimoire a few inches further under the bed, a pitiful attempt at stealth, but better than nothing. They marched in silence, only stopping to check under the snow for the presence of the white flower with red spots. It did indeed grow more abundantly the further they walked. Huxley instinctually breathed more shallowly, worried there may be trace amounts of poison in the air. Perhaps the masks worked well enough, and perhaps the snow was truly protecting them, but all he tasted in the air was the bitter cold. His nerves and adrenaline kept the worst of it at bay. His body was producing enough stress to cook a meal. It was a strange sensation, to be surrounded by both friends, and probably enemies. To know that he had help so close, but also was flirting with death. He couldn't describe it to himself. It was a rare and genuinely new emotion. "Anxious safety," was the best way to describe it, he mused. The barest smile escaped his lips only to disappear immediately for fear of breaking the seal on his mask.

The wind grew still, and only the sloshing of their boots could be heard. The eerie forest grew thinner. What were once dense trees now became intermittent. With every step, he disturbed the snow, and with every step, he could see white flowers with red spots. There was no other option now than just to trust that the masks would keep him safe. If not, he could never escape the poison. Abernathy hasn't made anything untrustworthy so far, he reminded himself. The ale was difficult to stomach, recalling how badly he reacted to it. It had lessened somewhat in the last few days but was still not easy to digest. At least he didn't get sick anymore. Suddenly, Onders stopped walking as did Elatress. The action was mirrored by Arktos. A few hundred feet away a plume of smoke escaped the trees and a bare outline of a wooden structure could be seen.

"He's here", Onders whispered. "Probably watching us right now." She motioned with her hands towards the house. "Move with stealth, strike as one, and draw him out into the open. Move him towards this clearing and I will dispatch him. Whatever you do, do not alert him to my presence. He will expect to be protected by his poisons and won't expect what we have in store for him."

"You're not coming with us?" Abernathy asked.

"No, I've told you the plan. Do it Norun." She commanded.

Elatress unlooped her hatchets. She was likely thrilled in a way Abernathy didn't want her to be at this news.

"Very well, come on." Abernathy motioned for Huxley to follow.

He took a few steps forward but Onders held up her hand. "Of course, you don't need an assistant. He will remain with me. Perhaps, he can split the Doctor's attention, if he sees me." Her voice was as cold as the snow around them.

Abernathy searched for a reason to refuse but only managed an, "Oh, fine then."

Onders had expected her orders to be followed and so they did. Ryla made no protest except to ask to lead. "I can see a number of landscapes coming out exquisitely in all of this white."

"Oooooo, like from the Lecture Hall?" Elatress asked.

"No, a portrait is different with each landscape," Ryla answered.

"Right, of course. Can I do the borders? I can make a river of blo-"

Onders shushed them and said, "I don't care, just get it done." She waved her hand as though to dismiss them. The four of them moved towards the house, leaving Onders and Huxley alone.

———————————————————————————————————

Elatress was muttering her mantra to herself as they walked. "...like me and other nice girls... I don't need to kill her." It had changed slightly, probably to fit the circumstance. "It's savages and beasts that kill for sport. I am not a savage or a beast...I am a nice girl." She continued muttering to herself and Abernathy gave Ryla an, "it's ok" nod at her visible confusion towards Elatress' state of mind. The trio and Arktos approached and split up as they got close. No lights were visible, nor any movement, but the fire was lit and issued a steady stream of smoke from the chimney. It was a small cabin, they may have even missed it if they hadn't seen the smoke on the horizon. It was surrounded by large plots of land covered in glass structures. The mist inside made the glass opaque, but huge amounts of plant growth could be seen. Each building was lush and green inside with a smattering of other colors adorning the leaves. No two plants looked exactly the same. Abernathy wondered what each one did and how violently they did it.

"...when I do kill it, I will cook it like a lady..."

"Is she going to shut up?" Ryla hissed, her grip tightening on her glaive.

Abernathy did have to agree. They were getting too close now for comfort, but he knew Elatress was almost finished. They paused and waited for her.

"I won't listen to or note its screams. I am doing this for survival only and not because it's in my territory. It is not important to store up fat for the winter, nor will my enemies be frightened by my many carcasses. Now silence." She closed her eyes and rubbed Arktos's fur. After a moment, she opened them again and nodded her head.

Abernathy would explain it to Ryla later, right now they had to deal with the man looking at them through the window.

———————————————————————————————

Onders and Huxley watched them leave. Silence settled in like an unwelcome guest, daring Huxley to ask it to leave. He stole a glance at Onders, but she didn't return it. Her focus was absolute, so much so that Huxley thought it betrayed her real motives. She was trying hard not to appear frightened but this was probably a big test for her. Onders had been an apprentice for a long time and was more than capable as an Ember, but she was held back and remained in a lower status. He didn't know how long that should last but she was well into young adulthood now like he was. There were all kinds of reasons she may have been denied promotion. He would have guessed it was her temper but in his experience, all Embers had bad tempers. No, her issue must be something else.

Onders pulled out her book and started taking notes. Huxley knew it was dangerous but he stole another look. And for the first time, she acknowledged him. Her pen stopped abruptly, and she snapped the book shut.

"You can remove your mask here Huxley. It is quite safe with this blanket of snow." Onders said while removing hers and Huxley then did the same.

"Don't you know that peeping at an Ember's Grimoire is dangerous?" She said overly casual.

He jumped in surprise and muttered his apology, "I wasn't looking."

"Of course, you weren't. After all, I'm just an apprentice Ember, not a full-fledged one. Why would my notes be of real worth? Is that what you meant? My secrets aren't worth stealing?!" A vicious edge creeped in. He heard her feet shift in the snow to face him.

He jumped but still tried to hide his face as he turned towards her. "Of course not! I just…I was curious but not trying to…uhh…I'm sorry."

She waved it away, but only before Huxley spotted excitement in her eyes and even a smile. What was happening here? He wondered desperately.

"One day, this book will be filled, and I will have a full Grimoire." Onders told him, her anger fading. She went on and said, "Have you ever seen one? They don't usually leave the college. I figure you don't actually have it. If you did, you would have been more impressive." She flipped through hers and said, "A passed-down line of ancient secrets and deep scientific knowledge, the root of understanding Magnincy itself. The college only has twenty that trace back to before the sundering and reformation of Magnadun. Three of which are believed to be written by the Kindler himself. The one who first lit the flame of knowledge in our hearts and raised us from the dirt. Fools still spend their time trying to track down lost ones; as though, such a treasure could be found casually."

Huxley gulped. His lungs constricted and he became dizzy.

"My master Maddox taught me this one, I can't create as wide a radius as he can. He once choked out an entire city block. At least, that's what he told me. It was likely only a building but the feat remains impressive."

Suddenly, Huxley realized what she was doing. It was the same thing done to him when he first entered the College. She was making the air hard to breathe. It wasn't his fear. It was her. He staggered backwards.

"Well, I guess it's not three anymore, it's two. One was stolen. And I believe I have finally cut off the thief from his friends and got him alone in the woods."

A concussive blast took Huxley off his feet and threw him into the air. He crashed through branches and slammed into the snow. The wind was knocked out of him, only it wasn't so bad because he already had lost it a few moments before.

"Are you awake?" Her voice called. "I'm not supposed to kill you. But who knows what will happen out here."

Huxley gasped and filled his lungs with frigid air that bit his throat on the way down. It was a bother that he was glad for.

"I didn't steal the Grimoire!" He answered back as he tried to find his feet.

Another concussive blast struck him, blowing huge swaths of snow into the air and shaking the trees around him. He slammed into the ground again.

"Stole, found or otherwise, it's not yours. It should have been mine! I put in the work, and who knows what fool thing you've done with it. You managed to steal some knowledge and thought yourself one of us!" She laughed derisively and sneered. "As though a fool, from Mayburn, could ever-"

A branch had fallen and struck Onders in the head. It knocked her to the ground but she found her feet again and recovered. She rubbed her head and turned towards Huxley, but he was gone.

"I'm so tired of being called a fool." He spoke into the air. Huxley had thrown himself behind a trunk that was barely thick enough to hide his body. At least, he hoped it was. He summoned wind pressures and sent his voice into it making it difficult to find exactly where it came from. "Fool enough to evade your Wardens and guards for months now!"

A forced laugh answered him back. "You think for one minute we didn't know where you were?! That girl is hard to track, but you! We found traces of your deeds all over. We just needed all of you out of Danador, and it helped that you and I were friends."

"Then why leave me alone to practice and not come get the Grimoire back." He whispered into the breeze, hoping she hadn't drawn a bead on him.

Violet smoke with a pop and crack sound emitted from various spots surrounded Huxley. She was teleporting like she has done before.

"We thought you'd do something stupid and blow up part of the city." Another pop and crack then from further away, "We figured you'd just make yourself go mad as all untrained Embers do," Pop and crack now closer, "...and we'd just come collect you. Why expend our efforts and flirt with madness when I could trust you would just do it to yourself?" Pop and crack, now just to his left. "Come out from behind that tree."

————————————————————————————————

The four of them regarded the presence inside. Abernathy didn't know what to expect with this man, but like so many things the Embers did, they likely didn't understand him as well as they thought they did. He waved heartily and bellowed "HELLO DEAR FRIEND! I am Abernathy from of the Norun. May we speak?"

Elatress and Ryla gasped and jumped backwards, and Arktos huffed in surprise. The man stood unmoved by the greeting.

"Abernathy..." Elatress whispered, "...he could kill us all."

Forcing a laugh Abernathy said "Who will kill us? A Doctor? Oh, sweet Elatress, you have forgotten, Doctors do the opposite of that." He swirled his finger around the side of his head mocking her. "We need his services. Tell me, friend!" He gestured with an open palm towards Elatress, "Do you have an opening for my companion here? She needs quite a few herbs, I imagine."

The figure shifted barely. Abernathy tensed and waited for his response. He was gambling big on this, but one thing he could count on was that Embers do not understand normal social situations. And if he could put him on the backfoot there he might have an opening.

————————————————————————————————-

Huxley knew he was out-matched, but perhaps if he kept evading her, Abernathy, Elatress, Arktos and Ryla would make it back. She had underestimated him before and it nearly killed her. It looked like she was about to make the same mistake. But he needed to stall.

"Is there even a Mad Doctor out here?" He asked as he emerged from the tree facing Onders head-on.

"Oh, he's mad, and a doctor of sorts, but it's his prison. He holed himself up in there after we tracked him down. He was happy to remain in there and grow his flowers, but lately, he had started healing people and sowing seeds of division. I was given this opportunity to return the Grimoire, be rid of the city's felons, and silence that doctor."

"They still won't make you an Ember, you know. You're being used. We all are!"

"NESCIENCE!" She screamed. "I will be an Ember!"

He summoned his bubble. He centered it on top of his head rather than his chest to allow his feet to be on the ground. It pushed the snow out of the way as he stepped. Onders was closer now, the wind had made it so that he couldn't hear her steps in the snow. The two faced each other, each shooting their hands forward grabbing Magnincy.

"Well, I am impressed." She sneered but showed gritted teeth. "You have managed to learn a thing or two. Did you break the branch or did it break free on its own?"

He tasted blood in his mouth. He spit it out and it caught on his shield.

"Ohh, your bubble is still there." Her sneer now was a full-blown smile, "Clearly you haven't learned much. It barely did anything last time. They were worried you'd be a challenge for me. The only challenge was getting rid of that oaf and drawing you out here..." She trailed off and cocked her head. "Is that my-"

Huxley flung his left hand through the shield to stretch a translucent tendril out. It wrapped around her right hand and yanked Onders off her feet.

"It is your shield, mixed with mine, Onders. I've learned from every encounter I've had. If you're paying attention you can learn a lot from people. The hexagon structure with pliability makes for a tough defense. It bends but doesn't break when attacked."

"You dare lecture me!" She threw forward her hands. One belched fire and the other screamed forth lightning. The bolt got there first and cracked into his shield. It knocked him backwards and he lost his grip on Magnincy. He wasn't hurt, but it had torn a hole in one of the hexagons but the others remained firm. Then the fire consumed it, wrapping the front half of the bubble and tearing it down. Though not fast enough, Huxley used that time to summon the full breadth of his knowledge. The pages of Grimoire rushing forward and the stars swirling begging to be used.

"We can learn from each other! We don't need them. Or to fight for their approval. We can ignore whatever game they are playing! You can teach me and I can help you." He pleaded.

The fire melted away his protection. A few tongues of flame managed to get inside where the lightning had struck. The heat was weirdly comfortable as a respite to the cold. It was then that he got his idea. He drew upon his knowledge and formed an icicle from the snow at the bottom of his shield. It wasn't much but would be a worthy dagger. Aiming clunkily, he fired it forward out of the lightning-torn shield towards Onders. The fire stopped abruptly just as his shield was reduced to tatters. It retained its loose shape but the fire left the inner honeycomb to only whisps and shreds. The smoke cleared, and he heard her gasping sharply. Finally, he could see her. Onders' hand was smoking from prolonged use and she had a small ice dagger stuck into her palm. It had melted considerably moving through the fire's vortex but it remained intact enough to do its job.

Huxley was stunned it worked so well. He had hoped for just a distraction, but this was far better. She yanked the shard out and closed her hand, her fist squeezing out blood through her fingers. A few drops hit the snow. Her face darkened, and she stepped forward. She shot her unwounded hand forward and grabbed Magnincy. Her eyes twitched and Huxley saw her look a few different places at once. *Was she slipping?* He wondered. He hadn't seen what he looked like when he went mad, but he guessed it probably looked similar to the way she did now. Suddenly, a new tactic came to mind. He didn't get a chance to employ it before his hands clenched onto his sides. She had pinned his hands to his thighs, with an unseen force bearing down on them. She tried to regain her composure of superiority but her face betrayed her inner rage. Huxley scoring a hit, or even worse proving a challenge, was upsetting her. And with his arms pinned he probably only had one option left. He had to get her concentration to break.

"You absolute-"

"Fool?" He interrupted. "Embers need to find a better way to swear. For all that reading you don't bother with vocabulary, do you? Fool this, and fool that! Even schoolyard bullies do better, and they are the most ignorant people I've ever met." He paused and said, "Oh ignorant means-" The pressure tightened and Huxley's wrists shook. He couldn't grab any Magnincy like this.

"I KNOW WHAT IT MEANS!" She barked and her composure slipped again.

He tried his best to sound like he wasn't in pain.

"Oh, and lightning and fire? The Amazing Guliford would have loved that; perfect for stage shows and children."

Her face turned cruel and she seethed, "I could create a lot more if you'd like."

"Of course, you can, that was the first thing I learned. It seems like kid's stuff, though."

Suddenly, understanding dawned on Onders. "You think you can upset me!?" Her voice was high and outraged. "You think you might be able to beat me? You are alone and without your stolen grimoire. While I have mine here to refresh me."

Damn, thought Huxley. He had forgotten she could do that.

Then he said "well reach for it then, use your bloody hand to grab it or the one you're holding me with. Go on." He smiled, still feigning how little pain he was in.

Her eyes narrowed and she opened her wounded palm. The blood remained but the wound had already closed.

"You know not who you jest with. I actually didn't want to do this. Our short time together has been fun. But we both have wants, and I want to be an Ember. And bringing back the Grimoire is the only way." She reached into her satchel and pulled out hers.

"Stop!" He pleaded. "Our time together was more than just that, wasn't it? What happened on that night? What had I misunderstood to change things so much?"

A boom shook the trees and snow, Huxley closed his eyes not wanting to see what she had produced when he found himself free. He looked around, the sound had come from afar. Onders had been shocked as well and dropped her concentration. Huxley used the opportunity to summon as much wind as possible. It wouldn't kill but it would disorient her. He used both hands and grabbed as much as he could of everything related to climatology and released it.

He sent himself flying backward as well along everything else. Snow buried him. His face stung with wind and ice burn. His adrenaline surged and he maladroitly pulled himself out. Onders had experienced the same thing as he had and pulled herself free of a snow bank.

"My Grimoire!" Her voice carried over the cold air with an icy hatred that Huxley had never heard before. She thrashed around in the snow looking for it. It wouldn't take her long to find it. The gust had caused most of the snow to be blown away exposing a thick field of white flowers with red spots. They were everywhere, hundreds, maybe thousands, packed together so tight they seemed to straighten up finally getting some sun. Then he tried something stupid.

"Oh, wonderful, a new Grimoire for me to study. I will add this one to mine. It's so small though, it won't be of much value." His lie was weak and under normal circumstances, his acting would not have sold it. But Onders was panicked.

Her screech thrummed his ears and she grasped at two hands of Magnincy and began reaching forward and grabbing more. Three, four, five, maybe six different stars of Magnincy swirled within her hands. Murder in her eyes, she drew back to release.

Huxley only had a moment to react, the stars in front of him were swirling wild and free, begging to be used. He didn't have a moment to decide. So he grabbed the one closest to him and released.

27

∽

Poison and Stories

"Vibrations within the nasal cavity produce neurochemicals and in-creased lymphatic circulation and melatonin production, it can also release endorphins, nitric oxide..." -**Page 118 Excerpt from the Grimoire**

Spores and pollen burst into the air. A yellow and greenish cloud encircled them. The newly exposed toxic flowers released their long-held death. Immediately, he felt his lungs scream in agony and blood vessels in his nose burst. He was not alone. Onders was suffering the same fate. She let go of her Magnincy in a wild thrash and it flew harmlessly into the sky. It likely would have killed him, but now that was likely to happen anyway. The pair both clutched their throats trying uselessly to find oxygen. Onders collapsed onto the ground but Huxley managed to stay up. His vision clouded and his heartbeat thumped heavily in his ears. He couldn't even hear his ragged breath anymore; it was overwhelmed by other parts of his body making their pleas. Knowing he was doomed, he waited for the end. His legs gave out but he managed to prop himself up into a sitting position, not wanting to leave an undignified corpse. "What a stupid thought." He said out loud. His voice was unrecognizable as his own. "Maybe I am the fool they always say I am." Onders lay motionless now. No, wait, her breath was still there, just shallow. So shallow, he almost missed it. One minute passed as he awaited death, perhaps the longest minute of his life. But he remained awake. *How?* he thought.

His vision blurred and much of his body's motor functions were unusable. He only retained simple thoughts and a loose balance. All at once, he felt himself moving through the air. Flying. He had a dawning of understanding, summoned Magnincy, and banished gravity itself. Flying through the air, he was the envy of all birds. Then, Onders joined him. Her blood-stained lips not speaking, eyes shut, but she flew all the same. The snow and flowers were far below them. Why had they ever fought when flying was an option? Up here, the cares and worries of the world seem so incon-

"Prophet please stop jabbering. I must concentrate." Grubmush said, placing him on the ground. With Onders next to him, the two lay in a heap. Grubmush bent low, wincing and looked them over. "Poison," he said, "The coward's weapon and the knife of the weak-willed. But you would not succumb to it. Clearly, my faith is well-placed. Faldurin merely wished you to feel pain on the inside." He thought for a moment, then his eyebrows raised and said, "To show that pain is not only external. The scars I collect and the wounds I endure are too shallow. I must learn internal pain and conquer that!"

Huxley was only half listening. He didn't pay attention to Grubmush but intuitively, he knew Grubmush was right. The poison was surging inside him. Huxley's breath was shallow and ragged, and the twisting in his stomach reminded him of something he ate or drank that didn't agree. If that wasn't enough, his vision swam in Magnincy. He kept his wits and mind as best he could. He had never used as much Magnincy as hastily as that before. He felt a small measure of contentment that he had survived the encounter, and even managed to hold his own against Onders. She likely had not taken him seriously as an opponent but now wasn't the time to be critical. He was just happy to be alive.

He glanced over at her. She lay slumped on the ground. It looked like she was tossed like baggage while Huxley was laid carefully. Blood had dripped from her eyes and nose. She lay unconscious with her eyes closed, but Huxley noticed her eyes were darting back and forth, lost in a dream or thought. Maybe she dreamt about the ocean and stars as he did. He coughed again and spit blood. He felt his stomach steadying and his muscles returning to his control. He moved to get up but Grubmush placed his enormous hand on Huxley's chest and pushed him back down. "Heal first, Prophet. It won't do to compound your injuries. Those do not bring glory, they only delay your growth."

Huxley was shoved back down easily. He thought, even if he had been at full strength, it wouldn't have been a challenge for Grubmush to hold him so he couldn't move.

He looked again at Onders and asked, "Is she going to live?"

Grubmush looked her up and down and sniffed the air. "Maybe." He said without much concern, "The poison is attacking her stomach and next her veins, most likely. If she hadn't been fighting, she may have lived but now in her weakened state...Faldurin may cut her from life and whisk her away."

"Right, whisk her away..." Huxley repeated. He was feigning understanding so as to not inspire a sermon from Grubmush to explain what he meant.

"We endure. We take all that Fladurin gives to us and come back stronger." Huxley focused on his breathing trying to get enough air into his lungs and exhale as many spores as possible. He tried to ignore Grubmush, but Grubmush was not easily ignored. He went on and on about wounds, healing and survival. It all seemed to make sense to him but Huxley didn't get how he lived his whole life around this religion. He chuckled to himself and thought maybe Grubmush felt the same about the worship of Embers and the knowledge they protect. Maybe he was just as foolish as Grubmush sounded.

Voices emanated from just past the treeline. They were gasps and shouts mainly. Snow flattened under beating footsteps and soon Arktos was upon him. Finally, someone bigger and louder than Grubmush. The gigantic bear shoved his nose under Huxley's head snapping it upward and seemed to be trying to crawl into Huxley's lap. Huxley couldn't figure out what the bear was thinking. If successful, the bear's weight would kill him faster than the poison might. The big ball of fur brought Huxley's mind out of the fog and made him feel a little clearer. Soon Elatress caught up and grabbed Huxley by the chin. She yanked his head upward and stared into Huxley's eyes. "How long was he in it?" She demanded.

"Maybe a minute", Grubmush replied.

She swore and grabbed a vial off of her belt. It was a light blue concoction that he had seen her carry before.

"It isn't as potent as the runestickle pl-" Abernathy protested

"Quiet! I know what he needs." Elatress spoke with the authority of a physician.

Abernathy held up his hands in surrender and said no more.

She uncorked it and poured it into his mouth. She held his mouth closed and said "Swallow it." Huxley jerked at first and fought off a gag reflex but then swallowed as instructed. It felt like a cold wave of water flowing down his throat, splashing into his stomach and following all the routes the poison did. He felt better almost instantly. A smile split his face and he looked up at her. She continued appraising his condition. "Breathe in deeply now."

He did as instructed. His breath was still ragged but considerably less than before. Elatress stood up and left Huxley. She wandered over to Onders and asked, "Same time for her?"

Grubmush just grunted.

She swore and looked at the empty vial she had given to Huxley.

"I don't have runestickle extract. Do you?" Elatress asked Abernathy.

"Ahh, no." He responded.

Her mouth dropped and she narrowed her eyes at Abernathy. "Then why did you bring it up?"

"I just thought you might have forgotten."

"Grim is the painting appearing, even now it becomes a reality," Ryla stated almost to herself.

Grubmush nodded in agreement. "Her wounds will take her under Faldurin's shadow. I will witness her passing." Grubmush stood up and walked over to Onders.

Abernathy looked like he wanted to say something, but not finding the words, he lowered his chin and averted his sight.

"Wait!" Huxley said. "Maybe I can help."

Huxley struggled into the wagon where he had stashed the Grimoire and searched under biology. He had seen Magnincy heal twice. Although he had no idea how he would achieve it. He barely grasped the subject let alone the knowledge to wield it. He flipped through the pages until he found the page he was looking for.

Abernathy spoke softly, "Huxley...I don't think you-"

"You can help!" Huxley said.

"Me?"

"Yes! I have an idea. If I'm reading directly from the Grimoire, and if you make yourself resonate like the other night, my mind can probably take it!"

"Huxley..." Abernathy's amber eyes looked kindly at the rapidly dying Ember. "This isn't something you can just try. It takes years, sometimes decades to achieve something like that."

Huxley knew there wasn't time to argue. He stared pointedly at Abernathy. His hands clenched tightly into balls, as he assured everyone, "I can do it. But only with your help."

Grubmush and Elatress nodded and looked at Abernathy.

Ryla hadn't stopped painting an imaginary picture of Onders death but stopped for a moment and said, "It isn't finished yet...it can still have a different subject."

Abernathy sighed and stated, "If she comes too and starts attacking again, you will regret this."

Huxley just nodded, accepting that potential outcome.

He began reading what he hoped was the right page. It was in human biology and contained nervous systems, circulatory and digestive. The muscles and skeletal were further in. This would have to do. While he searched, Abernathy did his best to arrange himself and the others to achieve what Huxley was asking. After a few seconds, they were all ready. Onders sputtered. She was short on breath; her eyes were now vacant.

"Ok," Huxley said. "Now."

Abernathy hummed outward at a volume that disturbed Huxley's concentration for a moment. Shortly after, the others joined, including Arktos. The similar feeling to the one a few nights ago enveloped Huxley. He read aloud from the Grimoire and his vision swam deeper and brighter than ever before with the stars of Magnincy. He felt himself rooted deep within his own mind. As he grabbed what he needed, he felt himself pushing even deeper. "How deep can I go?" The thought was terrifying. Pushing past his fear, he seized many handfuls of Magnincy and mixed them together. He grew closer and closer to the answer but found he still required more. He knew this could bring him to the breaking point. It felt like his mind was far away, rooted now in the Grimoire with only a small tether to sanity. Soon, even that faded away and the only thing that stopped the tide of madness was the resonance created by his friends. As he grabbed more and more, he realized he would soon be at a point of no return. It would have to be enough. It was not near perfect but it would have to do. The longer he took the further away she slipped which was forcing him to grab more. Her cells were degrading without oxygen, her brain was being choked, and her muscles were beginning to spasm. Each problem had a solution and each solution could be done only with Magnincy. The dawning realization that he would not be able to fix everything was sobering. Still, he had to try. He combined armfuls of Magnincy and released.

His mind felt deeply protected as the Magnincy surged, like a king hiding deep within his castle walls while being attacked on all sides. But even within his fortress, cracks emerged. The foundations shook and his mind bounced to every corner of his brain. Madness was invading from every weak spot trying to snake its way in.

Onders gasped and sat upright. She turned and wretched onto the ground. Huxley fell backwards, astonished by what they had accomplished. The group began talking wildly and Abernathy released his resonance. Huxley didn't hear them. Instead, he stared at his former enemy whose breath was given back to her. She held her chest in astonishment and looked back at Huxley like she understood what had happened.

Her eyes reclaimed some of their former senses and she narrowed them onto him and the book he held. "I knew you had it." She coughed.

"Yeah, well, if I didn't, you'd be dead." He replied.

"I'm barely alive.

"Don't thank me all at once."

"For what? For this passable job?" Her tone was incredulous.

"Passable?!" If Huxley had the energy, he would have balked, but Grubmush bent forward and picked Huxley up as easily as a parent picks up a child. Grubmush presented Huxley to the others like an offering. Slacked-jawed, with eyes wide, Huxley had no idea what he was trying to accomplish. All Huxley knew for certain was that Grubmush reeked of dried blood and sweat.

With bandages clinging loosely at his sides, Grubmush stated aloud, "Prophet of Faldurin's entire shadow." He spoke as if reading from a sacred text. Grubmush glanced at Abernathy, Ryla, and Elatress, "All of you are in his priesthood?"

Before Grubmush could continue, a polite cough interrupted his sermon.

It was the Plague Doctor. His mask was removed but the outfit was the same as the wanted posters. His face was a tangle of deep lines and patches of facial hair. His mouth was missing a few teeth which made his polite smile more off-putting than welcoming. His eyes however conveyed only sadness as he looked upon the two poisoned people in front of him.

"More victims of the Embers, and more casualties of their cause." He said and he sat down. He handed an ointment of some kind to Huxley and Onders and said "Dab this on your upper lips and breath from your nose for a few minutes. You will feel much better."

Sensing their confusion Abernathy said, "It seems our friend here isn't quite what we have been told. Would you like to explain?"

The Doctor looked around the group and said "It's been sometime since I have had company, my social skills are lacking."

Abernathy chuckled and said, "Then you are in good company. Please tell them what you told me."

The Doctor settled in while Onders and Huxley recovered. "I am an

Ember of the Arcane Flame. Or, at least, I was until I figured out what they were doing in there." He sighed and let a melancholy infuse his words. "I was expelled under threat of violence for disagreeing with their methods. Especially Maddox." Onders perked up defensively but was in no condition to argue. "After the world changed we saw it as our duty to help. We had never used the abilities much that Magnincy granted, why would we trifle with our own minds like that? Instead we collected knowledge and shared it hoping to raise up everyone as we had been." He paused but then went on, "It is difficult to illuminate minds that don't wish it but we still felt we must. Over the years we had limited success which drove some of us to try harder but some saw it as a confirmation of our own superiority. *Why would the Kindler let us succeed where others failed unless he chose us? Unless we are special?* They argued. But there were more of us that saw it for what it was. The Arcane Flame resides in all of Danador's children. The ability to wield it is only lost on those who don't dare reach for it. It starts as a small flicker in our chest and as our understanding of its light grows we are able to truly grasp it. All Embers do at some point. It is education that allows this and a secure mind. Those two things must be in concert. Education is easy enough but after the shared trauma we endured, finding people who would dare to reach outward became scarce. Some Embers began to hate everyone who wasn't like them. Even the Kindler. Deeming people to be beneath them only fit to supply their needs and the Kindler as some kind of enemy. Blaming him for not protecting us or for perhaps being the one who did the damage. It was impossible to know. They didn't see the flaw that focusing only on reaching for more left themselves untethered to what kept them sane. The power they grew was incredible as was their ability to wound. And wound they did." He sniffed, holding back tears at recalling the memory. "They drove young initiates to madness with overuse of their abilities, they would teach them concepts and knowledge far past their abilities and wait for them to break. Then locked them away to glean more knowledge from their ramblings. A broken mind can see everything around them. Which is detrimental to the person but bizarrely beneficial to those listening. You can advance your knowledge of the physical world immensely by just paying attention to them."

He adjusted uncomfortably in his seat and went on. "They began luring younger and younger iniaties in and repeating the process. Claiming the knowledge gained by their madness was worth more than they would discover through study alone. It was then that I realized I couldn't help anymore inside. I thought that maybe I could change their minds as a colleague, but madness takes more shapes than we can know. And a powerful man who is afraid will do anything to not be anymore. Maddox's ambitions grew towards mania. I believe he intends to weaponize Magnincy towards something that could damage Magnadun far worse than what has already been done."

Huxley was stunned. He had come so close to being one of the initiates driven to madness. Were they doing that to Onders? It didn't seem like it but after what he had been told, who knows?

The Doctor shrugged and said, "I thought, if I can't change them then I will try and create a world that is easier for people to dare to reach higher. Food, medicine....real security. But even that was too much for them. Perhaps they thought I would become a rival. Who knows. After enough close shaves, I moved myself out here and sent packages to the city through the forty-five to continue to try and help-" He made for his bag searching for something when a sudden blast tore through the air. The Doctor shuddered and stepped backwards. His hand automatically grabbed his chest in shock. When he looked at his hands they were covered in blood. The Doctor fell to his knees, his eyes rolled back and he collapsed, smoke emanating from his chest.

Onders stood, chest heaving from the poison's damage, unsteady on her feet. Seeing her work finished, her eyes turned to the rest standing before her. Her head jerked as her crazed eyes focused on one, then another, as though she were surrounded and under attack. She screamed as her hands thrashed into the air. Grubmush and Elatress leapt onto her and brought her down. Their combined weight slammed her into the ground. She laughed and tried to speak but only half words and thoughts sputtered out. Formulas, equations, weights, ratios, angles, aspects, she was seeing them all, Huxley realized. It was the same when he had attacked the Embers. Madness had taken Onders. She screamed again and again and again.

28

Pilgrim and Plans

"Think of it not as a punishment but as a thirsty man who drinks from a bucket instead of a cup. Thirst will be quenched but a mess is created. One only heat and towels may fix. And the only blame is on oneself." -**Page 6 excerpt from the Grimoire**

Onders continued her mad ravings in the back of the wagon. Abernathy had tied Onders to the post and deliberately tied her fingers and palms in a fixed position so that she couldn't grab any Magnincy should she become lucid again. It was uncomfortable to look at but Huxley agreed it was necessary. She was powerful and an attack now could make things even worse. Grubmush, now healed enough to be on his feet, insisted on walking. An embarrassed flush covered his face whenever they suggested he rest. Resting didn't seem to be Grubmush's favorite thing. They brought the Doctor back to his cabin and laid him to rest in his bed. The ground was far too cold and dangerous with spores to attempt a grave. Everyone but Abernathy agreed this was the best choice. It bothered him to agree not to bury him. He couldn't or didn't explain how it was wrong to him. Huxley expected it was against Norun tradition or at least against Abernathy's tradition. Practicality won out in the end. Disturbing the ground was too dangerous.

Huxley felt a fool on more levels than he had ever been accused of. His obsession with Embers seemed childish, his hopes of entry were naive and his association with Onders had become...he couldn't even sort his emotions on what that had become. She was a killer, a liar and utterly devious, but also wasn't she just a victim as well? How guilty was she of her own actions or was she being manipulated just like he had been. She had lived her whole life besides early childhood within the tower. In many ways, she was as ignorant as he was.

The decision was made then to leave and head back toward Danador. They would have to figure out just how badly they were in trouble. A dead doctor, a poisoned and possibly mad apprentice Ember *and* apparently they knew that Huxley was with them the whole time *and* in possession of the Grimoire. Suddenly, the Wilds were far more welcoming than home was. *Home...*Huxley thought. His heart lightened as he thought about it. The Gearbox had become a home to him. Definitely not what he had pictured at all when he had first left for Dandador, but he couldn't deny that it felt more like home to him than anywhere else now.

Elatress, Arktos, Abernathy, Ryla, Grubmush and Huxley traveled in silence. Arktos made the horses unbearably skittish so Elatress asked him to follow far behind. It did manage to make the horses move vigorously with his scent in the air. The group of outcasts were likely all thinking similarly. Would there even be a Gearbox to return to? Or would they be arrested at the gates?

Grubmush broke the silence.

"We rush the gates, destroy the guards, and take the college." He said definitively.

Abernathy coughed in surprise.

"We...might...not be able to accomplish that."

Grubmush's eyebrows raised in understanding "Ahh yes, violence. It always has to be the last resort with you folk. So what do we do first? Letters? Or do you sit down and non-violently talk about papers that are signed?

"You know Grubmush I'm starting to really understand you better. That IS what they do, isn't it?" Elatress joined in.

"Every time," Grumbush responded. "It is a hard thing to understand."

Abernathy sighed and looked at Ryla who just scrunched her shoulders.

Huxley finally said, "They want me...they've always wanted me. All of this is because of me. I'll turn myself in."

"Very wise prophet, then you can destroy them internally. Just as you deal with emotional and internal wounds. Something Faldurin has taught me about recently." Grubmush stated approvingly.

"Yeah, that reminds me, how are you not dead right now?" Huxley inquired.

"Because I endure, I always endure." His response was practiced. It sounded like the end of a poem or even a prayer.

Grubmush saw his confusion and said, "Not to be concerned Prophet, the pain is still resplendent and claws at my sanity." He lifted some of his bandages and showed Huxley the twisted remains of his abdomen. It shuddered as did Huxley. Grubmush had presented his body as though for inspection. Huxley nodded his head and that satisfied Grubmush. He lowered his bandages and motioned to Ryla. "Her one flaw was underestimating me."

"My flaw was not cutting you to ribbons!" Ryla burst out. "But I was trying to make something beautiful out of you."

"My rage was beaut-"

"You should have died!" Ryla interrupted. "Your obvious attacks were telegraphed all over your clumsy movements. It was simple predicting you! I won that fight. You barely troubled me."

Grubmush for once seemed dumbstruck. He thought for a moment and said, "You still think you won even after I let you think I had been mortally wounded? It's an ancient tactic, even the most vicious predators adopt that move. I figured one as skillful as you would have respected it."

Ryla's voice grew more rigid, "I respect someone who has grace and skill. You are the opposite of that."

"And I beat you anyway."

"You were skewered and gutted like a wild animal." She spat, "Your body lay broken at my feet. I could have cut your head off if I desired it. You only knocked me off my feet by sacrificing your body!" She paused and a deep loathing and suffering sentence escaped her, "I-should-have-made-you-the-focus-of-my-art."

Grubmush's face dropped upon hearing the last part. Not into fear but of genuine confusion. Even Abernathy had to admit not following the end. Sensing their confusion and that her supposed insult hadn't landed she shrieked and turned back around.

Grubmush let a second or two of silence pass and said, "I would be a beautiful subject of any painting...thank you." Gratitude heavy on his lips, he stood straighter.

He had heard her compliment him.

Abernathy stepped away and said "Ryla, I'm not sure he understood..."

Ryla swung her glaive again towards Grubmush and he caught the blade with his trident.

"Now look who is clumsy and predictable." Grubmush pointed out.

The two locked weapons and the horses whinnied.

"I...," Ryla stammered. "Perhaps, he is right."

Abernathy approached and placed his hands on both weapon shafts. "We are as good as caught if you two start fighting. Please...not now."

The two slowly lowered their weapons, agreeing, at least, to the "not now" part.

"Of course, you're not turning yourself in, Hux." Abernathy spoke up, "El and I have seen this day coming. It would have arrived had you been here or not. Being an enemy of the state is a ticking clock." Abernathy's tone was final but Huxley was far from settled.

"Even so, if I turn myself in they likely won't care as much about you all."

"Oh, get over yourself, Bookpile! We have survived this long and we will survive this too. Abernathy will make another deal with papers and agreements for whatever they want and we can carry on." Elatress glanced back at Arktos plodding along on their trail. "Besides, what good would it be to go get yourself killed."

"The prophet could never be-" Grubmush protested.

"Of course not." Elatress said, patting him on the shoulder. "But even still, we should not take chances."

"Ok, then," Huxley agreed, he did not like the idea of turning himself in but he didn't see a better option. "What do we do? You said you've been planning something?"

Abernathy scrunched up his chin in thought, "Yes, but obviously not like this. Pilgrims from all walks of Magnadun are in Danador seeking," he hesitated, trying to find the words, "I don't know how to describe it. They're not seeking the Embers, but that's what the Embers choose to believe. Something else summoned them. Some say they hear a voice calling." Huxley flinched. "With others, they see strange things in their dreams, and some others see things in the waking world." He didn't elaborate, but went on, "I can't say they are all fighters, and obviously not all of them will rally to a cause, but they all seem to have the ambition enough to journey here and reach for more than what they currently have. Magnadun and its people weren't always as they are now. When the world reformed, we lost more than our kin. Many of us lost our truest connection to Magnincy, all except the people of Danador. In fact, their connection seemed to grow stronger. Whatever happened cut us off and opened the floodgates for your people. It's why the Embers are so difficult to defeat. It would take an army, thousands strong, to overpower only a few dozen Embers." He rubbed his chin deep in thought "And even then I don't know," he added. "Their power is not exaggerated. Few of us have really seen them use their abilities to the fullest. Usually, those who do, don't survive. I suspect it's why Huxley has been able to excel so much in his growth. His connection to Magnadun and its power is considerable for someone who hasn't been practicing long. Normally, it takes many years to achieve such a thing. Grubmush may be on to something. I don't know if he's a prophet, but he certainly has an ability the Embers fear."

"The Grimoire has taught me most of it," Huxley admitted.

Abernathy shook his head at Huxley. "The book is helpful and gives you direction but a practitioner of Magnincy is more than that. They need to have the reach and ambition to grab..." He searched for the right word.

Suddenly, a frustrated voice broke out from the wagon and they leapt in surprise.

"Ahh, enough!" Onders yelled, "Your ignorance is worse than the creeping madness! You fools are fumbling at understanding letters while trying to read a book. You see nothing of the puzzle before you."

They all exchanged glances. Abernathy pulled back the flaps to reveal Onders still tied up, her eyes bloodshot with sweat drenching her face. She fidgeted back and forth, her madness appearing to have retreated but still, they couldn't be sure. She locked eyes with Huxley, narrowed them, and pursed her lips. Her cheeks flushed and she mouthed a few words no one could hear. Biting hatred and vitriol spilled out, Huxley had never heard such curses, even in his time as a city guard. When she had run out of the worst ones she said simply "How?!"

"How what?" Huxley asked.

"You should be a writhing madman, unable to separate your thoughts...how?" She spat.

"Maybe he's just a better Ember than you." Elatress teased.

Onders whole body surged forward and tripped over her own bindings. She smacked onto the wagon floors and found new curses; some Huxley had never heard before but her tone conveyed the meaning. Grubmush and Elatress laughed but Abernathy was stone-faced.

"Please..." he hissed, "Let's not make her angrier."

Emboldened, Elatress commented, "What? He obviously beat her in a duel. She's weaker."

Onders spasmed one more time but realized she was being mocked and decided on a new tactic. She got herself under control and adjusted her voice. Only her eyes betrayed what she felt inside. They blazed while the rest of her appeared calm.

"I could have beaten him at any time. He has access to a grimoire of immense knowledge. One, he used against me."

"Well, which is it? He had immense power or you could have beaten him?" Elatress teased.

It looked like she had a lot of pent-up frustration at the Embers and finally getting to be honest with one was exhilarating. Huxley confessed to himself, it was fun finally being able to not be in total fear of an Ember or what they could do to you. But he knew there would be consequences to such actions. He didn't regret fighting back, because he would likely be bound like she was, with no grimoire...or worse. It was then that Huxley realized that having a trapped Ember, may be useful to get some questions answered. She may just lie but maybe he could get a bit of truth. And he needed every bit of knowledge he could get if he was to survive the next day. He quietly shared his thoughts with the group and they all agreed to give him some time with her. Abernathy issued many warnings about not overreaching and Elatress strongly suggested not to get too close. Ryla and Grubmush seemed to think he would be just fine and offered no advice.

Onders had gone silent since Elatress had stopped provoking her. Huxley made his way back to the wagon and the others busied themselves with conversation to make it seem like they weren't eavesdropping. He pulled the tent flaps back and saw her wrists were raw from the effort of trying to escape. She kicked her legs upon seeing him. Why did she hate him so much? Was it just fury of being taken hostage or was it deeper than that? He had stupidly allowed himself to hope they had a pleasant relationship at least or maybe more than pleasant. The last few visits had made him believe that, but it was clear now she was just using him. He felt even stupider for longing for her kindness, even if it had been a lie. The person he had got to know in the Gearbox was a stark contrast to the seething individual before him now. He climbed into the back and sat at a safe distance.

"How?" She asked again.

He looked her over, curious at how promptly she recovered from her madness. He still knew so little about it. There were threats of it lasting the rest of his life but so far he had returned from it rapidly enough and she proved it wasn't just him. He remembered Palithur said something about the more you over reach the more you gamble with. Perhaps there was an exact ratio to power emitted and cost of sanity. And how fast you recovered was based on that, or maybe your age, or maybe how much you knew? It might be all of those things. He shook his head, it's probably an exact science that he didn't know the equations for. Like all things the answer was probably in more studying. But before he could do that he had to deal with her.

He turned his attention back to her. She seemed lucid enough. "You ok now? Are you seeing any equations? Any physics?" Her cold stare was his only answer and she asked again "How?"

Huxley ignored her question and reached under Grubmush's cot to grab the Grimoire. When he pulled it out, her whole body froze. She gained a sort of reverence, like regarding a holy book or artifact that was dear to her. Her face twisted and contorted upon watching him open it. Perhaps she felt he was desecrating it with his filthy, untrained hands. Short breaths escaped her lips as he casually flipped through pages. He met her eyes and closed the book. The two regarded each other for a moment and then he found her grimoire on the ground next to her.

"You. Wouldn't. Dare." She breathed, her words laced with rage.

Huxley held up his palm and said simply "No, I wouldn't."

"Good because I would-"

"Stop!" He barked. "Stop, or I will." She obeyed as commanded but her intensity remained. Huxley sighed heavily and said "I didn't want this. I don't want you in pain, and I don't want to exchange threats. All I ever wanted was to learn more. To answer some of the burning questions that my curiosity craves. The curiosity is a burning drive within me. I don't want to interrogate prisoners, I don't want to threaten you with Magnincy. It's not who I am. I thought I killed you earlier and it felt awful, perhaps the worst I have ever felt." He noticed her flinch. "Whatever it is that makes Embers hate everyone, I don't have that in me." He paused and thought for a moment discussing something internally. He came to a conclusion and calmly stated, "In a few moments, I'm going to untie you. You will be free to do as you choose. Last time you were free, you tried to kill me. This time, I hope we can talk. If not, we will fight again. It would be foolish since I am ready and you're surrounded...and if we're both being honest, I think you're close to the edge. You might not come back without resting longer."

He didn't wait for her to respond or even look at her as he spoke. He just reached over and loosened her hands and sat back down. She rubbed her wrists, wincing in the process. Huxley offered her a few bandages from the many they brought for Grubmush. She didn't reach for them, but he placed them next to her. Huxley went on, and told her, "Honestly, I have so many questions for you. My drive for knowledge is not solely for myself. I wish to return to Mayburn and help our people. I want to be able to defend them and bring the light of the flame of knowledge to them. I do not believe jealously guarding secrets is the path to accomplishing anything. I will start with answering your questions with no bargain for myself. Originally, I'd hold your questions hostage until I got answers of my own, but that would make me like them, wouldn't it? Knowledge shouldn't be a secret. If a people are to thrive, it needs to be shared. You want to know how I kept my sanity over you, right? How I *beat* you?"

She stopped rubbing her wrists and sat straightened in a dignified pose. Huxley had expected her next move would be to attack, but she didn't. She had her own internal battle and hesitantly answered him, "Yes."

It was likely she hadn't been offered many free answers before and suspected betrayal.

"Great," Huxley stated calmly. "I only have a theory and that will have to do."

She nodded her head for him to continue. "I don't deny you are more powerful than me. The power that you wield is overwhelming. I'm shocked you aren't a full-fledged Ember." She nodded again, swelling at his words. He went on. "I could not produce the sheer force you exert. The simple answer is that you overreached and I underreached and just outlasted you. The other simple answer is that, yes, I do have access to a Grimoire that I did *not* steal." He emphasized that point hard, hoping for acceptance.

"Those things are partly true but there may be an even more simple answer. You and I both know that the simplest answer is usually the truth." Unconsciously, she leaned in closer, eager to listen. "My quiver is bigger than yours, but your arrows are bigger than mine." He said with a satisfied smile. Her face dropped and she searched for more information. Huxley leaned back and smiled. "Get it? Like an archer?"

"No." she declared flatly, careful to keep her anger out of her voice.

Huxley's smile lessened and he said, "Magnincy are arrows that we can shoot. The bigger the arrow, the more damage. Your arrows are big. Mine are smaller but I have lots of them." He thought over the metaphor and seemed to confuse himself. This is what Guliford told him, after all. He was hoping it made sense. "I am more stable but weaker than you. I think I can fight for much longer but not produce what you can. Is that a clearer way of describing it?"

"Yes," She said but didn't seem quite convinced. He may have seriously messed up with the quiver metaphor. "But you are still more powerful than you should be. That Grimoire has provided you with tools far outside your scope. You must know how dangerous that is. And if you didn't steal it, someone certainly did. It can't be yours."

Huxley offered information again hoping to garner more understanding. He explained how the Grimoire came to him. She listened intently, nearly motionless as he filled her in. Even in her disheveled state, her grace captivated him. How come someone in such a state could be so alluring? After he finished explaining the broad strokes of what he had been through, she seemed satisfied. His story measured up to her expectations.

"And you think you are its heir? Based on what? That it fell into your lap?" She scolded.

"No, it was delivered to me by name." He answered. "If it was delivered to you by name, would you think for a second that it wasn't yours?"

"That proves nothing. It is just as likely it was stolen and hidden in the hands of someone who it was believed would not be likely to discover its secrets. It would be the safest place for such dangerous knowledge. It is Ember Maddox's Grimoire. He has filled it with his life's work of knowledge and understanding. He is unraveling without it. Our Grimoires are what keeps us grounded in sanity. That's how your quiver is so big. It's vital that we get it back to him. He could possibly destroy all of Magnadun if it stays in your possession. Do you understand my motives now?"

"You still don't understand." Huxley said, "The Grimoire helps, but it isn't the sole reason. I think I read about it on the first page of the Grimoire, here listen," and he quoted, "Reaching for what could be, while accepting what is, leads one to burn bright but remain the same, which is no bad thing." He looked at her and continued "From page one. I thought it was just flowery philosophy but I think my time studying is greatly punctuated by giving myself real time off from it. It has not been my singular focus. I have made friends, gone on adventures and enjoyed to varying degrees strange drinks and food. I am keeping myself tethered in that way. I don't think the Embers ever let themselves away from their drive. It makes them powerful but limited."

Huxley couldn't keep away his smile. Her eyebrows raised in interest at this turn and he stated, "See! Isn't this better than keeping knowledge caged up? We are understanding each other and not hiding it."

She rolled her eyes and said, "Did you hear what I said?! Give it to me and I will bring it to him. He may even let you go back to Mayburn!"

Huxley flicked open the Grimoire again and ignored her question. "What if it didn't belong to Maddox and he was the one who stole it?"

Onders' eyes widened. "Why would you think that?"

Huxley absentmindedly flipped through the pages. "What if he killed the original owner? What if it was delivered to him the same way it was delivered to me?" He opened a section and held it up. She looked away like she had caught someone exiting the bathtub. Huxley held it closer and said, "Look, different handwriting, different authors, different opinions. I don't think Grimoires are personal collections of a single person's thoughts. I'm sure yours is, but Embers grow so powerful because they share knowledge in Grimoires like this one. The rest of us scrape around for bits of knowledge we can call our own." She finally allowed herself to look at the pages, and her eyes swam over the information, eagerly drinking it up. As she read, her lips silently spoke the words she was reading.

Her eyes shifted from absorbing the information to looking at Huxley. "I...don't know," She confessed. "I hadn't considered that." He couldn't blame her for being excited to see new knowledge. He had chosen a section he expected she already knew about, but clearly, it wasn't as comprehensive. It felt good in a way to share knowledge with her. He knew the value of what he just gave to her but if it helped her to understand that an exchange would be worthwhile. It was certainly worth a shot, he thought.

Suddenly, the wagon lurched to a stop. Huxley heard voices and distinguished Grubmush speaking to the others. Onders looked at Huxley worried that they might bind her again.

"My kin arrived a few days ago...thousands sit in the forest ready to overrun the city and challenge its defenders. I must return to them and explain my victory inside the lecture hall. I must be allowed to preach my sermon to allow converts to our cause." He stomped through the snow to the wagon and opened the flaps. "Prophet, return with me and lead our people to glory!"

"Prophet?" Onders balked.

"Yeah," Huxley admitted thickly. "I guess I sort of am. But Grubmush, what do you mean your people are here? Like...the same army that attacked Mayburn?"

"Oh no, not at all prophet," Grubmush replied, and the two relaxed.

"Only a small contingent attacked your town. Our main force continued through the Wilds and camped outside the walls of Danador."

The two of them stared, but Onders spoke first, "Wait you TRAVEL through the Wilds? Why?! You must have lost hundreds, maybe thousands of soldiers."

Grubmush shrugged, "Hard to say, but we travel the new paths made by Faldurin when he reshaped the world. If we aren't strong enough for the road, then we will help nourish it."

"Nourish?" Huxley questioned but quickly figured out what Grubmush meant. "And you want me to travel, alone with you, to go see them? They are the ones that killed dozens of my friends and injured many more. Prophet or not, will they not kill me when I get there?"

"Kill a prophet?" Grubmush repeated, confusion oozing from each word. "I do not understand. How could we even accomplish that? You tore through our ranks with the cold fury of the winged and feathery god. No, they wouldn't dare." His face scrunched up in deep thought. "I am concerned you don't know your significance or much about your people. I was surprised a Prophet could be from Danador, but it is in line with what we suspect about your city. It has called to us since Faldurin split the world."

"Called to you?" Huxley inquired.

Abernathy and Elatress joined them now, and he nodded slowly, "Danador has called to many pilgrims. It is why I am here, and likely many others. Maddox is after more than just power. The Embers have a secret hidden in that tower. They are guarding something..." He trailed off looking at Onders.

She looked like she was about to deny it, but stopped. Her eyes searched for a response and then admitted, "There is something."

Abernathy's eyebrow raised and his mustache perked. Onders immediately winced as though she had just committed a crime and added, "I do not know what. Only that it is in our deepest chamber..."

She paused and was about to say something more but Huxley spoke first. "I've heard it."

Onders glanced up sharply as Huxley continued, "When I was tested I heard it." Huxley turned to Elatress, "When we traveled in the sewers I heard it. Huxley looked at Abernathy, "And I hear it in my dreams sometimes."

"The Prophet," Grubmush whispered.

Abernathy exhaled, like the last piece of a puzzle had just fallen into place. "Perhaps Grubmush," he stated, "but I do not think Huxley is unique. He may, indeed, have heard it like he says, but I have heard it too, all the way from my home. That's why I came to Danador. That's why I'm here," Abernathy admitted.

"I never hear voices, only visions and dreams of art; of what I can create, given resources and time," Ryla interjected.

"Well, I hear voices, but not one like you guys are describing." Elatress blurted out.

Elatress seemed to have an epiphany. "Wait...so I'm not the only one who hears voices? Because it's nice to know I'm not the only crazy person here."

Abernathy guffawed and said "El, I think you're still special. The voice we hear isn't telling us how to kill everyone right now…"

She shrugged and stated, "I couldn't get all of you, two immediately but Arktos would need to be here for the rest."

"Yeah, that isn't what the voice is telling us. Yours is definitely special," Huxley's tone held a customary hint of mockery.

"You could not kill me," Onders stated with certainty.

"You would need more than that bear," Grubmush added.

"Oh, you would be easy, you're still wounded. You were one of the two." Elatress told him.

He stood up and said "ME?! My wound is nearly healed." But standing up to his full height stretched his wounds and a small squirt of blood escaped his bandages. He didn't show it, but it must have hurt.

Abernathy put up soothing hands and gestured for everyone to calm down.

"It'd be easy, poison would go right in there." She pointed to Grubmush's soaked bandages.

Grubmush looked at his wound. "What poison?"

She drew four vials from her pouch and said "Any good Suminen always has a ready stock."

Huxley gaped at her. "You carry poison around?!" He stammered. "Like always?!" He used to think he understood her, but that confidence was waning.

"It saved your life!" She stated confidently to Huxley but her eyes remained on Grubmush as if she were still contemplating poisoning him.

"What? How?" Huxley demanded.

"Thanks to me, you built up a tolerance in your gut. Your lungs barely bled when you got poisoned by those flowers." She stated triumphantly.

Abernathy closed his eyes in dismay and sighed heavily, "Oh Elatress," Abernathy shook his head, "You haven't been…," Abernathy trailed off. He couldn't bring himself to say it. "I thought the boy just had a weak constitution," was all Abernathy could manage.

"He did!" Elatress exclaimed. "But I helped strengthen it....slowly...in his ale." She added, glancing around, wondering what all the fuss was about.

Suddenly, the weeks of sudden flights to the toilet, the violent wretches he tried to keep quiet in the bathroom, the general discomfort of drinking and eating in the Gearbox, all came back to him. No one would dine there if it always made them sick. But no one else ever seemed to, just him.

She had been poisoning him!

He shifted his gaze accusingly.

She saw his anger and reeled back, "What?! You'd be dead if I hadn't! Your lungs and gut were so weak, those flowers would have killed you!" She actually smiled, "I was expecting a thank you."

Abernathy launched into a speech about food safety and exposing poison in a restaurant but Huxley was only half-listening. The idea of traveling to go see Grubmush's people seemed like the safer choice at this point.

They continued to argue for longer than any of them wished. But the truth was, that they were scared. Returning to the city seemed like suicide, traveling to Grubmush's people was just as insane. They thought they could get back into the city easily enough except Huxley. The Embers wanted him. But if he did get in, what then? Travel to the college that is full of Embers? Together they might be able to take one, but all of them? Or the amassing army Grubmush told them about only a few miles away full of warriors that had already tried to kill him. It was only when it was pointed out that the subtle difference was that the Embers definitely wanted him dead and the others only maybe did. This was confirmed by Onders. Grubmush's people would only kill him if he proved to be weak. This was confirmed by Grubmush. Elatress seemed confident she could sneak everyone into the city through the Forty-Five like she had before. But to what end? There was no sense returning to the Gearbox as it may be a smoldering ruin by now.

They languished for what felt like hours. Nobody saw an outcome that was feasible. After what felt like ages, Abernathy perked up, and said, "I've got an idea...but it will take trust...lots of trust."

"In who?" Huxley was almost afraid to ask.

"Everyone here," Abernathy replied, "What is the only thing that could lure all of the Embers out? What has done it before?" A smile grew and his eyebrows raised in thought. " And how can we get Huxley in without being noticed?" His head nodding with each thought as he solved the problem. "We can empty the college, and get the rest of us inside the city. We can enter the tower to finally get some answers as to what is calling us." He looked around again and said "But I reiterate, it will take an enormous amount of trust from everyone here."

Huxley looked around. Abernathy and Elatress had earned it for sure, they'd always come through on their word. He didn't know Ryla well, but Abernathy seemed to think highly of her, which was enough for Huxley. But Grubmush...he didn't even need to say it to Abernathy. There was a host of reasons Huxley didn't feel comfortable with him. But the more Abernathy explained his idea, the more it seemed like it could work. Either that or Huxley had definitely gone mad and this insanity seemed rational. A knot formed in his stomach realizing that both may actually be true.

That left, Onders.

Onders, the Ember Apprentice who only recently tried to kill him. Huxley may have made some headway there but not enough to trust her with his life. He wanted to, it felt natural, in many ways she reminded him of himself. He could have been in this exact same spot. If he had been brought to the college and made to trust and follow the Embers as she had been...even now the idea of rebelling openly made his stomach knot up. But the Embers had shown they weren't the heroes he was led to believe. Huxley didn't know their true goal, but his was to get some answers to the identity of the voice and the reason someone sent the Grimoire to him. That would be hard enough without someone by his side he couldn't trust.

"You should just-" She started but Huxley cut her off.

"We're letting you go," Huxley stated pointedly.

Her eyes brightened and reclaimed much of their intelligence while still holding an edge of madness. She tried working out what was happening.

"I might be able to be bargained for or maybe used as bait to lure-"

"No, none of that." Huxley walked closer to her. "As I said before, if anything is to be gained here it's not by treating each other like Embers do. That just leads to madness, either from Magnincy or the regular kind. Listen to yourself....bargains? Threats? No, no more. I only ever wanted the strength and knowledge to defend Mayburn because it's my home. I'm not making enemies, I am only dealing with whoever tries to stop me." He looked at her again to make certain she was listening. "We're letting you go."

She took a few steps backwards. Huxley produced her Grimoire and tossed it to her. She snatched it out of the air and held it tight to her chest.

"You have many years ahead of you to fill this out, we could do that together, or you can keep doing as they ask. It's up to you."

Onders looked like she had more to say but couldn't decide how to start. She turned to leave but was unsteady on her feet. She stopped and asked Abernathy, "Are you going to kill Maddox? Is that the plan? Burn down the tower or something like that?"

Abernathy was uncharacteristically stone faced. His mirth was replaced with nothing. What should have been neutral appeared dark to Huxley. Was this his plan?

Before he said anything, Onders guessed his answer, "Good. I can help you get back into the city. Ryla will escort me with you as our prisoner. I was only instructed to kill the others specifically. The three of us could walk right in. If you corroborate that lie we will have no problems." Abernathy and Ryla agreed. That was enough for Abernathy anyway.

"Ok, then, if we are all in agreement I believe I can retrofit my first idea to work here. I was planning to have a small army of immigrants inside the city in about a year, but with what we have available to us now...it could still work. We will split into two teams. I will lead Ryla and Onders back into Danador so they stop looking for you three.

"And us?" Elatress asked.

"Oh, you are going to love your part, El." Abernathy said.

———————————————————————————————————

The groups all nodded in agreement. It felt less like a good idea and more like a desperate attempt to escape a burning building by breaking down the walls. Huxley couldn't believe what he had just agreed to. But with no other option that was less reckless, he had no other choice.

Before they departed Abernathy asked to speak with Huxley alone. It wasn't hard for them to find the space because Elatress was excitedly talking about the details.

"That was a decent thing you did for Onders." He squeezed his shoulder tight and said, "I have met and spoken to many pilgrims, meeting someone on a journey is always hard. You don't get to see the beginning or the end, usually just the messy part in between. That young lady is on a difficult pilgrimage within her own heart. We may never see where she ends, but I believe you may have made her journey easier."

"How do you know that Abernathy?" Huxley asked, trying to keep the emotion out of his voice. Seeing her leave hurt him. He was hoping it would have felt more like it had that night at the Gearbox. He wasn't even sure she wasn't planning on turning Ryla and Abernathy in the second they walked into Danador.

"Because of how she acts around you. You forget I've been in Danador for a while now. I've seen her and her master. Before you, she was far worse, like someone following a map that led them into deeper confusion, and totally immersed in their bias that it was the right path. You have changed her, we just have to wait and see how."

The party split on the road a little while later. Abernathy had attempted to convene them as a group to go over the details again but Ryla was getting anxious and Onders was already heading down the road. He shook his head, gave a hopeful nod to Huxley, Elatress, Arktos and Grubmush and said "I'll see you at the tower." And hustled back towards Danador.

Huxley watched Abernathy leave and got situated on the wagon headed towards an awaiting army of war hungry Dathu.

"He's gone", Elatress said.

"....what do you mean gone, Elatress?" He asked.

"Not here." She replied back in almost a whisper. She hopped up and sat on the front of the wagon, looking sullen, as though she had found a dead body. Huxley hoped she hadn't.

"It's over isn't it?" She asked.

"What? No, El. We just got started." He answered in surprise.

"No, this." She said. Her hands gestured outward, "The Gearbox, our time together. It won't be the same tomorrow. It might not even be there anymore" Her voice caught in her throat. It cracked but she didn't cry.

Huxley stopped himself. Sometimes he forgot she was still a kid in many ways. Her instincts and ability made him forget that. But just like Oakley, she didn't like change, especially when it involved her family.

Sitting beside her, he put his arm around her shoulder. Everything was moving so quickly. Abernathy had probably not stopped to talk her through this. He should have been the one too. He was so good with people. Huxley had no idea what to say. It was likely she was right, and it was going to get messy. A tear hit her trousers. Huxley decided to be honest with her.

"You're right. It won't be the same tomorrow."

She sniffed and whimpered, fighting hard not to crack into a full-blown cry. Why was she holding back? Wasn't it good to, "let it out?"

"But hopefully it will be better." He stated optimistically.

"What if I don't want it to be better?" She told him flatly.

"You don't?" He asked.

"I don't know...I just...it's the only thing that hasn't changed." She said, "Everything's always changing. I don't even remember anything from more than three years ago. Soon the Gearbox will just be a memory, and everyone might die tonight."

"Hey...no one's going to-," He didn't want to lie to her but he couldn't. Someone might die tonight.

She tensed and shifted in her seat.

"What?" Huxley asked.

"Scouts already..." She whispered into the wagon.

Grubmush whispered back. "Yes, they have been watching this area but they have not seen me yet.

"Why not reveal yourself now?" Huxley whispered back.

"They respect strength, not protection. If it looks like I'm protecting you it will make our larger goal more difficult.

If everything went according to plan, they would finally know what the Embers were hiding and perhaps even survive. The plan was so mad, the one thing they could be certain of, was that it was something the Embers would never expect.

29

Prophets and Betrayers

"Artistic expression is of no true value. It can serve to alleviate a belabored mind for a few moments but time spent creating is a waste. Fit only for charlatans attempting to mask reality instead of embracing it."
-Page 32 Excerpt from the Grimoire

The imposing stark gray walls of Danador greeted Abernathy, Ryla and Onders. They had not spoken much during their journey to the dismay of Abernathy. He had hoped to gain some more understanding of both of his companions. But neither felt much like talking. It was understandable, he was asking a lot of them and they had only recently shifted their allegiances, at least he hoped so. The walls had an illusionary effect that made them seem close and far away. As they approached, it seemed they could be a few hundred feet away or miles. The latter proved true and after hours of approaching the same walls they finally arrived. When they neared the final entrance, Ryla broke the silence.

"I cannot help you in this matter." She stated with a quiver in her voice.

"Which part?" Abernathy asked.

"All of it. I have lost something vital and only now have I recognized it." She said cryptically.

"It's fine, we don't need her to get in." Onders said dismissively.

"Good. Then I take my leave."

"Wait!" Abernathy yelped. "Just like that? What did you lose? We can help you find it." She hadn't been carrying much besides her halberd and a few personal items. "I don't understand!" He continued while looking.

Ryla's stance sagged. It seemed wrong, like a statue that began to melt under a beating sun. She always held herself at attention, and always seemed ready, but now...that changed. She sat down, crossed-legged and laid her glaive over her lap. She carefully removed her helm and sat it over her weapon. Her hair fell out, swished over her armor, it shone brightly in the sunlight.

"No one does. They never do." She answered to no one in particular, "Even my own people." She added. The tension eased and Abernathy looked pleadingly at Onders hoping she would let her speak. Ryla really was right. There may not be as lethal a fighter in all of Magnadun. Something suddenly made sense to Abernathy. It finally clicked why she would carry such melancholy.

He sat next to her, his metallic leg stepping heavily as he eased himself down. It didn't work great at such a sharp angle. He made a mental note to address that. "Valdannon folk have the most diverse and truly mind-expanding works of art. Not only have I not seen their equal, but nothing else even approaches what you do. It takes a vast array of skills and abilities to make any space into a work of art. I think they even arrange your trash beautifully....if such a thing can be done." She smirked at him and he returned it. They regarded each other for a moment, then he asked "But I take it your art isn't appreciated much there."

She sniffed and her eyes softened. She turned to look far away and said, "No one does, not even me. Just like Danadorians there are those of us that reach further and grab for more. But unlike Danadorians we cannot choose our subject of study. It chooses us. Painters, sculptures, blacksmiths, tailors, chefs and musicians and many more all make great use of it. But mine is nothing beautiful. My Magnincy is violence. It cost me everything, my family, friends, my home. We excel at artistry. It is as common to us as breathing. We see everything as it could be rather than how it is. And the greatest can even bring out Magnincy through their works. I found that I can wield Magnincy as well but, my art is a terrible thing."

The dying sunlight reflected as her eyes grew damp. "I hoped in Danador, the one place where no one seemed to care about art, I could find my place. My art requires violence, fighting, and battle. I am only valued for the pain that I can inflict on others." She sighed and said, "I am no more than a weapon to them...to everyone. When I see an opportunity for violence, my eyes drink in the possibilities. An intimate blade to the throat, a long slash across the belly, or a hate-filled strangulation. I can see the moves and the positions to bring those things about. It used to frighten me, but now I understand that it is mine to wield as someone wields a brush. My brush is my weapon. I paint well with it, and my palette prefers the color red." Ryla stood up abruptly and put her helmet back on. The Glaive swung outward and Ryla sniffed, clearing the emotion from her voice. "I must return. If I cannot find a home here then I will return and make a new one. My art may be reviled, but it won't be ignored. Farwell Abernathy."

Abernathy did not react and instead listened intently. This was the worst time for this, the pieces were moving already for his plan to work. But he was a Norun and Noruns help as best they can. Onders cocked her head either in interest or impolite amusement. Abernathy couldn't tell.

She got up to leave while looking at the flat gray of the walls of Danador, "I beat Grubmush in that arena. But I did not win the fight. I was hoping in Danador I would find a proper way to channel my art. The Wardens wanted me for violence and you folks, well it isn't so bad but I am not getting what I needed here. An artist must grow, an artist must create, an artist must be inspired. Stagnation is death. I have not grown sharper here, I have become clumsy and predictable. When you have a talent like mine, and it becomes clumsy and predictable, it is no longer a talent but a liability." She resigned herself and said, "I can no longer help you, only endanger you. I will take my leave for Valdannon immediately."

Abernathy began to protest but something stopped him. Her soul burned in a way that he rarely saw. If she was right or wrong, he couldn't be sure. But she was in absolute agreement in her mind, body and soul. It thrummed in unison at her statements. And he couldn't argue with that.

"Very well then Ryla of Valdannon. You have become a great friend and I will miss your company greatly."

Ryla left Onders and Abernathy at the gates of Danador. While it was the right thing to do for her, Abernathy pushed down the mounting panic at the implications. She was a vital part of the plan, for the first time in what felt like years Abernathy felt genuine and visceral worry. He was always the one to keep emotions in check but with Ryla swiftly fading into the distance... Now he had to solely rely on Onders! The plan had barely begun before it started to fall apart. He hoped that the others were faring better.

———————————————————————————————————-

Wood splintered as an ax cracked into the side of the wagon followed by several arrows. Elatress had warned Huxley they were going to get surrounded but he didn't think they would be attacked so suddenly. There were no warnings, no guards, just an assault. He summoned a defense and Elatress hopped to the top of the wagon. She drew a bead on a bush nearby and Huxley hissed at her to stop and, "Remember the plan!"

She hesitated and then had to swiftly dodge an arrow. She growled in anger but managed to deflect the next one with her hatchet blade. A yelp of surprise came from the bush and Huxley seized the opportunity.

"I AM THE PROPHET OF FALDURIN!" He screamed at the top of his lungs. "One whose internal pain matches any outward and it was I who wounded Grubmush so that he may endure!"

The attack stopped and a panicked conversation erupted. Moments passed and Huxley realized the insanity of what he just yelled. If anyone else heard him, he'd be locked up as a madman for sure. Of course, that might still be a possibility. This plan might actually be ample evidence he was stark-raving mad.

Men and women similar to Grubmush stepped forward. They breathed heavily and labored just as Grubmush did before a fight. They were certainly his kin. Wild beards soaked with bits of food and brush they had climbed through hung from their faces. Their muscles were toned and shaped like they had never lived a day of comfort in this life. Scars scored their bodies though not as comprehensively as Grubmush. They wore leather harnesses, mainly for holding weapons and they had fur covering their bottom halves that passed as pants. How someone could wear so little in this cold, astounded him still.

"The Prophet?" One asked through clenched teeth. "Grubmush was successful?" He asked with restrained rage.

"Of course, I was! Did you ever dare to think I wouldn't?" Grubmush said while emerging from the back of the wagon. A surprised rumble made its way through the foliage and more men emerged, flanked by a few women, all of them looked similar at first glance but they all had subtle variations he suspected that meant something. The furs were full of feathers like Grubmush wore. Their markings depicted many things, some accentuated qualities of their faces while others were recreations of terrible predators.

They all muttered amongst themselves, not as angry now.

"The Prophet?" The first who spoke repeated again but now like an accusation.

Huxley had prepared for this. "Yes, I struck Grubmush as Faldurin had and in so doing proved myself. You will take me before the rest and I will lead you to victory against Danador, we will prove Faldurin's might against the Embers."

His grand boast moved through the growing crowd. They silenced themselves as they considered it.

"Yeah, or else we will just have to kill all of you!" Elatress added brandishing her hatchets.

Huxley was so tense, he didn't register his surprise but his eyes did bug out a bit more.

Laughing erupted from their captors with the exception of the one who had spoken first. He waited for the laughter to die down. It didn't, it just shifted to excited talk about the Prophet and Grubmush's success. That didn't break the intense stare being directed at Huxley.

"What's going on Grubmush?"

He strode to Huxley's side and said "My claim is worthless without proof. You will be tested."

"Great," Huxley said. "Let me grab my Grimoire."

———————————————————————————————-

Abernathy and Onders were now walking right through the front gates of Danador. The Wardens barely spoke to her, and they certainly didn't talk to him. Onders shoved Abernathy along with increasing aggression. She might be enjoying this more than he felt was necessary. The only way to enter the city without setting off alarms would be if Onders was successful and had prisoners. They would assume she was more than capable of dealing with them, and when you feed people's assumptions they do what things do when you feed them. They grow.

When they entered the first rung of the city it was uncharacteristically empty. A few still roamed the streets but something had changed. There was a fear that permeated their movements. But more worrisome than that was where had everyone gone? It was a day that should have had the streets filled with commerce, he bet that there was a line outside the Gearbox now.

"The wardens are expecting an attack from the Dathu." Onders hissed. "They ordered everyone to shelter in place or take refuge in the Lecture Hall. The outer rung has many vulnerable people who lack proper defenses if the Dathu break through." She rolled her eyes and said, "As though that were possible. The college will have summoned every Ember today."

"How bad is it going to be?" Abernathy asked.

"For which side?" She asked.

"Both I suppose." Abernathy clarified.

"Embers have fought men like them before and won decisively, now they have discovered more and studied great amounts...Grubmush's people won't last long." She explained. "Now let's hurry to the Gearbox before the fires start."

———————————————————————————————-

Across all of Magnadun, Huxley could never seem to escape tests. He mused that maybe everyone had some kind of test for him to perform.

He found himself being judged again. Arktos and Elatress followed nearby, with Grubmush taking the lead. Elatress gently rubbed his back. Arktos shifted nervously surrounded by so many of Grubmush's people but kept pace. They were closer than they had thought to the main body of the army. He would have believed that an army of thousands would be so loud he would have heard them from miles away. They were far from silent, but the precision with which they moved was different than any army he had experienced. Most notably, they didn't speak much, communicating in short gestures and hand signals. Perhaps for stealth or perhaps it was their natural way of communicating. Hundreds of tents with small cooking fires littered the trees. They didn't choose small clearings or even chop down trees to make space. They just found places they would fit and set up camp. Weapons littered the ground around the tents, some hung properly but others were no more than tools sharpened to have a bladed edge. There were swords, hammers, axes, maces, clubs, and even bizarre spiked weapons he had never seen before.

It was then that he noticed what Grubmush told him to look for, siege weaponry. It was shocking that such an undisciplined army had siege weaponry. From his short study of military tactics and movement, he knew that in order to field weapons like that, there needed to be a complex structure of order. But their weapons looked ramshackle and their leadership nonexistent. There was so much he didn't know about the Dathu, and now he had to figure out what they wanted. If he failed, he would die by their hands like he nearly had at Mayburn.

Grubmush led them further into the encampment. Each tent emptied as they passed. When the crowd grew large enough that Huxley couldn't see through them, they came to a halt. Huxley looked for someone in charge. Or maybe some kind of council...elders...chief? None presented themselves. Their dress was all too similar to distinguish a leader. They moved into a large circle around him, the ones in front ducked low allowing those in the rear to see. Grubmush moved to the center of his people.

That made a strange kind of sense to Huxley, any kind of god that Grubmush followed wouldn't be one for lecture halls or churches.

Grubmush glanced around and stated, "I need to recapture the focus and integrity of my actions-"

The Dathu shifted uncomfortably and even called out arguments against him speaking. "Faldurin's strength flows through me but talking in words, that isn't who or what Faldurin is about. However briefly before the battle, hear me as I explain the Prophet! Would you like to hear the feathery gospel of Faldurin!?"

They roared. It sounded like the rage of battle which Grubmush accepted as a, "Yes."

"The funny thing about Faldurins beauty is that it's terrifying; terrifying beauty of violence and savagery! And in doing so we must all be, in our manners in all matters." He ticked off the points one by one on his fingers. "Discussions both violent and non-violent, in our dinners, both violent and non-violent, in our friendships both-," Someone interrupted him, "violent and non-violent?"

"Precisely! He gets it! Life can be violent or non-violent at all times. It is the way of Faldurin!"

Onders and Abernathy reached the second rung. It was manned by a skeleton crew of Wardens. The rest were likely busy elsewhere. He paused before they passed to take in the scene. The outermost rung was indeed empty in some way. Abernathy's heart lightened at seeing that. The poorest were always the most vulnerable when it came to war. They were always the ones who paid the highest cost. He was glad that the Wardens had sense enough to move them. A more calloused bureaucrat might think of them as pawns to slow down an advance. Here it was the opposite; they would be in the way of the defense. It would benefit everyone to clear the area so the Embers could make free use of their abilities. Even now, the Embers were positioning themselves high on the city walls, eager to prove once again that they were the undisputed rulers of Magnadun. Abernathy smiled, they hadn't anticipated Huxley or what he had had in store for them.

The two continued on, not quite running but moving as swiftly as they could without drawing attention. He moved, as fast as his leg would carry him. The sun had fully set by the time they made it. He breathed a sigh of relief upon seeing that the building was still standing. It was a little too much to hope that it wasn't ransacked but broken things could always be fixed. He laughed at himself for even thinking he would be allowed to continue his work after tonight. But it was his nature to see hope when there was none. Silver linings always colored his vision. It was a frustrating quality to some, but Abernathy couldn't help it. No matter the situation, there was always a way to see the good in something. Pleased with his fortune so far, he decided to push his luck. He crossed the street and entered the Gearbox.

The hearth had only a whisper of heat now amongst the chorus of cold that had filled the room. Despite the falling snow, the Gearbox seemed colder inside than out. Feeling this way was foreign to Abernathy. Usually, the fire burned so hot, fueled by his work downstairs, he wondered if cold had ever touched the place. It was one of the main criticisms he received during the summer months.

He had expected it to be burned down, but now, it was the opposite. It was frozen.

It was like all life had been pushed out and now the Gearbox was cold and motionless. When Abernathy walked forward, it felt like opening an ancient tomb for the first time, everything was stale. Physically, the Gearbox was mainly intact. Every drawer had been opened and every cabinet rifled through. But the main floor was no more disheveled than after a normal late night. That wasn't what he was worried about.

The metallic door leading downstairs had been shattered. He pulled back the tapestry next to the hearth where he kept his armor. It had, of course, been discovered, but they didn't know it for what it was. The ceremonial armor of the Norun people was a force to be reckoned with, but like all armor, it was who was underneath that mattered most. In this case, that was doubly true. The wearer brought it to life but he had outfitted the armor with numerous subsystems for battle. They had damaged through their search some of the plates, rigging and ammunition, but not the endoskeleton. It was the true strength of his invention. He would be vulnerable with the damage done but many of the systems were still functional with what was left. He donned his reduced armor and brought it to life. Its power gave his body strength and emboldened his steps. He flexed it back and forth, the chassis did as he willed it. Abernathy had hoped to never wear this inside of Danador, knowing that doing so meant he had failed in his mission. And he had failed in a way. This was certainly not the way he had hoped to win.

Casting a look around his ruined home and business was ample evidence of that. Pilgrims seeking refuge would find none now. Finally, after feeling the pain of his loss, he turned his attention to what he had truly been avoiding. The door to his workshop.

Shards of metal littered the entrance and only darkness emanated. Abernathy stood atop the stairs and looked down into his machine shop. He knew it was silly and he chastised himself, but a tear dropped from his eye. Crying over machines wasn't a good use of his time, especially with time being stretched so thin. But he couldn't help himself. Seeing his work strewn all over, wrenched out by hands who didn't understand what it could do, the help they could bring, they were treated like refuse. He examined his work on the ground and tried to determine how much was salvageable and how much was garbage. The ratio was disheartening.

The only good thing was, they didn't know what they were doing, so they had left key components intact. So much so, that Abernathy speculated he could still find a way out of this. His ammunition was the most important thing to consider now. With his tools in disarray, he wasn't sure he could make much more, at least not with any kind of stability.

Abernathy got to work and had made four usable pieces and five less than usable when the door to his study opened. He had only then realized his mistake. His focus on his shop led him to stop thinking about Onders and where she was. She had apparently been busy with her own work.

What little life had come back into the room, froze.

His body had to push through it as if it had thickened into gelatin. It would have stopped him entirely, if not for his armor. He gave it a surge of power and turned towards the open door.

Abernathy smiled and said, "Welcome to the Gearbox, Maddox,

Ember of the Arcane Flame and Chief Researcher of the Lost and Forgotten."

"No trademark?"

Abernathy's smile bled into a smirk "Glad you remembered. But my guess is that I've lost my status."

Maddox stepped forward and the air constricted further. "I've waited long enough to get my Grimoire back."

30

Sermons and Martyrs

"The dermal layer being the most effective safeguard to the internals must remain intact. Insufficient knowledge of the underlying cellular and molecular mechanisms of dermal repair can lead to infection, increased trauma and death." **-Page 145 Excerpt from the Grimoire**

Grubmush's people were strong, smart and direct. Subtlety had been lost on many of his people. It was one of the main points of his devotion to Faldurin. His sermon was confusing his audience. He had tried to make connections from their old ways to his, but his words were floundering. Subtly would need to wait until later. New breath filled him and gave him strength. His body lit up and he started again.

"When the world was sundered, all hope seemed lost!" He bellowed. His voice carried through the air and shook the audience. Any remaining murmuring ceased. His audience was captive like a field mouse in an owl's terrible talons.

"I do not know what you have been told has happened, but it is a farce. Only Faldurin, the great Owl god, knows, and I have been given his message." His hands pointed to the stars above, "Have you ever wondered who pecked through the darkness and allowed the lights of glory to shine through? Have you ever walked through the darkness only to find the stars, a comfort? Faldurin resides in Glory beyond the black veil of night. He pecked and tore holes in its fabric so we may see it but not enough to loosen its grip. It is up to us to reach for it. To see it. To grasp it."

"In time Faldruin grew disgusted with our weakness. Disgusted with our roofs, fires, and tools. We had grown soft. Soft enough that we had forgotten the ways of the Wilds. With one mighty gust of his wing, he brought all peoples together. With his perfect talons, he tore the world apart. And through his beautiful hoots, it was reassembled." A few laughs and a snort made their way through the crowd. It damaged Grubmush's focus. He pointed toward the source and said, "Only prey would not take me seriously!" He recomposed himself and went on, "Faldurin marked me two years ago when I completed my pilgrimage to his hunting grounds within the inner isles. I ascended his mountain, reached the summit, and called out to him."

He lifted his shirt showing his gnarled torso.

"With a silent strike, his talon tore away my innards and left me empty. He removed all that was and allowed for something new. A true follower. Someone who experienced his focus and sight. With my insides strewn over the ground, Grubmush the warrior died. I lay for, perhaps, days, Faldurin's own children made sport of what was once me. After my body had been made new, I awoke. Faldurin revealed the truth of Magnadun to me. It is only through conflict, we become perfect. He gave me this truth of understanding so that I may bring it to you."

He put his shirt back down. Whispers and hushed voices discussed what he had said. He didn't care, his people had come to follow him in a limited capacity. They craved violence for violence sake. They would follow anyone that gave it to them. And while Faldurin was certainly violent, it always had a purpose. He had to teach them that their strength needed purpose.

"Faldurin had made five worlds. And gifted them with individual powers. Powers that reflected his perfect nature. And for a time, all was good..." He let the moment hang. Knowing there was a "But" coming, he drew the silence out longer.

Finally, he said, "But weak men were able to worm their way into influences. They created shade when none was needed. They added more to their stomachs than what would fuel them. They sought out comfort rather than improvement. And their senses atrophied. Some people of Dathu remained true. Falrudin then placed me at the head of our army to show the way!" The crowd shifted uncomfortably.

"We have found our way through the Wilds. Fought and killed every beast, and we use it now as our roads! We met and scattered the Sumiens in open war. The Norun fear us so greatly, they won't leave their city. And the people from Valdannon...they have no warrior spirit." He spat on the ground, and said, "The only ones from there that can fight, they outcast! I met one recently in open combat. Ryla of Valdannon. She graced this city with her presence and she attempted to show them the way. And how did they react?! They treated her like a savage. I have been in countless conflicts. No one has spilled as much of my blood as she has, save for the Mighty Faldurin himself! Danador has lost its greatest treasure and embarrassed themselves by making her a lowly guard. She might have been able to preserve them all."

Grubmush fought to keep the emotion from taking over his voice. His passion was well-placed, but if he got out of control they wouldn't understand him. He pushed it down and tried to continue, but was interrupted.

———————————————————————————————-

Huxley realized what he might have been saying. It was likely time to do something. Prophets weren't meek and didn't wait to be asked. He got the feeling that the time for words was over as well. He walked out into the opening that Grubmush had created and silenced him with an outstretched hand. He was reaching for Magnincy. It swirled into his eyes and filled him with possibilities. It was never the same starfield, it always swirled and moved. Some sought his attention while others tried to avoid it. Grubmush had told him to make it obvious, as obvious to them as it was to him. But the way he did that last time was dumb luck and lethal force.

Then the memories came rushing back. The blood-splattered walls, the fallen friends, the smoking hole in the wall. Grief's invisible hand gripped hard around his heart. Was he really attempting to win over these people? Despite his growing understanding of Grubmush, he couldn't set these people loose inside of Danador. Even if their plan worked, how could they totally avoid killing innocents? The probabilities weren't promising. Stress and fear snaked through his body like poison infecting each part of him. The stars stopped swimming and began to shake, growing more pointed. More stuffed their way in, like foreign invaders, daring him to try to grasp them. He felt his mind itself shudder. When was the last time he rested? His vision shook, and he felt sick.

The warriors shifted and exchanged glances. Even, Elatress looked worried. She took two steps back as if in retreat but halted as Arktos moved forward. He made his way towards Huxley, not in his normal saunter but he was leaner and more precise in his movements. He rubbed his head under Huxley's searching hands and a small bit of the creeping madness abated. It served to pull him out of his dive, like finding a pocket of air while drowning. The great bear rubbed his fur under his palm and grunted a low rhythmic hum. Its tone reminded Huxley of Abernathy's song from the other night. Huxley still fought for control of his mind. New ideas and formulas were creeping in at the corners. It really had been too long since he had rested. His recovery from his poisoning could hardly be considered rest, more like a desperate attempt to cling to life.

A number of the warriors stepped forward. The ones that did were clad in brown and black furs with long pointed claws adorning their bodies. They raised their fists to the skies and began to breathe rhythmically as he had heard Grubmush do before. It had unnerved him once but not now. Now, it was a strange comfort. He wasn't sure if it was the prelude to a battle or a sign he was doing well, but it emboldened him either way. Huxley gripped Arktos' tuft of fur and reached towards a star that had been out of his reach moments ago. It tentatively made its way to his grasp and he pulled it down into his fist. Magnincy bobbed around inside his hand, it was definitely foolish to have reached for something he didn't totally understand. Before he released it, he felt Elatress in front of him. His focus had been on the stars so much he hadn't noticed her approach. She held out his grimoire. She didn't know what page to flip to, so she tried flipping through them all. His eyes scanned back and forth, reading his own notes, and from past authors, all detailing advanced chemistry and physics he only had a tenuous grasp on. The Magnincy grew impatient and ached to be released.

Suddenly, his mind calmed. He seemed himself again. Clarity cut through the fog and he knew what to do. The secret was his cells. When Elatress flipped to anatomy he yelled, "Stop!" He gulped and summoned his resolve. "This is going to hurt," He whispered. "Stand to the side, Elatress."

"I shall endure as Grubmush has!" He declared in a loud, commanding voice. Then, he let go of Arktos, seized his left hand forward to grab more Magnincy and released.

In a flash, he was skewered through his abdomen. It was the exact same spot as Grubmush. The crowd of onlookers gasped and Elatress leaped backwards. Her face instantly drained of color. A spear had been seized from the grasp of a nearby warrior and propelled through the air. It currently rested behind Huxley having made the gaping hole through Huxley. Huxley stumbled backwards, grabbed more Magnincy, and clumsily released it. His body quaked as he fell.

———————————————————————————————-

Elatress tried to block it, she really did. Spears were big and loud. Far easier than arrows, or darts. How had it moved so instantly? She watched Huxley collapse into the dirt. Her arms held still in disbelief that she had missed the spear. And now for some damn fool reason, her friend had just stabbed himself. She looked at Arktos who offered her no surprise like he knew it was coming. Why hadn't he thrown his big fat body in the way then? She swooped down to try to help Huxley...though she knew nothing could fix this. His eyes grew cold and lifeless, his breath was haggard as he spit blood involuntarily. She tried speaking to him but it was useless.

You knew this would happen.

She closed her eyes and shook her head. The voice refused to stay silent.

Now you're surrounded by them? How many is it? Oh my...that's a lot. The voice spoke.

"Five hundred and twenty-eight-here, with thousands more in the surrounding area." She answered.

If you had listened to me he would still be alive, you'd have a fresh kill and you would be safe.

She grasped desperately for Arktos. Grabbing handfuls of his fur as she pulled him close.

...not this time. It whispered in triumph. *You are mine now. We are going to rule the Wilds you and I. Everyone will fear our blades, all who enter our woods will be hunted by us!*

"No." She gasped.

You don't have a say in the matter anymore.

"I am not a savage or a beast...I am a nice girl-"

You are the most savage beast there has ever been! You are the Wild's unleashed, you are-

"NO!" She screamed. She released Arktos and fell to the ground squeezing the sides of her head hoping to push the voice out.

It laughed at her efforts and she felt it reaching deep within her. Grabbing hold of her muscles and testing them out like a puppet. Arktos huffed in anger, finally seeing what was happening. He laid down on her, not crushing her but allowing much of his weight to pin her. She screamed again but it was not her voice this time. It was someone else's, deeper...malevolent.

She felt someone's hands on hers, pulling her out from under Arktos. Arktos shifted his weight and allowed it. She knew who it was from his stance and gait. He walked away and came back again.

Huxley was alive.

———————————————————————————-

Elatress was herself once more, although that was the furthest gone she had ever been. Huxley was trying to lie still within a ramshackle tent tied with furs, skins, and other animal parts that he tried to ignore and didn't want to know more about. She was looking over his wound and poked it. He yelped and she jumped back apologizing, "It's just..it's not just a hole anymore. Shouldn't it be a hole? I've made holes in things and people so I know what they look like. Where's your stomach hole, Huxley?"

"Oh, it's there Elatress, I just did a patch job...probably too quick. But for now, they think I am who Grubmush says."

"A prophet?" She asked.

He winced again and said, "Yeah...I made the same wound that Grubmush talked so much about. The same that I gave to him, which is what started this whole thing. The only problem is, I can't heal as well as he can."

Elatress was looking close again and said, "But you've certainly done something." She moved to touch it again and he swatted her hand.

"Well, I took a big risk with Magnincy. I used up way too much of my stability. If I finished the job, I'd likely be mad. This was as much as I could risk. It looks ok from the outside but the inside is a mess."

"That's the important part," Elatress argued.

"Uh huh...it sure is, El." Huxley tried adjusting himself.

It had taken all of his strength to remain steady in front of his audience. He had been successful. They were moving on Grubmush's orders now. If anyone came into the tent, they would see how badly his body was doing. It might undo his rouse. His healing patch job was actually far more of a success than he had hoped for. After seeing Guliford, Grubmush and Onders all heal to varying degrees, he had made a few important connections. Healing a body may be the most taxing thing that could be asked of Magnincy. It's probably why Embers aren't known for it. The body can fix itself to a degree but if given the right program to follow, it will build new material. It built itself with the help of its mother at one point and it can be ordered to do so again. But what the mother knew instinctively, an Ember would have to know factually. Huxley had read quite a bit on this point but hadn't put together how valuable it might have been. If he could master biology, he might be able to save people from certain death. Another bolt of pain shot through his body. Cold sweat was soaking his shirt and Huxley couldn't focus again.

The sides of his mind were frayed and he felt himself teetering on the edge. If only he had been more clever, he may have found a way to prove himself without using so much of his sanity. Now, even basic Magnincy might send him over the edge. And the most important part of the plan was still ahead. Elatress had stopped prodding him. She dutifully sat by his side. Arktos had made his way to his bedside as well. Elatress opened the Grimoire and asked if he wanted her to read to him. The situation reminded him of childhood when his mom would ask in the same way. It was kind of her, and in truth, it did sound nice, but the likelihood of someone disturbing them was too high. He asked Elatress to stand guard and turn away anyone on orders of the Prophet. She reluctantly agreed and took her post.

The silence that had once been covering the army was now shaken loose like a rock smacking a hornets nest. Thousands of warriors were now in motion, weapons clanked and feet stomped. They were moving to war.

Huxley's mind raced as he prodded his wound. It looked ok, but internally it screamed in agony. "Foolish" he muttered to himself. It was yet another example of a good idea in theory. It saved his life, but they would know he had lied eventually. Elatress had taken her post outside and Huxley now fruitlessly flipped through the Grimoire. Healing wasn't really a subject covered in it. Biology yes, and perhaps it could be fueled by energy production. How to marry those two ideas, he wasn't sure. The body got its energy in different pathways than the kind that he needed. He made a note about it and chuckled nervously. Making notes was for the future, one that he wasn't sure he had. The Grimoire didn't help with his immediate problem, but it calmed his mind. He felt the madness abate, though it was still close. It was far harder to push out than the last time. Everyone had their limits despite his earlier successes. And he may have found his a little too early.

Suddenly, Huxley heard Elatress discussing something with the men outside. It sounded tense, but Elatress was holding her ground. He hoped it didn't turn violent. Just then a gust of wind hit him and Grubmush stood at his side.

He tilted his head and said, "Prophet", acknowledging Huxley's status.

Huxley jumped and screamed. How had he gotten past Elatress? She sees everything. At least, he thought she did. Grubmush was unapologetic, "Elatress is skilled but we have dealt with the Sumi since before you were born. They can be circumvented."

Grubmush looked over his wound and was amazed.

"Then why sneak in?" Huxley demanded.

He snorted, "Convincing Sumi's of non-violence is not a skill we have with them. Better to distract."

Huxley agreed, he wouldn't have convinced her no matter the story, she was on edge since he impaled himself.

After inspecting his wound, Grubmush pursed his lips and fixed his jaw. He stood straight and said, "I don't think what you did was wise."

Huxley only nodded and said "It seemed like the best way to prove I was a prophet."

Grubmush shook his head and said "You clearly have never met one, don't your people have religious ceremonies?"

"No, not really." He responded.

"Well, I shouldn't question your methods. But in the future I know that I was offering myself as a demonstration of both your ability and Faldurins wrath.

Huxley started to rise but Grubmush stopped him, "It doesn't matter. Our goal has been achieved. My cabal is ready to attack, and I will lead them. Their faith will waver if they see you still injured. Hold still, I will do what I can." He closed his eyes and started breathing in a manner that he had done earlier. It was ritualistic, but not anything Huxley could understand.

Could they really destroy Danador? Grubmush was certainly powerful, but he could never stand against several full-fledged Embers. Likely now, the walls were lined with the most powerful. They would never allow an invasion. "Your people may all be killed," Huxley told him, wary of how he might react.

"Yours as well." Grubmush replied.

"No," Huxley said "The embers-"

"Are powerful, but can be overwhelmed. We will lose many, but not all. Danador will be ours and its defenders we will crush. You and I will soar through the sky as Faldurins chosen talons. But that is only if we fail in our mission." He paused his breathing and said "And how could the Prophet fail?"

Huxley's stomach turned cold. The assurance in Grubmush's voice mixed with his faith in him made it seem possible. Had Huxley just rallied an army that could actually defeat the College of the Arcane Flame? The College's numbers weren't as full as he had thought they'd be. It was then that an old familiar feeling swam through him. Grubmush had placed his right hand onto Huxley and he felt his wound heal. It was the same feeling that Guliford had produced. No. Wait. Huxley thought. It was different. Guliford's was like a wave that demanded his body change. But Grubmush's was like a basket weaving around the wound. It wasn't fixed, it was bound. The body would still have to heal the rest, but it felt like it was sectioned off now, so he could focus on other things.

"Do not receive another wound there or use that spot to prove your word," Grubmush warned him, coming out of his trance-like state.

"As often as I can manage it," Huxley replied.

"Do not believe, you are well. For your kind, we can only help, not restore. You must endure alone."

"I...thank you Grubmush."

An uncharacteristic calm exuded from Grubmush, and he said, "We have grown in our knowledge of each other. I once thought you weak and you once thought me a savage. We were right in some ways but very wrong in others. I thank you as well."

Huxley nodded in agreement and lifted himself out of bed. It was a bizarre sensation. His abdomen wasn't in pain, but it didn't feel right. He would have to worry about this later. For now, Grubmush had given him some time. The wise thing to do would be to ask him how long this would last, but Huxley didn't want to know the answer. He had delayed too long already. Onders and Abernathy were likely already set and were waiting on him. Huxley fixed his shirt and grabbed the Grimoire. He made for the front of the tent where Elatress was in a screaming match with a small crowd. She seemed to be enjoying herself. She stopped when Huxley emerged and asked, "Ready to destroy Danador?"

It was then that the first fireball fell, followed by a rain of others.

Catapult's hurled attacks from the Dathu army. The attack on Danador had begun.

31

Ballistics and Bureaucrats

"The universal force that attracts all matter is one of the most power-ful structures in place within Magnadun if reduced to singularities. The matter within will lose concepts of space and time." **-Page 304 Excerpt from the Grimoire**

Huxley and Elatress watched as the city received its next salvo. If all went according to plan, this wouldn't last long. Huxley couldn't help feeling like a traitor to his own people. They did their best to protect everyone, but it was inevitable that people would die tonight. Tears welled in his eyes and were wiped away. He couldn't let anyone see them.

The Wilds were now choked with warriors all barely holding them-selves back from the attack. Despite no clear command structure, they held their positions and seemed to know when to move and when to halt. He wished he knew how they did that. Elatress, Arktos and Huxley made their way to the catapult lines with Grubmush. The first volley was a success. Small fires had begun around the city. If citizens had been watching, the fireballs could be dodged. Terror was the real weapon being employed.

"Where are the Embers?" He asked Elatress. "Did they take the bait? Are the coming to defend?"

She didn't answer. She had been helping load the next catapult. Abernathy's device looked ready, but Huxley nearly panicked just looking at it. He'd seen the prototypes plenty of times, but as toys with dolls inside it. He didn't like the idea of being one of the dolls. It was the only way if he wanted to get into the city undetected. THE GEARBOX ™ was plastered on nearly every inch of it. Abernathy had grown tired of his designs being hijacked, it seemed. Elatress made a few adjustments to the aim of the catapult and readied the release. She opened the cage and said, "Come on, just like Ballistics and Bureaucrats." She waved for him to step inside.

"And I will land safely?"

"Safely?!" She laughed. "Oh, Bookpile, no. Definitely not. You're being flung into a city that's on fire. You can die in lots of ways. Just make your bubble right before you land, and you should survive...right?"

"Uhh, Magnincy is near the edge for me right now."

She rolled her eyes and said, "Don't go crazy. Just try and relax." Her voice faded as she turned her attention elsewhere. "Oh. there they are." Huxley turned and saw the walls of Danador bespeckled with Embers. The whole college must have shown up. Having this part of the plan go right was exhilarating and dreadful. They formed up equal distance from each other, high up on the walls. He was reminded of Ember Palidthur showing up like he had hoped, except these Embers didn't waver. They stood as strong as the walls they were on top of, like a part of the structure itself. He counted about twenty, but it was hard to tell as the wall curved. He couldn't be sure how many Embers there were. Twenty against thousands? Danador may not survive the night.

As though in response to his doubts, an Ember closest to him produced three black orbs that swirled inward like tiny dark pools. They cracked with energy that gave them an eerie glow. They floated excitedly in the air until, all at once, they arced through the sky. They seemed to make no noise as they flew, but that may have been Huxley's internal panic. Each sphere landed deep within the trees. No crashing, no screams, silence. Then everything cracked. The trees, people, and ground around them bent inward towards the spheres. The warriors screamed as they were compressed together. It was as though the orbs had grabbed everything nearby and pulled it together. Nothing looked like it could have survived.

"Gravity," Huxley stated grimly. He had read only notes about it in the Grimoire. It was far outside his scope. Gravity worked in ways that befuddled all of the author's notes within. There was even a theory it could pull light. His heart began to pound and his body flooded with the urge to run. He took one step backwards and remembered his friends that had died in Mayburn. He recalled their screams, the loss, and his need to return an Ember. Mayburn deserved a real defender. If he ran now, he'd only return a coward. Huxley banished that thought and summoned what was left of his courage. He may not be up for defeating twenty Embers but Abernathy's plan just might. It was as though the Ember's counterattack signaled something because just after it landed, every warrior broke into a sprint. Thousands tore out of the tree line storming Danador.

"Anyway, as I said, relax." Elatress pushed him into the small box of Abernathy's design. It locked into place with a metallic thud. She knocked on it and said, "You fit? Feeling good?"

"Not at all." He said, not lying about either question. The newly cramped space and the task before him were nauseating. The Grimoire pushed against his stomach, making him feel nauseous. "I can't move my arms much and I can't really breathe. I won't be able to summon Magnincy here."

"Remember the plan. Form your bubble after it spits you out!" Her voice contained annoyance but was masked with false optimism. Was she genuinely worried for him? Two warriors picked up his cube and lowered him into the bucket. The arm and catapult shook under its weight. "Payload's ready," a warrior called.

"Hey, Payload, remember I'm great at the Ballistics part of Ballistics and Bureaucrats. I'll get you there. Besides, you can heal yourself right up if you smash into a wall." She made a few adjustments to the angle and grabbed the release. "Remember, we will be right behind you.".

"It's Huxley," He corrected her. "and I absolutely cannot heal myself if I hit a wall. It's not like that at all, it-"

She released the tension and Huxley flung through the air.

Wind screamed through the vents in his iron box, and his face pulled backwards, barely holding onto his skull.

He caught only bare glimpses of what was happening. The walls, wilds and fire all swirled around in a kaleidoscope of color. Huxley shut his eyes tight. It only served to make more confusion. Within seconds, his chamber broke apart. Huxley gasped as the sheer wall of wind hit him and snow stung his face. He instinctually grasped the Grimoire to keep it from flying away. Danador lay sprawled before him. He could see the rungs of the city as clearly as looking at a map. The only structure higher was the tower of the College with its ever-present torch. The Lecture hall was choked with inhabitants. His heart swelled with hope, it looked like the whole lower ring was evacuated. The Wardens were good at moving a city around it seemed. Snow covered the roofs of most of the lower-leveled homes. From the right angle, it looked like a blank white sheet of paper, except for the lamps that lined the main road leading toward the college. They burned all the brighter tonight, like the stars themselves.

Then Huxley's flight began to arc downward. The wind and snow shifted violently, and he fell. Around him, there were others experiencing the same fate. Warriors who had elected to be flung into the city. Only their cubes hadn't released them in the air like his did. He saw a few crash into the city streets and propel their contents outward. Some warriors even landed gracefully. Danador was growing far too close now and Huxley tried to remember what he was supposed to do. He had cleared the first rung of the city and descended into the second.

Summoning Magnincy, it swirled before him, making the houses below look like their lamps were still on. He remembered his attempt at landing in the snowbank and how that went. "Wider, stretch, viscous, and durable." He sized a few elements of Magnincy and cast them beneath him while fixing the point of it on his back. He turned and fell face up towards the ground. Seeing Danador climb up around him he looked at the stars, the real ones. The lights of the fires and the tower made it a little hard to see them but it was enough. Starlight washed over him and eased his mind. Falling towards what may be his death, he felt ok with it. Not the part about dying, but his plan. He was using a hybrid idea. It was the protective netting of the bubble but without completely surrounding him. Instead, making one area, he could be cradled like a hammock. The sides reached out far and wide with tentacles searching. When one touched a rigid structure, it sank into it. He'd sent twelve tendrils out hoping ten to grasp good and tight. Only three connected. One with the wall separating the rings and the other two with businesses. The fixed point on his back felt the intense pressure. It stretched, slowing his descent, but far too slowly.

He was going to impact any second, now. The street rushed to him and Huxley closed his eyes. Suddenly, another black orb imploded the buildings next to him and he flung up and to the side. His body changed trajectory in a wide arc like he had been caught and thrown upwards. The pressure pounded his ribs and flopped his body like a ragdoll.

His tendrils stopped him from smashing into the ground. He opened his eyes to find cobblestones a few feet away. He realized he'd been holding his breath for what felt like the whole flight. Exhaling sharply, he let his rigid body relax. When he got to his feet, his stomach finally caught up with the flight and he doubled over retching. Between bouts of sickness, he searched to clear his vision. A few mathematical formulas were edging their way in. He saw the trajectory of his flight based on the scattered remains of his pod and his landing zone. Elatress was really good at this, he thought. But soon, he was throwing up again. His landing idea worked almost as intended but it was too many tendrils. Scattered attempts aren't precise enough. *Fewer tendrils and more accurate shots next time*, he surmised.

When his body finally ceased removing his dinner, he wiped himself off and tried to get his bearings. The tower was obscured by the nearby buildings but he could see its fire illuminating the night. "Not too far, but not too close." He said. He reckoned he only had thirty minutes, or so before the meet up. The embers still continued their defense of the city, some even disappeared from their ledge, perhaps engaging closer now. The gravity orb had totally destroyed a piece of the market, perhaps three buildings all compressed into one. It looked like it missed any warriors, but it nearly got Huxley. He pushed down the urge to make notes on its effects in the Grimoire. His hand had already made its way to its bindings. "Later" he said, seeing a few more GEARBOX ™ boxes being hurled inside the city.

The sky was littered with pods flinging in warriors and Magnincy of all make and variety was there to greet them. The gravity orbs were only being employed by one Ember. Elsewhere, the Embers attacked with their own specializations. It was difficult to see exactly what they were using, he didn't move any closer to find out. His curiosity knew that would be suicide, no matter how fascinating it was. Two pods began their descent towards him. He held his breath again in hopes it was his friends. They fell far faster than he anticipated. The pods smashed into the ground shooting parts everywhere. A huge ball of brown fur was tossed out of one and the nearly naked body of Grubmush from the other. The brown ball rolled to a stop and flopped open revealing Elatress. Grubmush landed with a slide on the ice, looking no worse for the wear. Elatress and Grubmush nodded to each other while Arktos moaned.

Elatress gave a concerned look at the bear. "No lacerations, no fires, and no Magnincy, just bruises." Arktos protested her medical evaluation with a growl and she snapped back "What's the point of being able to withstand nearly anything, if you never try to do it? You grew this large for what then?" The bear didn't answer and Elatress's voice softened. "I'm sorry, I got scared as well. Thank you for helping me land so well. I couldn't have done it without you." Arktos brightened and the two rubbed foreheads. Grubmush straightened his loin cloth as it had been nearly ripped free upon landing. Huxley waved at them and crossed the empty streets to meet up. "I can't believe that worked. The odds of us all landing where we did and of us being uninjured..." He trailed off thinking of the ways it could have gone wrong.

"Odds?!" Elatress and Grubmush replied in unison.

They both protested at once. "I'm the best catapulter and judge of distance and space you've ever met!"

"We flew as the mighty Faldurin upon his holy quest! Our landing was assured before we even left." Huxley accepted their answers though they still left a lot of questions with no time to answer them. The party soon hammered the streets rushing towards the College.

Grubmush and Elatress easily outpaced Huxley. They hung back at the end of city blocks so he could catch up. Finally, they arrived at the main road of Danador, the one he had arrived by. What was once a bustling market with more people than air to breathe, lay empty of all of that. His spine shivered at the eeriness of the change. He studied the road. It felt like a trap, almost as if the road would never have allowed itself to be so empty. But there it was. Huxley carefully walked out to the middle. The straight lines of the cobblestone street beckoned him closer to the city. The main gates were wide open now. No Wardens manned them and no clips were required. If the street being empty chilled him, the wide open gates shook his core. The archway dimensions were fascinating. The angles were sharper than he would have guessed. The composition of the stone foundations and their iron oxide percentages were high, at least compared to the road. Huxley grabbed the sides of his head and closed his eyes. "You're slipping," he gasped. "You can't do this now."

His palpebral fissure height came in at nine millimeters. That was on the lower end of normal, but not an outlier. His split between the anterior lamella and posterior lamella of the eyelid was in correct ratios. "NO!" He screamed. "You aren't supposed to know what those are!" He told himself. "You can't collapse into madness in the middle of the street," he told himself.

But collapse, he did.

Huxley pulled himself up to his knees and flopped over onto his back. And once again, the stars greeted him. What kept him searching for them when he was near the edge? Even Magnincy took its form. Madness still clawed at his mind but found it couldn't grab hold when he looked straight up. He suddenly had an epiphany, or was it madness lying to him? Either the stars were too far away for him to make sense of them, or they reminded him of home and calmed him. Both ideas made sense.

Madness was breaking everything down to its core math and science, and he didn't doubt the cosmos contained plenty of that but it was so incredibly far away. Madness only broke down the stuff *closest* to him. It wasn't a perfect fix, because as soon as he didn't focus on the stars the rushing cold and snow offered up its compounds and makeup. Even a pod containing a raging warrior within flew past. Abernathy used metal with the chemical elements AI that was lighter weight than steel by one-third.

He refocused on the stars.

Their distance may be the solution but it also calmed his emotions. It was the same night sky he would gaze at in Mayburn, the same he grew up with, the one that hung over his home. It reminded him of Jonas and Bennett. The star light had long shone on them as they snuck off to get into trouble and watched over him as his father discussed life with him. The stars were home, even here in Danador amongst a siege.

Starting at his toes, making its way up through his legs, pelvis, spine and chest until it reached his head, he relaxed, and the madness abated. The formulas faded away and his heart slowed. A, "thank you," escaped his lips.

Inside his head, the now familiar voice responded, "Come find me Huxley the Heir."

The world faded back in around him just as the main gates of Danador were blasted apart. He shot upwards and looked down the main street. It was some distance away from him but he could see it. Hundreds of warriors poured into the city. The first few were instantly flooded by a liquid that dissolved them produced by an Ember atop the wall. It barely stopped the others from rushing over their former allies. This was the fight Dathu had been searching for. Elatress and Grubmush helped Huxley to his feet. Grubmush attempted to carry him but he fought his way out of his grasp. Feeling his time slipping away, he rushed past the opening and dashed through the industrial district unbothered by anyone else. He had fixed his gaze on the burning tower. Soon he would be inside the College of the Arcane Flame, and soon he would get his answers.

32

Insults and Wardens

"The Adherens junctions initiate and stabilize cell to cell junctions; they also facilitate adhesion of homoglomus cells in most tissues." **-Page 105 Excerpt from the Grimoire**

Huxley's legs ached and his lungs burned when they reached the inner circle. Their travel was uninhibited as Wardens had taken refuge and everyone else was likely holed up in their homes.

The inner circle was unguarded, like the rest. The pristine gates carved in splendor were now mostly covered in snow. When Elatress pushed on them mounds shook loose revealing the details. She didn't stop to look but it grabbed Huxley's attention. The carving was so unique to Danador. Art was considered needless work and didn't fit here. Most walls stood blank. Color was only applied to lure business or as a warning, not to be enjoyed. Carving a door only weakened the structure. If the purpose was to keep others out, then carving it made no sense. There was still so much about them that he didn't understand. It angered him that it had come to this. They could have gained so much more by sharing their wealth of knowledge. Instead, they hoarded it. All his life, he had only wanted to learn so that he could help. The answers always seemed just out of reach. And now that he had got a few, he knew he couldn't stop.

Answers were hidden deep within the college. The reason the Grimoire came to him, the reason the voice spoke to him, and the reason they were made to suffer, required answering.

The last time he was in the inner ring he couldn't help but marvel. It still impressed him, but now it was because of the emptiness. He looked immediately to the library and found it devoid of life. The books remained stacked high and categorized, practically begging him to come in. Grubmush muttered something about luxuries and comforts, ending his thoughts with a frothy spit.

Huxley shifted his attention back to the tower that stood taller than it ever had, looming like it was almost leaning down and threatening to fall on him. The three of them hadn't said it, but the second part of the plan was to meet up here and head in together. Only there wasn't a trace of the other members. If anyone was going to break from the plan, it would be Ryla or Onders, not Abernathy. He couldn't get over the feeling that something happened, something unexpected.

The inner ring was far better set up for a leisurely life. Business and homes were stacked like the first two but this was different. Gardens and benches with lamps burning were everywhere. Their yellow light reflected off the accumulating snow and gave everything a golden glow. His heart still longed for his foolish dream of strolling these streets, Grimoire in hand, and discussing ideas with fellow Embers. It may have been foolish, but he still longed for it. One day...maybe...if things were set right.

He saw Elatress and Arktos standing alone in a courtyard near the college with Grubmush stalking around, poking things with his trident. It was the same courtyard where he met Ryla on guard that first night he arrived. It looks so different now. Shoes now in hand, Elatress dug her feet through the snow. It took her a moment, but she found the rocky ground. She closed her eyes and put a hand on Arktos' back.

"Is he here?" Huxley asked.

"Not that I can see..." She muttered, "hang on..." She took a step back and crunched more of the snow.

A robed figure appeared from the dark and snowy skies. The snow didn't even make the characteristic "crunch" when he landed. It was like he weighed nothing at all. Huxley knew he would face at least one Ember tonight but it didn't stop his heart from racing. Whatever danger he had faced before, it paled in comparison to this. He had hoped to be backed up by everyone when the time came. The Ember stood as straight as the tower he defended. A sneer curled along his lips and his hands splayed his fingers outward in a hungry grasp. His customary hood was low though his eyes still had room to see. Elatress had already unlooped her hatchets, keeping them hidden inside her cloak. Huxley summoned Magnincy but didn't dare make a move yet. Grubmush and Arktos produced nearly identical growls.

Elatress whipped her head backwards to find two more Embers had appeared behind them. They were surrounded. One was shorter. His hood was pulled back revealing a pudgy face that was flushed in sweat and emotion. He was balding but retained the horseshoe ring of hair around his head. He didn't have the same disturbing calm as the first, but his eyes were just as confident. The other's body shape was lost inside his robes. The garment he wore was too big to discern much of anything, but a sharply pointed chin jutted out from within his hood. Then he re-membered them. These were the two Embers that he had attacked when he first escaped. His stomach fell and his knees wobbled.

Elatress brandished her weapons now and Arktos reared up on his hind legs. Grubmush moved first in a violent dash. It was the same charge he used in the Lecture Hall. The Embers did not look intimidated. An invisible force flung Grubmush into the air. It was the same feeling that Huxley felt that helped him land safely. Gravity. But moving upwards. It flung Grubmush far away in a wide arch. He bellowed in outrage but soon his howls were just an echo as the distance grew. Silence fell and was only interrupted by Arktos's murderous growl. The cold had finally made its way deep inside Huxley. His resolve faded away as he realized how out-matched they were.

"Lower your hands, boy." The first spoke, his voice vacant of emotion.

Huxley did as instructed. His heart screamed to fight but his mind knew he would only kill himself and his friends.

"The Grimoire."

It wasn't a question, just a command to the other two. The bald one seized Huxley while the other snatched his bag and pulled out the Grimoire. Huxley instinctually fought but it didn't do much good. Elatress was about to make her move when he caught her eye and shook his head. She probably knew as well as he did how hopeless it was. Luckily, she listened. The Ember unbuckled the Grimoire and flipped through it casually, finally after seeing enough, he nodded to the first and said, "It's Maddox's."

The thick-faced Embers grip tightened in anger, digging his fingers into Huxley's arms.

"Thief!", his voice whispered dripping with bile.

His sweaty hands now soaked Huxley's sleeves, making them damp. He had probably been fighting the Dathu already based on his current state. Could he be close to his limit? Huxley wondered. He tried searching his eyes for madness but they revealed nothing.

The first finally approached. He floated above the snow just inches off the ground. "Finally, he will have his Grimoire back and we can stop hearing his complaints. He was right though. The nescient brought it back to him." He looked over at Elatress who stood poised to strike. Arktos loomed but had fallen back to all four paws after sensing her hesitation. Far in the distance of what felt like another world, an eruption filled the sky, in a large bloom, like a flower made of fire. Screams echoed shortly afterwards and the Ember grew annoyed.

After a moment's thought, he instructed, "Bring the boy and the girl, leave the beast here, if it tries to follow, kill it. I must return to the wall." The ember seized Magnincy and flung himself upward into the sky.

Elatress looked expectantly at Huxley who still shook his head. Where was everyone? The answer was obvious. Onders. It was a mistake to trust her. She alerted the Embers and now they were caught. He gave up hope they were hidden nearby, Elatress would have sensed them. He knew that if these two Embers led him into the college, it would likely be his death. Perhaps he could wildly attack again? But before he could think of anything, he felt his hands bind. He was still in the sweaty grip of the pudgy Ember.

"I would greatly like to kill you before Maddox arrives, but I would also prefer not to waste my concentration on you two. But if you make this difficult, I will." His voice was choked full of malevolence, like a man who thoroughly enjoyed hurting people. Huxley couldn't claim to have met many who gave him that feeling, but right now, at this moment, he knew it was true. He likely had been fighting on the wall and came back here for this.

"Why not?" Huxley asked, taking a huge risk, "You seem well-practiced at it."

"Oh, I am, little thief." He answered, "And one more word from you and I'll show you how good I am at it. I could split your skin right down the middle." He snorted a laugh and went on, "Or I could just split you from crotch to throat. The bonds that make us up are easy to see, and it's even easier to separate them."

Elatress had had enough, "Bonds? I thought you were an Ember of the Arcane Flame. Huxley can do stuff like that. You must be a junior Ember. I've met one of those before."

He belched the word "JUNIOR!" back at her. Murder welled up within him. She had touched a nerve. Elatress was good at that.

The other Ember then said in a nasally voice, "Byrum...remember yourself."

Byrum apparently did not, because he continued summoning Magnincy. "JUNIOR!" He repeated again. His eyes crawled over Elatress' face searching it for something, his lips rapidly moving as though reading and then to Arktos and he did the same. "AH HA!" He barked. Then, Elatress' chin opened. A jet of blood shot out and it widened to the bottom of her lip and down under her chin. An identical wound burst out of Arktos as well. She didn't scream. She didn't even yelp. She just met his attention with defiance. It was Arktos that cried out.

His anger reached a boiling point and he said, "I can see what you are made of, every last spec of you. And I can split you in two with a gesture. Who should go first? You or the bear?" He didn't wait for an answer, "...now who is a junior?"

Huxley could see the wound truly wasn't deep, it seemed a clean slice, barely deeper than a shaving cut.

"Byrum." The second said again. "Maddox needs them breathing. Do not let her goad you! We have so many more to deal with."

Byrum let sputtered an incoherent argument. He said "But not the bear right?"

The second sighed and said "If you must."

Elatress cried out but Byrum's hands flash forward and began attacking Arktos. Similar cuts appeared all over him causing him to yelp in fear and confusion.

"Run Arktos!" Elatress screamed.

Akrtos considered it but couldn't leave her alone. He stopped crying out, replacing it with a guttural warning. The Ember hesitated, halting his attack. Then the second said again "Ok, you've had your fun. Do not overreach here." He huffed a few times in rage and shoved Huxley and Elatress towards the college leaving Arktos bloodied in the courtyard.

The college was just as Huxley remembered. It actually looked exactly as it did the first day he arrived. There was no sign of a conflict at all. The lamps burned bright, illuminating the shiny well-mopped floor. Their feet echoed over marble creating cascading echoes. Walters was even at his desk, writing from his long feathered quill. His face was so low, his long nose nearly touched the fresh ink. In fact, the evidence of a few faded dots of black on his nose indicated it happened frequently.

"You said you'd be more quiet next time?" He chastised.

Byrum barked back, "Like I take orders from you!"

"He was talking to me." Huxley corrected.

"Indeed, I was. You left blood droplets on my floor." He complained. The two Embers ignored him and pushed their captives towards the doors to the inner library. "Just a second!" Walters called out. "I need to record the visitors' names."

Huxley was shocked at his boldness. Would Wardens really be so dedicated to paperwork that they would give an Ember an order? It was peculiar, particularly with their captivity being so obviously different from a visit. Even more surprising, they stopped and did just as he asked.

The pointed chin Ember said, "Rules," under his breath to Byrum.

"Indeed, there are rules, Pictylon," Walters quipped with a chipper tone. "No worries, young sirs, just a moment. Bring them here, please. I even remember the first one." He looked up at Huxley, his deeply lined face scrunched tighter reminding Huxley of a maze again. His lips melded so well with his face that Huxley could barely discern that the warden was smirking. "Huxley Durant" Walters called out, "Of Mayburn, yes?"

"Yes," Huxley answered.

"Business?" Walters inquired.

"Uhh."

"You know his business!" Byrum seethed.

"Ah, yes, we will say parcel delivery."

Byrum snorted. Huxley wasn't sure if he actually got the joke. Walters seized Huxley's hand and drew him in closer, shaking it vigorously. "Welcome back to the College, I hope you stay longer this time." He released Huxley's hand. His firm grip had made an outline that slowly faded.

"And you young miss? Please mind the paperwork." He said motioning to the bloody drip from her chin.

Elatress stared daggers at him.

He then softened his gaze and said "Please."

"Elatress...DelaCourt. I don't have business here."

"Well, that isn't true, otherwise you wouldn't be here," Walters argued.

"Killing this fat idiot then!" She hissed looking backwards at Byrum.

"Hah!" He laughed, "Ok, we will say, seeking argument resolution."

Walters again shot out his hand and shook Elatress' hand. He pulled her in close and seemed to be trying to say something when Byrum made to smash her head against the desk. She sidestepped him and he lost his balance, stumbling onto the counter.

Walters laughed again, but stopped once he realized how angry Byrum was. He began picking himself up and Pictylon grabbed the two prisoners and shoved them forward through the doors. Huxley had finally, after months away, returned to the College of the Arcane Flame.

33

Knowledge and Nescience

"Arranging and leading a people is a difficult endeavor. One all leaders struggle with. Responsibility and leadership over another has ramifications not even the wisest can predict."
-Page 40 Excerpt from the Grimoire

Thrown onto his hands and knees, Huxley was finally in the room he had wanted to be in more than any other place. If only he was here under better circumstances. The library reached high above him, spiral staircases and narrow ironwork bridges crawled up its sides like vines. Lamps lit the way upward ending so high Huxley could barely make out the roof. His jaw dropped seeing the collections of vast knowledge. They were touchably close to him now. It wasn't possible to read it all, not with a hundred lifetimes, but he got the feeling he might have tried.

Unfortunately, he didn't think he even had the rest of his current life to read. The two Embers had adopted a sort of civility in front of Walters, which melted away once they were through the doors. They suddenly found themselves thrown against the ground and then into the library walls by an unseen force that even managed to shake a few books loose.

The books tumbled to the ground, surprising Pictylon, who yelped.

"Byrum!" He chastised.

Byrum's attention broke when he saw what he had done. He hurried to the fallen books, scooped them up, and placed them back. They both nodded in contentment after inspecting the shelves to make certain everything was back the way it should be.

"Jeez, they like books even more than you do Bookpile," Elatress commented dryly.

"The knowledge contained here can collapse the cosmos, you absolute cretin. It is not books we love, but the knowledge contained within." Byrum seized at multiple pieces of Magnincy and his expression turned dark. "I have this well in hand, Pictylon. You may leave for the walls. Maddox will be here soon. I want some time alone with them before he arrives."

Pictylon looked down his nose at Byrum and sneered, accepting whatever he had meant by that.

Byrum cleared his throat and said, "They may need you."

"I suppose you have this well in hand. Before I leave, I should return the Grimoire to Maddox's study." He stopped and considered the situation for a moment, "He will be angry if both are dead...though maybe, just cross if the girl doesn't make it." Pictylon exited with the Grimoire in hand leaving them alone.

Byrum grunted an acknowledgement and looked up. He gestured with his hands and Huxley heard something come loose. A wide cage shook to the ground containing a battered and bleeding Abernathy. His false leg was removed leaving only the stump. The rest of him had been battered, his cheeks were black and blue with blood soaking various parts of his clothing.

The two of them gasped at the sight. Elatress struggled against the force that kept her and screamed in anger. Byrum smiled and said, "Maddox caught him...the fool returned to his greasy little hole... as all the nescient do."

"Abernathy!" Huxley called out, "Are you ok?" But Byrum released something from his hand and Huxley's cheek split.

"Oh, no I am definitely the one asking the questions. I won't get the chance once Maddox gets here. Now, that one," gesturing towards Abernathy, "has already spilled his guts. Who is next to talk?"

Fearing more harm to Elatress and Abernathy, Huxley looked up and said, "What do you want to know?"

Another slice to his cheek emerged. "Ask me another question and that will happen to your eyes," He tutted, "Answers only."

"I am. I am the one to talk then!" Huxley stated through clenched teeth.

Byrum snorted, and said, "Of course you are. You're the only one *worth* talking to." The Ember then heard a shuffle of something upstairs in the library and shifted. Suddenly, Elatress spat in his face.

The Ember dropped his hands and let go of his Magnincy, his concentration broken. Byrum's face constricted tight, deep and utter shock overtook him.

"No. One. Has. Ever...you little rat!" He swept over to her and grabbed Magnincy again. "I will see to it that your body has no bonds left!"

His fingers began their terrible work when a book hit him in the back of the head. Byrum stopped and looked upward. Twenty feet above him stood Grubmush, in his arms he carried over a dozen books. Genuine curiosity broke through his rage as his face asked a question his lips did not.

"Books are the refuge of the weak!" bellowed Grubmush.

He scattered the books into the air, the pages flapping wildly in the wind. Byrum stepped backwards and flung Magnincy at Grubmush. The books burst into pieces as he made quick work of slicing them in half. The scattered pages fell like leaves in fall. Through the falling bits of parchment came Grubmush, his trident leading the way with his ceremonial owls feathers fluttering. The flurry of pages obscured Grubmush's assault. Byrum saw him a moment before he made contact and lashed out. A spatter of blood, and a clang of metal as the two impacted.

Byrum was slammed to the floor with Grubmush atop. His trident was split in half but his massive body crushed Byrum. Grubmush, unfazed by the impact, seized the Embers' hands causing him to shriek in pain. "Let's see what the soft man can do without his page-turning fingers!"

Grubmush crunched Byrum's fingers inside his own palms. Grubmush's fury was for the first time, the most welcome thing Huxley had ever seen. The predator-like intensity of Grubmush boring into his prey, made them seem less like combatants and more like wild animals. The Ember wept as he begged Grubmush to stop. Huxley suspected his words were as lost on him as a rabbit asking an owl to stop eating it. Blood dripped from Grubmush's face onto the Ember, and Huxley could see now that he wasn't totally successful in defending himself. His skin had split but was holding together. It didn't seem to hinder Grubmush. Sometime during the attack, Huxley had been released. He had hardly noticed. Elatress must have because she made straight for Abernathy. Together they removed his restraints and pulled him out.

Huxley reached for Magnincy but immediately felt madness invading, waiting just on the outskirts to take over his mind.

One or two uses without the Grimoire and I could be through, he thought to himself.

You are close now, find me! The voice spoke. It was the same voice that had been calling to him ever since he arrived in Danador.

Huxley gasped and was bathed in relief. The voice had, in fact, come from here. He looked to his companions for confirmation but they were busy. Grubmush was crippling Byrum and Elatress was helping Abernathy.

"How? Where?" Huxley responded. There was a pregnant pause and after a few seconds, it whispered, *Below. Follow the path.*

He remembered when Onders was testing him walking downward many flights of stone steps but it was hopelessly twisted and confusing. Perhaps sensing his hesitance, Huxley felt his head nudge towards a door to the side of the library. It may have even been the one he went through before but it was impossible to remember. *I will guide you*, It said, *But you must escape from him first.*

Huxley made for the door and said, "Oh don't worry about Byrum. Grubmush took care of him already."

"Not Byrum."

"Who then?"

Ember of the Arcane Flame and Chief Researcher of the Lost and Forgotten, Maddox, had heard enough. The air pulled from the room, replaced with a thickness that felt like they'd have to push through it. It became so difficult, in fact, that most in the room stopped moving. The only sound they made was their surprised gasps, which only made things worse. Each breath invaded their lungs and gummed them up even more. Maddox swept through the room, examining each of them like a scientist examining a specimen.

"I hope you understand the full breadth of the compliment you are about to receive though, the nescient rarely do...Abernathy, you impress me."

He smiled at him as he struggled with the rest. "I bet you orchestrated this whole fiasco, didn't you?" Maddox asked the question but wasn't really interested in the response. He leaned in, eyebrows raised as he examined Abernathy, surveying his face.

"The Norun..." he said but then acted like he was reading a banner "The saviors of Magnadun! What a joke. You would lick his boots and thank him for the chance."

Abernathy's eyes flared but the usual amber glow tinged brighter. Huxley realized he had never seen him like this before. Hatred spewed forth, the emotion like a foreign concept to Abernathy. Huxley had seen Abernathy frustrated, and even annoyed, but hatred was something new.

"There's the true man, I suspect. The one that hides behind free food and booze to gain loyalty. The one who came to Danador to destroy knowledge and claim headship of Magnadun. As I said before, I am impressed. You have managed much with little. A hallmark of the Norun I think. My Wardens were far too eager for the comforts you provided. They let their guard down. You got within striking distance of the tower and of our knowledge." He outstretched his hands reverently skyward. "We will destroy him."

Abernathy gasped and his eyes began to glaze over. "Your lungs are straining to pull oxygen. I imagine the burn is intense. The brute will last the longest but even his strength won't save him." He rounded on

Grubmush who was indeed thrashing to stay on his feet, "Your people are dying by the score against my Embers, burned into the streets having no one to blame but their own nescience. Never has a group of people rallied around their own stupidity as your own. I suppose it would be maddening to be that simple-minded. To see the creations around them, not understand how they work, then lash out like a fool. It's a common and predictable nescient trait. You created a simple religion around hurting oneself. Fortunately, such fanaticism has led you to kill yourselves so at least we won't have to go outside our walls to do it."

He rolled his eyes and turned to look at Elatress.

"At least your people have a use. Finding things is key for the serval class. It's why Ryla has worked so well for me. She has allowed my hand to stretch further than I thought initially possible. And, oh, the terror she creates! Having her stalk around talking about her paintings. Art is so strange to the populace that just her presence caused a stir."

Grubmush, Abernathy, Elatress and Huxley were all faltering. Their bodies wavered and began collapsing. "No! No, not yet." His fingers released some Magnincy and a breath of oxygen found its way to their mouths.

He looked Elatress up and down, sneered, saying, "You and Abernathy belong together. The two of you running around my city meeting with all the urchins, pretending to be beyond my sight. You even snared the thief for me."

Maddox was now overshadowing Huxley. "I wonder what stories you told yourself about my Grimoire. Young men are perhaps the easiest to understand, they want women, money or power. It's always one of those." He smirked and added, "Usually all three. But you wanted just the one, the same as I. That's why I know you so well. You stole power, claimed it as your own, and when you look at yourself in the mirror I bet you even call yourself a hero; someone destined for greatness. A nescient thief from nowhere grabbed something that others worked for and now claims he is someone special."

He grabbed Huxley's jaw, his spider-like fingers wrapped wholly around his face. "You are no one's heir. That note was written to me many years ago...I just never took it out." His clammy palm squeezed tighter as if to make the point for him. "I think I was being sentimental."

A sob crawled its way out of Huxley. He looked down, feeling his will giving way to sorrow. Deep down he knew Maddox was right. He wanted to scream and fight, but he knew. He was no one's heir, especially not whoever wrote the Grimoire. Through some mistake, it had been delivered to him. He let himself get swept up in the hero sagas that he consumed so often as a child. Perhaps he was the fool people so often told him he was. Which would be bad enough, but realizing that every-one believed it felt like a dagger plunged into his heart. They were going to pay the price for his foolishness. Tears stained the floor. Close to losing consciousness, Huxley collapsed.

You are an heir. The voice called again.

"No," Huxley stated in denial. "I can't listen anymore."

You are.

"No!"

Yes, It breathed. *He is telling you about himself. He is the one that stole.*

"How could you know that? How would you know anything like that?" Huxley demanded.

Maddox leaned in closer. Confused, it didn't take long for under-standing to dawn on him. Uncertainty cracked his calm. "Who are you speaking to?"

Then a breeze pushed its way into the room. Slow at first, but then it began sweeping the pages torn out by Byrum, swirling them around the room. Huxley's friends sucked air into their lungs. Maddox seized Huxley's hands trying to get him to release his Magnincy only to find he had none. Byrum lay passed out from the pain of Grubmush's assault. Maddox spun around to every corner trying to find who had given this room air to breathe when his own apprentice appeared.

"He's not the thief," Onders confessed.

Maddox drew up to his full height. Calm now restored, he shot his hands out and blanketed the room in thick air once more.

"He's also not a fool."

Huxley looked up at her but she was totally focused on Maddox, which was probably wise.

"It is the Embers who have been fools. Keeping knowledge hidden away and making others into slaves with promises you never intend to keep."

Maddox remained unmoved, "Ambition is critical in becoming an Ember, one cannot reach Magnincy without it, but yours has always been suicidally strong...which will be your doom today."

Onders stepped forward, "You don't know what he can do, do you? You never even bothered to find out. Huxley has figured out aspects of Magnincy you have been blind to...true nescience."

Maddox stiffened and set his jaw. His control wavered and just as Huxley was about to seize Magnincy, the stairway above came crashing down onto Maddox. It flung him a dozen feet away and he clattered to the floor. A faint humming from the other side of the room told him what had happened. Abernathy had moved it by exuding his spirit. He must be so exhausted, how could he have managed it? Maddox's Magnincy dropped from the air and Grubmush and Elatress sprang to their feet. Both leapt at the fallen Ember but were caught mid-air. He may have been injured but he was far from defeated. Maddox held them aloft and was about to speak when another stairway crashed toward him. Onders joined in with a stream of books that had fallen to the floor. They flowed on an invisible river directed by her and released at Maddox.

"Get downstairs!" Abernathy commanded Huxley. "We will hold him off."

"You can't beat him alone!" Huxley responded, "I can help!"

"None of this will mean anything if you don't get down there. Trust us! We can handle him...just hurry!"

He is right. The voice affirmed.

Huxley forgot his pain and forced his body up.

"Where do I go?"

The second door to your left.

Huxley sprinted for it when Elatress called out, "Wait! Huxley!"

"What?!"

"Open that other door first!"

He pointed at the one he was passing.

"Yes!"

He grabbed it and as soon as the door clicked, Arktos burst in, nearly knocking him off his feet. Blood-soaked and raging, Arktos had looked to have been trying to get in for some time. His claws and fangs glistened in the lamp light, gone was the gentle bear who would beg for scraps from under the bar. This bear wasn't the same one he knew. This one was a momma defending its cubs. Huxley actually felt a moment of remorse about letting it loose in the room. When Maddox cried out at the sight of him, it helped abate that feeling.

"Go!" Abernathy said as Maddox attacked again. The lanterns flared up and a net of fire began knitting itself around the room.

Huxley finally found his feet and opened the door the voice had told him to. Dark and ancient stairs greeted him as he dashed down into the depths of the College.

34

❦

Bioluminescence and Tunnels

"Luciferin or photoprotein/luciferase must interact to produce illumination. The enzyme interacts with the substrate affecting the release of chemical reaction." **-Page 437 Excerpt from the Grimoire**

Huxley's stomach dropped a few times as he threw himself down the stairs. He knew he was gambling with each step because his eyes hadn't had time to adjust and the only light was the bioluminescence of the lichen that grew on the stones. At a gentle stroll, it would be enough, but each blast from upstairs quickened his pace. He didn't know if his friends were dying trying to hold Maddox off. Onders proving trustworthy was perhaps the biggest surprise of the day. His thoughts turned to her and he stumbled again. He pushed such thoughts from his mind and forced himself to concentrate. Each passing moment increased the chances Maddox was killing them. There was little chance the Embers would take prisoners. Too much damage had been done. And so he hurled himself down the steps, in reckless regard for the insufficient light, following a mysterious voice that he was hoping would be the answer he was searching for. Perhaps, he might even find an ally to help in the fight.

The path twisted and turned, sometimes leading to larger rooms, but usually just down. *Follow the path,* it instructed. Huxley's plague of

405

questions bounced around inside his brain. Never had he communicated with a voice inside his own head. He couldn't be crazy because the voice seemed to know where he was going and seemed to know details that Huxley wasn't privy to. The line of illuminated fungi grew thicker the deeper he descended. The bricks blurred together and the air grew cold. It was not like the cold from a blustery snowstorm. This cold was old, like an ancient resting place that had grown lonely and forgotten. The kind of cold that hadn't been disturbed in years. He felt like he shouldn't be here. But onward the voice commanded, so Huxley followed.

His eyes were adjusting now and the mushroom luminescence filled each room. The greenish-blue glow now shined and grew thicker in corners. The stalks, he could now see, contained speckles of orange. The colors and light grew brighter and brighter with each new staircase he found. His eyes weren't just adjusting, the lichen was growing stronger.

You are close now, Huxley. Soon we will meet.

He entered a chamber that opened wide on both sides. Huge columns lined the room and propped up the ceiling. His steps were quieted by the mushroom covered walls in what should have been an echo filled room. He suddenly felt tiny after being so cramped in the hallways above. How could a room this big exist so far underground? Then he saw it. A wooden door adorned with carvings and crowned with lichen. It shone brightly.

You may need to shove the door...it hasn't been opened in many years. The voice was now so clear, he would have believed it was in the same room.

Huxley approached and asked, "These carvings...they're the same as above. What are they?"

They are symbols of understanding and praise.

Huxley raised an eyebrow, "Praise?" He pushed on the ancient door. It moved slowly, shaking off many years of dust and grout that had accumulated around its sides. Huxley slipped into the room and saw him.

"Grubmush wasn't entirely wrong about you Huxley. You are something of a prophet."

———————————————————————————

Grubmush found the fight he had been looking for all of his life. Once he thought it might have been Faldurin himself, but he was utterly ruined before he even saw her. That lesson had been instructional. An Ember, on the other hand, had flaws, though this one had yet to show his. Byrum had shown himself easy to goad and with a weakness for books. He was easily exploited and crumbled as all soft men do. Maddox was far different. He was angry like so many but kept his temper. He would attack but not leave himself open for counter. He was fighting balanced. Grubmush always favored attack as most had never been attacked by someone like him before and usually didn't know what to do. The exception was Ryla. She had predicted him as he was attempting to do now. How had she read him so well?

Maddox had shifted his tactics from denying everyone oxygen to ranged attacks. He may have surmised they didn't have arrows or other ranged weapons and so he adapted. For a book learner, he fought well. For that matter, the others were accomplished in combat as well. He only truly understood the bear, but Elatress spun and slashed like something from the wilds herself. Onders attempted to match her superior in ability, which was proving fruitless, though he clearly thought of her as the main priority. And Abernathy didn't attack at all. In fact, he had limped off once the fighting had begun. Grubmush hadn't thought him a coward before. Even wounded, a true predator could be dangerous, and Abernathy was the most wounded of all of them.

Grubmush was thrown again. The Ember had centered himself in the middle of the library and lifted high in the air. Many tendrils came from his chest and they swung around the room violently which provided both attack and defense. Grubmush was eager to destroy him. His hands felt light and empty without his trident. The ceremonial talon of the great Owl was gone. Hewn and broken on the floor, it lay useless but a true predator did not need his talons, he did not need his claws, his fangs, only his heart. Grubmush huffed deep, filling his lungs with Magnadun's renewing air and moved to kill the Ember.

Elatress had managed to keep away from the worst of it, both in the library and in her head but she was being attacked on both fronts. Her instinct was to hit her slower target with a hatchet throw, he likely didn't have the reaction time to dodge, but those arms were a problem. They seemed to instinctually act on his behalf. He seemed to care nothing for the preservation of the books that the others cared so greatly for. She hadn't accounted for that. She had only gained one good strike on Maddox so far when Arktos rushed into the room; he and Grubmush attacked together. She exploited that momentary lapse of concentration with a chunk out of his backside. She had hoped it was going to slow him down, and it had but only a moment. Maddox had resewn his skin though. Kill shots only then, she thought, or we could weaken him into madness. But how long would that take? No telling with this guy. No, she thought, better just chop his head off. Next time his back was turned, she would get it done.

——————————————————————————————————-

Abernathy could really use a drink. Not just a drink, but a whole night of drinking. And a spiced flank of meat. It didn't even matter what kind so long as it made his eyes water when the flavor hit. Normally, he'd want a fluffy mound of mashed potatoes with that but at this moment he wanted more of a sweet side dish. Glazed carrots or honey-drizzled asparagus, really anything with sugar poured on it.

His mouth watered as he lurched towards Maddox's office, leaving bloody hand prints and ample globs of whatever else was leaking out of him, along the way. He expected he was leaving the longest and most clear trail known to man. The only thing left was a sign saying, "Wounded Abernathy this way!" This had not gone at all to plan, though it hadn't gone totally off the rails either. He expected a fight, but he also expected to be armed. He was sure Onders had given him up when he was getting his armor. And she really had. *She's young and arrogant*, he thought, *she likely believed her plan was better.* In a way it was, the Ember's likely suspected something. At least this way she could have controlled more of what was waiting for them. She had been so difficult to read, even for him. She was so scared, and vulnerable, but equally brave and driven. Her sacrifice today was going to cost her more than perhaps anyone else, which was saying something. Her trust in them was a heavyweight, one among many that Abernathy carried. Bearing that, was part of being a Norun. It was who he was and it was his honor and duty to do so. Being worthy of it, was another matter altogether. So far every choice he had made, every sacrifice given, and every lie told was in service of getting to this moment. Standing inside this tower and freeing Danador, and by extension, Magnadun. All of that would be in vain if they died here.

Grubmush was flung through the wall cracking into the other side, stone and mortar crumbling on top of him. Abernathy turned to try and help but the Dathu was back on his feet before Abernathy could turn around. Grubmush bellowed from deep within. Abernathy could see Grubmush's soul shake. Of all the people in Magnadun, there may be no one who was less internally conflicted than Grubmush. Arktos joined him at a high rate of speed, and the two completed the hole in the second wall that Grubmush had started.

A crippled Abernathy would be no help here. He had to get to that office. Only thirty feet or so away now. They just had to hold on.

———————————————————————————————————————

Huxley stepped into his dreams. A vast ocean with stars reached far out before him. One step through the door, and he was already waist-deep. He was no longer in a chamber but somewhere else entirely. Perhaps, truly, it was his dream. Maybe Maddox had caught him just as he was stepping through the doorway, and he had been killed.

"You are not dead, and this is not a dream, Huxley." The voice clarified. It filled his mind and calmed him. It calmed him in such a way Huxley never thought possible. It reverberated through his body. His muscles relaxed, his heart felt emboldened and all traces of madness abated. He couldn't even remember what it had felt like, all he knew was he was centered in a way he had never been before. Stars above, stars below and somewhere there was a line of water that he waded through. How deep the water was, he had no idea. He could be swimming or flying. With each passing moment, he became less sure he even cared. He might have even fallen asleep if not for the crashes that shook the walls. It jogged his memory and brought him back to the purpose of his being here, though, it didn't seem important anymore, like a memory of another life. The stars danced around him like Magnincy, leading him forward. Each star was becoming more and more known to him each day. He could see them now, as pieces of information and subjects of science. The more known to him, the brighter it shined. But more than familiar, they were fast becoming a part of him. He felt less like he was seizing something and more like he had a place amongst them. It was like they were partners, both working towards the same goal. The stars stopped swirling at random and began moving together, striving towards a point, a singular star that shone brighter than the others. He knew what it was right away. It was the first piece of Magnincy he ever held and likely the most powerful. It burned brightly and the others circled it, making mesmerizing circles.

"Hello Huxley, welcome to my home."

"Who? Wha-"

"And your home is curiosity. It always has been, ever since you were a baby you wanted to know more. My inquisitive Huxley."

"My?"

The star's points softened as he got closer. The lines drew inward and redefined in shape. A body emerged. As Huxley drew closer, its shine lessened and he could see it for what it was. The place around him formed into a room. He was still in the tower. He was shin-deep in frigid water. And in the middle of the room was a man bound to a stone table. He had nothing but threadbare cloth covering him. He emanated light but it was focused now, understandable. It was a man, chained and facing upward. He turned his neck and faced Huxley, "Yes...my heir."

———————————————————————————————————

Abernathy DelaCourt of the Norun, Owner/Operator of the Gearbox ™ and the Grand Craftsman and Lord Engineer of Danador's Railways and Savior of the Crag Villages of Valdannon, was going to die in a hallway.

He knew this much blood loss coupled with, not-the-most-healthy lifestyle, wouldn't allow him to last long. Maddox was as powerful as he had feared. Before the world split, he may have been a match for him, or at least had put up a fight. Maddox must have spent the majority of the last twenty years studying. Not just studying but researching, fine-tuning, experimenting, and more important, he hadn't used much of it in practice. His mind was well-rested and ready to stretch itself. Abernathy was well acquainted with most sciences. His people may not have drawn on science for Magnincy but they had made great strides in it. At their peak, the Norun's technology far out-reached Danador. But they were far older and had a big leg up during their early development. The Embers of Danador had painstakingly acquired their knowledge. Through fair or foul they had gained it, and now Huxley threatened to undo all of their work.

As Abernathy collapsed in exhaustion, he couldn't help but be a little bit proud of what he achieved. Getting an Heir so far into the tower had always been a fool's hope, one the Norun didn't have much faith in, but it remained their duty to see it through. Abernathy felt his strength leaving and fought to keep his eyes open. Elatress, Grubmush, Arktos and even Onders were still attempting to win against Maddox. He was so proud of those kids. Their sacrifice and courage was more than what he deserved to be a part of. Darkness slithered its way into his vision and blood caught in his throat. Elatress was going to be ok, he thought. She has a new family that can help her. If she finally learns to open up and if she survives the day, she will be ok.

"You've made an awful mess of my floors, Abernathy," a warm voice spoke. "I don't have the time to mop this up."

Abernathy looked up.

Walters, the Ember's scribe and Warden stood over him, reaching down with his hand outstretched. Abernathy took it after a moment of disbelief. Walters lifted him up with a vigor that Abernathy would not believe rested in such a frail man.

"Your leg and armor were in my office. Maddox must think it's a storage shed." His face scrunched up tighter than normal, causing the lines to deepen so far, they disappeared.

"Uhh, right, it will take me some time to-"

"No, no, I brought them of course." He waved off Abernathy's thanks and said, "They smelled horrible. Please don't bring them back to the tower, ever." Walters finally let go of Abernathy's hand. He'd been shaking it the whole time.

"Heck of a handshake you got there, Walters." Abernathy eyed him strangely. He glanced down at the grip marks on his arm. The marks were still fresh, but fading.

"I do lots of writing, it helps."

Abernathy nodded, "It must."

With that, Walters turned to leave. Abernathy felt a bit of strength return.

————————————————————————————————-

Huxley staggered backward. The transcendent feeling of swimming in the stars faded and reality found him again. His memories and mind woke up. Totally rested, he questioned the man before him.

"I'm your heir?" Huxley repeated back as though he hadn't heard right.

"Yes." The man echoed again, but in a gentle tone that Huxley found disarming. It didn't frighten him, instead, it was like a concert of agreement.

"But, you are not my father, my father is-."

"That's not what makes you my heir."

Huxley blinked and began again, "But-"

"Come closer, my heir."

"I-"

"I can show you better than I can tell you." The man moved his body and the chains clinked but kept him secured. His body's movement disturbed the dust and dirt that had settled on him. How long had it been since he tried to move? The chains were secured deep under the water, thick and sturdy. They cinched his arms down in a manner similar to how they had tied up Onders, so she couldn't grasp at Magnincy.

Huxley moved closer.

"If I'm your heir, then who are you?"

"Your questions, do they burn within you as they did me?" He chuckled and said, "It's been so long since I've had a question...a real one anyway...be sure you want them answered. I know that burn, I miss it often. It drives you, makes you reach, makes you push, but the answer may not be the wood for your fire, but rather, a wash of water."

"I...yes?"

"Of course, you do. I only asked because it reminded me of what it felt like. One who has reached for the cosmos can never be satisfied without answers. The only problem is, you don't really know what question you want answered. You have to-"

Huxley stepped forward and interrupted, "How do I save my friends?"

He shook his head and said "No, you know that."

"How do-"

"No, you know that."

"If I-"

"No."

"How come it-"

"No."

Each "no" echoed, and Huxley stepped even closer, growing frustrated.

"Why won't you just tell-"

"You know why."

"I DON'T KNOW WHY!" He bellowed, "I DON'T KNOW ANYTHING! I'M JUST A FOOLISH KID FROM NOWHERE TO-TALLY OUT OF HIS ELEMENT, TRYING TO SAVE MY FAMILY AND FRIENDS! IT'S LIKE MAGNADUN HAS GONE CRAZY AND ONLY I'M TRYING TO STOP IT! IT'S NOT SUPPOSED TO BE THIS WAY!"

Huxley's voice rung over the stones and rippled the water and finally, the man breathed out satisfied and said, "Ahhh, you're looking right at it now."

"....what?" Huxley said out of breath and casting around for what he was talking about.

"Your question, *the* question."

Huxley tried to get a hold of himself, but he wasn't expecting riddles. His friends were likely dying only a short distance away from an Ember who hoarded every last bit of knowledge for himself. The city they were in was being attacked by a strange race of people who showed up when the world was torn asunder. A race who shouldn't even be here but whatever happened ... His thoughts trailed off as a question occurred to him.

"What happened to Magnadun?"

The man nodded and said, "Are you ready for the answer?"

Huxley nodded desperately. Deep down he wasn't truly certain he was ready, but he had no choice. Everything might depend on it.

"Touch my hand and you'll know."

———————————————————————————————

Abernathy did one last check on the fasteners. They held tight and strong. Closing his eyes, he hummed and found his resonance. It glowed outwards wrapping around his armor and infusing it with life. When he moved, it did so as a part of him, knowing intrinsically what he wanted from it without asking. He stood up to his full height, the boots of his armor bringing him well above seven feet tall. His weapons spun to life and the face plate snapped shut. "Time to be rid of this Ember."

———————————————————————————————

Elatress picked herself up off of Arktos. He seemed happy to have her off of him. Both of them were battered, but not broken. She had managed to avoid the Ember's most deadly attacks. For that, she credited her natural agility, but deep down she knew if she had his full attention she wouldn't have fared so well. Fights and brawls weren't that uncommon for her, but this was different. Maddox wielded strength that even the most savage beasts of the Wilds couldn't match. She watched as he broke off his attack on them and blew open the floor. Huxley was a success, it seemed but now had to fight Maddox alone. She instinctively reached for her hatchets but found only one. The other was likely lost in the rubble of their melee. Thousands of books lie in tattered ruins around her, pages and spines ripped to shreds. A few fires were beginning to take shape. She reached out and felt Grubmush under a deep pile of broken bookcases. He was badly wounded but nothing like the Lecture Hall. He would live. Even now, he was thrashing to escape. It was the other body that concerned her. It moved erratically and grasped at nothingness. Its steps were random and confused. Onders was wounded and in more than a bad way.

A gauntlet patted her on the shoulder. As Abernathy stepped beside her with heavy footfalls. He looked her up and down, "You ok?"

She shrugged, a motion he had seen many times before. "I'll live."

"Any episodes?"

"Yes, many."

"Are you going to make it?"

"It'll be rough...but yes."

He snorted through his faceplate. She could hear his mustache swish against the metal.

"I have to go deal with him. Stay here with Arktos, don't risk anymore, ok? You've done so well, little one."

She smiled.

Abernathy approached the newly destroyed library as Onders began to crumble under Maddox's attacks. She faltered and collapsed. Abernathy whistled as Maddox continued his attack, but now focused it upon the floor of the library.

"Nescience...everywhere." He muttered. "He was too stupid to see that we were trying to help him. Your little thief friend, *Huxley*, may have gained intelligence but he lacks the wisdom to use it."

"You have underestimated us at every turn," Abernathy stated, his armored legs stomping through the broken books and pages, "it is you and your kind that has been nescient. Now, a fully armored Norun stands before you...I won't go down so easily this time."

"Very well then, Norun, you will be the fir-" an orb cracked next to him spraying hissing green acid.

Maddox screamed and tried to summon Magnincy, but it had coated his hands and they were shaking in pain. Abernathy kept up the assault, his armor releasing orbs out from his shoulders, fed from a storage unit in the back. They lobbed through the air, each containing different chemical compounds. Alone they were harmless enough but once the seal internally was broken and they mixed...

————————————————————————————————————

The Norun would have to be wiped out. Abernathy had so much knowledge that he didn't. Maddox's mind shook. It had been many years since he felt strain like this. If he engaged with the Norun now he would lose. Not the fight but the war. The Norun would slow him down long enough for the heir to reach him. And he could not abide that. Maddox lashed out.

35

∿

Magnadun and Heirs

"Lighthouses are the most widely used beacons, however any easily seen mark will suffice. Guiding navigators to their intended destinations is their chief function. A beacon's job left undone can lead to sailors becoming lost, marooned or perished." **-Page 62 Excerpt from the Grimoire**

Huxley reached for his hand but just as they were about to touch, the roof split apart, sheared open in a circle. Lamplight flooded the chamber as Maddox descended into the room. Bloodied and disheveled. Malice twisted his face, as hatred curled through his body.

"NESCIENCE", He seethed.

"Huxley, touch my hand now."

"But what if-"

"No, you know that!"

"But-"

"Huxley now!"

Maddox's hands moved in a blur, seizing what looked to be dozens, maybe more, stars of Magnincy. He unleashed them as fast as he had grabbed them. Orbs, brilliant light, shards, gasses, and all manner of physics hurled toward him. Huxley stretched his hand forward and the two connected minds.

Maddox and his unleashed torments halted. The College of the Arcane Flame melted away and Huxley found himself among the cosmos. Not a dream, not a vision, but he was there. Looking down at Magnadun. It looked tiny at first, like a marble from childhood but it grew bigger so that he could take it all in. It floated in space, tranquil and still. From this vantage, the world seemed without a care that a bloody rage-fueled battle was happening on its surface.

"Beautiful isn't it?" The man asked.

"Yes," Huxley admitted.

"But badly and horribly scarred."

Huxley didn't know what he meant, it didn't look like that to him. He could only see a living breathing planet, more detailed and alive than any map could hope to produce. He managed to pry his gaze away.

"Is this a vision like my dreams or are we here?"

"Does it matter?"

"I-uh wait, that reminds me, what were my dreams?"

The man perked up and said "Ah yes, the further away you were I could only send images and feelings, the closer you got I could speak directly to you. Sorry if it scared you, it was my means of bringing you to me. I'm actually doing that with a few other people right now."

Huxley nodded acknowledging he heard him but likely didn't understand him.

"Are you God?" He asked next.

A warm smile formed and he said, "No, but I do know him."

"You know God?" And before he could answer Huxley blurted out, "He's not a giant Owl is he?!"

The man laughed and shook his head, "No but who Grubmush calls Faldurin is pretty close to the truth, she's like me. As for God...well...to you, he's God. To me he's-" But he caught himself, saying more than perhaps he thought he should. "Let's not get ahead of ourselves. No, I am not God. But I am part of Magnadun, and Magnincy itself."

The answer gave Huxley enough to process for perhaps a lifetime.

"So the stars?" Huxley asked.

"Which ones?"

"The ones I see that I shouldn't." He clarified.

"Ah!" The being chuckled. "Do you like them? It was my suggestion. When things get nebulous like amounts of knowledge and ability, I thought it best if we could see our options splayed before us. You know, so you can make the best choice. I chose the stars because of the link between you and him. But they aren't stars at all. Just representations of your accumulated knowledge that is your inheritance. He liked my idea so that's how we do it. It used to be so much more chaotic."

Huxley nodded but it was more acknowledging that he heard him.

The being sighed and said, "The cosmos is large, Huxley." He held his palm outward gesturing to everything, "And that is perhaps the most understated statement that has ever been. Let's, you and I, focus on Magnadun first."

"...ok" Huxley responded, feeling more than worried about the implications.

"And no, I am not a god or angel or anything like that. I am like you. A son of Danador who ascended. No more divine or less divine than you are."

"Am I at all?"

"Of course you are. We all were born under the stars and all of us have his light within."

"You sound a LOT like Grubmush now."

"Well, like I said, he's not entirely wrong. In fact, he might be one of the best teachers you can find for understanding." He waved that away again and said, "But like I stated before, let's not get focused on the wrong thing here. That tends to happen to us inquisitive types." He said with a smirk. "Maddox is still there, after all, and every moment we linger is another we can't get back."

"Time hasn't stopped? It feels like it has," then Huxley shrugged, adding, "I guess I don't really know what that feels like though."

"No, I just increased your perception and ability to process information. It feels slow because you can perceive and understand everything happening around you. Slowing time is really complicated, and I'm trying not to overwhelm you."

Huxley blinked and was about to ask a question but guessed the answer first.

"Huxley you're going to have to accept that you have real limitations. It is what you can do inside those limitations that is important. Everyone and everything has limitations. As a child, you thought your parents knew everything. As a young man, you assumed the Embers did. And now, meeting me, you think I do. The same way your parents didn't share everything with you as a child, is the same reason I don't share everything with you now. You have grown so much and are far more capable than you think. But I know you. I have watched you for some time now. You have achieved far more than the others."

Huxley's eyebrows raised.

"By that, I mean, there are many heirs. Everyone that receives a Grimoire, is an heir. It's a system we put into place to try and help ease a mind into the nature of Magnadun so we could expand knowledge. The way we used to do it was...abrupt." Regret passed over his face but soon vanished as he continued on, "Everyone has limitations...which leads me to your first question, the one that brought us here." He gestured over Magnadun. "What happened to it." His voice lowered as though whispering, but no one was around to hear them. Huxley thought it odd but was too interested to comment. "It is no secret it has shifted greatly. Please do not become frustrated with me, as an heir, you are owed an explanation but as a limited being, you won't understand all of it..." He smiled and said, "I did warn you."

Huxley nodded with acceptance.

"Magnadun wasn't always Magnadun, in fact, it used to be five different planets nearby each other, at least cosmically speaking. Each of the five peoples of Magnadun had existed on their own planets and communed with the Kindler...or God as you put it...but I call him the Kindler."

"So does Abernathy."

"Well, of course he knows his name." He said offhandedly then continued, "You see, being a higher being with near limitless capabilities, can be lonesome. One's mind needs stimulation, so he decided to create us. The only problem is, making something equal to yourself instantly is about impossible. It has to be grown over time. But how does one grow a race of people? The Kindler didn't know the answer to that question. (Remember what I said about limitations). But, he tried anyway. His idea was that he needed to start small and work his way up. He made the Norun first and communed with them directly, soul to soul. It worked, but still they couldn't understand all aspects of himself that he wanted to share with them. They only felt him in their own way. He had more he wanted from them. But they were incapable. So he created others. Those who could see his world for the artistic possibilities it could be, those who could see the brilliance of the science at work around them," He nodded to Huxley, "those that could take full use of their physical bodies and those gifted with perception so they could be totally aware of the world they'd been given."

He let that sink in a moment and then went on, "In these five peoples he was known, and they knew him. No one knew all parts of him, but he was happy with this arrangement as it could always evolve into something greater. He gifted his children five planets to live and thrive on. It went this way for many generations...until he was discovered. This is where my knowledge is limited but I will still try to answer your question. There are other great powers at work in the cosmos. I do not know if they exceed his or not, but they certainly did not agree with him creating us. Whether sentenced or asked, he was told to destroy us. When the time came, he couldn't. How could a parent ever do that to his children? But he was still compelled to act. In this, he destroyed the planets, saving a select few of the people from each. Those who had known him best were relocated. He sectioned off parts of the planet and made a new one, stitched together in a last-ditch effort to save at least some of us. Using intense growth and fecundity he sealed the separate pieces into...Magnadun."

Huxley's eyes saw it now as he never had before. The planet wasn't a planet at all, but an amalgamation of many! It made so much sense. The sudden appearance of the Wilds wasn't a random act but the act of a God. The Forty-Five must have been where his cut ran...and a chilling realization came over Huxley. "How many died?"

He nodded his head reverently.

"Now you see the source of the Embers' anger."

"How many?" Huxley pressed.

"Remember what I said about lim-"

"HOW MANY?"

He sighed, eyes welling up and his voice shook, "I can't know for certain...millions at least, perhaps billions." He stated.

Huxley stumbled backwards. He didn't even know that many people could exist. And they were all gone, just like that. Because God or the Kindler...got in trouble?

"Does it bother you that the Kindler is flawed? It is a troubling notion to wrestle with. I have found most people accept two outcomes, anger and an eagerness to see him destroyed as the Embers are trying to do, or a begrudging acceptance and willingness to work within that knowledge. I see the logic in both but doubt the Embers can be successful in the way they wish."

"You mean there's a chance? Can they actually destroy him?"

His face scrunched up. "I don't know if the Kindler can be destroyed...but I believe their plan has merit and can do enormous damage. The answer is, in a sense, perhaps, but not totally. It is more likely they will destroy Magnadun, and certainly Danador. That is why I have resisted them for so long and called out so loudly for you to come."

"Why me though? What makes me special?"

"It isn't that you're special. You aren't my only chosen champion. You are just the only one to be successful, so far. Like I said before, I have been sending out Grimoires to anyone who has reached for the truth of Magnadun. The difficulty of understanding the Grimoire coupled with the promise of what it can bring is the perfect kindle for Magnincy. Their hearts are calling out for what they know is there. Magnincy is your birthright. He has made you to wield it. It is birthed in you, and you are right to seek it. Not everyone is capable. In fact, most aren't. Magnincy is available to anyone, but only those whose minds reach for it; and I mean truly reach for the knowledge that is Magnincy. You have been doing that all of your life. In the world, before it was combined, Magnincy was taught widely and gifted to everyone who came asking. But the Embers, in their fear, wasted time hoarding the knowledge, suppressing any who they deemed unworthy. They felt they had to act now before the Kindler decided to change things again. Like many would-be heirs, they wanted their inheritance before it was time to receive it."

"But what if the Kindler really does destroy Magnadun again? Aren't the Embers a little bit right to try and stop him from doing that? Should I try?" Huxley asked.

"That question is what drives the Embers to commit the crimes they do...when you escaped that night you were nearly part of it. They have been capturing heirs, like you, who have come to the college searching for answers. Instead of training and teaching them, they just overload them and have their minds crack. When the madness takes hold they position assistants outside their cells to record their ravings. When a mind breaks and they see all that science can offer it is overwhelming to the individual, but a careful ear can learn much. Far far more than careful research, which can take years. But a broken mind can make scientific progress in moments. So the Embers break the young, like you." His face grimaced at the next part and he said, "Even now, there are scores of young people throughout the tower who will never recover. Shouting formulas, ratios, and chemical compounds. They have given Maddox so much knowledge he and his Embers have ascended into a true danger for their world. They just need another week or so. Getting close to a goal tends to make people lose sight of the details like how they treat people. Or capturing young men who have produced mighty amounts of Magnincy..."

"They were forcefully breaking people's minds to expedite their research?"

He nodded.

"And they only didn't catch me that day because I attacked rather than fight it?"

"Well, yes and no. The star that you flung at Onders is what gave them caution. It is rare." He explained.

Huxley blinked and said, "Wait! Yes, what was the star I threw that day? I didn't know anything yet, so how could I have used it."

He nodded and said, "That, I believe, is why you made it here today." He paused and looked for the right words. "It was the Arcane Flame."

Huxley looked down at his chest as though he could see it.

He went on, "It is perhaps the most artistic thing the Embers ever decided on. Every child of Magnadun has it in them. It is the desire to reach upward and understand their world. Some have far more that allow them to wield Magnancy. And some...are like you...who's flame burns so bright it can be wielded. You had no true scientific knowledge, but your body ached for it so badly you attacked with what you did have. It's dangerous to say the least, your body was not made to reach that far. Do it again and you won't come back I think, no matter how much humming or reading you've done. We used to use it to determine who would do my job. The embers see it as your potential. It takes exceptional amounts of ambition and stability. Perhaps you will take over for me soon..."

"Me?"

He waved his hand dismissively. "Don't worry about that now. For now let's focus on what's in front of us."

Magnadun dissolved and suddenly they were back in the chamber surrounded by water with stars reflecting and shining off the stones above. Maddox was moving toward them at a snail's pace, preceded by a mountain of Magnincy summoned by him. The moment this reached him, Huxley was done for. Sensing his fear, he looked at Huxley and reassured him, "Do not fear Maddox, he has let his fear turn to cruelty, hoping that it will save him. Fearful and cruel people can always be defeated by courage and kindness, and you have proven to have both."

"I appreciate that, but courage and kindness will not repel him, no matter how much I have."

He smirked again, "That is certainly true...Let me offer you a deal."

Eyeing the slowly moving wall of death Huxley figured he didn't have a choice. "I'll hear your deal." He stated.

"If you free me from my confines, I will let you understand the totality of the grimoire. All of its pages that you have memorized and agonized over. It will be as though you've had the privilege of education all of your life. Your understanding of it will be complete. But only for a few moments, I think."

"And once you're free, will you help me?"

"No...it would be unwise, I have been like this far too long...enslaved and tortured for many years now. I fear my own hand may bring about the same destruction you are hoping to avoid. It must be you...I have lived my time on Magnadun and done as I was asked. I need to leave...so if you free me, I will help you."

"But why only a few seconds? What can that do?"

"As I said before, you are like me. I am a human just like you, with the same capabilities and limitations. My mind was expanded to allow for the entirety of science to fill it. I can do the same for you, but only for a short time. Any longer, and you will crumble into more than madness." He saw Huxley's confusion and added, "Knowledge has to be earned over time, you were denied that. I can't undo the past, but I can allow you to be at your full potential for a short while."

Maddox drew closer. His rage and fear became overly apparent to Huxley. This man sought both of their deaths. Every decision he had made, every sacrifice and pain he endured, led him to this moment. Huxley reached out and allowed his mind to finally know everything.

36

Unlocked and Unbound

"Upon my death or madness deliver this Grimoire to its Heir."
-Slip of paper within the Grimoire

The pages of Grimoire flapped through his head and it was like he had written them himself. It was as though the world was strung together with tiny, invisible pieces that also were held together with even smaller pieces. Each one interacted with or rejected others; some had no reaction at all. Constant waves and pulses of energy, matter, and elements all weaving and combining. The forces of nature and reality all intertwined, he could perceive it.

Wait, not all of it. His knowledge was incomplete. Like the Grimoire, it had gaps in its knowledge. But the notes and theories written by other owners, filled in a good amount of what was missing. His mind suddenly connected all of the knowledge he had read countless times. Huxley's understanding had moved at such a sluggish rate, now it lay at his command, and not a moment too soon. Right, when it all clicked together for him, the man disappeared and time crashed back with a vengeance. Maddox's attacks, once seemingly so intricate and complex, were obvious and dull witted to him.

Huxley seized Magnincy as it presented itself before him. He flung a few elements out and rendered the bulk of the attack, inert. He completely wiped out what Maddox had summoned. The Ember hung in the air using a combination of air pressure density, individual weight mitigation and upward propulsion. It was clever, he didn't go all in so that if one failed, the others might make up for it. But it wasn't clever enough. Huxley waved it all away. Maddox plummeted. His rage bled into surprise and just a hint of fear. He splashed into the water and thrashed back to his feet. Huxley copied his technique though and added some flare of his own. He drew the damp air together under him forcing clouds to emerge. The warm and cold pushing together at his encouragement, sparks formed and rumbles of thunder issued forth. He smirked, "I've been told lightning is for simple trainee Embers who lack specialized knowledge. But right here at this moment, it seems appropriate, especially with you, knee-deep in water."

Maddox composed himself but couldn't help but sneer. "So...another Heir...another fool who thinks himself a hero. Another poor soul lied to by those that would condemn our planet to dust for their flawed god's miscalculations. Can't you see it now? Can't you see? I. CAN. BEAT. HIM!" Each word was a monument to his arrogance.

"You would have had all of Danador crawl around in the mud in service to you sacrificing our lives as you saw fit." Huxley reprimanded, "And in that way how are you any different than him?"

Maddox's face dropped, the heat of his anger draining into a cold, murderous pale. "Perhaps this god would destroy us. Perhaps he had no choice. I do not know him. But I do know you. And trading him for you would be true madness."

Maddox seized Magnincy again and before he released it said, "What do you think will happen? That you'll you become like us? A great hero to Danador? A great hero to Mayburn? You will never be as great as us!"

"Maybe I won't be great...but I can be passable." Huxley declared.

He let the charged air release into the water. There was a crack of thunder and blinding light. Maddox screamed.

Huxley launched out of the room. The air cracked into the void left by his sudden disappearance, and within seconds he emerged high over

Danador. He could feel his time slipping away. Guessing he had less than a minute before his knowledge left him. He shouldn't have paused to verbally spar with Maddox. Maddox's mind was slipping and his friends could take him now. But there were still sixteen Embers at war with Grubmush's people and they were losing warriors by the hundreds. About forty seconds remained...he would have to act fast. He shot towards the bulk of the Embers with the unlocked Grimoire fueling him.

————————————————————————————————————-

Onders, the apprentice Ember, who had betrayed her own master to help Huxley was gripped in madness. Elatress stood watching and felt pity. She once hated all of her kind, but then a begrudging friendship occurred, however brief. Now as she watched her grasp around muttering to herself, Elatress had the opportunity to be rid of her. Her hatchet practically begged for the job. Her eyes narrowed and she approached the defenseless girl. Her inner voice crept in, "You could be rid of so many problems with one swing. She wouldn't haunt Huxley's steps anymore. You'd be free to be a family. All of the Embers could be dead tonight. First her, then the other downstairs, the broken handed one that hurt Arktos, you could kill them all."

She saw it in her mind. It would be so simple. She stepped closer now within striking distance. Onders spouted formulas and elements. Her eyes swam in a sea of madness, not able to make anything out. Elatress raised her hatchet and their eyes met. Onders screamed. The scream was only matched by her own internal rage, "STRIKE HER DOWN! BEFORE SHE CAN RECOVER! DO IT!"

Elatress ached to strike. She knew this was her chance. She hated to admit it, but killing her in a fair fight might be impossible. Her hand twitched and the voice cheered her on. She raised her hatchet and began to bring it down when Onders voice croaked, "I'm sorry."

Elatress stepped backwards and stayed her hand. "You're SORRY?!"

But Onders slipped back into mad ramblings about formulas.

"You don't get to be sorry! You make one move to help us, and all of the sudden you're forgiven? You would have seen us thrown out of our homes and driven into the wilds! No." She said bitterly. "No, we need to be rid of you. No more haunting our steps."

"Pl..." her voice shook, "...please." She wheezed out. "Didn't....know...Huxley...was...." She spasmed violently and lost her thought.

Elatress seized her shoulders and said, "Didn't know what?!"

Onders was miles away in thought of something else. Elatress reached back and slapped her. Onders yelped and said, "Didn't...know...Huxley...was..."

"WAS WHAT?!"

"...right." A moment of cognizance stabilized her. "Right about everything...even about me."

"Right about you? What was he right about?" Her fits continued and she was unable to speak. Her inner voice crept in, it even used her own mouth to speak.

"That you were an enemy. That you were an Ember. That tonight is for killing." Elatress laughed and said, "Easier than rabbits." She lined up her blood-soaked hatched with an exposed neck.

Elatress' hand struck like a snake. It sank deep into flesh. Only it wasn't Onders. It was Grubmush's forearm, thrust outward in protection of Onders. "She is no killer now, and neither are you. Who lurks behind this young one's eyes?"

Elatress's body tensed and she tried to wrench away his arm. But it was too deep. "Leave my friend alone. Leave her mind now."

A gravelly chuckle came from deep within her, echoing like a deep cave. "She held me off for some time, but I am not far from being fully realized. I am the will of the Wilds. I am survival itself, born deep inside the heart of Magnadun. And now I wish to walk in her body...soon she will break and nothing will push me back down." Grubmush snarled and her eye twitched. She released her weapon. Stumbling backwards, Elatress looked at her hands and reached out for Arktos. The bear had made his way to her and she breathed easier. Both of their feral sides sated for now.

"We have to go..." Elatress said to Arktos. "We have to figure out what's wrong with me."

The bear growled an agreement and she collapsed into him weeping while Onders jabbered and bled.

———————————————————————————————-

Huxley channeled the flow of an Ember's attack, sending it skyward. The surprised Ember redoubled his efforts only to find the high wall he was standing on becoming unstable. He fell to what would have been his death but a pair of hands seized him from the air. Huxley sent him floating to the ground, landing inside a rage-fueled horde of warriors. Needless violence was not what Huxley wanted. It would just be a repeat of Mayburn only on a far larger scale. He needed to stop the fighting. He had his own idea, one not given to him by the Grimoire, but genius all the same. He knew what would stop them from murdering the people of Danador.

Huxley summoned points of light to surround him and emitted an outline of a great horned owl. Its wingspan covered fifty feet and a Magnincy-fueled screech reached every ear. "FALDURIN'S WRATH IS FULFILLED! Go now and rest brave warriors!"

They stopped immediately. One had already begun choking the frightened Ember but he released. At once, they all fell to their knees in reverence. Bowing low, they submitted their willingness to follow Huxley's commands.

He flew high and swift over the city, doing the same. He wouldn't have enough time to stop them all. Even with all this knowledge unlocked, he could still only move so fast. For everything, there were limits. He could increase his perception and information processing but it wouldn't work like that for them. They still needed a moment to see and hear him. Huxley swept through the city, rescuing Embers and Dathu alike. The outcome of this battle may have gone either way but it would cost thousands of lives if he couldn't put a stop to it. Everywhere he went, the warriors bowed in reverence and the Embers were too shocked to question.

Ten seconds left.

Huxley had only swept over about half the city. He summoned the last of his unmitigated power and formed what he thought the owl god looked like in the sky. Faldurin's spectral form flew to the burning Tower of the Arcane Flame. His wings beat like a hurricane and they snuffed out the eternal blaze. The stars instantly filled the void left by the ever-present flame. A terrifying cry of victory filled Danador. Faldurins talons now seized the side of the Tower and sliced it in half, collapsing it downward.

Three seconds left.

He realized his mistake after making such a dramatic decision. The top half of the tower was now falling onto the center ring of Danador, likely to destroy buildings and the people inside.

Two seconds left.

Huxley, as Faldurin, used his wings again to summon a tornado within the tower, all of the books and pages flung upwards taking the tower with it. For a moment, the sky was blotted out with paper torn from their bindings.

One second left.

He hurled the tower northward with a long line of trailing papers and books floating down in its wake. He didn't plot the trajectory, just sent it toward the wilds. Half a second later, it was gone, and Huxley dropped.

———————————————————————————————————-

Twice now Huxley had plummeted towards Danador. The circumstances though had changed substantially. The rain of pages fluttered towards the streets, flooding the markets and homes with knowledge. So many people would step out of their places of refuge and find long-hidden secrets and ancient texts just lying there. What may have cost many months or years wages, was now free for the taking. Of all the things Huxley had done, he'd never been more proud of himself. This would change everything. Clips would still be used, but what would happen to the knowledge economy? He couldn't worry about that now. He had a much more pressing concern.

The last time he fell toward Magnadun, was far more terrifying. For one, he was just hurled out of a metallic case and was edging on madness. But being so close to whoever he had met had made it seem like madness was impossible, more than that, it seemed madness didn't exist at all. That Magnincy and his mind worked together in perfect harmony.

He felt it shifting back to normal, the pages of the Grimoire becoming clouded again and the old familiar feeling of confusion returning. But it didn't always have to be that way. Knowing the utter power and freedom it contained, emboldened Huxley. He had only made it through a few dozen pages of the Grimoire during his brief stint of being unbound. What could he do with many years of it? He summoned Magnincy to solve the problem facing him now. How do I stop myself from splatting on the ground? The stars swirled into his view again and several options presented themselves. He learned from last time. Less scattered tendrils and more precise, strong shots. Fortunately, the remaining bottom half opening of the tower was now on his left and he plunged closer. Angling his body towards the hole was difficult. A few well-placed helpful gusts of wind and he made it inside. Huxley threw three strong tendrils upward and they found purchase. It slowed him dramatically, suspending him in the exact middle of the tower. Within seconds, he was hanging amongst many empty bookshelves with only a smattering of pages left. Carefully, he released tension in his tendrils and lowered himself down. It wasn't long before he was back on the ground floor. Blast marks, blood spray and rubble, were everywhere. His heart sank at the sight of it. But then, he heard a familiar voice.

"You sure do love making huge piles of books...don't you Bookpile?"

Elatress approached while flipping through one of the many to choose from. It was upside down, but she was deeply fascinated with it regardless.

Flinging himself towards her, he let go of his Magnincy and hugged her deeply. Initially surprised by his show of affection, she soon relaxed into the hug. "You ok, Huxley?"

"Don't worry about me, are you?"

"No, none of us are doing very well. I had what Abernathy calls, 'An Episode' But Grubmush helped me. He's around here somewhere." She stated. He caught sight of Arktos and Onders. Arktos was still covered in blood but was unbothered by it. His dopey bear face had returned. Huxley shuddered remembering him from earlier. Was he really sleeping so close to such a beast?

Then he saw Onders. "Oh, no." He remarked.

"Yeah she's bad right now...hey did you become an owl?" Elatress asked.

"Huh? Oh, yeah, sort of." But Huxley rushed to Onders' side. She was trying to read a book but its pages were missing. She was muttering at a fanatical rate about data and measurements. Huxley's stomach twisted into a knot.

"Onders?" He gestured for attention.

No response.

"Onders, It's Huxley." He tried again.

Still no response.

"You know...the thief fugitive?"

She stopped reading and closed the empty book.

Her mutterings continued but it seemed he had connected to a small part of her mind. He reached down and held her hand. It tightened around his, and for a moment, the two remained quietly sitting holding hands. Her hair had come out of the tight braids and now hung disheveled around her face. Her dark eyes fought for recognition of anything familiar. They searched as though trying to solve a puzzle.

Suddenly, her pupils dilated and she gasped.

"Cute...but foolish!"

Huxley laughed and felt exasperated. "Yes! That's me. Cute... foolish!" He dropped her hand and hugged her. "I'll get you through this. Don't worry, you will be ok, now. If you can hear me there. I won't leave you." She didn't acknowledge the hug or his words but something about her brief moment of recognition made Huxley know deep down, she would be ok. He just didn't know how long it would take, but he would be there for her however long it took.

———————————————————————————————————-

With a loud grunt, Grubmush worked the hatchet out of his arm. Looking himself over, he grew pleased. "Many tears and gashes. Both internal and external wounds. Both will serve me well." With each new laceration, he grunted approvingly. He even dug his fingers around in a few. "It seems books are far more dangerous than I anticipated. Cuts from paper are eye-wateringly painful. These sting sharper than blades! If I was naked during this fight, the pain would have been overwhelming."

He looked around for his weapon only to find the two pieces that remained. Holding them for a moment, as if saying goodbye, he laid them back down. Elatress made her way over to him and said, "Yeah, I think I lost one of my hatchets. Not sure where it went, and that is rare for me."

He said, "You limit yourself with dual chopping weapons. You should have a piercing and chopping, so you can kill more effectively. We can both look for more suitable weapons together." He handed back her hatchet which she took and inspected, "You may be possessed by something truly horrifying. Did you know this?"

She shrugged and said "Basically. I was hoping he would get bored and leave. I don't think he will though. I think he is getting stronger." He accepted her explanation needing more time to consider what it could be.

She looked at her remaining hatchet as though considering his advice. He was pleased to see her listening to him. Grubmush had excellent tactical advice, especially when it came to edged weapons.

He began extolling the virtues of options in bladed combat when a horn blast stopped him speaking and he stood abruptly. "My people have victory! Falurin's might has been proven!" He said, shaking his fists in the air. His sudden movement stretched open some wounds and he yelped. "Ahhh, papercuts! The newest form of pain to endure. I need to tell my people about it."

He slapped Elatress on the back and thanked her for her partnership in battle and made for the door. "Wait! Grubmush!" She called after him. "Are you leaving? Like all the way back to Dathu?"

"It is my home, and my people, though I believe I should stay with the Prophet." He said with a finality. "But I do not stay idle long, and there are many more warriors to encounter. I will spend some time with my people and celebrate our victory before returning to you." He nodded towards Huxley and Onders embracing and added in a whisper, "Tell the Prophet, I wished not to interrupt him, but that I will see him soon. I must leave Danador in victory and lead my people home."

Elatress nodded but couldn't help herself. "Well except for your fight with Ryla...you better hope you don't find her again."

He stiffened and said, "I WON that fight!"

"Not according to her, or your guts all over the ground."

"MY GUTS HAVE NOTHING TO DO WI-" But he stopped himself. "You're mockery will not bait me into violence. Peace has returned and it should be maintained for now."

She shook her head in a sarcastic agreement. "Bye, Grubmush, look out for Ryla."

———————————————————————————————————————

Huxley helped Onders into a chair and made sure she was comfortable. Elatress eyed the two of them. Seeing how he cared for her, she was glad she hadn't killed her. A sad Huxley would be a lot to deal with right now.

From the hole in the library, Maddox rose up. His robes smoking and reeking of acrid burns. His eyes were lifeless and his body swung limply held up by Abernathy's enormous gauntlets. "Well, he was a tricky one." They let go, allowing the Ember to clatter to the floor. Elatress ran over to Abernathy. His armor hissed releasing pressure while his chest and armor plating opened. She leapt up to him and the two hugged tightly. "Did we kill him?" She asked.

"Uhm, I can't be sure. His madness was getting to him but he didn't succumb. I think he is still breathing, pretty sure you broke quite a few of his ribs. I got one solid punch to his chest. Not sure he's ever been in a fistfight quite like that."

As though acknowledging it, the Ember hacked and gasped though it didn't help him. Elatress leapt off the armor and ran over to the Ember, and delivered a swift kick to his gut causing him to scream.

Abernathy yelled "OK! HEY NOW! We won El! There's no need for torture and cruelty."

Huxley made his way over, still keeping an eye on Onders, not wanting to stray far from her. Maddox spit blood and wheezed. He really might be dying, Abernathy thought. He didn't want that but had limited options at the time. Maddox had adapted to his chemical bombs. He was dangerous. Even now, barely hanging on, Abernathy feared what he could still do. Elatress' kick brought him back to consciousness. Abernathy slipped off his armored gloves and pulled them over Maddox's hands. Without the connection to Abernathy, they ceased allowing him to grasp anything. He hummed the wrists to lock tight so they wouldn't slip off, an adequate prison for now but something more permanent would have to be figured out.

Maddox began to cough as he came to, but his coughing soon turned to rhythmic muttering. Soon it became full-blown raving. Abernathy had never seen an Ember go mad like this. He nodded to Elatress to be ready for anything. Blood stained his teeth as he looked upward towards his ruined tower, the wealth of its knowledge strewn about all around him. His failure was complete.

37

Wretches and Reunions

"The nature of the Kindlers' work can be known. If not in this lifetime than another. It is the duty of all the learned people then to raise up and lead the next Embers that burn the Arcane flame of knowledge within. So that its light can connect with the one who made us." **-Last page of the Grimoire**

The sun shone in bright streaks setting Huxley's room aglow in golden rays. The melting snow outside reflected the light, casting even more through his window. The warmth of his bed told him where he was before his eyes opened, and the strong smell of tobacco wafting told him he wasn't alone. The intake of breath through a pipe and the subsequent crisp burn of its contents was unmistakable.

"How bad is my stomach, Abernathy?" Huxley asked.

He heard him start and cough, perhaps not realizing Huxley had woken up.

"I was hoping you could tell me." Abernathy said, "El says you did that to yourself? In an act of 'Utter stupidity for an even stupider religion,' uh, she says."

"It's only stupid if it doesn't work," Huxley explained. He didn't lift his head up from under the blankets. It somehow felt like if he did, he would have to engage with the mess he created, both in his body and of the city.

"It certainly did that. You have quite the following now." Abernathy continued, "Grubmush has been hard at work extolling your virtues to his flock. And their number has grown quite a bit since the battle." He laughed, "Even some Danadorians have joined, if you can believe it."

"How long have I been asleep?" Huxley asked. "And how long-"

"Huxley," Abernathy interrupted, with a tone that Huxley couldn't place. "A lot has happened since. Some of it may be too much to bear in your weakened state. Why don't you focus on healing up for a while."

"Thank you for asking, but you already know my answer, right?"

Abernathy puffed deeply again and said "Yeah, I thought as much. But we Norun have a tendency to try and protect people from time to time."

Huxley was reminded of something. He pondered it while Abernathy puffed. "Did you know I was in almost this same circumstance a few months ago?"

Abernathy chuckled, "How could any of this be something that has already happened to you?"

"When I woke up after the battle in Mayburn..." He paused, remembering, "And I was forced to stay and recover. I got in over my head then. I suppose I am far deeper now. Especially now that I have to go back and face them."

"Will you not be viewed as a hero? Did you not promise to go train and become their defender? I bet you could make good on that promise." Abernathy reasoned.

"Well, yes...but also no." Huxley strained. Indecision clouded him. "How can I go back there now after all that has happened? To just sit as Palithur does and wait for the next attack. Especially now that I know that more calamity could be upon us. It seems wrong."

"Wrong to make good on your word?" Abernathy asked.

"No, it's just that everything has changed. It's not so simple." Huxley said. "Especially with the Embers. I always thought so highly of them. Were they always out for themselves? Did every Ember think so little of the common people?"

A commotion began downstairs that intruded on their conversation. Both ignored it. It wasn't bad enough to go check on yet. And it seemed every time he woke up there was a commotion so it could certainly wait.

"No. In fact, their history tells us that they were in fact the people you thought they were. Celebrating learning, growing, and taking hold of their inheritance. But trauma changes people. So starkly, in fact, that they can hardly be blamed for their reaction."

"Not blamed?" Huxley asked. "They were-"

"Of course, they are responsible for their actions, what I meant was..." Abernathy had difficulty finding the right words. He settled on, "If you witnessed what happened to Magnadun, as you witnessed your city in flames, and you had the power to change that...you would."

Huxley didn't speak, he tried thinking it through.

"What I mean is, Maddox was doing what he calculated to be the best choice for everyone. True, he hurt many people getting there, but in his mind, it was an acceptable loss in order to stop another catastrophe. It was partly hubris, but I would like to think it was also a love of Danador's people that drove him. Even if it drove him to vile acts on its behalf."

"How do you know that's how he viewed it, Abernathy?" Huxley asked.

"Ah, that is one of the many gifts I have been burdened with. I can't read minds but I can see far more than most. It is how I trust so many people. It is how I knew you were a good one right away."

"You read my soul?"

"You don't read a soul like a book. Souls are far more complicated than that. But after many years of practice, I found I can get a good measure. I did in you, Elatress of course, even Maddox. He wasn't acting in hate all of the time, though it was a core part of his drive. Almost no one is entirely evil. *Almost.*" He closed his eyes and shook his head. His mustache waved back and forth comically.

"You now carry a similar burden that the Norun do, Huxley. Never knowing how best to help and where to properly place themselves. It is a heavy thing to decide and only you can do it. Perhaps you will come to a wise conclusion in your time of rest."

Huxley could hear him shift his tone while he spoke. He was trying to get him to relax again. As though hearing his thoughts, Abernathy apologized, "Sorry, as I said before, I am often compelled to try and help people."

"Yes. I have seen that. Can we talk about that? About you being a Norun and apparently God's favorite people or something like that."

The puffing stopped. Abernathy readjusted in his seat. Huxley, still not emerging from his cocoon could hear the creak of the leather as he found a new spot.

"How much did he tell you?"

Huxley hadn't really processed what he was told yet. It had been interrupted by the fight. It felt like way more than he could even understand. "Not sure how much or how little...other planets, the Kindler making mistakes, us connecting with him differently."

Abernathy nodded and said "That is a relief. I have had so few people to talk about that with. It's bizarre knowing someone is from another planet and not acknowledging it, you know?"

"I really don't," Huxley admitted.

Another guffaw of laughter erupted and the sound of furniture moving in the Gearbox. It didn't sound concerning, but it was definitely too early in the day for that.

"Well, you do now." Abernathy chuckled but saw Huxley didn't quite think it was funny and stopped. "Right then, the Norun?"

Huxley wanted to hear all of it.

"The Norun were the first created among all of the Kindler's children. Being the oldest and farthest established, we took on the burden of leadership when things were upended. It's not that we are his favorite, it's just that we connect with him best." He paused to see if Huxley reacted but he just listened intently. "Right, hmm, that usually frustrates people."

"Well, up until a day ago, I wasn't sure there was anyone out there in the stars," Huxley explained.

"Yeah...yeah that's quite Danadorian of you. Anyway," Abernathy went on, "The story goes that when the Kindler wanted to make children, he lacked the ability to make us exactly like him. There are many debated theories to that end, but the point is, he made us anyway. The Norun were able to exude our soul's energy freely and without much fear of overextending ourselves. Norun rejuvenate each other by virtue of our company and ease of understanding. It was when we exuded outward that we could feel his own spirit touch ours. It was as though you were hugging the cosmos themselves. And for a long time, that was enough. Ambition, it seems, could have been our greatest enemy. After a few generations, the Norun found their souls' energy could do more than just connect with each other and god. We could extend our will and intention. Mechanically speaking, it could provide power to a society still firmly in the stone age. Naturally, it caused us to accelerate far faster than any other society that had to start with the basics. It gave birth to wildly gifted engineers and thinkers all while staying close with the one who gave us that ability." He puffed a few more times and his brow furrowed, as he arrived at a less pleasant thought. "I will never know why that was not enough."

"Not enough?" Huxley asked.

Abernathy didn't respond, he just went on "Just like you, we have our own form of madness. It is different from yours. When you overreach your mind draws in too much scientific knowledge. Knowledge that is at work all around you. Sharp minds can retreat inward and depending on how much they overreach, they can find sanity again."

He ran his fingers over his mustache. His normally shaved chin now sported several days of growth. The pipe smoke was beginning to accumulate around him making him look similar to when Huxley first met him.

He began again, "But the Norun can lose the tether to our bodies. Our souls can reach so far, they can become lost and wander. Being separated from one's own soul is an existential crisis that shakes you permanently. We become wretched things." He stopped shaking away an ugly memory and resumed, "Our best guess is that enough souls, over time, became untethered, never returned, and found, or perhaps stole new bodies. Or maybe they merely floated out into the cosmos looking for the Kindler.

It's guesswork at this point. Stories started to crop up about things like that with more frequency.

A loud and boisterous man began laughing and telling a story at what was probably the bar. His voice muffled by the layers of separation, it rang as vaguely familiar to Huxley but he was too engrossed in what Abernathy was saying. "The Kindler tried to fix it by raising up the best of us to be beacons. Those of us that burned brightly, and helped others to do so, in turn. That was who you met underneath the college. A chosen person. A beacon. He sent out Grimoires to all legs of Danador in search of people like you. His job was to inspire all and to keep those near him grounded and sane. These beacons of sanity were an excellent fix for a time. They helped to heal our people, and now that we are aware of it, they did the same for all of the Kindler's other children. Someone to show the way or at least keep them from madness. I expect when you spoke to him, you have never felt more grounded."

Huxley had shifted his feet and slid out from the covers of his bed and placed them on the floor. "Yes, it was like I didn't have a care in the world, and I could make sense of everything."

"Exactly." Abernathy remarked, "Now imagine you had that in every major city, and it wasn't hidden away?" He took a long slow draw from his pipe and when he breathed out, he accompanied the smoke with, "We could have been so much more."

Huxley asked, "So it was difficult, for a while, then the Kindler made beacons to help fix people. So why did that not work?"

"The same way it happened here. Ambition, greed, and lust for power. It's almost always those things that ruin people." Anger crept into his tone as he went on. "With that much power and that much at stake, things went wrong for the Norun, and they went exceedingly wrong. We had a few beacons that grew selective, and reached further than they should have."

"Did they also go mad?" Huxley asked.

"Do you know how bad it can be when a god's chosen ambassadors go mad?" Abernathy asked, "So bad that it can send reverberations into the cosmos."

"But he is god? Can't he just fix them?"

"An excellent question, Huxley," Abernathy said, pointing his pipe at him. "But we don't get to know stuff like that. We only get to know what happened. Apparently, in his wisdom, he decided to, destroy, hide and remake Magnadun into what it is now."

"So what now? Can we fix it?" Huxley inquired.

More voices filled the Gearbox, but the first one only raised his volume to speak over the crowd.

Abernathy laughed and said, "You are growing powerful, but fixing a planet is probably outside your scope. No, we need to help whoever we can with what we have. We can fix planets later."

"Like Elatress?" Huxley asked, "She's not getting better, is she?"

"No. I had hoped normalcy would help her. But I think that was wishful thinking. Her problem is far outside my abilities or yours. But together we might be able to find a solution."

Huxley nodded, "Now, that is a problem that is right in front of us."

Abernathy began to stand up and said "Not in front, but probably on the roof or something like that." He dusted himself off, allowing the soot that had accumulated on his chest to fall to the floor. Huxley stood and stretched only to collapse back onto the bed in pain.

"Whoa, now! You still have to heal up. It's going to take a while, lad. Probably, a few weeks. But I think the Hero of Danador and Mayburn has earned a few weeks off."

"But, surely you need help downstairs?" Huxley stated, holding his wound as the near riotous group of morning drinkers had all but filled the Gearbox in a roar chanting something he couldn't quite make out.

"Most definitely, but not from you. I need you to study the Grimoire and all the other knowledge we've acquired." Abernathy explained.

Huxley's face fell. Last he saw it, the Grimoire was in Maddox's hands and after everything that happened, he had lost sight of it. His eyes widened in shock, could I have sent it flying with the rest of the tower!?

Abernathy laughed heartily and said, "whoa, calm down, now, I've got your book. I even flipped through it. I can't make sense of most of it. Pretty advanced stuff in there. Of course, I know the engineering and math bits but not much else." He handed the Grimoire to Huxley and indicated, "If it's still a mystery to you, I can probably teach you those parts."

Huxley perked right up, "Yeah that would be great actually, I'll have to find other teachers now too"

"I can think of a few," Abernathy told him. But for now, just take some time and heal."

The window panes shook under the thumping of movement and timber of the rowdy crowd that was growing more impatient by the minute. Surely, they had drinks and food for them all? It was the Gearbox, after all.

Huxley held the Grimoire in his hands. It looked a little more scuffed, with a few cracks in the leather and marks on the binding, but ok overall. He cracked it open and leafed through. The experience was totally different than the first time. It had a deeper familiarity to it. Not just the pages that he had read over repeatedly but a sense of belonging, of ownership. He really was its heir, one among many, it seemed. He wondered how many other Grimoires were out there with people struggling to understand them just as he was. Perhaps now, he could reach out to them? Or maybe it was time to return to Mayburn and do as he originally promised.

The boisterous voice asked a question to the rest of the room and they responded with the first understandable words since it started. "Yes! Get him!"

The swift clatter of boots came up the stairs and was followed by a chaotic rap on the door.

"Hux! Huxley!" He recognized the voice now. "Everyone's here to meet the Hero of Danador. I told them I know you and we're best friends. Come on man, don't make me a liar." A thud and smack sounded under the door and the speaker yelped in pain. "Ow! Ok, yeah, fine. Bennett's also here and it's super important that he tells you something."

Huxley smiled. Mayburn had come to him.

"Yeah, Jonah. Just give me a minute, I'm still in bed." Huxley announced.

The door opened anyway. Jonah strode in followed hesitantly by Bennett. Huxley's heart swelled at seeing his friends. The two took in Huxley, beaming with pride.

"Did you really blow up the tower and become an owl?" Jonah asked.

"Kinda yeah." He said sheepishly.

Bennett looked shocked and Jonah pushed his hair back and said, "Jeez and we thought you killing a few people was crazy! What did that book teach you? Maybe I need to read it too."

Bennett approached Huxley and sat at his bedside. He reached down and shook Huxley's hand. He looked like he was about to speak but only pointed to his throat. Huxley was confused for a moment, then Jonah said, "Oh yeah, he, uhh, didn't recover so well. But it's ok, I'm talking for him a lot these days. We're even working out a hand signal system. He didn't like to talk a lot anyways."

Bennett nodded in agreement.

Abernathy introduced himself and welcomed them to the Gearbox before departing so that the boys could be reunited. Before the door closed, Jonah began "You have GOT to hear what happened in Mayburn since you left-"

Bennett waved at Jonah who uncharacteristically stopped and gave his attention to Bennnett. He placed his thumb with outstretched fingers on his chin and then on his forehead.

"Ah! Right. Sorry Hux. They finally caught up to you. Let's get breakfast together afterwards."

As Jonah and Bennett left, Huxley was confused as to what Bennett meant. A moment later, he got his answer as his Mother and Father stepped through the door. Tears in their eyes, no one spoke. Huxley's father walked forward, sat next to him and said "Son, can you ever forgive me?"

"Forgive you?" Huxley asked. Remembering the last time they spoke, he had lied to them, attacked his father and ran away.

His mother nodded furiously but couldn't speak.

"Yes...everything we have done to quash your curiosity...your ambition...your drive. If the stories are true, then..." He began to sob and managed to finish with, "We held you back from who you could have been because we were afraid."

Huxley felt nothing. Not in a vacant depressed way, but that too many emotions were present to take center stage. They all fought for the front but they were all too powerful to lose to the other. Seeing them here, and hearing this from them. He did his best to explain.

"No, dad..." he said, placing his hands on his. "Yes, I was able to do much here. But it was because of how I was raised that helped me do it."

His father looked back confused. "Everyone here was so mystified by my ability to wield Magnincy but I didn't do it like everyone else. It was because of my start that I had a greater handle on myself. It was because of...you."

They were confused, he scolded himself, they don't know anything about Magnincy but they knew their son. At least an aspect of him. He tried again.

"My loving home, and life with you, flights included, are what made me able to handle this enormous stress of Magnincy. The other Embers train with a ferocity that I never had but they were also pulled from their families at a young age. They never knew any kind of normalcy. It made me think I couldn't be like them. And I can't, but I can be better." They still looked confused but were coming around to understanding. It was then that he remembered the first thing he read besides the note in the Grimoire. He looked at them and said, " 'Reaching for what could be while accepting what is, leads one to burn bright but remain the same which is no bad thing.' That's page one of my Grimoire. It means that while others reached higher than me they lost what 'is' faster than I did. I have learned to burn bright but remain the same. And I have you two and Oakley to thank for that. It might have hurt at times and it even might not always have been the best but, it was right for me."

His father nodded and his mother burst into uncontrolled tears.

Oakley couldn't wait any longer, being an eavesdropper as she always had been, she slipped into the room. She had a dagger around her waist band.

"Did Elatress give you that?" He asked.

She nodded her head and said, "She said I should be armed at all times, she's my favorite person ever now."

The Durant's spent the next few days in Danador making plans for Huxley to come home soon. But acknowledging how difficult that might be. His mom had told him that Palithur was even coming to Danador to see if he could help. That he was a "changed man" since Huxley left. Huxley didn't understand if that was for the better or otherwise, she just kept saying he was changed. Huxley wanted to return home and make good on his promise but felt responsible for the mess he created here. The main focus being Onders. She was still deep into Madness, with only slight improvements. Abernathy, Elatress and Huxley all took care of her while she stayed in the Gearbox. It might be many weeks for her to recover...or maybe not at all. Huxley felt that burden heavily as he would most likely have been caught and killed by Maddox without her sacrifice.

His main goal had always been to protect his home from people like Grubmush, but after everything he had learned...he did not think they would be a problem anymore. The problem was much larger.

The streets of Danador had become chaos, the Wardens had all but left since that night in the tower. What few Embers remained were seen through town but had nowhere to go. A few attempted to wrestle leadership back but no one would have it. The worst was all the information he had distributed. Stories of Magnincy were popping up around town, causing the homeless Embers to try and start their own schools under their tutelage. His solution may have been right at the moment but it brought a host of other problems. And Elatress wasn't getting much better. In fact, even for her, she had been becoming more erratic lately.

Magnadun was also far bigger and more complex than Huxley had realized. What he had seen could not be forgotten. But for now, he needed to focus on what was right in front of him while also having a global view of things. Were there beacons left out there? What had Abernathy been talking about in his homeland? And where had all the Wardens gone too?

Bennett and Jonah only stayed a few days because apparently they were in charge of Mayburns militia now. Bennett had proven to be a great military leader with Jonah as his second in command. The Durant's spent the next week together at the Gearbox as Huxley took them through what had happened to him. When they returned home they couldn't help but look at him differently. Certainly as a man now, but also a son who had found his own path. As someone who perhaps was more than just passable.

Epilogue

The stench of death hit the dock before the ship, but it did its best to keep up. The harbor master approached the vessel waving his hand back and forth, hoping to clear the miasma. He had watched it approach and became concerned. It carried a verdant and citrine hued cloud. Not wanting to endanger his employees, he had them hold back while he approached. They did not argue. If they let this ship dock and whatever it carried made its way into the city, he'd be exiled to the outer ring, maybe thrown out altogether. His crew were good at their jobs but hardly sharp enough to sniff out smugglers using theatrics to scare people and this almost surely was. Or more likely, urchins from the Forty-Five sneaking in. He searched the hull for a name and found only a handful of scratched-out letters.

Boots slammed onto the dock next to him. A woman materialized through the haze. Dull hair the color of dried blood sat under a tricorn hat, her blouse, a dingy white, and a saber, hung on her hip. She sported a few loose bangles on her arms that jangled as she walked. Her boots reached up to just past her knees and thumped with each step. Dozens of vials adorned her belt as well as were tucked into a bandolier across her chest, sporting a rainbow of colors. Most had liquids but some were just powders. The harbor master took a step back and held up his quill and notepad.

Projecting confidence he asked, "Captain and vessel?"

"Oh, the captain...the captain didn't make it." She looked around and stated in a smooth voice, "That's him over there." She motioned to a corpse with sickeningly gray skin hanging over the bow. "I tried but he just kept on dying. Revived him three times, if you can believe it."

The harbor master tried to remain composed at the sight but the smell was beginning to take a deep residence in his lungs. It was only then that he could see the rest of the crew on deck. They had shared their captain's fate. He wasn't sure it was theatrical smoke anymore. He might have made a serious mistake dismissing his crew.

He coughed and said, "And...vessel."

"Oh, I never got the vessel's name," She told him offhandedly, and continued, "Look, if you go ahead and ignore this and let me enter the city, I'll push this boat back off your dock and let it float downriver. You can say it never docked here and we can both go on our merry way."

"What you're suggesting is-"

"Illegal, yes. Are there laws here though? It seems like the city is run by no one anymore. But to sweeten the deal, I'll give you this." She pulled out an orange-tinged vial from her hip pocket. "It will clear out that feeling you're having in your lungs which is causing your breathing problems. Remarkably good work holding it together, by the way."

His composure broke and he snatched at the vial.

She yanked it back and said, "Ah ah. Do we have a deal?"

He nodded his head and grabbed the vial. The woman turned and grabbed a bag off the dock. Put a bilge hook against the hull and pushed it back into the river. The harbor master, amid coughing fits, drank down the contents of the vial and watched the diseased vessel disappear towards the bend in the river.

I'm not evil, Harvey thought. Everyone always yelled that at her. Evil implied dislike. She didn't particularly dislike anyone. She was just good at her job and people always got in the way of it. There were going to be a lot of people that got in her way on this next job. And way more are going to yell things at her, mostly untrue things. But they will yell it all the same.

Even now, she thought, rolling her eyes. The dock crew watched their boss clutch at his throat and gag. Their vile threats against her were being thrown with such aggression but none of them dared approach. She rested her left hand on her cutlass and ran her remaining fingers over the vials she carried. None of the crew found their courage. *They never do.* She thought dismally.

She looked for the ever-present college tower and found nothing. "Huh, so it really did happen. I just have to meet the person that did that. I'm pretty sure Elatress is wrapped up in this, and I need to take her home. You boys know where a girl named Elatress is? Traveling with a bear? No?"

They shook their heads.

"That's ok. I can find anyone. And now that Danador is in such disarray, it will be even easier."

Acknowledgments:

Writing the Grimoire's Heir was difficult and easy. Both are true at the same time. I have always wanted to write and to complete a story of this length, and every time I finished a page it felt like a victory. But as anyone who has tried something new and innately vulnerable, (especially with the "arts") can tell you, my inner critic was viscerally mean. It took many years to silence myself enough to write and many more to tell people about it. The following people have been instrumental in getting The Grimoire's Heir finished and I am truly appreciative.

First and foremost I have to thank my wife Rachel for this book. She endured years of me wringing my hands and constantly doubting myself. She was my grounding and constant source of encouragement. I would have deleted this story many times if it hadn't been for her. She may have sacrificed more than I did in getting this made. Thank you Rachel.

Caleb, Caiden and Coraline thank you. Your constant interest and unwavering support has been of paramount import. Hearing you three chat about being able to read it soon and your growing interest in the narrative has kept me writing.

Caiden and Caleb, your fascination and aligned interest with all things "nerdy" has kept me inspired and yours has been one of the voices I draw on when writing Huxley.

Coraline, Elatress is doubtless you in another life in many aspects. Whenever I didn't know what to write for her I would think about what you would do and it came to me.

Erik and Lindsey Hesselbirg and Olivia Parsons, you were my first real readers. The fear and trepidation I had melted away when I sent my pages to you which I think speaks to your friendship. Thank you for being my first critics and for giving so much of your time to helping me sharpen the story.

Joe Clement, thank you for dealing with many phone calls where I ramble about specific parts of my story without much more context. And for allowing me to text you every morning with my new word count to keep me going. You are a great friend and a peerless bro.

Steve Carter, thank you for being the realest pushback on ideas. And also allowing me to text you everyday with word counts. Your encouragement helped me get over the finish line. Your humor and charitable nature were greatly appreciated.

And of course my mom Dorothy who was the first one to teach me to love literature.

Lewis (Chris) Pennington who gave me great advice in how to push through to the end. When I was floundering, your encouragement helped me to persevere.

Olivia Parsons (Again) for drawing the first image of Huxley! When this surprise showed up in my inbox I was floored. Not just at the skill and talent but at the sheer generosity. Thank you.

Gabriella Grullon for your amazing cover art. Seeing you constantly share your art with the world has helped me to share mine.

Olan Rogers, even though we don't know each other, your artistic journey and inspirational videos helped me to be brave enough to finish this story. If ever I was stuck I would try and imagine how you might respond. Your ability to bare your heart motivates me to do the same. And for you hopefully not being mad at my use of the name "Hammersnow". It was used in respect and thanks for all of your inspirational work.

Dynamite Roasting Company, for allowing me to drink coffee and sit at your tables while typing away. I must have written 70% of this book in your lovely building and I thank you for it.

And of course Chewy for keeping my feet warm while I type and grumbling at me when I've neglected walks, you helped me get my steps in while trying to be an author.

And to my GoFundMe backers:
Anthony Rodriguez
Melissa Parker
David Price
Nicholas Stevenson

Steven Carter
Cosmo Crowe
Kamryn Cieply
Erin Whitney
Phillip Johnson
Julie Brentise
Gregg Harding
Peter Jensen
Adam DeKleine
Alee Rose
Mandy Intravaia
Joyce & Charlie Milling
Aaron & Katie Tyson
Emily Honeycutt
Erin Portner
David Bentley
Susan Bryan
Gregg Harding (Again!)
Illy pennington
Casey Stoterau
Sarah Lima
Garrett Walston
Michael Williams
Dorothy Johnson
Justin Wood
Jake Rhinehart
Dane Haskell
Erin Carr
Wanda Adams
Katie Douros
Ryan Carlson
Reid VanGilder
Ryan Patterson
Kyle Jensen
Jon Meisner

And also the anonymous donors who I left anonymous but wanted to thank as well.

I never knew I had so much support and good will from you guys. This has been the sweetest outpouring of love. Thank you.

Craig Walston lives in Black Mountain North Carolina with his wife and three kids. This is his first novel and is planning many more to come. He is an avid Sci-fi and Fantasy fan that wants to push the genre further. You can find out more about his upcoming projects at www.CraigWalston.com